continued . . .

By J. R. Ward

The Black Dagger Brotherhood Series
Dark Lover
Lover Eternal
Lover Awakened
Lover Revealed
Lover Unbound
Lover Enshrined
The Black Dagger Brotherhood: An Insider's Guide
Lover Avenged
Lover Mine
Lover Unleashed

Novels of the Fallen Angels
Covet
Crave

Writing as Jessica Bird
Heart of Gold
Leaping Hearts
An Unforgettable Lady
An Irresistible Bachelor

AN
IRRESISTIBLE
BACHELOR

J. R. WARD

Writing as Jessica Bird

A SIGNET BOOK

SIGNET
Published by New American Library, a division of
Penguin Group (USA) Inc., 375 Hudson Street,
New York, New York 10014, USA
Penguin Group (Canada), 90 Eglinton Avenue East, Suite 700, Toronto,
Ontario M4P 2Y3, Canada (a division of Pearson Penguin Canada Inc.)
Penguin Books Ltd., 80 Strand, London WC2R 0RL, England
Penguin Ireland, 25 St. Stephen's Green, Dublin 2,
Ireland (a division of Penguin Books Ltd.)
Penguin Group (Australia), 250 Camberwell Road, Camberwell, Victoria 3124,
Australia (a division of Pearson Australia Group Pty. Ltd.)
Penguin Books India Pvt. Ltd., 11 Community Centre, Panchsheel Park,
New Delhi - 110 017, India
Penguin Group (NZ), 67 Apollo Drive, Rosedale, Auckland 0632,
New Zealand (a division of Pearson New Zealand Ltd.)
Penguin Books (South Africa) (Pty.) Ltd., 24 Sturdee Avenue,
Rosebank, Johannesburg 2196, South Africa

Penguin Books Ltd., Registered Offices:
80 Strand, London WC2R 0RL, England

Published by Signet, an imprint of New American Library, a division of Penguin
Group (USA) Inc. Previously published in an Ivy Books edition. Published by
arrangement with the author.

First Signet Printing, July 2011
10 9 8 7 6 5 4 3 2 1

For my Bluegrass Family, with love

Dear Readers:

An Irresistible Bachelor is the fourth of the first quartet of books I wrote, and to be perfectly honest with you, by the time I finished drafting the manuscript, I was pretty sure my career as a published writer was going nowhere. Well, to be honest, it was going somewhere . . . right into the sewer.

Way to start this on a high note, right! Wait, stick with me, I'm going to get to how hot the hero is, I promise. . . .

Here's the thing. Most books are written well in advance of publication, and when I handed *Bachelor* in to its editor, it was clear that my print runs were declining, my sell-throughs were bad . . . and I was not likely to have my contract renewed. Which meant I was out of a job and wouldn't have a home for my material anymore.

Ultimately, this hitting rock bottom was the single best thing that has ever happened to me—because it forced me to get really clear really quick on what my strengths and weaknesses as a writer were and, thereafter, reinvent myself. (The irony, of course, was that the following spring, the book was nominated for the RITA, which is the Romance Writers of America's big national award.) I firmly believe that the incredible success of my Black Dagger Brotherhood books and my Fallen Angels series would not have come about without the singeing fear that hit me as I was working on *Bachelor*.

The idea that every book I write could be my very last has stuck with me—as has the idea that playing it safe with plotting and conflict is not the way to go for my stories.

On that note, about the hero! I remember being utterly in love with Jack Walker. First introduced properly in *An Unforgettable Lady*, he's your quintessential wealthy businessman, and in a lot of ways, he harkens back to the heroes I loved when I started reading Harlequin Presents a million years ago. Back in the early and mideighties, there were a lot of aloof, powerful men just waiting for the right women (come to think of it, there are still a lot of them out there on the shelves right now!) and I thought that shark-in-a-suit routine was just fabulous.

But here's the thing. During the editorial process, Jack actually got watered down a lot. He was much darker in the first draft—his self-destructive streak was more pronounced, and he was hotter-tempered and more edgy (remind you of certain alpha males with fangs and/ or wings I write about?!). With *Lady* and *Bachelor*, I was already heading in the direction that I give free rein to in the Black Dagger and Angels books, and sometimes I've wondered how different Jack's story would have been if I'd been able to tease out more of his intensity.

I still think this is a great story, however, and that Callie Burke's down-to-earth innocence is the perfect foil for his worldly persona. Callie's a great heroine ... and she happens to be in a profession that I'm absolutely fascinated by. As an oil painting conservation and restoration expert, she is doing work that has always captivated me— and I was so lucky, while doing research on her job, to get a chance to visit the conservation department of the Museum of Fine Arts, Boston, and to meet with their head conservationist. What an amazing afternoon that was—as well as a bit of a shock. When I arrived, he met me down in the lobby and took me to a back elevator. That thing was the size of an RV, and just as the doors were closing, someone yelled out to hold up. From around the corner, a man came forward with this huge rolling pallet, and as he pushed it in ... I realized that it had a Monet on it that was big as a desktop. Along with about four other paintings. Okaaaaaay. It was my first and only time going anywhere with $100 million worth of art. And I remember glancing over at the conservationist, who was chatting up a storm, and thinking ... Buddy, do ya see what's next to us?? But he was used to it! And come on, it's not like you could strap those puppies on your back and hoof it up a set of stairs. . . .

I digress, however. The main conflict between Jack and Callie comes from the fact that she's the product of an illicit love affair and is trying to keep that a secret to protect her half sister, who's been really good to her. Jack, on the other hand, is deciding whether or not to run for governor—and if he does, the press is going to delve into every part of his life . . . including who he's dating.

At the time I was writing *Bachelor*, I was still pretty much seat-of-the-pantsing it when it came to the drafting. I had developed only a rather loose outline for the book and, as usual, handling the conflict between the hero and heroine was my big weakness. Naturally, when I got toward the last quarter of the story, I realized that I didn't really have much of a dark moment. Which is like buying a pair of jeans that doesn't have any material where the seat is: In romance novels, the standard rhythm is two people meet, they fall in love, BANG! something drives them apart . . . and then they come together at the end for their happily-ever-after.

I had no BANG! in this book.

Enter my first stab at "credible surprise."

One of the things I think good writers do is they create shock points in books—things that are seemingly out of the blue, but ultimately make you think, Well, hell, I should have seen *that* coming. I mean, that's life, isn't it. How many times have you been going about your merry business when suddenly something happens and you're like WTF! Except then as you go back and look at what led up to it all, you realize the event or the conversation or the reversal of fortune (for good or bad) was inevitable.

For a credible surprise to work, it absolutely must be believable in the context of the world you've created. Set your book in the Adirondacks and have a massive L.A.-style earthquake wipe out a town: Surprise? Yes. Credible? Ah . . . not so much. Assuming you're not in a paranormal world with some bad guy who's got a really powerful wand up his or her sleeve.

When it came to *Bachelor*, I can remember feeling really stumped at the big, fat nothing I'd whipped up. For Jack to go against what he'd promised Callie (namely that he wouldn't make up his mind about his candidacy before she decided if she could trust him fully with her secret) would be totally unheroic. So he couldn't be the one to blow the whistle. And his close friend Gray Bennett was set to be a hero in a future book (assuming I ever got published again). Callie would never say a word.... What the hell was I going to do?

At this point in my career, I was still trying to "think up" books, i.e., I was trying to manufacture specific endings and force characters into places I thought they should go (as opposed to just letting them do what they're going to do and getting out of the way). (P.S. I've had much better luck NOT thinking.) Eventually, however, it dawned on me: Jack's mother, the evil witch, could blow them apart. Perfect! The first credible surprise I ever tried. Not a big one, granted. But her announcing his candidacy before he was ready was exactly the kind of obstacle that Jack and Callie's story needed. Was it believable? Yes. Did it come out of nowhere? Well, for Jack and Callie it sure did.

And yes, they worked through it, and they did get their happily-ever-after.

Man, do I remember feeling out of control as I came up to that announcement scene. And I guess that's why I'm such a careful outliner now. I can't write well if I'm not really grounded in the levers and pulleys of a book's inner mechanics. Now I know that the better prepared I am, the more I can let myself go ... if that makes any sense.

After I was released from my contract, which happened, just as I had suspected, shortly after I turned this manuscript in for production, part of my restructuring myself as a writer focused on how to identify, magnify, and resolve conflict between characters. Which, in retrospect, is ironic. I spent a lot of time and money getting and reading books on the craft of writing.... I even ended up sitting down and deconstructing, chapter by chapter, the plotlines in some of the books that I loved the most . . . and yet I ended up as a writer taking all that formal stuff and all the "rules" out of my process and my plots.

It's weird, though. Courtesy of all that studying, I changed my game big time. I used to hate conflict. Now when I write, I wallow in it. Big emotions on the page used to scare me. Now I'm addicted to them. And finally, going dark used to be something that I was steered away from. Now that's where I'm most comfortable—because I know that the inevitable redemption at the end burns all the more brightly for the contrast.

I truly hope you love *Bachelor* as much as I do. I think it's a very solid book, and rereading it now makes me see a lot of where I eventually ended up. This was the big turning point where everything changed for me, and for that alone, Jack and Callie will always have a special place in my heart.

And, well, I still love a hot guy in a suit—whether it's made of worsted wool or black leather. . . .

Happy Reading,

J. R. Ward
January 2011

1

THE WOMAN came to him from the shadows and he knew her by the red of her hair. She moved slowly, deliberately, toward him and he released his breath with satisfaction. He wanted to ask her where she'd been because he'd missed her.

But the closer she got, the less he felt like talking.

As she stopped in front of him, he reached out and ran a finger down her cheek. She was achingly beautiful, especially her eyes. They were spectacular blue, a shade that perfectly complemented the auburn waves that fell past her shoulders. He wanted her. No, he *needed* her.

Her smile deepened, as if she knew what he was thinking, and she tilted her head back. Staring at her upturned mouth, at her parted lips, a wave of urgency shot through his body. Giving in to the hunger, he put his hands on her shoulders and pulled her close, wanting to take what she was offering quickly before she disappeared again.

Bending down, he felt anticipation and something else, something that made his heart pound with more than lust.

Jack Walker's eyes flipped open. Caught up in the raging hunger in his body, he wasn't sure whether he was truly awake. Or where the hell he was. He knew the bed wasn't his own, but not much else.

He looked around at the dark shapes in the room.

After a few deep breaths, the patterns made sense to him. He was at the Plaza Hotel in New York, in the suite he always used when he was in town.

And the woman he still wanted so badly it hurt had disappeared into thin air. Again.

He stared up at the ornate ceiling in frustration. He hadn't slept well the last two nights and he needed some sustained shut-eye soon. He didn't have much patience to begin with and lack of sleep wasn't getting him any closer to Mother Teresa territory.

The dream was driving him crazy.

Every time it was the same. Just as he was about to kiss her, right before he knew what she would taste like, he'd wake up slick with sweat and in a hellacious mood.

Jack pushed a hand through his hair. Without a suitable target for his frustration, he seethed in the darkness.

He'd met the woman only once and he hadn't thought she'd made that big an impression on him.

Restless, he had to fight his way out of the sheets that had gotten tangled around his naked body. When he was finally free, he walked over to a bank of windows and looked outside. The view was characteristically New York. Skyscrapers reaching toward the heavens, taillights flashing in a maze of asphalt down below. It was late at night, but the city was still hopping.

A couple of days before, he'd come down from Boston expecting to meet with his college roommate, who was now a top-notch political consultant, and to buy back a family painting. Picking up a subconscious sexual obsession had sure as hell not been on his itinerary.

But at least the meeting had gone well. And he'd gotten the portrait.

Last night he'd been the successful bidder at the Hall Foundation's lavish gala. The painting was John Singleton Copley's masterful rendering of Nathaniel Walker, a Revolutionary War hero and one of Jack's most prominent ancestors. He'd paid almost five million dollars for it, but he'd have gone higher. The painting should never have left the family and he was the only one who could afford to get it back.

Which would have been a surprise to anyone other than his immediate relatives.

Since the day his father had gone discreetly bankrupt, Jack had been shelling out his hard-earned money to protect and fortify his family's legacy. To be properly sustained, the proud heritage and luxurious lifestyle of the Walkers required a tremendous, unceasing river of cash. Among the gene pool, however, there was a dearth of earners and a plethora of spenders. Jack was on the short list of the former.

His father's poor asset management and the financial realities of keeping up the Walker Theme Park had helped to ensure that he didn't turn into yet another useless blueblood. Instead, he was a hard-hearted, competitive SOB who had a reputation for winning at all costs. It had been an evolution his father, Nathaniel James Walker VI, had never approved of, but then, the man's opinions and choices had usually been poor in Jack's opinion. Nathaniel Six, as he'd been known, was the epitome of the Old Guard philanthropist. He felt there was only one proper thing to do with money: Give it away. A gentleman simply didn't tarnish his hands with the ugly business of making the stuff.

It was an entitled way of looking at life, and one that had resulted in his father being much celebrated by the universities, libraries, and museums that were the fortunate recipients of his largesse. Unfortunately, all that philanthropy had also landed him dead broke by the time Jack was twenty-five. The painting had been one of the first things sold to keep up the charade of limitless wealth.

Although Nathaniel Six had been dead for almost five years, Jack could clearly imagine how conflicted his old man would have been at the first Nathaniel's return. The patriarch's picture was back in the family, but thanks only to Jack's dirty hands.

What a catch-22, he thought, thinning his lips.

Shaking himself free of the past, Jack figured he shouldn't be quite so pleased with himself. He'd got the painting, all right. And the goddamn dream.

He'd gone to preview the piece at the Hall Foundation before the auction, expecting to quickly verify it was in reasonable shape and move along. He'd done the former, but in the process had met the art conservationist who'd been keeping him up nights ever since.

He'd first seen her as she'd been backing out of an office. She'd turned around, her deep red hair swinging over her shoulders, and their eyes had locked. He'd been intrigued, as any man would have been, but it wasn't like she'd struck him dumb with her charms.

His old friend, Grace Woodward Hall, president of the Foundation, had introduced them. The woman, Callie Burke, was an art conservationist, and on a whim, he'd invited her to come with them to view the painting. Standing over the canvas, he'd been struck by her thorough commentary on the condition of the painting and her assessment of what needed to be done to properly care for it. He'd also liked the way she'd looked at the portrait. Her eyes had clung to his ancestor's face, as if she were utterly entranced. When he'd asked if she might like to conserve the work, though, she hadn't seemed interested and they'd gone their separate ways. At least until his head had hit the pillow that night.

He'd laughed off the dream at first, pleased to find that at the age of thirty-eight his sex drive was as high as it had always been. With each passing night, however, he lost more of his sense of humor. He'd decided the one saving grace was that they'd never meet again, so eventually he'd forget about her.

But then last evening, after his successful bid at the auction, his friend Grace had brought up the woman again. Grace had urged him to follow up with this Callie Burke, stopping just short of asking him to do it as a personal favor to her. Evidently, Grace felt confident that Ms. Burke could do the work and pushed him to look into the conservationist's background so he'd know just how talented she was. By the end of the evening, he'd agreed to play along though he still had no idea why it was so important to his friend.

Looking out over the city, he figured that he'd check into the conservationist's background tomorrow, and then he'd go find her and ask her again. He wasn't much for giving people second chances, but maybe now was a good time to give it a try. He had to admit he'd been rather touched by Grace's ardent support of the woman.

And the dreams? He wasn't going to worry about them. Hell, he didn't even like redheads.

"Jack?"

He turned to the bed and looked at the dark shape of Blair Stanford. His fiancée.

"Sorry I woke you," he said as she sat up on her elbows.

"Are you okay?"

"Yeah, I'm all right."

She reached a hand out to him. "Come back to bed."

Jack slid between the sheets and felt Blair put her arms around him.

"You're tense," she said softly, stroking his chest.

He wove his fingers through hers. "Go back to sleep."

"Is there something wrong?" she murmured. "You've been tossing and turning every night for the past few days."

"There's nothing to worry about."

He stroked her forearm, trying to get her to relax, but she propped her head up on her hand.

"Jack, we know each other too well for secrets."

"True. But who says I'm hiding anything?" He smiled at how her short blond hair was sticking out at right angles. He reached up and smoothed the sides down, thinking she wouldn't have stood for that kind of disorder if she'd known about it. Even in the middle of the night.

Blair stared down into his face for a long time. "Are you rethinking our engagement?"

"What makes you say that?"

She hesitated. "I was very surprised when you asked

me to marry you and we haven't really talked about it since."

"We've both been busy. That doesn't mean I'm having second thoughts."

What he really wanted to say was that she should know by now that he didn't do "second thoughts." Having made the decision that it was time to get married, and having found a woman he wanted to be his wife, he had everything arranged.

"It's just that . . ." Blair shrugged. "I didn't think we'd ever take this step. I keep wondering when I'm going to wake up from the dream."

He touched her shoulder, feeling the tension in her. "Where's all this anxiety coming from?"

"I never thought you were the kind of man who'd settle down. There were a lot of women before me."

"Come on, you know the stories of my love life are vastly overblown."

"Maybe so, but there was plenty to go on. And it's not just the women. You're a traveler."

Jack laughed and thought of his twin brother. "That's Nate. He's been around the world how many times? Four, now?"

"That's not what I mean and you know it. You've always been restless."

He thought about the odd mix of blood in his veins, the DNA of WASP aristocracy and Portuguese fishermen combined. She was probably right, though he'd never thought about it before. He did have a seaman's need for freedom, just like his brother, but he'd tempered the drive with his strong will and a healthy dose of avarice.

"Well, restless or not, I'm staying with you," he told her.

He heard her sigh in the dark. "I just want you to be sure."

"You know how I feel about you."

"You don't love me, Jack."

The quiet words hit him hard. He opened his mouth,

not sure what he was going to say, but she put a slender fingertip on his lips.

"It's okay," she whispered. "I've always known."

He grabbed her hand and kissed it, wishing he could tell her otherwise. There were so many things about her that he liked and respected. She was a business success in her own right, running a thriving interior decorating company. She had fantastic style and grace. And she was both caring and understanding, two things he was going to have to rely on in the upcoming twelve months. In all likelihood, he was going to run for governor of the commonwealth of Massachusetts and he knew she would handle the stress of his candidacy with the same calm confidence with which she managed everything.

He valued her. He enjoyed having her in his life. The fact that he didn't love her was the only thing missing, but he didn't consider it a problem. That particular kind of passion just wasn't something he had in him. For any woman.

"So maybe the question is more, why are you marrying me?" he asked.

"Because I love you and I think we make a good team."

"We *are* a great team."

"So talk to me. What's wrong?"

He shook his head resolutely, not about to tell her he was dreaming of some other woman. "Blair, trust me. There's nothing going on that you need to be worried about."

"Okay, okay." She ran a soothing hand over his shoulder; it was something she did a lot. She had a way of handling him that he liked. Calming, but not patronizing. "But I hope you'll tell me at some point. I prefer to know bad news sooner rather than later."

She lay down and gradually relaxed against him, her breaths becoming deep and even.

Jack stared at the ceiling as she slept in his arms. When he finally closed his eyes, visions of the redhead drifted into his mind.

It was just a dream, he told himself. The images, the sensations, had more to do with his libido than some woman he'd met for how long? Ten minutes?

Besides, he'd always preferred blondes and he had a loving, wonderful one right here in his arms. He was a man with a plan and nothing was going to change the course of his life.

2

CALLIE BURKE stepped out into the brisk October wind and pulled up her collar, feeling the rough scratch of it on her neck. The old wool coat had been her protection against cold, windy New York winters for years, just one more thing in her life that she needed to replace and couldn't afford to.

She glanced back at the art gallery she'd worked in for the past eighteen months and put her hands into her pockets, feeling her last paycheck through her mittens. Stanley, her boss, her *former* boss, hadn't wanted to let her go. Business, however, was slow because of the bad economy and he hadn't had much choice. People just weren't buying like they had during the dot-com years, and financial reality had to prevail over all the interpersonal stuff.

She sure could have used more notice, though. Just this morning, she'd gone in assuming her job was secure.

Stepping forward, she joined the grim rush of pedestrians.

The gallery had been a good place to work. It put a roof, however modest, over her head and kept her in the art racket, even if she wasn't doing conservation projects. The place was also located in the Chelsea section of Manhattan, only blocks away from her apartment.

And she'd liked Stanley in spite of his theatrics and his codependent relationship with Ralph, his teacup poodle. She hadn't been all that fond of Ralphie. Four pounds of bad attitude backed up with a bark that could shatter glass just wasn't endearing—no matter what Stanley said.

Callie grimaced, thinking she would miss the place, and then pushed the temptation to sink into self-pity aside. She had real financial problems. Even with the check, she had only about seven hundred dollars to her name and rent was due in a week.

She thought about what she had to sell. There wasn't much back at her apartment. Her mother's jewelry had been used long ago to pay off medical bills. Callie's furniture, which had come from thrift stores and flea markets, wasn't going to bring more than two cents. And her old TV had been stolen months ago when her apartment was broken into.

The fact that the thieves hadn't taken anything else showed how little the rest of her stuff was worth.

She tried to think about her options. The thing she knew for sure was that she didn't want to go back to that depressing little hole in the wall she lived in just yet. There was no way to find strength or courage there. What she needed to do was walk around for a while and hope her head cleared.

As she marched through the chilly air and thought about employment opportunities, she wondered why she couldn't have gone to school for something a little more lucrative. Art conservation, however passionate she was about it, however good she was at it, was hardly a run-of-the-mill career to support yourself with. Accounting, law, medicine. At least in those fields, you could get work almost anywhere and be pretty well paid.

Landing a conservation job, however, was like getting struck by lightning, and this was why she'd ended up at Stanley's gallery. While going through NYU's conservation program, she'd interned at MoMA and received some great experience working under experts in the field, but with her mother so sick, she hadn't wanted to move out of the city when she got her degree. The field was competitive enough to begin with, but because she needed to stay where she was, her prospects were even more limited.

Callie stopped in front of one of the more prominent galleries, thinking they might need help. Maybe a receptionist. Or someone to empty the trash. She didn't care. Aside from her very real financial imperative, she just wanted to be around the art. She went inside, but was told that they had laid off their receptionist two weeks before. When she asked, halfheartedly, if they knew anyone who was hiring, the shake of the head and lowered eyes told her that many of the galleries were in the same shape as Stanley's.

Just keep going, she thought as she reemerged into the cold. At least if she wore herself out, she'd sleep tonight.

She was strolling past a newspaper stand when she saw a picture that stopped her. Picking up the paper, she looked at the face of Grace Woodward Hall.

Her half sister.

The stunning blonde was in a gown at a podium, addressing a crowd of the city's most influential people. According to the caption, the picture had been taken at the Hall Foundation's annual gala, and Callie was shocked when she read the article. A killer had tried to attack Grace in her office and she'd been saved when her bodyguard had taken him down. Also, it appeared that her marriage to the Count von Sharone was over and her soon-to-be ex-husband was shopping around a tell-all book about her.

Focusing on the picture, Callie was glad she'd finally introduced herself to Grace and sorry that the woman's life was in such turmoil. After years of reading about her half sister in the society pages, Callie had never expected to meet her, but things changed when their father died. She'd become determined to see her next of kin up close. Just once.

Grace was Cornelius Woodward Hall's daughter. Callie was his dirty little secret. At birth, she'd been given Burke, her mother's name, and the lies that began with her first breath had followed her into adulthood, creating a wild disparity between the kind of life her half sister lived and the kind Callie struggled through. Despite the fact that Cornelius was worth close to a billion dollars, lavish financial support for his illegitimate daughter was out of the question. When he was alive, he could barely stand to be in the same room with her, as if she were too obvious a reminder of the double life he was leading. Anything that would have increased her profile was to be strictly avoided.

Although, even if he had wanted to be generous, such gestures probably wouldn't have been accepted. Her mother's pride had cut off much of what Cornelius had tried to give his lover over the years. Extravagant gifts to her went unopened. A fancy apartment was left uninhabited. The only thing she'd accepted was the payment for Callie's college and graduate school tuition.

And some jewelry that had ultimately helped to ease her death.

Callie read on. The article mentioned that at the gala's auction, Jackson Walker had purchased a portrait of his ancestor, Nathaniel Walker, the Revolutionary War hero.

Jackson Walker.

At the sight of the name, she felt like a blast of hot air had hit the back of her neck.

"Hey! Are you gonna buy that or do you want me to get you a chair?" the stand's owner barked at her.

Callie put the newspaper down and kept going.

She'd first learned about Jack Walker through the gossip columns years ago. He came from one of America's most famous families and had more money than most small countries. He was also too damn handsome for anyone's good. For years, he'd been a notorious bad boy and the tabloids had carried endless stories about his women. He'd tended to date models, actresses, and debutantes; usually more than one at a time. The ensuing catfights and his casual dismissal of jealous rages had probably moved more newspapers than the exploits of Bill Clinton and Jennifer Lopez put together.

Needless to say, it had been a surprise to meet him in person.

Evidently, he and Grace were friends and he looked like the kind of man Grace would know; everything about him was expensive. From his fine, tailored suit to his polished shoes to the leather briefcase he carried, he was from the world of privilege.

And in all his finery, he was precisely the kind of man she avoided.

Okay, maybe *avoided* was the wrong word, because billionaires didn't cross her path very often. But all that money, all that smooth confidence, was a red flag. Her father had taught her everything she needed to know about rich men, and little of it had been good.

But she had to admit Walker *was* attractive. Aside from his physical attributes, he spoke with the authority of someone used to being followed, in a voice that was seductive even when he was talking about nothing sexual. She could have listened to him speak for hours, his words enunciated with that aristocratic drawl, a signet ring flashing gold on his hand as he gestured.

And then there was the way he'd looked at her. He'd met her eyes directly and it was as if he'd really *seen* her. As someone who was used to being sidelined, she thought it was nice to be noticed. Especially while standing next to a woman like Grace.

It had been another surprise when he'd offered her the job of conserving the portrait of his famous forebearer. He made the proposal even though he didn't yet own the painting, taking for granted he'd prevail in the auction. Considering the kind of money he had, she supposed no price would be too high for him.

But she'd walked away from the proposition, in spite of the fact that it was a plum job. It wasn't that she couldn't handle the project. She'd worked under some renowned conservationists during school and had tackled some very difficult restorations. The Copley, though dirty and in need of a cleaning, wasn't a big deal in terms of technical difficulty.

Callie just wasn't in a big hurry to work for the man. She knew how the Jack Walkers of the world operated, having had to deal with them on occasion in Stanley's gallery. Having had one for a father. They thought of themselves first and that meant there was always an angle and always a demand. He probably treated his employees as if they were disposable and found fault with even the most successful of efforts.

Maybe she was wrong. Maybe Walker was a perfectly nice man who just happened to have built a business empire. Maybe he was honest and forthright, a beacon of human virtue laced up in a Savile Row suit. Maybe he was closer to Nelson Mandela than Donald Trump.

But more likely, he was a tough guy in gentleman's clothes and not someone she should work for. Getting mixed up with Walker had *Bad Idea* written all over it, even if she could have used the money.

Abruptly, Callie turned around and started for home. She reminded herself that walking alone through the city on a cold night could only get her two more things she wasn't interested in: a case of pneumonia and mugged.

Besides, she had more important things to worry about than the real or imagined character defects of some man she was never going to see again. She had to think about shelter. Food.

She shoved her hand into her pocket and felt the lining give way.

Clothing.

3

Jack stood in front of the dingy six-floor walk-up and frowned. The front door hung off-kilter in its jamb, a pile of Chinese food leaflets littered the stoop, and the place looked as if it was sagging in on itself. He went up five stone steps and leaned in, looking through grungy glass. A bald lightbulb hung over a battered set of stairs and a decrepit tile floor.

He went over to an intercom with a row of buttons below it. There were no names attached to the thing so he punched a few randomly. He wasn't surprised when there was no answer. He hadn't expected it to work.

With a curse, he stepped back and looked up again. He was finding it hard to believe that the conservationist lived in such a building, so he took out the slip of paper he'd written her address on. After double-checking the street and the number Grace had given him, he thought maybe it was a working studio.

A cold gust of wind shot down the street and he glanced in its direction. He'd tried calling Ms. Burke a number of times throughout the day, but hadn't gotten so much as an answering machine. Since he was going back to Boston tomorrow, he'd figured his best shot at reaching the woman was to do a flyby in person, but it appeared, unless he was prepared to do a little breaking and entering, that he'd reached another dead end.

He tried the front door in case its lock, like so much

else, was broken. When it held fast, he figured enough
was enough.

He didn't have any more time to waste. If she was so
damn hard to find, it was her loss. Crumpling the paper
in his hand, he started down the steps.

Just as he hit the sidewalk, a woman rounded the corner at the far end of the block. He was about to look
away when he caught a flash of red hair and his breath
left him in a cloud of mist. An image from the dream,
of pale hands touching the skin of his stomach, brought
him to a standstill.

Christ, he told himself, don't think like that.

He watched as she moved between two parked cars
and crossed the street, her head down as if she were
deep in thought. It wasn't until she was halfway to him
that she lifted her eyes, caught sight of his limousine, and
stopped dead in the middle of the road.

"Hello," he called out, raising a hand. "You're a hard
lady to track down."

She frowned and looked to the left and the right.

"Yes, you," he said, smiling.

When she started walking again, it was much more
slowly.

"What are you doing here?" she said.

He narrowed his eyes, taking in every detail of her.
Her cheekbones and the tip of her nose were glowing
bright red from the cold. Her hair, which fell past her
shoulders, was being tossed around by the wind. Her
blue eyes were regarding him with open suspicion.

She was as beautiful as he remembered and he had to
wonder if her body was anything like what he'd dreamt
of. He couldn't make out anything under her enormous
coat and he was surprised at what she was wearing. The
thing was old and shaggy, a mottled brown tent that
did nothing to accentuate her dramatic coloring or her
curves.

"Well?" she prompted him. "Why are you here?"

He lifted an eyebrow. People didn't tend to address
him with annoyance in their voices.

"As I said before, I want you to conserve my painting."

The cool glance she shot him wasn't encouraging and he felt himself gearing up for a lively negotiation. Which was just fine with him. He loved a good barter, whether it was over a company, a stock position, or a piece of art. The tougher the battle, the sweeter the reward when he won.

She walked up the stone steps, not even looking at him as she passed. "I told you, I'm not interested."

"I find that hard to believe," he said sharply. "Considering the way you stared at that portrait."

As she turned around, he knew she was itching to get rid of him, and her impatience made him want to pull up a chair and hang around for a while.

"I'm not right for the job."

"Then you have a low opinion of your capabilities."

"It has nothing to do with my skills." She brushed a strand of hair out of her eyes.

"Come on, you're dying to work on that painting."

She got out her keys and pivoted away again. "I'm not prepared to take the assignment. Thank you."

She was putting her hand on the doorknob when he took the steps two at a time and reached out for her arm. The moment he touched her, he felt her stiffen through the sleeve of her coat.

"Let go of me. Please."

As she refused to meet his eyes, he grew curious.

"Tell me, what have I done to earn this animosity?" He dropped his hand and threw her a smile.

"You show up uninvited on my doorstep," she retorted. "I've told you no and you're still standing here. You're obviously prepared to pressure me into working for you for reasons that I can't begin to guess at. Why should I welcome you cheerfully?"

"Are you always this wary?"

"When things don't make sense to me, yes."

"So how's my offering you the job of a lifetime senseless?"

"Because I don't believe in miracles."

"Atheist?"

"Realist."

Jack grinned. He liked her resistance, even more so because he could tell she wasn't nearly as tough as she was pretending to be. Her face might have been composed but those eyes of hers were bouncing around, touching on his face, the top knot of his tie, the width of his shoulders.

"I think you can do the work."

"Based on what? You must be a quick study because we've only met once before."

"I'm considered to be pretty astute."

Her head tilted to the side, as if she were waiting for him to prove it.

He shrugged. "I know you graduated at the top of your class, with highest honors, from NYU's master's program in conservation. That's a damn good indicator of interest and aptitude. I know your professors liked you and thought you had talent and a willingness to work. I also understand you interned under Micheline Talbot and Peter Falcheck on some very complicated, high-profile projects."

Her eyes skipped away to the front door of her building. She was no doubt eager to put those keys in her hand to good use. "How did you find out all that?"

"The head of your former department holds the Walker Chair in Art History. He was amazingly forthcoming." Her lips pursed. "Anyway, I took that track record, thought about the way you looked at my ancestor, and came to the conclusion that as someone early on in her career, you might appreciate a shot at the big leagues. That's pretty sound reasoning, don't you think?"

The strand of hair was back in her face again, blowing into her eye. She pushed it away, obviously aggravated.

"Listen, Mr. Walker, your new acquisition is an extraordinary piece of history. One wrong decision or badly executed maneuver and the loss would be monumental."

"Scared?" he taunted mildly. As she stiffened, he

smiled. He was more than willing to use her pride to his advantage.

"Of course I'm not scared. But you need someone—"

"So if you're qualified, interested, and able, that means only one thing."

"What's that?"

"You have another reason for turning me down. What could it be? I wonder."

"I don't like you," she blurted. As soon as the words came out, her cheeks reddened even more. "What I mean is—"

He laughed. "You don't know me well enough to dislike me."

"I'm not so sure about that," she muttered. "I don't tolerate playboys all that well."

His smile faded. "What makes you think I'm a playboy?"

"I'm also considered pretty astute," she said, lifting her chin. "And I'm a very good reader."

As she eyed him with another challenge, he was less than amused. Living down his past had been getting on his nerves lately.

"But I haven't done anything to offend you personally, have I?" he drawled. "Haven't propositioned you for sex. Haven't touched you in an inappropriate manner."

He'd made love to her in his sleep, sure. But that didn't count.

When she remained silent, he smiled grimly. "Maybe the problem is that *you're* attracted to *me.*"

Her mouth opened in a rush of indignation. "I don't think so."

"You mean I shouldn't assume you're just playing hard to get with all this latent hostility?"

She shook her head in disbelief. "You know, I'll bet you assume anyone in a skirt is attracted to you. Which is the hallmark of a playboy, I might add."

He gave her a level stare. "Well, now that I know what you think of me, I'm going to give you a little something to chew on. I think you're looking for excuses not to take this job and it would be a shame to turn down something so important on the basis of fear, don't you think?" He took out his business card and pressed it into her hand. "This could make your career, and you know it. Call me tomorrow with your answer."

"I gave you my answer."

"Think about it."

"I have."

"Well, think about it some more," he shot back.

As she glared up at him, he could tell she was framing another argumentative response and thought, if she wanted to keep going, he was more than willing to indulge her.

For some reason, the heated exchange made him think of Blair. When he got wound up, she tended to become easygoing, moving like water over his sharp edges. This woman, on the other hand, was meeting him head-on. Facing her determination, feeling the strength inside of her, he felt very much alive.

Abruptly, he grinned. "You know something? I like you."

"No, you don't," she said quickly, her eyes widening.

"Yes. I do."

Another gust of wind shot down the street and that length of hair flipped back into her face. Without thinking, he reached out and tucked the strand behind her ear.

The simple gesture brought their volley to a halt.

She jerked her head away, but his hand went with her, following the silky waves of red down to her shoulder.

He looked into her eyes. They were glowing with alarm and something else. Something heated. He had a passing notion that he should be very careful around her, but then her lips parted and he lost his train of thought. The lower one was fuller and he felt an urgent need to test its softness with the pad of his thumb. With his own mouth.

Abruptly, he realized he'd leaned forward, as if he was going to kiss her.

Jack quickly stepped back and pushed a hand through his hair, thinking she seemed as dazed as he was.

Pointing at his card, which she was gripping tightly, he said, "Call me tomorrow."

And then he left before she could give the thing back to him, walking briskly down to his limousine. As soon as he got inside the car, he glanced at the seedy building. The front door was just shutting.

He let out a curse.

Jesus, he'd nearly kissed her.

Any more clear thinking like that and he was going to end up in some serious trouble. He'd come here to talk about a job. Not to cheat on his fiancée.

"Let's go, Franky—we're late."

"Sure thing, Mr. Walker."

The limousine surged ahead.

He had just twenty minutes before he was supposed to meet Blair and that new client of hers at the ballet, and now he had even more reason not to look forward to the evening. He didn't like having to sit still for so long and the dancing never really held his attention. He was looking at a good two hours with nothing to do but mull over what had just happened on Callie Burke's doorstep.

He shook his head, telling himself he shouldn't make a big deal out of it.

Besides, he had a feeling he'd won. His instincts told him she was going to call tomorrow and say she would do the work. In the end, her ambition and her attachment to the painting would win out over her suspicions of him. And courtesy of her commitment, he would be giving someone a leg up, something his father had maintained was completely outside of his character. He'd also have taken care of Grace's request.

So he was doing the right thing. In spite of that flash of insanity back there.

Jack relaxed and leaned back against the leather seat. He told himself the only thing he had to worry about tonight was how to feign interest in a bunch of men with stuffing down the front of their tights.

As Jack Walker's limousine drove away, Callie stood in the lobby of her building, aware that she was trembling. She told herself that whatever was going through her body was not attraction. It just couldn't be.

People shivered in the cold, she thought. That had to be it.

Oh, hell, who was she kidding.

She glanced at his card. Jackson W. Walker, CEO, The Walker Fund. There was a Boston address underneath his name and title.

Even the paper was expensive, she thought, testing its creamy stiffness.

Although she could still remember how good his cologne had smelled, it was hard to believe that he'd come looking for her. She couldn't have been more surprised if Bill Gates had been standing in front of her building, and it had taken all of her self-control to walk up to him.

The man made her nervous, but then, why wouldn't he? He was offering her something she wanted badly. He was rich and that meant he had power. And she sensed that he was the type who got whatever he wanted out of life—even if someone else paid for it. Which pretty much described her father in a nutshell.

Mostly, though, it was because when she was standing in front of him, she felt like someone had hooked a pair of jumper cables to her toes.

He was right. She wanted to work on his painting. Desperately.

But turning him down *was* the right thing to do. Her financial straits put her in a position of vulnerability, of wanting to believe in miracles because she was in need of one. Coming home to him and the job offer of a lifetime just seemed too good to be true.

Or maybe she was making excuses. Maybe she *was* a little scared to tackle something like that portrait on her own. And maybe her attraction to him was just one more hazard in a minefield of complications.

She put his card in her coat pocket, the one that didn't have the hole in it, and checked her mailbox. After taking out two overdue bills, she walked up the six flights to her apartment. The stairwell smelled of Indian cooking from the family who lived on the first floor, and turpentine from the artist who lived on the second. As she opened the door to her studio, the dog across the hall started yapping and its owner, a frail, older woman, chastised him in her surprisingly hardy voice.

Callie shut the door and leaned back against the wood. She could hear the shower dripping in the bathroom.

Taking off her coat, she went over to her bed and sat down at the foot of it. She looked at the bureau she'd bought for fifty bucks and painted herself, the carpet remnant she'd commandeered from Stanley when he'd redone his office, and the bedside table made of cement blocks and a piece of wood.

Where the old TV had been.

Then she glanced over to her closet, at the Chanel pantsuit hanging from the top of the door. From across the room, the jacket's buttons glowed gold in the light, the two linked Cs on them clearly visible. The thing looked as out of place as that limousine had in front of her building.

The suit was Grace's. Callie had been soaked the day they'd first met and Grace had lent it to her. Letting herself flop back on the bed, she figured the cost of the thing could probably cover the gap in her rent and keep a roof over her head for two months.

After an hour, she grew cold and curled on her side, pulling her blanket over her legs. As she stared across the shallow expanse of her room, she hoped the solution to her problems would come.

And that it wouldn't involve Jack Walker.

*   *   *

It was sometime around four a.m. when she made up her mind to take the job. The deciding factor wasn't money, although that did play a role. The Walker portrait was just too enticing, and if she turned down the opportunity because of a lack of faith in her abilities or a hyperbolic reaction to some man, she'd never forgive herself.

Having come to a decision, she had plans to make. First of all, she'd need help. Fortunately, she still had good relationships with her professors at NYU, and if she got into trouble with the conservation, she could always turn to them. She was also willing to bet she could ask for some work space and use one of their microscopes. Supplies would be covered in the cost of the project, so she wouldn't have to worry about out-of-pocket expenses, and she was pretty damn sure none of Jack Walker's checks would bounce.

As for him, she wasn't going to see him much at all, hopefully no more than once when he dropped the painting off and then again when he came to pick it up after she was finished. Maybe he'd show up for a visit in between to monitor her progress.

Surely she could handle that amount of interaction.

In a flash, she pictured him as he'd leaned forward, in that crazy moment when she could have sworn he was going to kiss her.

Maybe she could handle seeing him that often.

Callie stayed awake until the sun came up, thinking about the things she needed to buy or borrow. After she'd finally formulated a way to make all the pieces fit together, she called his office number and was surprised when the phone was answered by a secretary, even though it was the weekend.

When she gave her name, the woman said, "Oh, good. He's been waiting for you."

Music came over the line, something classical and rather grand. Callie managed to swallow even though her mouth was dry.

"Good morning, Ms. Burke." Walker's smooth, gently

mocking voice came through the phone and went right down her spine.

"I'll do it."

There was a soft laugh of satisfaction and then he was all business. "Fine. Let's meet, ten o'clock, at the Plaza."

She frowned, looking down at his card. "I thought you were in Boston."

"No, still here. Ten o'clock? We'll meet in my suite." When she hesitated, he said drily, "If it makes you more comfortable, I'll get a chaperone. And I'll make sure the bondage masks and the handcuffs are put away."

She gripped the phone. "Very funny."

Callie wrote down the name of his suite and hung up the phone, her heart racing. When she put her hand on her chest and felt buttons, she looked down at herself. She'd slept in her clothes.

Well, not really slept.

Debating the wisdom of what she'd agreed to do, she went into the bathroom and turned on the shower. As she stripped, she considered critically the black pants, white button-down, and black sweater she'd inadvertently used for pajamas. They were modest, nondescript. There was only more of the same in the closet.

She wished she had something chic to wear when she met with him. A getup that would help give her some of the backbone she was going to need when she sat across from the man and tried to pretend she was every bit as sophisticated as he was.

She peered out at the Chanel suit and smiled, figuring Grace probably wouldn't mind if she threw that puppy on one more time.

4

CALLIE WAS right on time when she walked into the Plaza Hotel. The first thing she did when she got inside was take off her coat and fold it so that the satin lining, and not the furry outside, showed. After she found the elevators, she took one high up into the building and stepped out into a lofty hallway. A series of brass signs on the wall helped her find her way.

As she was walking along, a blond woman in a sleek red suit and matching coat approached in a wave of perfume. The blonde's hair was cropped short, emphasizing her carved cheekbones and tilted eyes, and her jewelry was discreet but expensive. The woman looked over and smiled with a nod.

Callie mimicked the cool upward tip of the chin, thinking she'd have to remember the gesture, and kept going. A little farther down, she stopped in front of a set of double doors marked "Greenough Suite."

She raised her hand to knock, but a voice stopped her. "Are you looking for Mr. Walker?"

Callie turned around. A maid holding a set of towels was looking at her with pleasant inquiry.

"Yes, I am."

"He went out about an hour ago. He should be back soon, but I can't let you in."

"That's okay. I'm happy to wait out here."

After the maid left, Callie leaned against the wall,

cradling her coat in her hands. She was thinking about what she would say when she saw him and remembered the woman in the red suit. How would someone like her greet Jack Walker?

Whatever the words, they would undoubtedly strike the perfect note. Just like the woman's clothes and hair had.

"Sorry to keep you waiting." As she jerked at the sound of Walker's voice, she let out a squeak she could have done without. "Didn't mean to sneak up on you."

She opened her mouth, but any cogent thought stalled as she took a good look at him. The black T-shirt and running shorts were a surprise. And so was the sheen of sweat over his skin.

But his body was what really got her attention.

My God, she thought. He was an athlete under those expensive suits.

The man's shoulders were wide and solid and his arms showed a heavy network of veins and muscle. She couldn't help but glance farther down and noted that his stomach was as flat as the wall she was leaning against and his thighs were corded with strength. He looked like some kind of well-made machine, all superb working parts that had just passed a rigorous test down on the streets of New York.

Callie looked away, aware she was staring. "Would you like me to come back in a half hour?"

"Why?" He opened the door.

"So you can, er, get ready."

"Don't worry. I'm fast with a bar of soap."

Now, there was an image she could do without.

"Are you coming in," he prompted as she stalled in the doorway, "or are we going to do this in the hall?"

She kicked her chin up and brushed past him.

As she stepped into the suite, her feet slowed. It was a palace, room after room of cream and gold with mahogany furniture and thick swaths of brocade drapes. She could see a dining room, a sitting room, and a bar. In a far corner, there were a couple of other doors that probably led into bedrooms.

"I've ordered us breakfast," he said as he sauntered across an Oriental rug that complemented both the pale walls and the dark furniture. "If they come, will you let them in?"

She nodded and put her coat down on a chair.

When she heard a door shut, she started to study the suite in earnest. She figured she might as well take a good long look because she didn't know when she'd be in a hotel room like this again. A flash of color caught her eye. Lying on the glossy surface of a side table was a woman's scarf and next to it were a pair of heavy gold earrings. Callie walked over for a better look. They were beautiful, expensive things and it was easy to imagine the kind of woman they belonged to.

She was willing to bet whoever it was didn't have a hole in the pocket of *her* coat.

Were they his girlfriend's? His lover's?

Or was he married? No, that would have made it into the papers.

Once again, she thought about him reaching out and touching her hair the night before. Remembering the way she'd felt, she found the stories about all those women floating in and out of his bedroom totally believable. In that moment as he'd come toward her, his eyes hooded and fixed on her lips, his broad body throwing off waves of heat even through his clothes, she'd had no interest in turning away. She'd been ready to put her hands on those shoulders and pull him to her.

Which proved that he was dangerously attractive and she was clearly out of her mind.

A soft bell chimed and she crossed the room to let in the waiter delivering their breakfast. She stood to the side and watched as he set up a spread on the dining room table. Silver, crystal, porcelain plates, and heavy linens were arranged with precise, efficient movements. The guy was in and out in less than ten minutes and he didn't hover for a tip, which was a good thing; she had little to offer him.

Grateful for something to do, Callie sat down at the

table and poured herself some coffee. She was lifting the china cup to her mouth when Walker came back into the room.

"Good. I'm starved."

Her hand twitched and some coffee landed on her plate in a brown puddle. She muttered a curse and debated about whether to clean it up while he sat across the table from her.

"Do I make you that nervous?" Walker said in his deep voice.

She glanced up without meeting his eyes. His hair was damp and his crisp white business shirt was open at the collar, revealing the skin of his throat. She smelled his aftershave, something subtle and expensive.

Yes, she thought.

"No," she said. "Does that disappoint you?"

He smiled. "Now, why would I want to make you uncomfortable?"

He poured himself some coffee and then picked up a basket of breads and pastries and offered it her. She hesitated.

"Not eating?" he prompted.

She snatched a cinnamon and raisin bagel before realizing what she'd picked. She hated raisins, but she wasn't putting it back—that was for sure.

He put a muffin on his plate and ladled some cut fruit out of a silver bowl. "I'm glad you're coming to work for me."

"I'm looking forward to it," she said from behind her coffee cup.

"Really?" he drawled, starting to eat. "You still seem conflicted."

"How's that?"

"You haven't looked me in the eye yet."

Callie frowned and forced herself to meet his steady gaze. She noticed flecks of green and yellow in the hazel depths staring back at her.

"There, now, that's not so bad, is it?" he teased with a smile.

"Mr. Walker—"

"Jack."

"Jack," she repeated, "why don't we talk about the job?"

"You don't want us to get to know each other a little bit?"

"That's not what I'm here for."

He shrugged while spearing a strawberry with his fork. "So loosen up. Live a little. You might even like me if you got to know me."

"I doubt that." She shook her head, wondering if she was ever going to learn to think before she spoke to the man. "Listen, I—"

"I'm hurt, Ms. Burke," he murmured. "Or may I call you Callie?"

She rolled her eyes. He didn't seem hurt. In fact, he looked perfectly content as he munched on his breakfast.

If this guy has a tender ego, Callie thought, I'm the tooth fairy.

She gave it another shot. "No offense, but I'm really just interested in the painting."

"Well, maybe I want to learn a little more about you."

"You know my professional background. What else is there?"

He shot her a dry look. "You don't like to talk about yourself?"

"Not to you, no."

"And why is that?"

"Because I have a feeling that anything I say might be used against me."

He laughed, a big, easy sound. "I'm not the police. You're not a criminal. At least as far as I know."

As he smiled at her, she made busywork by spreading cream cheese on the bagel. "So about Nathaniel—"

"You are bound and determined not to enjoy breakfast with me, aren't you?" he said laconically.

"I can't imagine I'd enjoy anything with—" She flushed as he sent her a sharp look. Waving her hand in the air, as if she could erase her words, she muttered, "I'm sorry. I shouldn't have said that."

He considered her for a moment. "You're very honest. And you don't let yourself get pushed around, do you?"

Callie's mouth almost dropped open. Both because he seemed to approve of her candidness and because he was so off base.

How little he knew, she thought, putting the knife down. She'd had to absorb the fallout from her mother's emotional theatrics for years. She'd accepted being relegated to a shameful footnote in her father's life without ever challenging him or telling him how much it hurt. Hell, she'd taken the brunt of Stanley's peevish nature day after day without sticking up for herself.

But Jack Walker didn't need to know all that. And she was quite content to relish his misunderstanding in private.

"Why is it so important that I work for you?" she asked abruptly.

He picked up his cup and she saw his gold cuff links flash.

"We all need a start in life," he said. "You've worked hard and you deserve a chance to make a name for yourself. You've interned with some of the best in the field, but you need to branch out and do something that'll get you noticed. Make your mark."

It was sound advice and a generous inclination on his part. But she didn't know him and he didn't owe her, and that meant the pat explanation didn't hold water. She wondered if Grace had said something. Was he doing this as a favor to her?

"What did Grace tell you about me?" she asked.

He regarded her evenly. "That you're a friend of hers. That you're talented. That it was important to her for you to have a chance at this project. Why?"

"Nothing." She tried to sort through the implications of Grace having a hand in her career. She appreciated the support, although she'd have preferred to get the job solely on her own merits. But maybe she had. Jack Walker didn't seem the type who'd hire anyone on the basis of sentimentality.

And now she better understood why he'd tracked her down.

"Is there a problem?" he asked as she stayed silent.

"I just don't want to be a charity case," she blurted.

He frowned and then laughed.

"Then you'll be pleased to know that my lack of philanthropic interest is legendary. You've got the credentials and you're going to work for every penny. My money's far too important to me to have it any other way." He gestured at her clothes. "Besides, if you can afford to wear Chanel, you're not exactly starving. Although I have to say, I'm surprised you have a workshop in such a worn-down building."

"Workshop?"

He frowned. "The one in Chelsea."

Callie almost laughed. He thought she worked where she lived? It was certainly conceivable. There were a lot of artists' studios in her neighborhood.

She was about to disabuse him of the error when she decided to keep quiet. There was no reason to tell the man her life story, and if he thought she had money, it worked in her favor by putting them on more equal footing.

As she fell silent again, he let out a frustrated noise. "Fine, no more chitchat. When can you start?"

"As soon as you want me to."

"Can you be in Boston the day after tomorrow?"

"Boston?" She stiffened.

"The painting is going to be shipped to my home on Tuesday."

"Oh. I'd assumed it would stay here."

"I don't live here."

"But you could have the portrait bonded and leave it with me," she said hopefully.

"That's not what I had in mind."

And she could tell his mind was made up. "This changes everything."

"Why?"

"All my contacts are here. My, ah, work space. My tools."

"None of that will be a problem," he said smoothly.

Maybe not for him, she thought.

"I'll see to everything for you," he continued. "And I'd like you to stay at Buona Fortuna while you work."

"Where?"

"My house. *Buona fortuna* means good fortune in Italian. My great-great-grandmother had a fondness for the Renaissance period." He took another croissant from the basket. "I'm going to dedicate studio space to you, get you whatever equipment you need. You can set up everything exactly as you want it."

She pictured herself sleeping under the same roof as him and the pool of heat that set up shop in her stomach made her want to get away from the man, not move in with him.

"I don't know whether that would be such a good idea. It could be at least six weeks. That's a long time for a guest."

"True. But it's a big house."

Yeah, well, the damn thing could be the size of a football field and it would still be too small, she thought.

"I don't know."

"I won't charge you for the hospitality," he said with disapproval. "If that's what you're worried about. I'll still pay you the same."

And then he named a price that almost made her fall out of the chair.

With that kind of money, she wouldn't have to worry about rent for a year and then some. She'd be able to do a job search in comfort. She could start a nest egg.

Callie tried to keep her voice level. "That's very generous."

"It's the going rate for a professional. And remember, I'll get you anything you need for your work on the painting."

She hesitated, finding it hard to imagine doing the job in a private home. It wasn't impossible, but it would complicate things.

"Why is it so important that the work be performed at your house?"

"No museum is going to get the mistaken impression that my painting is hanging on any wall but my own. I've been burned a few times, having to wrestle pieces back once they'd been conserved, even if I've footed the bill for the restoration. The attachment can become personal for some conservationists and their museums, which is another reason why you're attractive to me." There was a slight pause. "You're unaffiliated with an institution, so there'll be no confusion."

"But I'll need equipment that will be either prohibitively expensive or hard to get."

"There are no such things," he said, pouring himself some more coffee.

Taking a sip, he looked at her over the rim and she shifted her eyes to his pinkie ring. She was close enough to see that it had a crest on it and she thought that with the money and connections he had, there was probably nothing Jack Walker couldn't get his hands on.

No material possessions, at any rate.

"If there's something you absolutely can't do on-site, we can take it to the MFA. I've already spoken with their head of conservation and he's offered to help even though I've made it clear that I'm going to have an independent do the work." He wiped his mouth on his napkin and leaned back in the chair. "So, you see, everything is arranged. All you need to do is show up."

Callie wavered, thinking the job was taking her in directions she wasn't entirely comfortable with.

Moving sharply, Walker threw down his napkin and got to his feet. "I've got a meeting in ten minutes. I know my terms are generous so I'm not inclined to negotiate. Are you in or out?"

As she measured his expression, she realized he was

totally prepared to walk away, and that eased some of her concern.

She took a deep breath. "Where should I meet you in Boston?"

Showing no particular reaction, he walked over to a desk.

"My house is in Wellesley. We live on Cliff Road." He bent down and wrote something with a gold pen. "That's the address and phone number. I'll make a point to be there by five on Tuesday."

He handed her the paper and she squinted at the wide scrawl. His handwriting was barely legible.

"Is this a nine?" she asked, surprised at how sloppy it was.

He nodded and smiled. "My penmanship has always been awful. It was one of many things my father never liked about me. A therapist would probably tell you my enduring carelessness is a passive-aggressive expression of independence targeted at a dead man. But I reject that theory out of hand."

She couldn't help it. The corners of her mouth lifted.

"You don't smile very often, do you?" he said softly.

Callie folded her napkin and stood up, clearing her throat. "Thank you for this opportunity."

Walker extended his hand to her and looked darkly amused as she just stared at it. When she finally stuck her hand out, his fingers wrapped around hers and she felt a surge of warmth shoot up her arm. She pulled back quickly and went over to pick up her coat.

He frowned as he looked at it.

"May I help you with that?" he murmured.

She shook her head, draped it over her arm, and headed for the door.

"Callie?"

She halted and looked over her shoulder.

Jack Walker stared at her for a long time, his eyes lingering on her hair and then moving downward. She shifted her coat so it blocked his view of her body, feeling as though she was being measured against something. She wondered what the standard was.

When he said nothing, she got antsy. "Good-bye, Mr. Walker."

"Jack. Call me Jack."

She didn't bother replying and left his suite quickly.

As she rode down in the elevator, her body shaking and her head in a fog, she had to remind herself that she'd survived a hell of a lot worse than the job offer of a lifetime. Just because her new boss was capable of melting paint off a wall with those hazel eyes of his didn't mean she should be overwhelmed.

She just had to be strong.

And, fortunately, she'd spent a lifetime in training for that.

Jack stared at the door.

She was really quite attractive. He'd never bought that whole passionate redhead cliché, but there was a real fire in her. He loved how she stood up to him and the fact that she fought harder whenever she was especially uncomfortable.

Was she with someone? She didn't wear a wedding ring, but maybe there was a boyfriend in the picture.

He frowned, thinking that shouldn't be relevant.

The phone rang and he answered it. Grayson Bennett, his college roommate, was on the line.

"I've cleared my calendar," Gray said. "I'm ready to spend the next month or so assessing your candidacy in Boston."

"Excellent. What's the first order of business?"

"We're going to set up your exploratory committee. We'll pull together ten or twelve people from different sectors in the state and do a quiet assessment of the landscape. We need to know who will back you and who's going to be trouble, what kind of money we can raise, how you're perceived. Should take four or five weeks."

"When are you coming in?"

"Tomorrow night. I'm staying at the Four Seasons."

"You bringing female company?" As a resounding no came over the line, Jack laughed. "No more—what was her name? Sarah?"

"Sophia. No, she's gone. She was starting to talk rings, and as you know, I'm allergic to diamonds. She's a good woman—for someone else."

After they hung up, Jack headed for the bedroom to finish getting dressed. For a long time, he and Gray had shared the same view of marriage, namely that it was right for other people. But hell, if he could change his mind, so could Gray.

Just not when it came to Sophia, evidently.

The grandfather clock in the corner started to chime and Jack hurried up.

In a few minutes, he was going to meet with two brothers, one a physician and the other an engineer. Bryan and Kevin McKay had devised a new, faster, and cleaner way of processing blood products like plasma and platelets. They had the proper patents, so the intellectual property rights were sewn up, and with some good contracts with a few hospitals, they had an income stream. Currently housed in a small shop on the West Coast, they wanted to expand and they needed some big money. If they had the right mix of debt to equity and some reasonable growth projections, Jack figured there was a potential to make some money.

He was looking forward to the meeting and there was no better way to spend a Sunday afternoon as far as he was concerned. One of the things he liked about the venture capital business was that it was twenty-four/seven. There was never any downtime, no wasted moments, always something that needed to be done. Sundays, holidays, birthdays, weddings. He worked through them all.

Hell, the day his father had been buried, he'd spent half the wake in his study setting up the funding for a tech firm down in Atlanta. But that hadn't just been about business, he supposed. He'd found it difficult to mourn someone whose sustained disapproval had marked his life so indelibly, and getting some work done had seemed like a more productive use of time than faking sorrow.

Bad family dynamics aside, with every sunrise, there were places he had to be, things he needed to accomplish, people who wanted to get to him and his money. It was a nonstop, frenetic ride with no clear end in sight. In all that swirling chaos, he found purpose. He knew being governor of Massachusetts would be just as complicated and demanding. And if he ever made it to the Oval Office, the stakes would be astronomical.

Jack slid a silk tie around his neck and faced the mirror. He couldn't wait for the future.

5

ON TUESDAY, Callie took a train up the coast of Connecticut to Boston's Back Bay Station and then transferred to a commuter rail line that took her out to the suburbs. As she stepped off in Wellesley with her old Samsonite suitcase and a toolbox full of supplies, she stared up a steep hill.

Now she knew why they called it Cliff Road.

By the time she walked up to a pair of stone pillars bearing the right number, her arms were going numb and she had pins and needles in her shoulders. She dropped her load and looked down the driveway. There wasn't much to see. The strip of asphalt disappeared into a thicket of underbrush and trees.

She picked up her things again and started down the last leg of her journey. She told herself, as she had innumerable times during the trip, that everything was going to be okay. She was going to do a good job and Jack Walker was going to be too busy running his business empire to bother with her.

And even if it was awful, nothing lasted forever.

When she rounded a corner, uneasiness came over her like a curse.

"Good fortune" my foot, she thought, looking at the mansion.

The house, which was painted a dark gray, was a towering mausoleum as it rose from its stone foundation.

There were porches and cupolas and a tower at the top and the various eaves and corners threw off a host of shadows that made the place seem even gloomier. The grounds didn't help lighten the mood any. They were austere, with only clipped bushes and beds of pachysandra to soften the mansion's footprint. But at least there were several big trees on the property. The oaks and maples arched their limbs over a lawn that was big enough to play pro football on and the grass was just as well tended as any playing field's.

She started walking again. The drive was a good hundred yards long and it split to wrap around the house. The left half went to the garage, which was two stories high and had four bays. The other led under a porte cochere that shielded the main entrance of the mansion. She went to the right.

When she got to the heavy front door, she dropped her suitcase and toolbox. Reminding herself she was an invited guest, not an interloper, she let the brass door knocker fall.

A woman in her forties answered it. As she looked Callie up and down, her eyes weren't unkind, but they weren't exactly warm, either.

"Yes?" The air of purpose about her suggested she worked at the house, though she wasn't wearing a uniform.

"I'm Callie Burke."

"The conservationist?" The woman's expression changed to one of surprise.

Callie nodded.

"Oh—ah, he told us you'd be coming." The woman frowned, taking in the orange suitcase and the furry coat. "Mrs. Walker was looking forward to your arrival."

Mrs. Walker?

"Actually, I was expecting to meet Mr. Walker."

"He's not home yet. She is here, though."

Surprise, surprise, Callie thought. She hadn't read that he'd been married, but then, she hadn't been picking up the paper as much as she used to. The idea that he had a wife made her feel more at ease in a way.

Unless he really had been about to kiss her in front of her building, in which case she felt worse.

An awkward silence followed, until Callie said, "Is there something wrong?"

"I'm so sorry. I should be more . . . Welcome to Buona Fortuna," the woman said, extending her hand. Her eyes began to warm up. "I'm Elsie, Mrs. Walker's personal secretary. We were expecting someone a little . . ."

"Older?" As the woman nodded, Callie smiled and shook hands before stepping inside. "I can understand that."

Once her eyes adjusted, she saw glowing mahogany walls carved with deep reliefs, a stone fireplace that ran from floor to ceiling, and a lot of heavy European furniture. It was like walking into a Renaissance exhibit at a museum.

And just about as cozy.

"Mrs. Walker will be down in a moment. Why don't you wait in the solarium and I'll have your bags taken upstairs?"

Callie nodded and shrugged out of her coat.

"You can give that to me. Do you need anything?"

She shook her head. "No, I'm fine."

"The solarium is through there, past the library, and out the other side."

When Callie finally found it, the bright, sunny room was a relief. The solarium, with its glass walls and pale slate flooring, looked as if it had been decorated by someone else entirely.

Someone who hadn't been born a Medici back in the fifteenth century.

There were chintz chairs and a comfortable sofa to sit on, and white wicker side tables supported lamps made out of Oriental vases. She took a deep breath. The warm, humid air smelled of the flowers that were growing around the room in perfectly maintained beds.

She was looking through the glass at the undulating lawn when she heard soft footsteps. She turned, very curious about who exactly Jack Walker had married, and found herself meeting the soulful eyes of an Irish wolf-hound. The dog was about the size of a small pony and covered with a shaggy gray coat of fur. He wagged his tail in a tentative welcome.

"Well, hello," she said softly, getting down on her haunches.

The dog approached, moving in a slow, loping walk. His head was taller than hers as she kneeled in front of him, but though his size was daunting, his eyes gave him away. They were limpid pools of friendliness.

She was stroking his head when a voice cut through the room.

"I see you've met Arthur."

Callie looked over into an impeccably aged face. Her first impression was that the woman had once been incredibly beautiful. The next was that the proprietary glare coming out of her brown eyes was about as welcoming as a Taser gun.

My God, she thought, this wasn't his wife.

The great Jack Walker lived with his *mother*.

She wanted to laugh, but knew the outburst wouldn't have gone over well. Mrs. Walker looked as if she didn't find much humor in anything.

"So you are the conservationist my son has chosen," the woman said, stepping into the room. Her stark white hair was pulled back from her face and the severe style showed off her set of spectacular cheekbones. She was wearing a tweed pantsuit that had the clean lines of haute couture and there was a lot of heavy gold jewelry around her neck.

She was right out of central casting. The quintessential grande dame.

Callie got to her feet. "Yes, I'm Callie Burke."

"You're a little young for this, don't you think?" The comment was followed by a chilly little smile.

"I can do the work, Mrs. Walker. And your son is confident of this or he wouldn't have hired me."

The smile disappeared. "You do realize that Copley was the painter?"

As if Callie might have mistaken the thing for a Le-Roy Neiman.

"Of course."

"Well, it's Jack's money wasted if you fail. Not to mention the loss to the art world, which would be significant. But I'm sure you'll perform to the best of your abilities."

Callie lifted her brows.

Well, at least you didn't have to dig for her put-downs. Anything more obvious and Jack's mother would be burying a knife in her chest.

Though she was tempted to shoot something back, she forced herself to keep quiet and was surprised as the dog leaned against her legs. She put her hand down and stroked his ear, appreciating his support.

Mrs. Walker frowned.

"Arthur seems to like you." Her tight lips suggested that the virtue he'd found was a mystery. "I'll let Elsie show you to a room. Jack just called me. He told me to apologize on his behalf because he will be late tonight. I'm going out, so you will be alone."

Now, that was terrific news.

Jack's mother walked away, but paused in the doorway to give Callie the once-over again. "Wherever did Jack find you?"

At the local pound for starving artisans, she wanted to toss back. One more week of no work and they were going to gas me. He saved my life!

Instead, she just let the woman go. She wanted to tell the venerable Mrs. Walker exactly what she could do with her attitude, but that was just going to make the next six weeks even harder to get through. Besides, she'd endured worse than what Jack's mother could dish out. Growing up she'd worn thick glasses, braces, and bad clothes, and her father had never shown up on parents' days. Bullies were the same whether they were in the school yard or a solarium.

Anyway, it looked like she didn't have to do much to get back at Mrs. Walker. Callie's mere presence in the house seemed to be revenge enough.

Elsie came back in, looking tense. "You can follow me."

Arthur came with them. When they got to the front hall, instead of going up the massive staircase, they continued through an ornate, golden dining room and into a restaurant-quality kitchen.

Elsie led the way over to a cramped set of stairs. After going up two flights, they emerged into a bare hall lined with six doors. Unlike the rest of the house, which was festooned with antiques, here there were no paintings or rugs. It looked downright institutional.

Elsie opened a door, revealing a single bed, a dresser, and a table. The walls were white, the floor made of more bare wood, and there was a radiator under the window that was making a hissing noise. Callie saw her things in the corner.

Servants' quarters.

She looked at Elsie. The woman was obviously embarrassed as she pointed down the hall.

"The bathroom's three doors down to the right. You'll have to share it with Thomas, but don't worry. He's a neat freak, even if he looks like a Hells Angel."

Callie cocked an eyebrow.

"Thanks for the reassurance," she murmured, as she went in and sat on the bed. It made a rusty squeak and Elsie winced.

Callie smiled up at the woman. Whatever her feelings about the accommodations, she wasn't going to be rude to the messenger. "This will work out just fine. I'm so tired, I could sleep on the floor."

The bed let out another protest and she eyed the pine planks, thinking that might well be where she ended up.

Elsie started to back out of the room.

"It's the rest of the staff's day off. I'm leaving now, but I'll be back tomorrow," she said, as if she felt like Callie needed a friend in the household. "If there's anything you want, just ask me. I'll make sure you're taken care of. Oh, and there's plenty of food downstairs. Help yourself."

"Thanks."

Elsie stared at her for a moment and then left, looking as if someone had asked her to leave a stray puppy by the side of the road.

Callie stood up and glanced out the door, wondering whom she was sharing a bathroom with. Trading off shower time in the morning wasn't exactly what she'd had in mind. But then again, had anything concerning Jack Walker gone according to her plans so far? Not hardly. She should be getting used to surprises.

Besides, she was just an employee, not a guest. And one good thing was that the chances of Mrs. Walker showing up in this part of the house were slim to none.

So maybe it was for the best.

Arthur, who was roaming around the room, investigating corners and sniffing under the bed, looked up as if to inquire whether they were heading down to the kitchen.

"Sorry, Artie. I need to get settled first."

The dog heaved a sigh and fell into a heap at the foot of the bed. With his head down on his massive paws, his eyes followed her as she unpacked.

Parceling out her meager wardrobe into the dresser drawers, Callie wondered how long it would take for Jack's mother to get out of the house.

Rule number one with bullies: A good avoidance strategy can nip a lot of conflict in the bud. She was just going to give Mrs. Walker a wide berth.

Callie pictured the woman's haughty, disapproving face and grinned.

Kind of like you would with any other type of WASP.

6

JACK PULLED his Aston Martin into the garage and got out. He'd expected to get home much earlier, but the negotiations he'd begun with the blood brothers weren't going as well as he'd hoped. There were some issues with their debt financing structure that were going to make securing a large, unfettered interest in the company close to impossible. The McKays had borrowed money from a legion of family members during their research and development phase and had given away a substantial amount of their shares in return.

Hell, he'd be lucky to get a quarter ownership of the thing, which would hardly justify the nine-digit investment they needed.

He'd learned long ago not to put his money into anything he couldn't get it back out of. His father had taught him that lesson. The first hundred thousand the man had "borrowed" from him had been lost into the ether. After that, Jack had required that some transfer of property, either real estate, jewelry, or art, occur in his favor before he wrote a check to Nathaniel Six.

God, his father had hated him for that. But the elder Nathaniel had been more horrified at the thought of going to a bank and begging for money from people he wouldn't have sit at his dinner table. Jack owned everything by the time Nathaniel Six died. The cars, the houses in Wellesley, Palm Beach, and the Adirondacks, the art collection, his mother's big jewels. His father, after starting with millions of dollars in the 1950s, had just under a hundred thousand dollars to his name when he was buried.

Jack activated the automatic door and heard it shut with a rumbling sound as he walked over to the porte cochere.

Having the Copley portrait in his possession meant everything to him. As soon as the painting was conserved, it was going back over the mantelpiece in the living room where it hung when he and his brother were growing up. In reclaiming the first Nathaniel, he felt like he'd closed the circle and all of the financial chaos his father had caused was over. Finally.

As he let himself in the house, he called out, "Callie? Hello?"

When there was no answer, he put his briefcase down and walked through the living room to the library, then through the den and the solarium. Lights were on in all the rooms, but she was nowhere to be found. When he got back to the front hall, he looked up the stairs and wondered if he should go hunting for her among the guest rooms.

A picture of her in one of his beds brought up images he was determined not to dwell on and he was debating the merits of going upstairs to find her when he realized something was missing. Where was Arthur? The dog was usually waiting at the door for him.

Jack headed to the kitchen. Next to the sink, a bowl, plate, and fork had been carefully washed and left to dry, so he knew for sure she was in the house. No one else would have left dishes out like that. His mother rarely set foot in the kitchen and certainly never cleaned up after herself. The staff had the day off and Elsie would have gone home to have dinner with her own family.

He was resigning himself to a search of the guest rooms when Arthur came down the back stairs.

"What are you doing up there?" He bent down as the dog ambled over in his heavy way.

"He was with me."

Jack's head shot up.

Callie was standing at the foot of the stairs, wearing jeans and a navy blue fleece pullover. Her hair was all around her shoulders and he stared into her eyes, testing once again whether he had the color right, whether they really were that beautiful blue.

They were.

Before the silence continued for too long, he said, "I'm sorry I'm so damn late."

She shrugged. "Artie and I have had a fine evening, although I suspect he'd have preferred my dinner be a little less leafy. He doesn't seem to be a big fan of salad."

Jack's eyes narrowed as he assessed her mood. She really didn't seem perturbed. She'd been perfectly happy in an unfamiliar house all by herself, with just his dog as company.

So all that independence wasn't just an act, he thought.

"Are you already setting up your workshop?" he asked, nodding at the stairs. "I thought being over the garage would suit you better, but if you'd rather be in the house, that's fine, too."

Her brows lifted. "Actually, I've been reading about Copley and trying not to fall asleep before you got home."

He gave Arthur a sound pat on the ribs and straightened.

"So what are you doing in the staff quarters?"

"That's where my room is."

Jack frowned. "What the hell—" He stopped himself. He didn't have to ask who'd put her up there. "You are not staying in the staff wing."

And he and his mother were going to have a little talk in the morning.

Callie pushed her hands into her pockets. "I'm quite comfortable up there."

"Don't be absurd." He started toward the stairs. "Let's move your things."

She raised her hands. "Look, I really don't care. All I need is a place to sleep."

"How can you say that? I'll bet the last time you stayed in a room like that was back in prep school."

"I didn't go to prep school," she countered softly.

Jack stopped, frowned again, and then kept going. "Whatever. Come on, let's go."

He strode past her, thinking his mother's ability to stick her nose into things was unparalleled.

When he got to the head of the narrow stairs, he headed for the open door. "Where are your clothes?"

As she came into the room, she gave him a steady look. "In the drawers."

He glanced over at the small dresser. "Where else?"

"Nowhere else." She went and opened a drawer, gesturing over the shirts and sweaters that were neatly folded. "Just here."

Well, this was a new one, Jack thought.

He was used to women who needed a moving van to go away for the weekend. She was staying for a month and a half and her things fit in three drawers.

"You're a light packer."

She shrugged. "I don't need much."

"What about your tools?"

"In the closet."

"So let's pack you up," he said impatiently.

She regarded him evenly, as if weighing the inconvenience of moving against having to deal with him, and then she went over to the closet and took out a battered Samsonite suitcase that surprised the hell out of him. He'd have expected a Louis Vuitton matched set or even a bunch of Coach bags. Instead, her piece of luggage was ancient, orange, and looked as if it had seen a lot of cargo holds.

As he watched her move her clothes around, he realized something.

Whatever her relationship was with Grace, wherever that Chanel suit had come from, Callie didn't have much money. The things being taken out of the dresser were clean and serviceable, but inexpensive. There wasn't a lick of couture in sight.

When she was finished, he couldn't keep his voice from becoming gentle. "Do you have everything?"

Her eyes rose to his and narrowed, as if she'd caught the change in tone and would have preferred if he'd stayed impatient. After nodding with a strong chin, she picked up the suitcase and a wooden box covered with paint smudges, and headed out the door.

"Let me take something for you," he said as she banged her way down the narrow staircase.

"I've got it."

"At least let me take the suitcase."

"If I can get this load from Penn Station to your house, I can move it to another bedroom."

Penn Station? Jack frowned, picturing her with the heavy burden, transferring trains and walking through Back Bay Station. He had a feeling she'd probably skipped the taxi and taken the commuter train out to Wellesley, too. Which meant she'd also dragged the weight all the way up from the base of Cliff Road.

Damn it all, he thought, as he led her through the kitchen and up the main stairs. He assumed she would have flown in and taken a limo out from Logan Airport.

He felt like a heel.

"You should have told me if you needed transportation," he said. "I would have sent my plane for you."

He heard her stop moving and looked over his shoulder.

"I don't need any handouts," she told him. "I got here just fine on my own."

"But that's not the point. I could have made it easier on you."

"I'm not interested in easy."

He thought that was obvious, going by the luggage dangling from her hands. As she stared back in silence, her determination not to rely on him in any way irked the hell out of him.

"Struggling needlessly isn't the only way to become

a martyr," he said drily. "You could strap on a hair shirt and live on top of a pillar for a month or two."

She shored up the load, reminding him of how much she was carrying. "Tell you what. When I need to be rescued, I'll let you know."

He scowled and kept going, knowing it would be a cold day in the devil's living room before she would ask him for anything. And why that defiance bothered him so much, he couldn't fathom. Maybe it was just a tremendous change from what women usually expected of him.

Hell, even Blair, who was hardly a lightweight when it came to taking care of herself, relied on his jet, his contacts with Fortune 500 companies, and his connections in the art world. And he didn't mind that at all. In fact, he liked it.

When he got to the top of the landing, he took a right and led her down to the best guest room in the house. As he opened the door and flipped on the light, he heard her gasp.

The Red Room was a real showstopper, he thought, which was precisely why he gave it to her. If she wouldn't let him help her overtly, he was determined to take care of her through back channels.

Callie stepped inside and slowly dropped her load. The delight on her face made his chest swell with pleasure because he'd finally done something that made her happy.

The room was decorated in deep red and burnished gold. In the center, there was a mammoth canopy bed in the Jacobean style, a little something that his great-great-grandmother had imported from an English castle. A fireplace, made of rich russet marble, was set with logs and above its mantel was a painting of the Madonna and Child dating to the sixteenth century. The best detail, though, was the stained-glass window that faced the front lawn. Framed in swaths of thick red silk, the built-in seat under it had pillows of every size and shape to lounge on.

"Goodness," Callie breathed, going over to the fire-place and then the window. Her next stop was the bed. She ran her fingers up the teak supports and over the acres of tasseled velvet that hung from the top. "This is magnificent."

As her hands stroked the rich cloth, Jack found himself wanting to remember exactly how she looked in his favorite room in the house.

"Red suits you," he murmured.

She went back to the fireplace and her eyes widened as they took in the painting. "Is this a Caravaggio?"

He nodded. "What do you think of it?"

She was silent for a long time. When she finally spoke, her voice was commanding and he smiled, thinking it was how he sounded when he talked about mezzanine debt and interest rates.

"It's magnificent, clearly from the height of his prominence. But I'm shocked at its location. Is this fireplace ever used?"

"No. I've had it sealed."

"Good. Repeated, radical changes in temperature are death to an oil painting." She flashed her eyes over at him. "You should have this conserved. When was the last time it was cleaned?"

"My great-grandmother bought it in Italy in the nineteen twenties. I don't know that anything's been done to it since."

She made a disapproving noise in the back of her throat as she studied the work more. Her absorption was total, her breathing shallow. He figured a stink bomb could go off in the room and she probably wouldn't notice.

This woman was pretty close to fantastic, he thought.

"So, Callie, maybe we should go through the whole house together and you can tell me what else needs attention."

"Be happy to." She went over to the window seat and looked through the small clear windows on either side of the stained-glass panels. Arthur went with her as if to supervise, putting two paws on the cushions and arching forward, almost as tall as she was on his hind legs. Callie's arm stole around his scruffy neck and she patted his shoulder absently.

As Jack stared at the two of them, he knew he should go. There was something altogether too appealing in the picture they made.

"The painting's arrival was delayed," he said. "It's supposed to come tomorrow. But I can show you the space over the garage first thing in the morning."

She looked over her shoulder. "Great."

"The bathroom's through there." He pointed over to a paneled door. "And I'm across the hall if you want anything."

Her eyes skipped away from his as she straightened. Once again, he had the impression she'd wait until the house was burning down and she'd run out of water before she'd knock on his door.

What would it take for her to open up? he wondered.

"Do you need anything?" When she shook her head, he undid his jacket and started to loosen his tie. "Listen, I'm sorry I wasn't here when you arrived."

She shrugged. "It really wasn't a problem."

"My mother—"

"Is a lovely lady." She cocked an eyebrow at him, daring him to call her on the bluff. It was obvious she was going to take the high road, and he respected her for it.

But he wasn't going to stand for her being disrespected while under his roof.

"If you have any problems with her, let me know."

"Now, why would I have to do that?" she returned softly.

Whether she was talking about his mother's bad behavior or coming to him, it wasn't clear. Probably both.

There was a long pause. When Callie's eyes shifted to the bed, becoming wide and pleased again, he thought it was highly probable that she lived in the building in Chelsea.

The very place he'd told her he was surprised she'd even have a work studio in.

Christ, he wished he could take that little zinger back.

"Come on, Arthur," he said, going to the door.

The dog looked over at Callie and then back at him with a discerning eye.

"Here, boy," Jack said, patting his thigh.

The dog lowered his butt to the floor and Jack measured the defection with a grin. "He likes you."

"I like him."

Callie looked down at the dog with nothing but warmth in her face. There was no not-so-subtle caution. No closure. Just a small, secret smile meant only for Arthur.

No wonder the beast had fallen in love with her, Jack thought. Man or dog would be enchanted with such a look.

"Good night, then," he said.

"Good night." She was still smiling at Arthur as he shut the door.

Standing in the hallway, he hung his head and looked down at his wing tips. He should not be interested in another woman's smile.

Hell, he shouldn't even be *noticing* another woman's smile.

He shook his head. At least he hadn't had any more of those dreams. Since Callie had agreed to come to Boston, his subconscious had stopped running the Playboy Channel.

But it was a damn shame his memory was so good.

The sound of the front door being shut brought his head up. It had to be his mother, home from the symphony. As he headed downstairs, his mouth was set in a grim line.

She was just taking off her coat when she saw him.

"Jackson, darling, how was your day? I saw the Carradines—"

"Why the hell did you put her in the staff quarters?"

His mother's eyes rounded in surprise. "You mean

the conservationist? Darling, she's here to work, isn't she? She's not a guest."

"She's here at my invitation. She's staying in the Red Room."

Mercedes paused as she measured him and then resumed putting her coat away. "As you wish. It was never my intention to upset you."

"You didn't upset me—you insulted my guest and pissed me off."

Jack turned to go back upstairs, thinking it was better for them both that he get away from her. He really didn't appreciate her games and he was feeling particularly protective of Callie.

Probably because she'd handled his mother's affront with such grace.

"Jackson, don't be angry," Mercedes called up after him. "How was I to know? I mean, she doesn't exactly look like a guest of ours, does she?"

Jack paused and glanced over his shoulder. "She is a guest of *mine*. Staying in *my* house. So she's going to be treated properly."

His mother lost a bit of her bravado. "Jack, I had no idea she was so important."

He turned and kept going, not trusting himself to respond.

After his father died, it had seemed a little much to kick her out of the house she'd lived in for some forty years. At the time he'd also figured keeping her at Buona Fortuna would save him the cost of funding yet another household. With no money of her own, and no skills to offer in the workplace, she couldn't support herself, and it wasn't as if she could sponge off her other son. Nate wasn't making the kind of income that could maintain the lifestyle she'd become accustomed to. Jack was her meal ticket and all three of them knew it.

He shook his head. She was a perfect example of where beauty and brains could take a person. Unlike Nathaniel Six, she hadn't come from wealth. For all her haughty airs, his mother had started her life in the fishing town of Gloucester, the fourth child out of six in a family of Portuguese fishermen. Her one goal was to get out into the big world, so at fifteen, she'd changed her name from Myrna to Mercedes and vowed to find her destiny somewhere far away from her roots. When she was accepted to Smith College on a scholarship, she'd been ready to make her mark.

Or put her mark on an eligible man, as was the case.

Jack's father had fit the bill nicely, coming from much wealth and being of the Walker name and legacy. They'd met through friends when Nathaniel Six came over from Harvard one fine, spring weekend of his senior year. Her beauty caught his eye and her aggressive nature had ensured he didn't have the opportunity to stray. Three months later, she dropped out of college and they were married discreetly at the Episcopal church in Osterville on Cape Cod.

It had proven to be a good match, Jack supposed. His father hadn't been bothered in the slightest by her background. In fact, he'd been more than happy to have her on his arm while he taught her what she didn't know. And, like the outstanding student she was, Mercedes soaked up the lessons in better living and then exceeded all expectations. By her thirties, she'd firmly established herself in Boston's social set. In her forties and fifties, she joined the right nonprofit boards and became respected for her civic contributions. Now, in her early seventies, she was held in esteem by the WASP establishment, courted by climbers, and generally regarded as the arbiter of taste when it came to judging which holiday parties were worth going to.

Her ascent was something she was no doubt proud of, but it was only a victory of appearances. Though her determination had carried her to heights of wealth and social power she hadn't dared dream of as a child, nothing could change the fact that she'd been born into the working class. Jack had always thought it was a truth she despaired of even though no one else seemed to think twice about her modest beginnings, at least not in her immediate family. In fact, Nathaniel Six had regarded the wife he'd transformed into the toast of Boston society as a badge of honor.

Frankly, Jack didn't know how she'd withstood all those years of condescending affection.

The trade-off, though, was one hell of a lifestyle.

As he went down to his bedroom, he was convinced that Mercedes and Callie had a humble start in common. It made him wonder why, assuming Callie could have used the money, she'd turned him down twice before accepting his generous job offer.

He paused outside of her door. While he was trying to see through the wood, his mother's voice drifted down the hall.

"What are you doing?"

He wanted to snap at her to leave him the hell alone. Instead, he went over to his own door and said smoothly, "I thought we already said good night."

"Jackson."

"What?"

"She's not your kind, Jackson."

He shot a glare down the hall. Mercedes was standing under the light at the head of the stairs, her face drawn in dramatic shadows, her cheeks hollow, her lips painted red with the lipstick she always wore.

When he didn't reply, she spoke with urgency. "You must always remember. You carry the Walker legacy."

"You don't need to remind me of that. Not when I'm cutting all the checks to keep it alive."

He was opening his door as she came down the hall at him. "I heard about Blair tonight. Why didn't you tell me yourself?"

Jack crossed his arms over his chest, trying to think whom she could have heard it from. They hadn't kept the engagement a secret, but there had been no wide announcement, either.

"It really isn't relevant," he said.

"You're getting married. Of course it's relevant." Her eyes started to light up with an enthusiasm that exhausted him. "When is the date?"

Ah, yes, the precise question he wanted to avoid. He told himself this was because he didn't want his mother meddling in his and Blair's affairs, but the image of Callie flashed in his mind and wouldn't leave.

"We haven't decided."

Mercedes frowned. "Have you made announcement arrangements yet? What about the papers?"

"I haven't contacted them."

She smiled. "Well, no worry. I'll call tomorrow—"

"No, you won't."

"Jackson, this is—"

"None of your business, Mother."

She rolled her shoulders back and arched her elegant brows. "Well."

Jack smiled grimly while the silence stretched between them.

If she wanted to wait for him to give her free rein with the planning, she'd be sleeping out in the hall, he thought.

Mercedes's chin rose. "No announcement, no date. Why did you bother to ask her to marry you?"

As he refused to entertain the question, he watched a subtle triumph flare in his mother's eyes and thought her accuracy for finding vulnerable points was a gift. For her, at any rate. He supposed that everyone needed a hobby and his mother's favorite one was exposing people's weaknesses.

Though why the hell she couldn't take up knitting like every other seventy-year-old was a crying shame. After all, she'd still get to use needles.

"Sleep well, Mother," he said, stepping into his room.

"Please, Jack." The aggression drained from her face, revealing an impotency she must have despised feeling. "I only want to help."

"Then let us handle it. We'll let you know if we need you." He shut the door firmly.

7

CALLIE CAME awake with a jerk. She had the eerie sense she was being watched, and when she rolled over, she ran into a furry face and a lolling pink tongue.

"What the—"

Bolting upright, it took her a moment to remember where she was and that Arthur had stayed with her during the night. His tail wagged shyly, as if he was dismayed and a little hurt by her reaction.

She leaned forward and put her hands under his ears. "Sorry, Artie. I'm not used to waking up next to a man."

His tail went back and forth with a wider sweep as he rose on his hind legs and put the upper half of himself on the bed. As she rubbed his chest, she looked out the windows. By the pale gray in the sky, she guessed it was probably around seven.

"I imagine you want to go out." She didn't have a lot of experience with dogs, but figured his visit to the bed wasn't just a social call.

She was pulling on her jeans when she heard a knock at the door.

When she opened it and Jack was on the other side, she had her second jolt of the morning. He looked sexy as hell. His hair was still damp, the dark waves thick and shiny, and he had on a black sweater and blue jeans. The casual clothes looked good on him.

But what wouldn't, she thought, eyeing the span of his chest.

He smiled and leaned against the doorframe. "Good morning."

"Yes?" she said, aware that she was staring and unable to help it.

"I've come for my dog."

"Ah—he's right here." Obligingly, Arthur appeared in the doorway.

"Did he keep you awake? He chases groundhogs in his dreams a lot."

Callie shook her head and tried not to smile, thinking if she felt more comfortable with the man, she might have asked how he knew they were groundhogs. "I sleep through anything."

"Good trait to have."

The conversation stalled and she began to fidget while he continued to look at her. She racked her brain for a way to get him to move along. She was quite sure there were more amusing things for Jack Walker the great to do, none of which would involve her standing awkwardly in a doorway, trying to make small talk with him.

"Why don't you meet me downstairs," he said finally. "We'll head for the garage and you can set up your workshop."

"The sooner, the better," she said under her breath.

Both his brows rose. "Are you always so focused?"

"I just want to get this job over with," she blurted. "What I mean is, I don't want to waste any time here." She shook her head. "Rather, I really—"

"Should I take your rush to get out of here personally? I wonder." He straightened from his casual pose with a half smile. "Come on, Arthur."

Callie watched him and the dog go down the hall.

She had to admit, she liked the way he moved. What she wasn't quite so fond of was his habit of staring at her. She couldn't begin to imagine what he found so fascinating.

Although the larger problem, she supposed, was her

response. The warm feeling that came over her skin and sank into her bones was disconcerting.

Mostly because she wouldn't mind getting used to it.

Shutting the door, Callie knew she shouldn't deny the truth. She was attracted to Jack in spite of his past with women and all his money. Part of it was physical, of course, but after last night there was more. His indignant response when he saw where his mother had put her showed that her comfort and her pride mattered to him. His sensitivity had been unexpected and the fact that he'd wanted to take care of her had been . . . appreciated even as she'd made a point to prove her independence to him.

She shook her head and reminded herself whom she was dealing with.

An exhibition of good manners didn't mean he'd turned into Prince Charming. Ruthless men could still be polite. After all, her father had possessed the manners of English royalty and still managed to cheat on his wife for decades. Romanticizing Jack Walker was not in her best interests. If she really wanted to take care of herself, she'd work long hours and get out of his house as quickly as she could.

So yes, the man certainly could take her desire to get his project done fast personally.

After showering, she grabbed her toolbox and went downstairs, unsure of exactly where she was supposed to meet Jack. She listened and heard a voice down at the far end of the house. Following the sound, she eventually found him in his study.

He was standing behind a large desk, facing a set of French doors that were hung with maroon velvet drapes. The room was paneled in a dark wood and had a spectacular domed ceiling on which a scene of cherubim and clouds had been painted. Across from the desk, there was a black marble wet bar and a bank of TV screens that were silently projecting MSNBC, CNN, and CNBC.

She was about to knock on the doorjamb to get his attention when he barked into the phone, "I don't give a damn what he said. He cooked the numbers, so I'm not doing the deal. Tell him he can find another sucker."

She noticed that he had the receiver tight against his ear and his free hand was cranked in a fist.

This, she thought, was the real Jack Walker.

Abruptly, his body tilted forward, as if he was actually standing in front of the person he was yelling at. "Look, I've got a half a dozen other deals going right now, so I only have two more words to spare on this one. Fuck. Him."

Callie jumped back as he slammed the phone down.

"God *damn* it." He raked his hand through his hair and wheeled around, grabbing something off his desk.

The moment he saw her, he cleared his throat. "Callie."

"Why don't I come back?"

"No." He let the paper fall out of his hand, watching it land on the desk. "No."

He put his hands on his hips and released a slow, deep breath. When he looked back up at her, the aggression was mostly gone.

"Let's go."

As he walked past her, she gave him plenty of space.

Leading the way to the garage, Jack was struggling to control his anger. Thanks to the financial muscle he had, most people didn't screw with him, but desperation and money could make fools out of almost anyone. If he was going to stay on top of his game, he needed to remember that happy little fact and not be so surprised when someone tried to do a nasty on him.

But hell, he'd done his homework on that deal. He'd dedicated resources. He'd expended time and thought. To discover at the tenth hour that he'd been lied to was a real insult. It had happened before and it would happen again, but that didn't mean he had to like getting served bullshit. And if his reaction had been hotter than usual, it was because he was frustrated that he or one of his people hadn't caught the problem sooner.

He looked at Callie, who was apparently fascinated by the grounds. Her eyes were focused anywhere but on him, making him feel like some kind of thug.

"I'm sorry you walked in on that."

He was rewarded with a quick glance. "I know you're a hard-core businessman and all, but it's hard to imagine what could be that upsetting."

"You ever stand to lose a hundred and twenty-five million dollars?"

Her eyes widened. "Ah, no."

"Well, that'll light a fire under you. Trust me."

They got to the garage and he opened the door for her.

"What exactly do you do?" she asked, going up first.

He struggled to answer the question while watching her hips shift from side to side.

"I invest in privately held companies in return for an interest in them. The profit is made when they go public."

"Is the Walker Fund a big deal? No offense, but finance isn't my field."

"When properly leveraged, I can command over ten billion dollars."

"Oh." She paused at the head of the stairs as if trying to come to terms with the number. When she looked up, she exclaimed, "This is wonderful!"

He lost the remnants of his anger as she put her toolbox down and walked around. There were windows on every side of the open space and the peaked roof stretched the ceiling upward to a shallow point. He'd had a long wooden table set up and had brought up a few different chairs for her to choose from. There were also a couch and a couple of side tables.

Her footsteps made a clicking sound across the glossy floor as she explored and he watched her with a greed that worried him.

"This is going to be just perfect," she said, looking outside. "Plenty of light."

"I'm glad you like it. When I had this space winterized last year, I put in a bathroom with a shower, and there's also a stereo system hardwired into the walls."

"This is all so surprising," she said, running her hand absently across the table.

"What is?"

Her head jerked around as if she'd abruptly remembered she wasn't alone.

"Nothing." She faced him, all business. "I have a list of the equipment I need. Some of it I have to get before I can do any work on the painting at all."

"Fine. We can go to the MFA this morning."

She nodded and pointed to a set of double doors. "What's through there?"

"Just a closet." He walked over and opened it up. Inside were four Rubbermaid bins, and she seemed curious as she looked at them. "I believe the bottom two are stuffed with some needlepoint pillows my mother has no use for. The others are full of old family papers."

"Really?" She went inside and lifted the lid off the top one. "Have they been cataloged?"

"Not that I know of."

"They should be."

"Do you want to do it?"

She glanced over her shoulder. "Are you serious?"

"Of course. And I'd pay you for the work."

She shook her head. "Absolutely not. I happen to like making order out of chaos, so this would be a nice diversion for me. Besides, I don't have a background in document preservation. All I could do is sift through the papers, put them in piles, and get them ready so someone who knew what they were doing could go through them."

She got up on her tiptoes and leaned forward, putting her arms inside the box. He heard papers sliding against one another with a graceful sound and then a harsh noise when the container slipped. She started to fall forward.

Moving on instinct, Jack grabbed her around the waist from behind, pulling her back. His first thought was merely to keep her upright.

But as her body came up against him, his brain pretty much shut down.

As they made contact, he heard her gasp and felt like doing a little heavy breathing of his own. The fit of her against the cradle of his hips was seamless, and she must have been as struck by the sensation as he was because she didn't struggle as much as he didn't move.

He couldn't have counted the number of heartbeats that passed while they stood together.

Now would be a good time to let go of her, he told himself. All he needed to do was drop his hands and step back. Make some smooth comment about her throwing herself into her work.

Instead his fingers splayed over her waist, measuring the subtle undulations of her rib cage as well as the softness of her sides. He felt her body expand with breath. When she still didn't pull away, he leaned into her until his chest was against her back.

Don't do this, he thought. For Christ's sake, don't you dare do this.

But his body was taking over, drowning out sane thoughts and moral reasoning, replacing them with an insane need to take her. He couldn't think about the implications of what he was doing. He wanted her and that was all he knew.

Moving slowly, Jack brought his hand to the weight of her hair and he swept it aside to expose the skin of her neck. He bent down, bringing his lips close to her ear.

"Callie."

"Let me go," she whispered.

"Callie." His voice was low, vibrating with what was happening between them while he apologized for what he was about to do. "I'm sorry."

He pressed his lips against her skin.

Her breath left in a rush and he kissed her neck again, stroking her with his tongue. When her head fell back, he put his arms around her, his hands wide across her flat stomach.

As his lips came down once more, her head started

moving back and forth as if she were struggling to argue.
Seizing the moment, he turned her around. Her eyes
were luminous with heat even as he got the sense that
she was a hairsbreadth away from bolting.

Keeping his eyes locked on hers, he lowered his head
and lightly put his lips against her cheek. Small kisses,
designed to calm as well as arouse, brought him to her
mouth. He hesitated.

At the core of him, he knew what he was about to do
was very wrong.

You bastard, he thought, as he lowered his lips to hers.

Callie's mouth trembled under his as he softly kissed
her, and the sigh that came out of her was all the permission he needed. He kissed her again. Stroking, cajoling,
gently.

He knew damn well the restraint wasn't going to last.
With every little kiss, his self-control was slipping away,
transforming him from a rational human being into a
fully aroused male with exactly what he wanted in his
arms.

Her lips parted without warning and his tongue
slipped between them. He groaned as he felt the warm,
slick glide of hers and all he could think of was getting
her skin next to his. Riding a surge of lust, he tightened
his hold until her breasts pressed against his chest.

Holy Christ, he thought. Nothing in the dream had
prepared him for what she actually felt like, and he
thought of the sofa across the room. Had he closed the
door downstairs before they'd gone up? The last thing
he wanted was to be interrupted.

But then she pushed him away with a moan and
stumbled out of the closet.

Jack cursed as cool air took the place of her warm
body and reality came back with horrible clarity.

Before turning around, he took a deep breath and re-
arranged himself. He didn't think facing her with a rigid
erection was going to make things easier for either one
of them.

Man, he'd blown it.

She was pacing around the studio when he came out of the closet.

"I'm so damn sorry," he said. "I don't know how that happened."

Well, actually he remembered the whole thing from start to finish. What he should have said was that he didn't know *why* it happened. Getting used to monogamy with Blair had taken some time, but he'd never slipped up. Not once. He couldn't believe he'd just broken the commitment he'd made.

"I can't . . . ," she started and stalled out. "This isn't going to work. I need to go home—" She pressed her palms to her cheeks. "God! I should never have let that happen. I'm— I don't even know you."

Jack was struck with an absurd desire to recite his vital statistics. Height, weight, Social Security number, date of birth. Marital status.

He winced at that last one.

"It's my fault," he said. "You didn't do anything wrong."

He saw her eyeing the toolbox and then the stairs.

"Wait a minute. Let's not blow this out of proportion." The last thing he wanted was for her to go. "Just because I kissed you doesn't mean you have to quit."

"Quit? If I leave now, it is not quitting. You tried to take advantage of me."

He frowned and spoke too quickly. "You weren't exactly fighting me back there."

She let out a disgusted noise. "Thank you for pointing that out. That makes me feel *so* much better."

Jack cursed to himself, thinking he should be more of a gentleman. "I'm sorry. I'm not exactly thinking clearly right now."

Hell, he was lucky he could string a sentence together. Sexual frustration was making his temper short. Worse, in spite of everything that was wrong about them being together, all he wanted to do was get her back in his arms. Naked.

He had to shut his eyes as another wave of hunger pounded through him.

Maybe he should just let her go. Show her the door. Get her out of his life.

Because things like that kiss didn't happen by accident. He'd been wondering what she'd feel like in his arms for real since that moment on her stoop back in Chelsea. And it was a damn tragedy that what had just happened between them had more than lived up to his expectations.

"Should I expect you to try and kiss me again?" she asked.

He opened his eyes and wished like hell he could give her the ironclad answer she was looking for. But at the moment, he wasn't feeling particularly trustworthy.

He dragged a hand through his hair. "I'm in a relationship. I'm engaged to someone—"

"You're *engaged*?" she said incredulously. "Oh, my God."

Her hands were back on her cheeks and she looked for a moment as if she might be sick because now she was eyeing the bathroom, not the stairs, with desperation.

"Listen, I'm not in the habit of cheating once I make a commitment."

"Oh, really," she tossed back. "So all those stories about your love life were made up?"

"I said once I *commit.*"

"Well, you certainly don't do that very often, do you?"

She crossed her arms over her chest. He couldn't blame her for looking at him with disdain, and meeting her narrowed eyes wasn't easy.

"Tell me, Jack, what exactly are you going to tell your *fiancée* about this?"

God, he had no idea.

"I'm not sure."

"Probably nothing, right? Which is precisely how all those women ended up fighting over you like they did. No doubt they all thought you were their one and only."

"You shouldn't believe everything you read."

"If I cut out a quarter of what I've read about you, there'd still be plenty to go on. Like the time one of your girlfriends chased a half-naked actress through the Waldorf Astoria lobby? And what had that lovely Cameron Diaz wannabe been wearing? A feather boa across her breasts and a pair of your boxer shorts, isn't that right?" Callie put her hands on her hips. "That was a personal favorite of mine. Featured in *People* as well as the *New York Post*."

He swore out loud, long and hard. "That was *years* ago. And she was wearing my pants if I remember correctly."

At the time, he'd found the incident hilarious. After the great chase had begun, he'd sat back in his suite and waited until either his pants came back or the woman he'd been dating for six weeks did. Now, in retrospect, and especially in front of Callie, the theatrics seemed immature.

He took a deep breath. "I'm not like that anymore."

"Are you sure about that?" she muttered.

"Back then, I never would have apologized to you because I wouldn't have felt badly. Now I do. I know I don't have a lot of credibility when it comes to . . . things like this, but you've got to believe me. I had no intention of going down that road with you."

She stared at him, measured him. "Have you ever cheated on . . . her before?"

"No. And I never planned to." He walked over to the couch and sat down, putting his elbows on his knees. "I just got caught up in the moment and I made a mistake. I don't know what else to say."

Her gaze shifted to the window, and, after a moment, returned to him. "I'm not like those women you're used to. I'm . . . just not."

No, he thought, she certainly wasn't. She wouldn't put up with being used and he had no desire to treat her casually, either.

"I know that," he replied. "I found it impossible to turn away from you. That's my weakness. Not your fault."

Her head lowered and she stared at the floor for a while.

"If I stay, it's for the work. Not because I'm interested in playing games. I don't want you to do that again."

He frowned. "You mind if I ask why not?"

"What kind of a question is that?"

"What I mean is, do you have someone in your life?" He didn't really think she'd answer him, but he wanted to know.

"That's totally irrelevant. Because even if I were alone, that doesn't mean I'd be looking for you."

He had to smile. "You've made that very clear."

Gradually, the tension left her shoulders and her chin started to drop.

"So, can we be friends?" he asked, surprised to realize how much that mattered to him.

"No, we can't be friends." Her eyes drifted back to the window. "You and I, we are never going to be friends."

He didn't like that answer.

"Why not?"

"We have nothing in common."

"Untrue. We both like art. Dogs. Grace Woodward Hall. I'm sure the list could go on and on."

She shook her head. "I work for you. Just like the other hundred or thousand or however many people make up the Walker Fund. I'm simply one of many—"

"No, you aren't."

"—and I want to stay that way."

"Have you always preferred anonymity or is this just a special case because you want to avoid me?"

"This time I'm choosing it."

Jack's hunter instincts sharpened. "And when was it not your choice?"

Quickly, she turned away. "This conversation is over."

She walked across the room and picked up her toolbox, putting it on the table with a declarative sound.

He studied her for a moment, wondering what had caused her retreat. What exactly she was hiding.

"Tell me something."

"No."

"You don't know what I'm going to ask."

"And I don't care."

More gently, he said, "I just want to know. Did you get hurt by someone?"

She looked over at him, her eyes sparkling with outrage. "You're out of your mind—you know that?"

He stood up. "I'm just thinking it might explain something."

"And what exactly do you think needs explaining?"

"Why you pulled back from me."

The blush that came to her cheeks was just about the most attractive thing Jack had seen in a while. And it was confirmation, regardless of whatever denial she was about to throw at him, that she'd felt the same way he had in that closet.

Her chin rose again. "Maybe it's as simple as I didn't like it."

"That wasn't what it felt like to me."

"Then maybe you just enjoyed it enough for the both of us." Her eyes flicked down to the fly of his pants.

The idea that she'd felt his arousal made him clench his teeth with need.

He knew he should back off. He knew he should just let it all go because if he pushed her too far, she was fully capable of walking out on the project. On him.

But he just couldn't. Her defiance captivated him, making the compliance he got from other women seem pale and uninteresting.

"Callie, I don't care if you pushed me back because you don't like me or because I was inappropriate or because I moved too fast. All of those are no doubt true. But I would appreciate some honesty. You liked it when I kissed you."

She gave him a righteous huff. "You ever have trouble fitting that ego of yours indoors?"

He shook his head slowly. "Not in a place the size of Buona Fortuna. I'd probably have a hard time with a ranch or a split-level, though."

She opened her mouth to speak, but then a smile tugged at the corners of her lips and she turned back to the toolbox.

Damn, but he wished she'd share the expression with him.

Jack took a step toward her and then forced himself to stop. "Listen, there's nothing wrong with pleasure, and most people, when they're lucky enough to find it, don't want to stop. Unless, of course, they're already with someone or they've been hurt before, which brings me back to my point. You are one of the most defensive, closed women I've ever met. It makes me think that someone's done a number on you."

She glanced at him over her shoulder and the smile was gone. "I have no intention of discussing my personal life with you. It's none of your business as it doesn't impact our *professional* relationship. And I am not defensive!"

He cocked an eyebrow and smiled softly.

She cleared her throat and looked away. "Maybe I'm just wary of strangers. Which is a very healthy thing."

"Does that mean, if you knew me better, you wouldn't be so cautious?"

She laughed, and the rueful edge to the sound was a relief to him. "I'm always going to be wary of you."

"Callie. Look at me."

It was a while before she did.

"I really am sorry. And you can trust me. With anything. With your life. I'm not going to hurt you."

She frowned and chewed her bottom lip. Seeing her white teeth come out over the softness of her mouth made him forget his good intentions for a split second.

Her voice was almost a whisper when she finally spoke. "But you kissed me while knowing you were engaged. Didn't you?"

He shut his eyes. She had him on that one.

She began taking small jars out of the toolbox and lining them up on the table. "Maybe we should wait for the painting to arrive before we go to the MFA. And I— ah, I think I'd like to get set up now."

It was an effective change of subject and suggested she wanted some time alone. He knew he couldn't force her any further, but sure as hell hoped she took what he'd said to heart. In spite of his actions.

"I'll leave," he said. "But I want you to know that I'm glad you're staying. And that I really do want this to go well. For both of us."

When she didn't respond, he walked across the room. Pausing at the head of the stairs, he said, "Callie?"

She looked up. "What?"

"Are you with someone?"

As her face reddened, he told himself he was stepping over the line again.

Although not as much as when he'd kissed her, he thought drily.

"What I mean is, do you need time off? Or to have someone come visit?" He spoke casually, trying to cover his tracks.

Because he wanted to know for himself, not to be gracious.

She frowned before responding. "I was planning on working right through."

"And any visitors?"

She went back to the toolbox, pulling out wooden sticks and wedges of cotton. "Ah—no. No visitors."

The shot of satisfaction that went through him made Jack want to curse.

Get the hell out of here, you idiot.

This time, he left quickly.

8

As JACK walked back to the house, he looked up at the dull, cloud-covered sky and knew that getting Callie to stay solved only part of the problem he'd created.

What the hell was he going to tell Blair? The only explanation he could think of was that his self-control had slipped.

Which was no explanation at all.

Staying faithful to Blair had never been a problem before. When she'd asked him for monogamy a year ago, he'd agreed to the request and been faithful ever since. He'd wanted her to be happy, and besides, he'd begun to think about settling down with her anyway.

Since he'd made the commitment, he'd had plenty of opportunity to fall back into old habits with the ladies. Just last week he'd had another offer, as a matter of fact. Down in New York, at the Hall Gala, Candace Hanson had cornered him and suggested they put an elevator to good use. Take a little trip up the building while she went down on him.

It was curious, he thought. Candace was beautiful in a very made-up, carefully tended kind of way. And she'd obviously been interested and willing. Able too, no doubt, considering all the men she'd been with. Yet he'd found turning her down ridiculously easy.

There had been a lot of Candaces. Lovely women with a variety of angles and agendas, all willing to give him whatever he wanted. The fact that he'd walked away from them had been a testament, he'd assumed, to his relationship with Blair. But maybe he just hadn't been truly tempted. Except he just couldn't understand it. After a year of saying no to obvious offers, he found it a little hard to believe that he'd blown his perfect record on a woman who was at best ambivalent about him.

No, ambivalent was the wrong word. Callie was quite clear about what she thought of him and absolutely right to be wary, he thought. Because he didn't feel all that honorable when he was around her.

As Jack stared at the clouds rolling by, he really wished he hadn't lived up to his reputation back there.

Maybe the whole engagement was a mistake. An exercise of good planning over emotions. He heard Blair telling him he didn't love her and thought he could have made a major miscalculation.

He had been rather laissez-faire about the engagement from the very beginning. He'd asked her in front of Grace and her bodyguard, for Christ's sake, which was neither private nor particularly romantic. And he hadn't been very enthusiastic when she'd asked him when they should have the ceremony. Or where.

When Blair had questioned him that night at the Plaza, he'd gotten defensive, presumably because he felt so sure of it all. But maybe he just didn't want to look at what was going on between them for fear of seeing everything that was not.

And Blair was right to be surprised that he'd asked at all. When they'd first gotten together, he'd given her his antimarriage speech, the whole thing about the trip down the aisle being nothing more than the first step toward divorce, and therefore, a financially unattractive proposition for him. He'd had no interest in getting hosed by an ex-wife, not after working so hard for his money.

Had his fundamental opinion of married life changed? He supposed it really hadn't. But his father's death had made him start to think about the future. About children. For the sake of his unborn sons and daughters, he was willing to take a shot at the flawed institution and he knew no other woman who'd make him a better wife. Hell, maybe he and Blair could beat the odds and stay together for the long term.

Maybe he'd eventually fall in love with her.

The problem was, as he thought of Blair now, he could feel nothing but guilt in his chest. There was no spark, no wild passion, just deep fondness.

Although surely the remorse meant something, he thought.

But then again, you could feel like an absolute ass and regret something you've done without being *in* love with the person.

And what about Callie? Jack's conscience forced him to consider whether her elusiveness was her appeal. If it was, he hardly had a reason to make any big changes in his life. Or hers. Or Blair's. If everything with Callie came down to his love of a good chase, there could be one and only one outcome. He was known for getting what he wanted, and once he reached his goal, it was only a matter of time before he moved on to the next target. The cycle had ended up making him a lot of money.

And getting him branded as a playboy.

Jack shook his head, knowing he needed to take a deep breath and calm the hell down. He was skidding out of control, which was a pretty reasonable response when someone's life had taken a sudden lurch from its plotted course. But he didn't need to throw out everything he'd planned just because of one kiss.

No matter how good it had been.

He was not breaking off his engagement. And he wasn't going to tell Blair a thing.

He didn't relish being a liar, but there was no reason to burden her with his mistake. She'd be hurt, and as long as he had no intention of doing it again, he didn't want to put her through the pain.

And it would never happen again. He wasn't going to

blow everything he'd committed to just because he liked a good chase. Because that was all the kiss was about.

As for Callie?

His breath left him in a rush and he figured his self-control might need a little help. If only there was a way to make her less available—

Gray Bennett was in town, he thought. And handsome. Single.

Maybe his old friend was someone she'd like. If he could set the two of them up, that would mean he was covered on all fronts.

Totally committed to his fiancée. With Callie being otherwise occupied by a charmer.

Jack started walking toward the house with purpose in his stride.

Callie watched Jack stop and look up at the sky, his body pulled into an arc. He stared at the clouds for quite a while and then marched across the driveway as if he was prepared to go about his day.

She glanced back at the closet where the lid to the box she'd opened was lying on the floor. She went over and put it on tightly, trying to ignore the symbolism and wondering whether she was doing the right thing in staying. Replaying their conversation, she realized he never had promised her that he wouldn't kiss her again. And now she knew that he had a fiancée in addition to his god-awful reputation. Based on both of those two facts, she should probably be packing up and getting back on the train as soon as she could.

Because she had a funny feeling about Jack Walker.

Yeah, it's called dislike, she told herself.

"Oh, hell," she muttered.

Yes, she disliked the man, but that wasn't the only thing she felt. She might as well admit it. He was sexy as hell. And he was a great kisser.

But then, practice makes perfect, she thought with a grimace.

She went back to the window and looked at the looming mansion. The idea that she'd end up a bit player in some terrible Gothic drama made her smile, especially as Arthur came over and leaned against her thigh.

Somehow, it just wouldn't be the same if the dog was a golden retriever, she thought.

As her hand went down to his rough fur, she tried to imagine the situation if Jack weren't involved with someone else. What would she have done then?

She was a grown woman. She was attracted to him. Putting aside her throwback ideas about romance, namely that sex without love was probably just pointless, mildly aerobic exercise, she had to wonder what would be so terrible if they followed a string of kisses like that into bed.

Not that she had anything to compare it with, but she knew he'd be a fantastic lover. He moved with a slow confidence she found incredibly erotic. Just remembering how he pushed back her hair and put his lips on her neck was enough to make her rethink whether she'd done the right thing in pulling away.

Okay, fine, she was pathetically attracted to him. But what if he knew the truth? What would he think if he found out she'd never had sex before? God knew that piece of news had put a damper on things before.

Ending up a virgin at the age of twenty-seven hadn't been a goal of hers; it had happened by default. Years of caring for her mother, going to school, and having a job all at the same time had pretty much shut down her social life. She'd also been trained since birth to keep a low profile so she never courted attention. And she knew her relationship with her father had something to do with it, too. She just didn't trust men.

Her one serious sexual experience had been an awkward straining in the dark with a guy she'd seen for a little bit in college. She'd decided to sleep with him because she liked him and she figured it was about time, but things had come to a screeching halt when she'd explained he was about to be her first. It wasn't fun to watch him throw his clothes back on like they were flame retardant and he was standing next to a Molotov cocktail.

Later, she learned that he'd been dating her only because he wanted to get back at the woman he was really interested in.

It would have been a mistake to have made love to that guy, but she'd always wished she'd had some experience. Previously, it had been because she felt isolated from what every other woman her age was doing. Now she wished she had some perspective on what it had been like to be kissed by Jack Walker.

Maybe what happened in that closet was nothing special. No doubt it hadn't been extraordinary for him. He'd probably had as many erotic experiences as she'd had nights alone.

Bondage masks and handcuffs, indeed.

She frowned, wondering why she was wasting her time. Jack Walker *had* someone in his life. And he obviously felt something for the woman because he'd seemed genuinely sorry he'd taken things where he had. Maybe he was merely a good actor but she actually believed he regretted the fact that he'd cheated on his fiancée.

All they needed to do was keep things on a professional level. And once she got to work, the days would fly by and the project would be done before she knew it. He probably wasn't going to give the kiss another thought. So neither would she.

As for the friends idea? She had to wonder whether men like Jack Walker had friends, the kind you called when you were in trouble or when you needed a laugh. Even the super rich needed support, she supposed, but it was hard to imagine him ever turning to someone else for help or comfort. He was just too self-confident. Too in control.

Although it wasn't as if her own address book was full. She didn't have many people in her life, especially now that she'd left Stanley's gallery. There was . . . Grace, she supposed. A distant cousin or two. But for Callie, friends were tricky because they got involved in a person's life, and hers was hard to explain in a lot of places.

So no, even if she wasn't attracted to him, she and Jack Walker couldn't possibly be friends. He was already asking questions and those shrewd hazel eyes were way too observant for her comfort.

Callie frowned, seeing a delivery van come rambling up the drive and stop under the porte cochere. Leaping into motion, she took comfort in the surge of excitement because it had nothing to do with Jack.

"Let's go welcome Nathaniel," she said to Arthur. The dog pricked his ears, ever ready for an adventure, and happily raced for the stairs.

The deliveryman was opening the van's rear doors as she came across the driveway. Jack emerged from the house at the same time and she noted that he'd changed into a suit and tie. She tried to remain calm as their eyes met. Predictably, he seemed totally at ease.

The portrait had been shipped in a wooden crate and the cumbersome load was lowered to the ground on a mechanical pallet. After sliding the heavy weight onto a dolly, the deliveryman followed Jack over to the garage. Together, they rolled the painting up the stairs and hefted the crate onto her worktable.

As soon as the other man had left, Jack offered her a hammer. "You want to do the honors?"

She took the tool from him and began to pull out the nails along the crate's edge. When she'd worked around the perimeter, they lifted off the top together and she pulled back the packing material.

Nathaniel Walker's beautiful, brooding face was revealed and she couldn't keep a small sound of pleasure from escaping her lips. She leaned in close to the canvas. With his wavy dark hair and his heavily lidded eyes, he and Jack looked very much alike.

"This is such a remarkable work," she murmured. "I can almost see him breathing."

The Revolutionary War leader was seated on a chair, head turned so he was staring out of the painting. He was dressed in a black suit coat and had on a frothy white shirt that came up high on his neck. The silver mirror in his left hand was also facing toward the viewer, a symbol of his work as a glassmaker. His other hand hung off the arm of the chair in an elegant drift of pale skin. The background was dark, practically black, although Callie knew that with proper cleaning it would become less dense.

She reached over to her box of tools and supplies. Strapping on a headset that carried a magnifying glass and a light, she began to scan the surface of the painting, immediately identifying the pattern of craquelure, or small fissures, in the paint. This complex network of fine cracks was expected and confirmed the painting's age. As she continued her examination, she was able to see that the brushwork was masterly and the colors were blended with confidence. She couldn't wait to strip off the old layer of varnish that had yellowed and get a real sense of the hues and tones Copley had used.

"You're really in your element," Jack said softly.

She looked up, having forgotten for the moment he was even in the room. He had settled against the wall, one foot resting on the toe of a wing tip, arms crossed in front of his chest. A half smile stretched his lips and his eyelids were low, suggesting he'd been deep in thought as he'd watched her.

Feeling vulnerable, she reminded herself that reviewing the painting was part of the job, not a private moment for her. Still, she felt like he'd seen her without her guard up and it made her want to banish him from the garage.

She took the headset off, tossing it into the toolbox. "He looks great and he traveled well. I'd like to go to the MFA now."

"Sure thing."

They were heading to the stairs when he stopped. "I'm really happy you're the one doing this. I like the way you look at him."

When Jack started walking again, she followed more

slowly, intrigued that a man whose world revolved around money had such sentimentality in him.

"Your father's name was Nathaniel, right?" she asked, taking the banister as she went down the stairs.

"Nathaniel the sixth, as a matter of fact." He opened a side door into the garage and lights came on automatically as they walked through. Parked inside were two Jaguars, a pickup truck, and some kind of sports car, the likes of which she'd never seen before.

"Why weren't you the seventh?"

Jack stopped in front of the sports car. "My brother was born before I was. He got the name."

"I didn't know you had a brother."

"He keeps a very low profile." Jack opened the door for her.

"Now you've got me curious."

She watched him go around to the driver's side, a smile on his face. "Nate's a great guy, but he's got a bad case of wanderlust. I don't get to see him half as much as I'd like."

She slid into the car and felt like the seat had been custom fit to her body. Impressive, she thought. "What does he do?"

"He's a chef." Jack got behind the wheel.

"You sound proud of him."

"I am."

The doors shut with a muted sound and she breathed deeply as she put on her seat belt.

"Hmmm. I love the way this car smells. All this leather . . . It's beautiful. What kind is it?"

"An Aston Martin DB9."

The engine came to life in a deep growl that faded to a soft purr. As they headed down the drive, Mozart filled the air and she stroked the butter-soft hand rest.

One minute later she was gripping the damn thing for dear life.

After screaming down Cliff Road, Jack shot into traffic on Route 9 and proceeded to dodge around other cars like he was playing a video game. The man was a menace behind the wheel and Callie thought the only saving grace was that the sports car probably had top-of-the-line air bags and plenty of them.

As they swerved around a truck, she looked over at Jack in alarm. He was calm, whistling under his breath with the music.

He glanced over at her and frowned. "Are you cold? You look uncomfortable."

He reached for the climate controls.

"No! I'm fine." Anything to keep him looking forward, with both hands on the wheel.

"You don't look fine."

"Fear of imminent death does that to me," she said as she was pushed against the door when they jogged around a VW Bug.

Jack nodded. "The traffic around Boston takes a while to get used to, but it's not much better in New York. Those cabbies can be heavy-handed."

This was being said while he cut off a bread truck and then threw on the brakes as they came up to a stoplight.

Callie jerked forward and thanked God for the seat belt running down her chest. Catching her breath, she looked at him. "You know, there's a middle ground between the brake and the accelerator. You don't have to always pick one."

He seemed surprised. "I'm making you uncomfortable?"

"G-force wasn't something I expected to experience in a car."

He let out a short laugh as the light turned green. She braced herself, but he eased them forward.

"Sorry about that. I usually drive alone."

"Probably because people are afraid to ride with you," she said drily.

He looked over at her. And then grinned.

She flushed, wishing she could be indifferent to him, wishing that his smile didn't make her feel as if they were sharing some kind of intimate secret. She looked out the window. They were passing neighborhoods and small shops, the road being an odd hybrid of a small highway and a regular municipal street. As she focused on the passing view, distraction was the landmark she was searching for.

"So how did you get into conservation?" he asked, as if he sensed her desire for a diversion.

"I started out studying art history. I loved the lectures. Sitting in a dark room, seeing beautiful works of art up on the screen, the professor's voice low in the background. I used to imagine that I might someday own paintings like the ones I studied. Pretty soon, I found out how much they cost and knew the only way I'd ever get close to them was if I worked on them." She paused. "You know, you have some very special art in your house."

"Thanks."

"I mean, the Canaletto in the front hall alone is . . . spectacular. The Titian and the El Greco in the dining room."

She felt him look at her. "Did you see the Rubens in my study?"

Her eyes widened. "Don't you ever worry someone is going to steal them?"

He shook his head as he pulled up to another light. "The man who wired the MFA did my house. The paintings are bolted into the walls with weight-sensitive alarms. They're going nowhere."

"Has your family always collected?"

"Yes. My great-great-grandmother was the first to focus in on the Renaissance period. She donated some of her collection to the MFA when she died, which was fine with my great-grandmother, who just filled up the wall space again. The thrill is the hunt, of course."

Callie shifted in the deep leather seat, wondering what it was like having so much. She had no intention of asking him, however, because she didn't want to seem like a rube. Dignity, after all, was one asset the rich and the poor could both have.

She frowned, thinking of the past. Maybe that was why her mother turned down so many gifts. Her father would show up at the door of their apartment bearing a small, foil-wrapped box or some huge package with a bow on it and her mother would just shake her head.

"Is that how you met Grace?" Jack asked. "Through the art world?"

Callie hesitated, wishing she was a more confident liar. "You could say we met through the Hall Foundation, yes."

"She speaks highly of you."

"She's been very kind to me."

"Grace is like that. Good person all around."

In a flash, Callie wondered whether Jack and her half sister had ever been together. They seemed perfectly suited.

"She's stunning, too," Callie murmured. "Certainly fits her title."

"I thought she was divorcing the count?"

"I mean about being one of the world's most beautiful women."

With no turn signal, Jack hung a U-turn and then pulled into a parking lot next to the low-slung pale buildings of the Museum of Fine Arts. He shut the car off and released his seat belt while she stared ahead.

"Callie?"

"What? Oh—right, we're here."

He gave her an odd look as they got out. "You okay?"

"Yeah, sure. I'm fine."

She just wasn't one of the world's most beautiful women and wondered why she suddenly seemed to care one way or the other. God knew, she didn't pay a lot of attention to her looks, usually.

But then, Jack was making her think about all kinds of unusual things.

As soon as they were inside the museum, people started coming up to him. He seemed to know everyone by name, and the respect with which he was treated spoke volumes about what he and his family must have done for the place.

She and Jack had just emerged from the cloakroom when Mrs. Walker strode into the lobby. She was talking and gesticulating wildly while being trailed by a staff member who was taking notes. Jack's mother was dressed in a black suit and had an exquisite tangle of pearls around her neck. She looked fresh and elegant, as if she'd stepped out of the pages of *Vanity Fair*. The staff member just looked pooped.

When she came to a halt next to her son, Mrs. Walker waved the minion away with a flick of the wrist. "Have you come to talk with Gerard?"

Callie knew she was referring to Gerard Beauvais, the head of the MFA's conservation department. Callie had heard of the man but never met him. A legend in the art world, he was responsible for conserving the work of some of the most important masters: da Vinci, Rembrandt, Michelangelo.

Jack nodded. "I thought he and Callie should meet."

Mrs. Walker's brows lifted. "Perhaps Ms. Burke will consent to his assistance. Assuming she's open to collaboration."

Callie felt her stomach knot as Jack shot his mother a level stare. "Did I happen to mention that Callie worked with your friend Micheline Talbot on the conservation of the torn de Kooning?"

Mrs. Walker's eyes flickered just enough to show that she did indeed recall the project.

"You remember that painting, Mother. It's at MoMA," Jack prompted smoothly. "You told me that Micheline had gone on and on about how she couldn't have done the job without her assistant. That the young woman was talented as hell and a pleasure to work with, right?"

Callie held her breath, wishing he'd drop the subject.

"Remember. Mother."

"Yes, yes, of course. It was an extraordinary result."

"So I think Callie and Gerard will get along just fine."

Mrs. Walker brought a hand up to her hair, smoothing back what was not out of place. "I'm sure you do. Now, if you will excuse me, I'm going home. The executive committee meeting went on longer than it should have and I'm tired."

Callie flushed as Jack's mother walked away. The woman hadn't made eye contact with her at all, as if Mrs. Walker could make her disappear by ignoring her.

But Jack had made sure she was noticed. Had stuck up for her.

She glanced at him. His eyes were narrowed as he watched his mother go into the cloakroom.

"That wasn't really necessary," Callie said softly.

"Yes, it was."

"I can take care of myself."

He looked at her. "I have no doubt of that, but my mother is not going to be your problem. Come on, let's go to Gerard's office."

Jack led them past the guard who checked tickets and through an exhibit of African art, to an elevator big enough to park cars in. The thing was huge, its ceiling some eighteen feet high. As they lurched upward, she could feel him staring at her.

"What?" she asked.

He put his hands into the pockets of his fine suit. "Why don't you want me to protect you?"

"Because I shouldn't get in the habit of relying on you when it comes to dealing with your mother." She paused. "Although it was a nice gesture on your part."

"I'm sorry—did I hear that right? You actually approve of something I've done?"

"Don't let it go to your head," she replied, hiding her smile.

He laughed. "With you around, I don't think either of us have to worry about that."

She lifted her eyes and was taken aback when he looked at her grimly.

"Tell me something, Callie, what's it going to take to get you to like me?"

"Why do you care if I do?" she asked, surprised by the question and his intensity.

"I like a challenge," he said, that grin of his returning.

"Then go climb a mountain."

He laughed again. "I think you're far more interesting and I'm not crazy about heights. Now, answer my question."

"Why don't you take a shot at mine for real, first?" she tossed back.

"Okay." The smile stayed in place, but his eyes grew somber. "When I showed you to your new bedroom you were delighted, but I know you would have quite happily stayed in the back rooms. You haven't once asked me about paying you the money we discussed. And my dog loves you."

"So maybe I'm laid-back, fiscally irresponsible, and have kibble in my pocket."

"Mostly, though, I'm fascinated by you."

The elevator came to a stop.

"You can't possibly be serious," she muttered, trying to ignore a sudden pounding in her chest.

As the doors opened, he held them at bay while she walked out.

"But I am," he said, falling into step beside her. "You are one very unusual lady."

She could feel the heat hit her face.

"Where's the office?" she asked pointedly.

It was a relief when he walked ahead and stayed quiet.

She wasn't in a big hurry to tell him that in order for her to like him he'd have to morph into something other than a devastatingly handsome and wealthy man who'd kissed her like she'd never been kissed before.

He'd have to go from being an Aston Martin DB whatever to a Chevy Chevette.

9

THEY WALKED through a rabbit warren of offices that was broken up by floor-to-ceiling shelves filled with a jagged, colorful array of books. When they came to a set of double doors, Jack rang a bell on the wall. Moments later, the metal panels were opened to reveal a small, older man. Under his sparse, graying hair, his face was surprisingly young looking, mostly because of the enthusiasm in his eyes.

"Jackson, how are you?" The man's voice was high and lilting, marked with a subtle French accent, and the hands that reached up and removed a pair of tortoise-shell glasses from his nose were beautiful enough to have been a woman's.

So this was Gerard Beauvais, Callie thought as she shook one of those hands after Jack introduced them. She tried not to get swallowed by hero worship.

Beauvais smiled at her as he motioned them inside. "Come in, come in. Please."

There were six workstations in the room and at each one a person dressed in a smock was leaning forward toward the surface of a breathtaking work of art. She saw a Pissarro and a David held upright in vise grips and several paintings lying on tables. The place smelled like chemicals, and as her nose tingled, she thought back to her days at NYU.

Only this was no classroom.

This was where Beauvais had carefully repaired the Fra Filippo Lippi that had been splashed with acid. It had taken him two years to find a way to mitigate the damage and conserve what was left of the paint, but the wait had been worth it. He'd also stabilized one of da Vinci's rare self-portraits in the lab. Da Vinci's experimentation with paint mediums meant that his exquisite labors could sometimes be ravaged by fading and flaking. Beauvais's work on the chemical composition of the master's oils had been revolutionary.

"Your mother is being so generous," Gerard said to Jack. "As always."

Jack cracked a dry smile. "I can only imagine."

"I mean, loaning the Walker painting to us after conservation, how gracious. It will look stunning next to Copley's Paul Revere. They are perfect companions." Beauvais smiled. "We will throw a party, yes? Something to properly welcome Nathaniel back to Boston."

Callie noticed Jack's eyes narrowing even if Beauvais did not.

"And you," the man said to her. "I am great friends with Professor Melzer. He speaks very highly of you and that is a rare recommendation indeed. You must be anxious to get down to work."

She felt blood rush to her face. Or maybe the tingling meant it had left her head altogether. "I'm going to do my best. But I have to admit, I'm nervous."

"Good. Good, good! You should be." He wagged his glasses at her. "We should all approach the canvas with sure hands, a clear mind, and palpitations in the chest. It is a sign that you understand the value of what you can do for a painting and the destruction you may cause if you are not reverent and careful. *C'est bon!*"

As he beamed at her, she was quite sure she didn't view her fear with the same kind of optimism, but she felt herself relax a little.

"Now, tell me, what of the painting? Have you examined it yet?" Small, rapt eyes searched her face.

As she nodded, she cleared her throat, feeling like she'd had an oral exam sprung on her.

"The canvas is solid and the paint is holding together nicely for the most part, but the varnish layer is yellow and dingy. Technically this will not be a complicated job, but the significance of the painting makes the project rather daunting." Enthusiasm warmed her voice. "The work is obviously from the period before Copley left for London because his style is still maturing. Even so, the brush technique and use of color are incredible. I can't wait to see what Nathaniel's face looks like under the old varnish."

"Anything else?"

She stared at the man. His smile was just as warm but his eyes had narrowed.

"Not yet." She hesitated. "Is there something I should be looking for?"

He shrugged but kept his voice low and his eyes on Jack, who was scrutinizing the David. "I examined the painting myself once. In the late nineties. After the Blankenbakers purchased the portrait from Jack's father, they hung it above a fireplace in their Newport house. They came to me because they were concerned about the effect of the fluctuating heat and changes in humidity it had been subjected to. We did not do a cleaning, so I know less than I would have had we performed such work. I will say, however, that you would be wise to pay particular attention to the surface texture."

She opened her mouth to speak, but he looked passively at Jack, who had turned back and was heading for them.

"Discretion among owners is prudent. Especially when things are not clear," Gerard said softly. He gave her his card after he'd written something on the back. "There is my home phone number, as well as the one here in the lab. You must call if you have trouble or if you require another set of eyes. Particularly if you are tempted to go into the paint layer. As you are well aware, that should not be done lightly."

Jack smiled as he approached. "So, we were wondering if you could spare a— What kind of light did you want?"

"A halogen steam lamp," Callie said. "And a microscope as well, if you don't mind."

Gerard smiled, nodded, and worked miracles. Twenty minutes later, Jack pulled the Aston Martin around to a rear entrance and a microscope was eased into its trunk. The light and stand were too big to fit in the car, so they were to be delivered that afternoon.

As they were leaving, Gerard took Callie's hands in his and looked down at them. "These, along with your eyes, are the most important tools you have. Call me if you need help. Do not be afraid."

As he squeezed, the full weight of the job hit her and she wondered whether she was up to the task.

"Ah, *cheri*, it will be okay," he whispered, as if he knew she wouldn't want Jack hearing him reassure her. The lilt of his accent was musical. "You have done this before and you will do fine. There is love in your eyes when you speak of the painting, and you would never hurt what you love, would you?"

She shook her head with a series of jerks, worried that if the man were any nicer to her, she might burst into tears.

"So go now, go and do what you have been trained to do. And know if you call me, I will come."

He squeezed her hands again and then went back into his museum, a slight man with the bouncing walk of a child.

Later, as they waited for a break in traffic, Jack said, "You've got a hell of a glow going."

She glanced over at him. "What? Oh—Gerard. He's just so amazing. And surprisingly humble."

"The great ones always are," Jack murmured as he put the car into gear and eased them into traffic. "What were you two whispering about?"

"He was just giving me some advice."

"Good man to take advice from."

She nodded and tilted her head toward the back of the car. "Generous, too."

His brows tightened. "Unfortunately, I'm going to have to disabuse him of the notion that my portrait is going to hang next to Paul Revere. Damn it, my mother's ability to commit the assets of others is unequaled, at least now that my father is dead."

Callie waited, hoping he would continue, and was disappointed when he didn't. She shifted her gaze to his hands on the steering wheel. She wanted to ask him to elaborate, but then he changed the subject.

"By the way, I was wondering if I could introduce you to a friend of mine."

She looked at him with surprise, thinking that taking on another private client after she finished the Copley conservation would be great. "Of course. But are you sure you don't want to wait until after you've seen some of my work?"

"This isn't about work."

The Aston Martin darted out in front of a truck and Callie gripped the door again.

"Gray was my college roommate and he's an all-around good guy. He lives in New York, but he's going to be here for the next couple of weeks. I think you two might get along."

Jack wanted to set her up on a date?

"No pressure, of course," he said, glancing across the seat at her. "I just thought maybe we could invite him out to Buona Fortuna. You could meet him, see if you like him."

Callie told herself this was normal. This was how people met other people. Through friends. Contacts.

Business associates.

And it proved how serious he was about keeping things between them . . . out of the closet, as it were.

"Er—okay."

Jack focused on the traffic again. "Good. That's just great."

*   *   *

The next morning, Callie had just settled in front of the painting when the garage door opened down below. She got up and went to a window, just in time to see the Aston Martin shoot down the driveway. She was watching the taillights disappear when Arthur came over and nudged her thigh with his head.

Work, she thought. She had work to do.

But it was hard to think about the job.

Yesterday, when she and Jack had returned from the museum, he'd helped her set up the microscope, and after it had arrived, the light as well. In the course of getting her workplace organized and removing the portrait's massive, gilded frame, he'd asked her innumerable questions about the project. He wanted to know what the process for cleaning the painting was going to be. What kinds of solvents she would use to remove the dirt and old varnish. What type of new varnish she would apply at the end to protect the fragile, original oil paint.

Given what had happened that morning, she was surprised by how comfortable she'd felt around him. He was witty and charming and had smiled at her with respect as she answered each of his queries. And the best part had been the sense that he was hitting her with all the questions simply because he was curious, not because he didn't trust her.

He'd been on his way back to the house when she'd asked him how to work the complicated stereo system. In the process of showing her how to turn the thing on, he'd discovered that it wasn't working, and that had led to him going up into the shallow crawl space over the room. She'd played nurse to his electronic surgeon as he'd banged and crashed around overhead, trying to get the speakers to receive a signal.

The cursing that had drifted down through the ceiling had been priceless and when he'd reemerged, cobwebs hanging from his hair, his beautiful business shirt and slacks covered with dust, she'd had to laugh.

Still, he'd got the damn thing working.

By the time they'd gone back to the house, dinner

had been served and cleared. Jack had parceled out some leftovers and overdone it with the microwave, and they'd laughed as they tried to chew through the rubberized chicken. Neither of them had wanted to take a shot at the flaccid, weary green beans.

As much as she'd tried not to, she'd thoroughly enjoyed his company.

Callie shook her head and went back to the painting. She really needed to get started.

Positioning the microscope over the top right-hand corner of the painting, she brought the paint surface into focus by twisting a pair of knobs. Her eyes sought out the craquelure, memorizing the pattern of fissures, their direction, their depth. Inch by inch, she surveyed the surface of the portrait and meticulously recorded the status of the varnish, paint, and canvas support. This documentation, as she'd explained to Jack, was the first step in any conservation.

When she got to the mirror Nathaniel was holding, she frowned and cranked the microscope closer to the canvas. The paint layer was thicker in this area, suggesting an extra coat had been applied. The craquelure was different as well, the pattern tighter and the direction subtly dissimilar. She told herself she was imagining things, but further inspection only confirmed what had gotten her attention. There was something faintly inconsistent about the paint layer over the glass portion of the mirror, a slight change in the texture of both the brushstrokes and the cracks across the surface of the painting.

Callie pulled back and looked at the portrait with her naked eyes, telling herself not to get worked up. The difference was very subtle and it could be explained by a function of the paint itself. The mirror was one of the few pale parts of the painting, aside from Nathaniel's face and hands. Maybe Copley had used a different kind of oil base for the lighter hues.

She bent down and checked the forehead, cheeks, and chin of the face. The cracks were all consistent with the rest of the painting, which kept her suspicions running instead of slowing them down.

She retrained the microscope on the depiction of the mirror.

The change was so slight that, if it was an alteration, it had been made a long time ago. Or by an expert. And the varnish across that part of the painting was consistent with the rest of the work's surface. She'd just read in a book on Copley's work that the Walker portrait had last been conserved and revarnished some seventy-five years ago. The change, therefore, could be no more recent than that.

Callie sat back and stared off into space, wondering why the inconsistency hadn't been noted during that prior conservation. The book had mentioned details about the condition of the painting back then, but there had been no reference to any discrepancies in surface texture.

And Gerard Beauvais had seen something, she thought.

She recalled what he'd said about where the painting had been placed in the Blankenbakers' home, over a working fireplace. Such temperature fluctuations could have been the catalyst that revealed the retouching. Which would explain why the last conservationists didn't mention anything.

Maybe it was something as innocent as a repaint by Copley himself. Painters, even great masters, did that frequently. Not liking a shape or a tone, they would paint over what work they had done. Over time, as the paint layer aged, these changes could become more obvious, appearing as shadows in pale backgrounds or as pockets of disruption in the craquelure just like the one over the surface of the mirror.

Thinking perhaps the explanation was as simple as that, she recalled one of the things Professor Melzer had drilled into her. When you see hoofprints, don't think zebras.

It was good advice, she told herself. But damned if she wasn't skeptical anyway.

She spent the rest of the day on her preliminary review of the painting, going over every square inch of the canvas, searching out areas of chipping or flaking, discoloration or fading, changes in brushstroke. Her notes were as copious and objective as she could make them.

When she finally had to stop because her back ached from stooping over the microscope, she stood up feeling pleased. The painting was in good shape and she'd confirmed that there was no extensive work that had to be done. A removal of the old varnish and a cleaning, followed by an application of a new coat of varnish to protect the surface would be all Nathaniel would need.

She felt better able to complete the project and figured she'd probably need only another day to finish the documentation. And then the real fun would begin.

As she left the garage, she decided not to tell Jack about her suspicions. The chances of her making a neophyte mistake and jumping to a wrong conclusion were very real. And you didn't tell a man who's just spent five million dollars on a painting that it might have a flaw, based on a single inspection done before the thing was even cleaned. You waited until you were 100 percent sure and backed up by half a dozen other professionals in the field.

Wearing hockey pads was probably a good idea, too.

On Saturday, Jack hung up the phone on his desk and stretched in his chair. He was doing a deal with Nick Farrell, the renowned corporate raider. The guy was offloading his interest in an international conglomerate and Jack was happy to take the shares off his hands. The company owned various European wireless and fiberoptic networks and would fit in perfectly with Jack's private portfolio of international broadcasting and TV stations. Farrell was going to realize a hefty profit and Jack was positioning himself to be one of the largest providers of electronic media and Internet service on the European continent. It was a good deal for them both.

Except at the moment, Jack was feeling nothing of the triumph he usually did when an acquisition came together. He leaned back and listened as the grandfather clock across the room began to chime.

Five o'clock. Which meant he could have a bourbon.

He walked over to the wet bar, poured himself a good portion of Bradford's best, and sat back down behind the desk. The liquor burned his throat as it went to his gut.

In spite of his success, he was feeling unsettled and vaguely aggressive and he knew precisely the cause.

When his phone had rung an hour ago and his caller ID had spelled out Blair's cell phone number, he'd let it go into voice mail. He'd done that a lot lately and he'd gotten into the habit of calling her back at her hotel when he knew she wouldn't be there. The decision not to tell her what had happened with Callie was harder to stomach than he'd thought and he knew he couldn't put off talking to her indefinitely.

After another hit of bourbon, Jack lifted the phone and his fingers punched out a familiar pattern.

Blair's voice was sharp when she answered. "Hello?"

"Sorry I missed your call."

"Finally, it's you! Hold on— Listen, Joey, I need those light fixtures now. Karl wants me to show him this suite at the end of the week. I don't care if you have to gold leaf them yourself. It can't wait." She let out a laugh. "Sorry about that, Jack. Things are pretty crazy here."

"So Graves is as demanding as I've heard." He brought up his glass again.

"But not impossible. He has high standards, but if you meet them, he lets you know it."

Jack moved his chair around and looked out the window behind his desk. The light was just beginning to fade from the sky. "So how're you holding up?"

"Other than the not sleeping? I'll get through it somehow— Here, wait a second. No! No, I want the dark green in velvet. The gold is the brocade," she yelled to someone in the background.

"You sound busy."

"I am," she said, sounding tired. "I knew going in that redecorating the Cosgrove Hotel was going to be a big project, but Graves has moved up the date of when he wants to reopen. I've only got a couple of months to do what would normally take a year."

"If he drives you too hard, let me know and I'll take a hunk out of him. Me and a couple of my buddies could do a hostile takeover of his company and bounce him out on his ass in a heartbeat."

She laughed. "Thanks."

"When are you coming home?"

There was a hesitation. "Actually, I was thinking I would stay in the city for the next couple weeks, even through Thanksgiving. We're picking colors and fabrics and I've got to get to Karl whenever I can. His schedule's ridiculous, but he insists on being the decision maker about everything. He's offered me an old suite in the hotel."

Jack told himself that the feeling in the pit of his stomach was from the bourbon. It was not relief because she was staying in New York.

"Sounds reasonable."

A flash of movement outside caught his eye. He watched Arthur go bounding after something and he wondered how the dog had gotten out.

When Callie came across the lawn, Jack sat upright and leaned toward the window.

"You sure you don't mind?" Blair said. "It will be a while until we see each other."

"No, that's fine. Really."

Arthur ran back to Callie, dropped a stick at her feet and backed up, poised to run. She picked the hunk of wood up and extended her arm behind her. With one strong, fluid motion, she let the branch rip, flinging it a tremendous distance. The dog surged forward, his head tilted to the sky.

While Callie watched Arthur go, a gust of wind swept some of her long hair into her face, and with a laugh, she pulled the red waves back and tucked them into the collar of the fleece she was wearing. She got down on her haunches as the dog raced back toward her.

"Jack?"

He came to attention. "Yeah?"

"I'll definitely come for the holiday party, though. You're still having your usual blowout this year, right?"

"Yes." He shifted the phone to his other ear and tried to think of something to say to her. Usually it wasn't tough.

"Jack? Are you sure you're okay with me staying down here? I could just take the shuttle back and forth if it really bothers you." As he tried to reassure her, his voice must have tipped her off. "Jack, is everything all right? Did the painting arrive safely?"

"Nathaniel's back in Boston and in one piece."

"And did the conservationist come?"

"Yes, she did."

"I can't wait to meet her. I saw Grace yesterday and she told me Callie's quite lovely. Hey, did you know that Grace is seeing someone? She didn't have time to give me a lot of details, but she looks very happy. We met him. At Newport."

Jack frowned. "The bodyguard? Jesus. He was a tough character."

"Well, Grace is certainly in love with him. She just couldn't stop smiling and I was so happy for her." The phone was muffled as Blair yelled out another set of commands. "Listen, I've got to go. Why don't we talk later on tonight?"

"That'd be great."

"I love you," she said before she hung up.

Jack put the phone down and stared at it. The conversation was typical of the ones they shared. Easygoing, warm.

Placid.

He turned back to the window, watching Callie and Arthur play.

Nothing was easy with Callie. He felt as though he had to work to earn her smiles, her laughs, her respect.

But when she'd send one of those rare, wide grins his way, he felt like he'd been blessed.

As soon as he finished his drink, he headed back to the bar.

This was wrong, he thought. This was all wrong. He wasn't supposed to be thinking about another woman and having Blair look unexciting by comparison.

With his glass full again, he went to the window and watched Callie pick up the stick and throw it toward the house. As Arthur sprinted across the grass, she caught Jack's eyes through the window and froze. He lifted his hand.

She waved back and then moved out of sight.

With studied effort, Jack tried to think of all of the things he liked about Blair: the shape of her eyes; the way she dressed; her sense of style. He heard the rhythmic inflection of her voice and the slight lisp that marked her *th*s.

He couldn't remember either of them raising their voices at each other, and considering all of the tension in his household and all the conflict in his business life, that calmness had been a welcomed change. With Blair, it had always been smooth sailing. Smooth as glass.

And maybe a little flat.

"Jackson," his mother said crisply from the doorway. He looked around. She was wearing her mink and pulling on slim leather gloves. "I'm going out for the evening. Thomas has prepared a buffet for you."

"I'm sure Callie and I will enjoy it," he said, swirling the bourbon in his hand.

His mother's lips tightened. "I had Elsie mail the invitations to the holiday party today. I used the standard list."

He nodded even though he didn't care and she knew it.

"You know, I really wish you'd take more of an interest," she said, easing one of the gloves down the back of her hand. "Your father was so very helpful. With the guests, the choice of food. He was such a master at these things."

Jack shot her a dry smile. "So paying for it isn't enough?"

Her eyes lifted from the glove. "Really, Jackson, that's uncalled for."

"Sorry." He rubbed the bridge of his nose and sat down in his chair. "Long day."

He heard her come farther into the room, her high heels clipping across the marble floor until they were silenced by the rug behind his desk. When he felt her hand on his shoulder, he looked up.

"You know, Jack, I do appreciate all your hard work." Her eyes were as soft as they ever got. "Your father may have been blind to everything you have done for this family, but he never knew what it was like not to have money. I, on the other hand, have never forgotten."

So she remembered after all, he thought. His mother, the well-composed illusionist, had kept a little of her past with her.

Jack reached up and put his hand over hers. The bond of work, of industry, of pressing the limits because they were there to push against, was something they would always share. His drive and ambition had been his inheritance from her and they sure as hell had proven more lucrative than what had been left to him in his father's will.

From the doorway, Elsie cleared her throat. "I'm sorry to bother you both, but I'm going home now. Unless you need anything else."

Mercedes snatched her hand back, and before she turned around, her face settled into the elegant mask she showed the world. "No, we're fine. Have a good evening."

Elsie bowed a little and then left.

His mother walked back across the marble.

"By the way, you'll never believe who I'm having dinner with," she said as she went to the door. "Senator McBride."

Mercedes waved one of her gloved hands and disappeared down the hall.

Jack frowned, wishing his mother was eating with just about anyone else in town. Jim McBride was on the short list of people who were being approached to serve on the exploratory committee. The invitation was supposed to have been extended sometime this week.

Which meant if his mother asked the right kinds of questions, she would find out Jack was thinking of running in the next election.

She wouldn't be totally surprised. He had a feeling she might have guessed he wanted to try his hand in politics. He'd deliberately cultivated connections in the Massachusetts statehouse in recent years and had hosted many dinners with powerful legislators and lobbyists at Buona Fortuna. But that wasn't the same as her knowing his plans outright.

In order for him to declare his intentions in a strategic way, he and Gray needed to first assess his chances of getting on the ballot and then the odds of him winning. The exploratory committee would be responsible for rating him against the competition and for doing their work in confidence and with discretion.

His candidacy's groundwork needed to be established *quietly*, something his mother knew little if nothing about. Jack was going to tell her he was running only right before he publicly announced it, and he hoped like hell McBride wouldn't let the cat out of the bag, assuming the guy knew anything.

After Jack heard the big door close, he picked up the phone and called Gray. When he hung up, he went to look for Callie, feeling relieved and pleased with himself.

McBride hadn't been asked yet, so he knew nothing. And Gray was more than willing to meet an attractive redhead.

10

"OKAY, ARTIE, my arm's about to fall off." Callie bent down and gave the dog a hug. He was panting heavily, his breath coming out in bursts of steam. "Besides, we're about five minutes away from pitch dark. You'll never find it."

She heard a car and looked up as a Jaguar with Mrs. Walker behind the wheel went down the drive. She hadn't seen much of the woman in the past couple days and was hoping it was the beginning of a trend.

She was walking toward the house when the door opened. Jack was on the other side, the light from overhead illuminating his face. He was smiling at her, a drink in his hand, as she came up to the doorstep.

"I talked to Gray. He thinks he can get free for dinner tonight and should be here in a half hour," he said as he shut the door behind her.

For some reason, the fact that Jack had followed through on the setup bothered her.

Having just finished the documentation portion of the project, and being cross-eyed from so much concentrated work with the microscope, the last thing she felt like doing was meeting one of his friends. Or maybe the idea of being charming in front of Jack and his college roommate was what exhausted her. Pretending to be interested in one man's conversation while ignoring her attraction to another was going to require more coordination than she felt like she had.

She told herself that none of it had to do with the fact that she'd been looking forward to having dinner with Jack alone, which was what they'd been doing the last few evenings. He tended to stay at the office rather late and she'd been putting in long hours with the portrait. When he'd come home, he'd check on her progress with the painting and then they'd eat in the kitchen while trading stories about their days.

She'd pointed out just last night that his skills with the microwave were showing improvement and his obvious pride had made her smile. Apparently, his incompetence was from lack of practice. He'd told her that he usually didn't get home until ten o'clock at night and ate at the office, but now he had a reason to leave earlier. He evidently liked their talks as much as she did.

In those quiet moments, she felt as if she was truly getting to know him, and what she was discovering was a surprise. Yes, he was a tough-as-nails businessman, but people mattered to him. One of his senior management team, the Walker Fund's general counsel, had a daughter who was dying of a neuroblastoma at the age of six. Jack was beside himself with grief for the family and she'd never forget the expression on his face as he'd described how helpless everyone felt. All the money and the power in the world were not going to save the little girl. Connections had gotten her treatment at the Dana Farber Cancer Center and had ensured that she'd been seen by the best Harvard-trained specialists in oncology and pediatrics. But she was still going to die.

Callie could have sworn Jack's eyes had watered briefly while he'd talked about the situation, and it had taken every bit of her self-control not to reach across the table and take his hand.

Arthur was another one of Jack's soft spots. The other night the dog had come inside with a limp. Jack had gotten down on his hands and knees, in his suit, to look at the injured foot. As he'd gently probed the area, Artie had capitulated to the examination with total trust, even as he winced while a thorn was taken out. When it was all over, Jack had put some bacitracin in between the pads, wrapped some gauze around the wound, and then fed Artie some filet mignon from his own plate. That night, the dog had wanted to sleep with him.

"Hello?" Jack prompted.

She shook her head. "Sorry. Hey, what's that fantastic smell?"

"Thomas's marinara sauce, I believe."

"Thomas?"

"Our erstwhile cook." He frowned. "You haven't seen him during the day?"

"No, I stay up in the garage."

"All day long? Until I come home? Don't you eat?"

She shrugged. "I lose track of time and forget."

"Where's your watch?"

"I don't have one."

He grumbled something under his breath while taking her elbow and urging her ahead. The contact burned and she closed her eyes briefly, letting him lead her into the kitchen.

"I think you will like Thomas."

As she fought against the urge to lean into Jack's body, she thought maybe it was a good thing this other guy was coming. Maybe she'd really like him and her mind would get taken off of Jack.

When they got to the kitchen, she was surprised to see a man with only one arm holding a pot of boiling water over a sieve in the sink. She doubted she could have handled the load with two hands, but the guy looked perfectly at ease as he tipped the handle and sent a torrent of hot water and pasta over the lip.

"Thomas, I've got someone for you to meet."

The cook looked over his shoulder. He was probably around sixty, she thought, and had a face like a bulldog with the short, stocky body to match. She caught a glimpse of a tattoo peeking out from under his short-sleeved shirt and noticed there was a small gold hoop in his earlobe. She never would have guessed a rough-neck like him would be in charge of Buona Fortuna's kitchen. She imagined the chef would have been some whip-thin Continental with a haughty attitude to match Mrs. Walker's.

Thomas sent her a grin and Callie liked him on the spot.

"So this is who's been stealing food out of my refrigerator," he said. The man had a terrific New England accent marked by flat vowels and hard, lingering consonants. "Every morning I come down and fruit's gone out of my bowl, someone's been into the eggs, and bread's gone. Just like there's breakfast being made."

He put the pan to the side and came over. His kitchen whites were spotless, she noted, except for the dish towel that hung from his belt and had a couple of red smudges on it.

As they shook hands, she noticed that he had a tattoo of an anchor on the inside of his forearm. A seaman, she thought.

"So what are we eating, chef?" Jack asked, going over to the cupboards and taking out a pile of dishes. He proceeded to set the low-slung oak table that was in front of a bay window.

"My marinara sauce. For a cold night like tonight, it's just what you need before hitting the sack."

Jack clapped him on the shoulder. "Bless your heart. I'm starved."

"Yeah, it's your mother we can't get to eat around here." As Arthur came over to Thomas and looked up at him, the man laughed. "But this one, we can't get to stop with the munching. Can we?"

The dog waved his tail and licked his chops.

"So what are your plans for tonight?" Jack asked as he pulled out some linen napkins.

"Got a date with the sweet Angelina."

Jack laughed. "She's still around?"

"Son, you don't turn down a woman like that. She's got special skills with her—" Thomas paused and glanced at Callie. "Er—she's a great conversationalist."

Callie grinned as the man took off his apron and

tossed it into a hamper in the corner. "I'm heading up to shower and then I'm going out. Don't wait up."

"Wouldn't dream of it," Jack replied.

"Nice to meet you, Callie."

She waved. "Same here."

When the lights dimmed, she looked up in surprise. Jack came over, lit the candles on the table, and offered her some wine. She decided to hold off on the alcohol until his friend arrived. Suddenly, the intimate atmosphere seemed a little overwhelming and she wanted to keep sharp.

This was not about her and Jack, she reminded herself as they sat down. He had a fiancée and she was waiting to be introduced to his friend. This was absolutely *not* about the two of them.

"You're really going to like Gray," Jack said. What followed was a long list of the man's attributes, including some anecdotes about Jack's college days that had her listening more for clues about Jack than anything about his friend.

"And I told him all about you."

"What did you say?"

"That you are smart and—" He cleared his throat. "And that you're beautiful."

She slowly lifted her eyes to his face. He was staring at the deep red wine in his glass, swirling it around so it caught the light.

"So, how are you and Nathaniel getting along?" he asked brusquely.

"Fine." She was more than happy to talk about work. "It's taken me a while to finish the overview, but it's important to be precise during the documentation part of the project. I took pictures of him today and I'll start working on the canvas tomorrow."

There was a brief silence and then she asked, "What was your day like?"

Jack smiled and started to remove his cuff links. She heard one hit the table with a solid sound.

"Not all that good." He took off the other one and

started rolling up his sleeves. The backs of his arms were covered with fine, dark hair and she had to look away. "The blood brothers are still driving me nuts, I think interest rates are going to go up, and my assistant gave notice because she's going to start business school in January. On the other hand, one of my main competitors got indicted for fraud. How's that for a day? The best thing that happened was I got to picture someone I dislike in horizontal stripes. Oh, but my brother's coming for a visit soon."

She fiddled with the silverware in front of her, turning the knife over and over. "Really? Tell me more about him."

"We're twins." He laughed as she glanced up. "I didn't mean that. Well, we look nothing alike if that makes any sense. He's a hell of a cook, as I mentioned. Thomas taught him the basics and then, after he graduated from Harvard, he went to CIA."

"He was a spy, too?"

"Culinary Institute of America."

"Ah." She smiled. "You two must be close. Or at least I've heard that about twins."

"We are, even though we don't have a lot in common." Jack's voice took on a hard edge. "Although our father didn't like either one of us, so that's something."

Callie frowned, trying to imagine how a parent couldn't be proud of everything Jack had accomplished. Ten billion dollars was a lot of money for one man to be able to throw around. "But why?"

He shrugged. "I was too aggressive. Nate was too laid-back. In retrospect, I think my father got along better with women his whole life. He probably would have been easier on daughters."

The phone rang and Jack reached over to the wall. When he hung up, he looked out of joint.

"Gray's not coming. He said to tell you he was sorry and that he's looking forward to meeting you."

"Oh."

Jack frowned for moment, but then went over to the

stove, where he put some pasta into two bowls and ladled on the sauce. After he'd served her and sat down
with his own food, she thought it all looked too good to
be true. The candlelight. The steaming bowls of pasta.

Him.

"Wine?" he asked.

Yes, she could certainly use a drink right about now.
"Please. But white, if you don't mind. My head doesn't
like red."

Jack went over to a wine refrigerator and pulled out a
bottle. As he opened it at the table, her eyes lingered on
his hands, tracing the thick veins that ran down his arms
and into his fingers. She thought of what he'd looked
like after returning from his run. All sweat and muscle.

"Is it hot in here?" she asked abruptly.

"You want me to open the window?"

She shook her head as he poured. When he was
seated, he raised his glass in a toast.

"To Nathaniel."

"To Nathaniel." Their glasses met. And then their
eyes did.

Looking across the candles at him, she thought the
scene felt very different from their usual routine.

She quickly took a drink and focused on her glass.
"Good Lord. What kind of wine is this?"

He said something in French and followed the grand
title with the year she'd gotten her learner's permit to
drive a car.

"It's, ah—very nice." And no doubt the best wine
she'd ever had.

As she tried the pasta, she let out a small moan of
appreciation.

Jack looked up. "I feel the same way. The man's a
genius."

"How long have you known him?"

"He's been here since the seventies. He could be a
chef in any first-class restaurant, but he works best by
himself. But what about you?" He switched the subject
deftly. "Do you have any siblings?"

Callie swallowed a mouthful that had turned flavorless. She bought herself some time by drinking a little wine.

"I have a half sister," she said quietly.

"Are you close?"

"Ah—it's complicated. But I like her very much."

He nodded and let the subject drop, only to bring up something that completely wiped out her appetite.

"What about your parents? What are they like?" He was twirling pasta around his fork casually, but she wasn't fooled. He was waiting for her answer.

"They're both dead."

He lowered his fork. "I'm sorry."

She shrugged. In the dim light, she was stupidly tempted to talk. About her mother, at least. But then she eyed the empty place setting, where his friend should have been, and reminded herself that an accident of fate had put them alone together. This was not some magical beginning for them.

"Thanks, but I'm doing okay."

"So who do you go to when you need help?" he asked. "Who's there for you?"

She took a good long drink. "I, ah—I don't know how to answer that."

"You could try a proper noun," he chided gently.

She smiled, thinking when he got playful like that, he was pretty damn near irresistible.

"I try to keep to myself," she said.

He frowned and tilted his head to one side. "What kind of men do you go for?"

She looked at him in surprise. "What kind of— God, I don't know."

"Come on, there must be a set of characteristics you find attractive. Looks, humor, money—"

"Definitely not money."

He smiled and picked up his glass. "So that takes me out of the running."

"You're out of the running because you have a fiancée." As soon as the words were out, she wanted to curse. "What I mean is—"

Jack took a fast drink. "I know, I know."

There was a long silence.

"So back to your men. What's your type?"

Callie shook her head at his persistence. "I don't have a type."

"Everyone does."

"So what's yours?" she countered quickly.

"Touché. But how about you go first this time?"

When she just smiled and stayed silent, he laughed.

"Don't tell me you can't take what you dish out?" As she remained quiet, he said, "Fine. Why don't you tell me what you think my kind of woman is? But remember, charity begins at home and you're under my roof."

She hesitated. "Are we talking about the new, improved, socially responsible Jack Walker? Or the playboy whose pants have been known to run through hotel lobbies without him?"

He laughed. "For both our sakes, let's keep it current."

"Okay." She took a long drink from her glass and was surprised when she emptied it. "I'm sure you'd want someone who shares your background and values, who's beautiful, socially adept. I can't imagine you'd waste time with a dummy, so she'd have to be smart. And I think it would make it easier for you if your mother approved, although I doubt you'd make that a condition."

His eyebrows rose and she got the impression she'd nailed the answer.

"May I have some more wine?" she asked quickly.

His lips lifted. "Of course. If you answer my question."

"I just did."

He smiled. "I still want to talk about your men."

Well, that was going to be one short conversation, she thought wryly.

Shifting in her chair, she noted that he seemed content to wait her out.

"My wine first," she prompted, tipping her glass forward.

He poured and then looked at her directly. "So?"

She shrugged. "There's nothing to tell."

"Or nothing you want to share."

"The end result is the same, isn't it?"

"You are so damn elusive," he muttered. "Getting information from you is like pulling an oak out of the ground with a shoestring."

She had to smile. "Interesting way of putting it."

"You frustrate the hell out of me."

"So maybe you should give up."

He shook his head, looking at her through his dense eyelashes. The hazel in his eyes burned. "Sorry, Callie. I'm not that kind of a man."

She pushed her wine away abruptly and stood up. "It would probably be better for us both if you were."

When she made a move to go past him, he reached for her hand. His grip was warm. Urgent. "Don't go."

She knew if she looked into his eyes, she'd be lost, so she stared at one of the candles, watching the flame undulate slowly. The air seemed to have suddenly thickened and her lungs felt tight.

"I really wish you hadn't kissed me," she murmured.

The bold statement was followed by an absurd urge to smack her palm over her mouth.

"Tell me," he said softly, "are you looking for another apology for what I did? Or is it because you can't quite get how it felt out of your mind?"

Through the candlelight, his voice drifted up to her, embracing her.

She tried to take a deep breath. Her heart couldn't seem to decide between beating triple time or stopping altogether.

"Callie?"

Warily, she looked into his eyes. Crazy things started to swirl in her mind, like images of herself leaning down toward him.

She watched his gaze go to her lips. As his eyes darkened to a near black, she had the sense that he was as conflicted as she was.

Callie shook her head, trying to get her hand back.

When he didn't let go, she stopped and asked, "What are we doing here?"

"I wish to hell I knew."

And then he got to his feet and pulled her to him.

Putting his hands on either side of her face, he bent his head and she closed her eyes, lifting her mouth for his kiss even as she told herself it was wrong.

He already had a woman. A fiancée. This was all wrong.

Still, when the kiss didn't come, she was bitterly disappointed.

She lifted her lids. He was poised, inches from her lips, his eyes burning. But he came no closer.

Riding a wave of insanity, she grabbed his shoulders and pulled him down so she could kiss him. He resisted for a split second and then crushed her to him so they were hip to hip, chest to chest. His mouth was hungry on hers, his tongue sliding between her lips, his hands digging into her hair. She moaned and leaned into him, feeling the length of his body against hers, so solid and strong.

"God help me," Jack groaned while he pulled her shirt free and slid his hands onto her bare skin. "You feel too good."

He pressed her up against something, maybe the wall, his hands coming around to her stomach as he kissed her neck. His lower body was grafted onto hers, the hardness of him pressing into her, and she only wanted him closer. Naked. Inside of her. She held on to his shoulders with all her strength as he slowly moved his palms upward to her breasts. He spanned them with his hands, cradling the sides in his palms, but he didn't actually touch them. She strained against him, wanting more.

With a moan, he stopped kissing her and rested his head on her shoulder, breathing heavily. The sound rushed in her ear, as loud as the screaming in her blood. As he struggled for self-control, she didn't know whether to be grateful or not.

"This isn't right," he said roughly. "We shouldn't be doing this."

But then his thumb moved over to her nipple. It was the gentlest of brushing, but it made her want to cry out in triumph and need. She arched back, trying to give him more room, and found herself in full contact with his erection.

Abruptly, he pulled away and put the distance of the kitchen between them. She stared in shock at the retreat, wondering what had made him stop, as shame cut through her sensual fog.

But then his mother walked into the room.

Callie tried to gather up her composure, to look something other than thoroughly kissed and achingly frustrated in front of Mrs. Walker. Heading back to her chair, she surreptitiously pulled down her shirt, glad that the woman tended to ignore her presence.

Thank God Jack had heard the front door open. She sure hadn't.

"Well," Mercedes said. "Isn't this cozy."

Callie was grateful for the dim light as she picked up her fork and pushed the cold food in her bowl around. She had no doubt that her face was showing what her body was still feeling, and no mother needed to see that.

Especially not Mercedes Walker.

"You're home early, Mother." Jack's voice was dry and Callie risked a look at him. His face was utterly composed, as if nothing had happened at all. Considering the hoarse rasp of his voice just moments before, his recovery was downright astounding.

"I wasn't feeling well."

Callie glanced over at the woman. She looked perfectly fine.

For someone who was thoroughly pissed off but hiding it well.

Mercedes's eyes were shooting messages at Jack and it was pretty clear what the gist of them were. The woman obviously didn't like the intimate atmosphere in the kitchen, didn't approve of her son having quiet dinners with someone other than his fiancée. She no doubt would have fallen over in a dead faint if she'd walked in on them while they were actually kissing.

Then again, Callie would probably have passed out, too.

An awkward silence ensued while Mercedes glared at her son and Jack leaned back casually on the granite counter.

So this was how the upper classes fought, Callie thought. No yelling, no cursing. Just a lot of chilly glances and the rank odor of disapproval filling the room.

"Did you want something?" Jack said smoothly.

Mercedes took off her gloves with sharp movements and pushed them into the pocket of her fur coat. "No."

"Good night, then."

"Good night, indeed," Mercedes snapped before turning on her heel and leaving.

Callie took a deep breath and stared at the remnants of their dinner. The half-eaten food in Jack's bowl. The candles dripping wax. The napkins that were lying on the table.

Such a fine meal, she thought. Or at least it had started out that way.

"You okay?" Jack asked.

She nodded even though she was far from fine. Now that she was thinking more clearly, she had to wonder what would have happened if Mercedes hadn't come home. Would they have ended up in a bedroom somewhere? Was she really that reckless? To lose her virginity to a man with no relationship, no declarations of love? No chance of a future because he was *engaged* to someone else?

Unfortunately, when she remembered what it felt like to be in Jack's arms, Callie thought, yes, maybe she was that rash. And maybe she should thank his mother for being an intrusive pain in the ass.

Jack cleared his throat. "Brace yourself. I'm about to apologize again."

Callie looked up at him. "This time, you have nothing to be sorry for. I was the—ah . . ."

Aggressor was probably the right word. God, she wanted to cringe.

Jack shook his head and came over to the table. She thought for a moment he would take her in his arms again, but he only cleared his place setting.

As he went over to the sink, he flipped the lights on and she blinked from the glare. He paused and then slammed his bowl down with force, making her jerk in surprise as pasta jumped out and landed on the counter.

"Damn it, I don't want to ... want you like I do. What's happening between us ... It isn't right."

"I agree," she said quietly. "We should— Ah, let's just forget about it."

His face was harsh as he stared at her over his shoulder. "You think that's even possible?"

"Do we really have a choice?"

In the awful silence that followed, she helped him clean off the table. As soon as the job was done, she dropped the napkins on the counter and headed to the door.

"Good night."

He didn't stop her. "Good night, Callie."

11

JACK WADDED up the napkins, threw them into the hamper, and shut off the light. Instead of heading for the stairs, he went out a side door. The last thing he wanted was to get into a bed that was only the width of a hallway away from her.

The cold wind cut through his clothes and he liked the sting of the night as he walked aimlessly across the lawn. Distantly, he heard cars go by, the sound of Route 9 a soft, unceasing hum.

She wanted him to forget? He'd have more luck turning back time.

When a light came on in Callie's bedroom, he stopped and watched the shape of her body as she moved around. When she paused by the window, he stepped deeper into the shadows. She seemed to be scanning the night.

Forgetting her was just not an option.

And he knew playing Peeping Tom was only going to push him further into the clutches of insomnia, so he headed for the garage. Hitting the light switch and climbing up the narrow stairs, he looked at her carefully arranged work space.

Brown jars of liquid were lined up neatly to the left of the painting, as were an assortment of brushes, wooden sticks, and cotton swabs. The microscope, which had been poised over the painting surface, had been put aside and he saw that a breathing mask and some rubber gloves had been brought out. He picked up a notebook and flipped it open. Her notes on the portrait's condition were voluminous, her writing very neat, her statements almost lawyerly in their tone and accuracy. She'd ordered the documentation under headings like "Surface," "Edgewrap," "Soakage," and "Thread Oxidation." In talking with her about her work, he'd been surprised at how scientific the terminology was. She knew a hell of a lot about chemistry, for instance, and had been able to describe at a molecular level what would happen when the solvent she was going to use hit the old varnish and liquefied it.

She was, he'd learned, incredibly smart.

As well as sexy as hell.

He closed the notebook and put it back.

Damn it. If his mother hadn't come in, he would have taken Callie on the kitchen table. On top of the damn dishes. He'd been so driven to have her, he hadn't cared where they were.

He shook his head. He had to talk to Blair. He could have put one slipup with Callie behind him. Two was a trend he couldn't live with.

It was not going to be easy. No matter how carefully he expressed himself, he was going to hurt a woman who loved him, and that made him feel wretched. He also knew there was a possibility she'd end the engagement, and he wouldn't blame her if she did.

As the deep growl of a car sounded out in the night, he glanced at his watch, surprised Thomas was home so early.

Before Jack turned off the lights, he looked back at the table, picturing Callie bent over the painting, totally absorbed in her work. He thought about her losing track of time and not eating properly and realized there wasn't a clock in the place, not even a digital readout on the stereo.

He lifted his arm and took off the Patek Philippe wristwatch he wore. He'd bought it when the first company he'd ever invested in went public and made him a millionaire a couple of times over. It was gold, with a black alligator band, and he didn't take it off except for when he showered, even though it was waterproof to some ridiculous depth.

He laid it faceup next to her can of brushes, hoping she'd use it until he figured out what kind of clock to install for her. The thing kept perfect time, and with any luck, she'd know when it was lunchtime now.

Jack was just stepping outside as Thomas got out of his car. The Pontiac GTO was the man's pride and joy. Deep purple with lots of chrome, it was the quintessential muscle car.

"You're home early, old man."

Thomas let out a shout of laughter. "They call her the fair Angelina, not the faithful. Found another backseat she was interested in trying out."

"Sorry about that."

Thomas grinned and ambled over. "S'all right. There'll be others."

They walked into the kitchen together.

"Beer?" Thomas asked, throwing open the fridge.

When Jack nodded, a bottle came flying through the air at him. He caught it, opened it, and sent it back across the counter. Thomas tossed another at him.

"So that conservationist's a looker," Thomas said after a deep draw.

Jack frowned, twisting his cap off. "Yeah."

"How're you two getting along?"

"Is that an honest question or a leading statement?" Jack tipped the bottle back, swallowing hard. It was better than cursing.

"Lil' bit of both. Right now, you're prowling around like you're on a short leash with a plate of food just out of reach. So it makes me wonder."

"You're reading into things."

"Don't think so."

Jack was sorely tempted to go with a lie but he knew he wouldn't get away with it. Not with Thomas. The man had known him his whole life.

"It's no damned good." Jack shook his head. "And

the timing is awful. Just when I decide to settle the hell down. I thought I was through chasing women."

"You're lucky it happened now. Before things got permanent."

"Is this why you never got married?"

Thomas grinned. "Naw. I never got married because the woman I loved wasn't interested in me."

"Really?"

"I know. Can you believe it? With all my charm." Thomas arched his neck to finish the beer. His eyes had a faraway look in them when his head came back to level. "She wouldn't have me. Thought she was too good for me and was probably right."

"What happened to her?" Jack polished his beer off and put it down.

Thomas shrugged. "What does it matter?"

"Maybe you could have a second chance."

"There are no second chances, Jack-o'-lantern," the man said, using the old childhood name. He tossed his beer into the trash. "I'm heading upstairs. Night."

"Hey, Thomas?"

"Yeah?"

"If Callie doesn't surface around noontime for some eats, bring something up to her, will you?"

Thomas smiled, long and slow. "Sure thing."

When the man went up to bed, Jack headed to his study and called Blair's cell number. It rang three times and he got voice mail. He tried the Waldorf, where she had been staying, and then remembered she'd moved into the Cosgrove. When the front desk answered and he asked for her, they transferred him immediately, but there was no answer.

He checked his watch. It was 10:30. She was probably still hard at work.

Jack rubbed his hand over tired eyes. It was a good thing she hadn't picked up. He was in a rush to get through the hard conversation and might have been inconsiderate enough to try it over the phone.

Besides, his mind was as clear as silt.

*   *   *

The next morning, Callie left her room quickly. After what had happened the night before, she would rather not run into Jack. Or his mother.

She was surprised to find Thomas in the kitchen, but he explained an early night had meant he'd been up with the sun and in the mood to make bread.

She grabbed a piece of fruit, because it was the only way he would let her go without making her breakfast, and went to the garage. Arthur was excited by the rush, prancing alongside her.

When she got upstairs and sat down in front of the painting, she saw a heavy gold watch set carefully beside her tools.

She picked it up, recognizing it immediately.

"Oh, Jack."

She'd spent most of the night sitting on the window seat, a satin pillow cradled in her arms, Arthur asleep on the floor next to her. In the quiet hours, she'd attempted to negotiate a compromise between what was good for her and what she wanted. It was like trying to broker peace between warring tribes.

Which was a bit of a surprise considering how clear-cut the situation was. She knew it would be crazy to think Jack would end his engagement. So if she were to get involved with him, she was just going to end up exactly where her mother had. As second best to a rich man's better half.

She was going to have to make it her business not to get caught alone with him again.

Because she obviously couldn't trust herself. And if she let Jack kiss her again, if she let him touch her body, God forbid if she let him make love to her, she was bound to start confusing the intense physical sensations with emotions. Wasn't that what the naive always did and why first loves were so painful? If her heart got involved, she'd feel a hell of a lot worse than sexually frustrated.

Hell. *If.*

She had a feeling it was too late for *if.* The man captivated her with all of his contradictions, with his hard shell and his soft touch. He was like no one she'd ever met and not because he was rich and powerful.

But he was never going to be hers.

With a deep breath, Callie set the watch back where he'd left it, trying desperately not to get lost in the thoughtful gesture.

Staring at the painting, she attempted to find the appropriate enthusiasm for the adventure she was about to embark on, but it was a while before she was ready to get started.

With the documentation finished, her next step was to strip off the dirt and the old varnish layer. First, she needed to determine what kind of varnish had been applied and choose a solvent that would be strong enough to remove the protective coat but not so intense as to take off any of the paint layer. She was going to use the lower left-hand corner to do the testing, in an area that would be covered by the frame.

When she'd finally gotten into bed the night before, she'd reviewed the painting's records one more time. The varnish had been applied in the early 1930s, at the time of the last cleaning, and this meant it was made of natural compounds. Nothing synthetic would have been used back then and she'd come prepared with chemicals that were appropriate to remove a tree-sap-based resin.

She had six different solvents of graduated strength and she picked out the weakest one, opening the lid and releasing the familiar sweet, chemical smell. Before she set to work, she opened two windows a couple of inches to make sure that Artie would have plenty of fresh air. Strapping on her breathing apparatus, which would filter the vapors as she worked so closely over the solvent, she plucked a wooden stick from the can and wrapped a small amount of cotton around one end. She dipped the bud, as it was known, into the solution and gently brushed over the canvas. She wasn't surprised when there was little effect and moved up a grade.

After considering the effect of the stronger solvent, she went back to her jars and readjusted the strength one more time to settle on the perfect composition to dissolve the varnish layer safely. She was careful to document the chemical compounds she tried out, noting when she had reached the right balance.

And when she had, she ventured out onto the painting proper. Whenever the bud became too dirty, she disposed of it in a sealed jar, wound another one on the stick and kept going. This was the part of her job that she loved the most. The quiet, the intense focus on such a small area, the delicate work, the solitude. It gave her peace, focusing her mind while she used her hands. The world and her problems faded into the distance, no longer crashing cymbals, not even a whisper.

It was just her and the painting.

While she worked, her eyes traveled over the portrait intermittently. She was learning the landscape of the masterpiece, the vast darkness around Nathaniel's head, the dense grays and deep blacks of his jacket, the frothy cream and white of his shirt. His tormented, handsome face was her favorite part. She was enchanted with the faint blush of pink across the cheekbones, the dark velvet of his pupils, the thick browns and blacks of his hair.

It was quite possible she'd be in love with him by the end of the project, she thought, looking into the eyes again.

They were so like Jack's.

A couple of hours later, the quiet of the studio was broken.

"Hello?" Thomas's voice barreled through the silence. "Mind if I come up?"

"Hi! You're always welcome."

She got up, as did Arthur. The dog had been a patient observer throughout the morning, and as he put his front paws out and lowered his shoulders in a big stretch, he looked as if he had high hopes for the man's arrival.

"I've brought you lunch," Thomas said as he clomped

up the stairs. He was carrying a picnic basket and a phone jack.

Arthur loped over to him, ignoring the wire and sniffing the wicker. His wagging tail suggested he was touched by the gesture.

"That's awfully nice of you," Callie said, accepting the food and frowning as Thomas got down on his hands and knees under her table. "But you didn't have to. Er— Is something wrong?"

"Just hooking up a phone for you." His head popped up and he nodded at the basket. "Would you mind? It's in there."

She laughed and took out a small cordless unit. "But I don't really need one."

"Jack called this morning. He wants me to install one for you."

"Oh."

When Thomas was finished connecting the wires, he checked for a dial tone. "You're all set. Now, I've got a message from Jack for you. He wanted to know if you'd meet him in Little Italy for dinner tonight. At seven, at Nico's."

Nico's. At seven. Her heart skipped a beat.

At least they wouldn't be alone. Restaurants had people in them. Lots of other people.

"Okay."

"And don't worry about getting there. I'll drive you. Hey, can I look at what you're doing?"

"Sure."

As Thomas studied the portrait, Callie set the basket down on a side table. Arthur put his snout right next to it, as if to remind everyone of the pivotal role he was going to play when it was opened.

She was stroking one of his ears when Thomas looked up. "How long did it take you to do those four square inches?"

"A couple of hours."

"You've got some work ahead of you," he said with a grin. "I better get out of your hair."

"Thanks for the lunch. And the phone."

"No problem."

Thomas went over to the stairs and paused. When he looked back at her, his eyes seemed somber, as if he was debating the merits of saying something. Evidently he thought better of it, because he just lifted his hand in a wave and disappeared.

Callie stared into Artie's brown eyes, telling herself not to get worked up.

It was just dinner, she told herself. In a public place. Where they couldn't possibly get into trouble.

She tried not to think about what it would be like if Jack happened to be a free man and they were going to go out somewhere together.

It would be nice to go on a real date with someone, she thought. She'd enjoy getting dressed for a lover. And she wanted to walk into a crowded restaurant where a man would look up and take her into his arms with his eyes. She wanted to know what it was like to feel that she was beautiful to someone and had been eagerly waited for.

Callie cursed under her breath. Of course, as she spun the fantasy, Jack was sitting at the table, and the image made her think of her parents.

And all those nights her mother had made herself beautiful for someone else's husband.

Preparing for her father's arrival usually started in the late afternoon, and as her mother had prepped in front of the mirror, pleasure made her normally dull eyes shine. Callie would always help her decide what to wear and how her hair should be worn, but no matter how considered the choice, a change would always be made at the last minute. A different dress, another pair of shoes, hair back instead of down.

Unfortunately, more often than not, the nights had ended with a delay, an apology, a letdown. The disillusioned undressing had been terrible to watch.

And yet she'd spent decades waiting for the man.

Callie had often wondered why, at least until she'd met Jack.

The answer, she now knew, was passion. When her parents had been together, there had been magic and sparks and tenderness, even with the perennial conflict. Her father had been very tall and statuesque, a power-ful man with a deep chest and a low voice that rumbled like thunder. Usually, he was very serious, but under the right circumstances, her mother could shake him out of his somber moods. Callie suspected that must have been part of the attraction for her mother. Transforming someone so great, so powerful, even if it was only for a short time, must have been meaningful.

And perhaps the passion, the emotion, the laughter, was what her father had lacked in his bigger life, but found in their tiny apartment.

Callie shook her head, thinking she would never know. Maybe he'd had those same things at Grace's house, too.

Arthur butted his head against her hand, but when she went to scratch the scruff under his chin, he looked pointedly at the picnic basket.

"Right." She snapped to attention and opened the thing up. Tossing him a strip of chicken, she started in on the salad while deciding it was time to take a break. She was contemplating a walk when she remembered the documents that were in the closet.

When she was finished with lunch, she lifted the top container off the stack and muscled it over to the couch. As she removed the lid, there was no sense pretending she wasn't preoccupied with going out to dinner with Jack, and she figured she could handle sorting paper with a scattered brain.

It was safer than playing around with chemicals and the painting—that was for sure.

12

LATER THAT evening, Callie stared at her reflection in the bathroom and played with her hair. Up? Down?

She let it fall across her shoulders, knowing it shouldn't matter.

Two minutes later, her hands were propping it up on her head again. She couldn't help herself and a lot of it was pride. She didn't want to meet Jack looking anything less than composed. Refined. Elegant.

Although she was going to need a different wardrobe to really pull it off. She'd settled on a black skirt that fell below the knee, a white blouse that was pretty nondescript, and a black sweater to wrap around her shoulders. The black tights and shoes were also garden variety. Regarding herself in the bathroom mirror, she figured she was one step away from looking like a nun, saved only by the red fall of her hair.

Definitely down, she thought. And lose the old-lady tights.

She ran a razor over her calves, put on some nude stockings, and slipped into a pair of shoes with a modest heel.

Throwing on her coat and picking up her purse, she headed for the stairs quickly because Thomas was waiting for her. She was about to hit the top landing when Mrs. Walker's voice stopped her.

"Going out this evening?" The woman stepped into the hall and looked over what Callie was wearing.

"Yes. I am."

"With my son?"

Callie lifted her chin. Rule number two when dealing with a bully: Show no fear.

"Yes."

"Well. You've certainly made an impression on him. I imagine you must be quite pleased."

As if Callie had set out all along to seduce her son.

"If you'll excuse me, I don't want to keep Jack waiting." She turned and started down the stairs.

"Don't fool yourself, Ms. Burke. My son is very much in love with his fiancée. There is no hope for you."

Rule number three for dealing with bullies: If you have to set them straight, do it firmly. Any weakness is perceived as an opening and will immediately be capitalized on.

Callie looked over her shoulder and spoke clearly. "Please don't take offense at this, but you are presuming a hell of a lot of things for no good reason. Good night, Mrs. Walker."

She forced herself not to race down the stairs. The last thing she wanted to do was slip and fall, and her legs already felt like pipe cleaners.

It was a relief to find Thomas in the kitchen wearing a biker's jacket, all ready to go.

"You're going to like Nico's," he said, holding the back door open. "The owner's a friend of mine. Best osso buco in Little Italy."

Waiting outside, with the motor running, was the Pontiac GTO she'd seen in the driveway earlier.

"Nice car," she said, getting in.

"You've got excellent taste."

Twenty minutes later, he piloted them through a cramped network of streets and stopped in front of a bright red door.

"Thanks for the ride." She got out and waved as he screeched off.

She went inside Nico's, and when her eyes adjusted to the darkness, she saw a fleet of tiny tables and doz-

ens of waiters dancing around with trays held high on
their shoulders. The place was packed with people talking and laughing and there was some kind of fabulous
opera playing in the background.

No, wait. That was one of the waiters singing.

"Welcome!" A man came up to her and smiled. "I am
Nico! Come this way, Ms. Burke."

"How did you—"

"He is right, of course. The red of your hair. Beautiful!"

Bemused, Callie followed the man past a bunch of
people who were obviously waiting for tables and she
looked for Jack in the crowd.

But he wasn't there and she wasn't led to a table. Nico
went straight through the room and into the kitchen.
There, at a linen-covered table in the back, Jack was sitting down and laughing at something one of the cooks
had said.

"Mr. Walker is an old friend," Nico explained with a
smile. "So we always make a special place for him."

Nico took the coat from her shoulders just as Jack
turned and saw her. He stopped laughing and seemed to
take a breath. Abruptly, the noise of the kitchen quieted
down and she felt the eyes of the staff on her.

"Go to him, yes?" Nico prompted with delight. "He
has been waiting for you."

Jack got to his feet, his eyes traveling up and down
the length of her. He was wearing a black suit, a crisp
white shirt, and a brilliant red tie. For some reason, he
seemed even taller than she remembered.

Oh, God, Callie thought. Yes, she wanted to go to him.

As she walked to the table, she heard the chefs go
back to work, which was just as well. Jack's attention
was quite enough for her to handle.

"Hello." He came around and pulled out her chair.

He was about to sit down again when his face broke
out in a grin.

"Gray! You made it." The relief in his voice was obvious.

Callie looked down and saw the third place setting.

So that was it. He'd wanted to set her up with his friend and was giving it another shot.

Right. Good.

As she turned around, she made sure her smile was in place.

Well, at least Gray Bennett was easy on the eyes, she thought as she looked at him.

Jack's friend was tall and had hair that was lightly graying around the temples. His pale eyes were sharp, his suit pin-striped and beautifully tailored, his tie perfectly knotted. She could see instantly why he and Jack might get along.

"Jack's told me a lot about you," the man said, offering her his hand.

"Oh, really?" She felt nothing as they touched and was a little disappointed.

But the night was young, she thought.

As she went to sit down, Jack and Gray both reached for the back of her chair. With a dark laugh, Jack stepped back and let his friend settle her into the table.

Gray smiled at her as he took a seat. "I understand that you worked on the de Kooning with Micheline. She's a very close friend of mine. She restored two of my family portraits."

Of course. Bennett as in Bennett Trust Company. As in the Bennett School of Private Industry at Harvard University.

She frowned, thinking she'd also heard of Gray Bennett himself, but not in the financial sector. What had it been?

"Would you like some wine?" Gray asked, picking up the bottle of red off the table.

"She only likes white," Jack said, taking her glass and filling it from a bottle of Chardonnay he had cooling in a stand.

By the time the antipasto course had been eaten, Callie was surprised at how easy Gray was to talk to. He was interested in what she said, asked questions about her work and where she was from, but didn't probe the way Jack did. And when he talked about himself, she figured out why she knew of him.

Gray Bennett was a heavy hitter in politics. As a consultant specializing in elections, he knew a lot about Washington, and she was fascinated by his juicy stories about the political world, even if he edited out some of the names. As the entrées arrived, she decided that having dinner with him wasn't quite the chore she'd assumed it would be.

Jack was the one making her uneasy. He was a constant source of movement, tapping his foot on the floor, folding his napkin again and again, rearranging his place setting. He looked like he couldn't wait to get the meal over with, and as a plate of pasta was set before him, he told the waiter to start preparing the dessert.

Gray grinned at her. "You'll have to excuse Jack. He hates downtime. Any wasted moment is a crime to him."

When Jack's mouth tightened, Gray cocked an eyebrow at him. "Do you want to leave? I can assure you, Callie and I will do just fine on our own."

Jack looked as if that was about as attractive an option as staying was. He brushed a hand through his hair and seemed tired. "Just ignore me. I've got a lot on my mind."

Gray looked across the table at her. "Did he tell you we were roommates at Harvard?"

When she nodded, the man poured himself a little more wine and settled back in his chair. "Did he tell you how we were almost expelled?"

"No, I didn't," Jack said.

"Ah, good. A fresh slate." Gray rubbed his palms together. "Picture this. It's right before Christmas break, around midnight. Jack, his brother, Nate, and I decide that we've had enough of studying. We head out of Eliot House, convinced there has to be more to life than Aristotle, Homer, and their crew of deep-thinking, toga-wearing wordsmiths."

"I think I was studying stats, actually."

Gray waved Jack into silence. "We end up at the

boathouse and decide that taking a shell or two out on the Charles will be a great way to burn off some energy. The three of us get on the water in separate boats and decide we'll race between bridges. Losers have to take off a piece of clothing after each sprint. The winner gets bragging rights and seventy-four dollars and fifty-three cents, which was all the cash we had on us at the time."

"God, do you remember how cold it was that night?" Jack interjected.

"Now, Nate and I, we know who we're going up against. Jack was captain of the varsity crew team. The man could row anyone under the table. Hell, he probably still can. In light of his scary skills, we made him start twenty yards back. But you cheated, didn't you?"

"Like I had to with you two lightweights?" Jack was warming up now, his eyes flashing. "I don't think so."

"So we start racing," Gray went on. "After four laps, Jack is fully clothed, Nate and I are rowing without shirts and shoes. A crowd starts to gather on one of the bridges so, of course, we start showing off. Jack didn't lose once, but Nate and I put on one hell of a strip show at the end of each pass. We were down to our underwear when the accident happened."

Callie glanced over at Jack and saw his smile dim.

Gray also got more serious. "Nate was taking off his boxers and waving them to the crowd when his shell tipped. I can still see him right before he went in, tilted at a totally wrong angle, arms pinwheeling, eyes wide. He hit his head on an oar as he went into the river. Before I was even out of my seat, Jack had whipped off his jacket and plowed into the water. How cold was it?"

"Probably forty-five degrees. It hadn't frozen yet, but it was close," Jack said, bringing his wineglass to his lips.

"Anyway, Jack dragged Nate back to shore. The police, alerted by the rowdy crowd, showed up just as they collapsed on the ground next to the bridge. The two of them got carted off with the lights going. It was very exciting."

"At least they gave us blankets."

Gray looked at his friend thoughtfully. "I've never seen anyone move as fast as you did."

"It was my brother in that river."

The two fell into silence.

"You were very lucky," Callie said, imagining what could have resulted from such a plunge into that kind of water. "But what happened to you, Gray?"

"Nothing." He grinned widely. "I'm no dummy. As soon as I could see Nate was fine, I hid under the bridge in my boat until the fervor died down. Snuck the shell back in the boathouse. Was never caught."

Jack smiled. "Isn't that just like a consultant."

"Hey, I posted your bail."

"Yeah, you did. My father had no interest in taking care of that. He told me later he would have preferred we'd spent the week in jail." Jack looked over at her. "Fortunately, the charges of public indecency and misuse of private property were later dropped, but only because one of my crewmate's fathers was the judge. Harvard put us both on probation."

"We were heroes that last semester in school," Gray said, with a chuckle.

When dinner was over and their plates were being cleared, Gray had started to talk about his vacation home in the Adirondacks.

"It's been in my family for generations. Jack's spent a lot of time there, although Blair hasn't been there yet, has she?" He leaned back while a cup of cappuccino was set in front of him. "We'll have to get the two of you up this summer for a proper vacation. Come for a week."

Callie looked away quickly as Jack made some noncommittal reply. Gray pressed on. "You know, I think she'd really like it up there. She strikes me as the kind who'd be just as comfortable in hiking boots as she is in a ball gown."

Jack's response was quiet, something along the lines of agreement.

"Callie, have you met his fiancée yet?" Gray asked.

Her heart stopped and she could feel Jack's eyes

burning from across the table. She forced herself to look up and smile. "I haven't had the pleasure, no."

"You're going to love her. She's a remarkable woman. And a terrific match for Jack, considering what he's about to get himself into."

As Gray turned and cocked an eyebrow in inquiry, Jack cleared his throat. "I haven't mentioned anything, but we can talk about it in front of her."

What she would have preferred, Callie thought, was having no more talking at all.

"In all likelihood," Gray said, "our friend here is going to run for governor of this fine commonwealth next year."

Callie glanced across the table at Jack.

Political ambitions. How appropriate, given his family's history.

She tried to picture him leading the state and could see it clearly. He was charismatic, smart, compelling. And he probably wasn't going to stop there. Knowing him, he would shoot for the Oval Office.

Jack nodded at his friend. "I'm pulling together my team now. Gray's going to make himself indispensable, aren't you?"

"And you're going to need all the help you can get. This is going to be a nasty fight, considering who the incumbent is."

"Who will you be facing?" Callie asked.

"Bill Callahan. Better known as Butch Callahan," Jack answered. "He likes to play dirty, and fortunately, I'm not put off by a good fight. I'm going to enjoy trying to beat him."

She thought back to him in his study, phone up to his ear, looking like he was about to reach through the wires and grab someone around the throat. And then she saw him crawling into the ceiling over the garage, determined to fix the stereo even if it took him all night. He was the kind of man who would stand up to anything and persevere until he had what he wanted. She figured whoever he was up against had better watch out.

Gray shook his head. "Like I said before, you're going to have to be prepared to have some serious mud thrown at you. Butch and his buddies are going to get into everything, especially your, ah, past."

Jack frowned while his friend looked at Callie.

"But fortunately, his wild days are over. There's no more carousing with the ladies and Blair is a great asset. Photogenic as hell with a background that's clean as a whistle. She also happens to be a fine person, which is the most important part."

"How about dessert?" Jack asked.

How about getting the hell out of here, Callie thought.

As Jack nodded to the waiter, she had no idea how she was going to sit at the table for another moment. It was a relief when they were finally done and Jack, who insisted on paying, left to find Nico.

Gray regarded her steadily and smiled. "I'm in town for the next few weeks. Would you like to get together again?"

She hesitated, but then Jack came back to the table.

"Yes, I would."

"Yes, what?" Jack asked.

Before Gray could say anything, she stood up. "This has been lovely."

Which was partially the truth. Under different circumstances she would have enjoyed getting to know Gray. He was charming and witty, though he could have been a troll for all the attraction he had for her.

No, she saved her lusty thoughts for the unattainable. Lucky girl that she was.

After they thanked the chefs and Nico, she and Gray waited outside the restaurant while Jack went to get the car.

"So how do you like working for Jack?" Gray asked.

"I love the painting." It was as close to the truth as she could get at the moment.

"It is a masterpiece. When Nate Six went bankrupt, he sold it off and Jack was infuriated. At the time, he was just out of business school and starting at J. P. Morgan in New York. He was working his tail off, but he didn't have enough money of his own to meet the asking price. He's waited for years to get that portrait back."

Callie stared at Gray in surprise. Bankruptcy and the Walker name were two things she never thought would get linked.

"How did Mr. Walker go—what—er, what did Mr. Walker do for a living?"

"Not much. And I don't mean that pejoratively." Gray rubbed his jaw and then shrugged. "Well, maybe I do. He was a philanthropist. The man donated money to charities and universities as if it were his profession. He funded the Walker Chair in Art History at NYU. You went there, right? So you must have heard about it."

"Yes." She cleared her throat. "If Mr. Walker lost his money, how did he pay for . . ."

She didn't go any further. She couldn't believe she'd started to ask such a nosy question.

"Jack. Jack paid for everything. Still does."

"Mr. Walker must have been grateful." In spite of what Jack had said about their relationship.

"Not in the slightest. He thought Jack was a money-hungry reprobate. It was ironic as hell. If his son hadn't been so strong in business, Nate Six's declining years would have been spent in something far more modest than Buona Fortuna." Gray shot her a meaningful look. "Jack's dad was a bastard, to be honest, and an alcoholic. I don't think many people outside of the family knew how bad it was. In public, the man was a perfect gentleman. He saved the ugliness for those closest to him."

"How awful."

"Yeah. I like to think Jack turned out all right in spite of his father, not because of him. Although I worry."

She waited for him to explain.

"About what?" she asked after a moment.

Gray crossed his arms over his chest, his eyes staring through the people walking past them.

"He's under a lot of pressure. The Walker Fund employs several hundred people, for example, and I know he feels personally responsible for each one. If he runs for office, someone's going to have to take over for him and no one will ever match his commitment. And if he wins, he's going to have to think seriously about the future of his business." Gray frowned. "Hell, there's the election itself. I know he thinks he's prepared for it, but I'm not sure he really understands how bad it could get. He's an extraordinary man, but everyone has their limits and stress does funny things to people."

There was a pause.

Gray looked over at her, smiling slowly. His eyes took on some heat. "But enough about Jack."

Callie heard the purr of the Aston Martin as the car came around the corner, and she was kind of relieved.

"It was nice to meet you," she said.

"My pleasure, I assure you. I'll call you at Jack's." With a small bow, Gray opened the door to Jack's car and offered his hand to help her inside.

"You want a ride?" Jack asked, bending across the seat to meet his friend's eyes.

Callie shrank back, trying to avoid contact with him, and saw his mouth tighten.

"Thanks, but I don't think I could fit in that backseat. Besides, with the way you drive, it's safer to go through the back alleys on foot." Gray shut the door with a smile and strode off in the opposite direction.

Jack put the car in gear and they hadn't gone two yards before he asked, "So what do you think of Gray?"

"I think the two of you were separated at birth," she said, looking out her window.

On the sidewalk, people were milling around in the cold, going in and out of restaurants. A couple caught her eye, a man and a woman walking close together. He was staring ahead, she was looking up at him, and they both had wide smiles on their faces. They were young, she thought. Midtwenties. So close to her own age.

"But what about him," Jack prompted. "Any chemistry?"

The girl hip-checked the guy, pushing him off balance,

and he threw his arm around her, bringing her close. As the Aston Martin rounded the corner, she lost sight of the couple.

"Callie?"

She shook her head. "Sorry. I got distracted."

"By what?"

Dreams, she thought. My own and others'.

"Nothing. Gray's likable. Very smart. Handsome."

Jack looked over at her sharply.

When he refocused on the road, he muttered, "I suppose he is good-looking. But you should know his appendix scar is frightening."

As he maneuvered them onto a highway of some kind, she had no idea where they were and was glad the traffic was light. She leaned back against the soft headrest, hoping he'd get them back to Wellesley in one piece.

Blair. His fiancée's name was Blair.

How proper. How elegant.

But what did she expect? That he'd marry an Irma? A Gertrude?

As visions of a long-limbed, well-dressed socialite with perfect diction and an impeccable bloodline went through her head, Callie closed her eyes and prayed for a distraction.

Maybe she'd still find one in Gray Bennett, she thought.

As he drove them home, Jack was feeling less than satisfied with the obvious success of the evening.

So. She thought Gray was handsome.

That bastard.

God, he wanted to kick himself for bringing them together. Now that his plan for hooking her up might be working, he hated that she thought some other man was handsome. Smart. And what else? Oh, likable.

Likable. What the hell did that mean?

Jack glanced over at her. She had her head back against the rest and seemed to be looking out the window. Streetlights and the headlights from other cars flared over her features.

"Callie?" She tilted her head around. "Are you going to go out with him?"

She shrugged and turned away.

He stared at her, trying to divine the answer in the lines of her face.

"Jack! Watch out!"

He snapped his head forward and wrenched the wheel, just in time to swerve and miss a car that was broken down at the side of the road.

"Christ," he breathed as the screeching faded. "That was close."

Callie clutched her chest with her hand. "You've got to learn to slow down."

"I know."

And he probably had to stop making brilliant plans, too.

They were silent until he pulled into Buona Fortuna's garage and shut the car off.

"Thanks for dinner," she said, opening her door.

"So are you?" he asked.

Callie stepped out and bent back down into the car. A long, thick curtain of red hair fell forward and swung in the air. He wanted to thread his fingers through it, pull her down to his mouth, and kiss her until she didn't think his friend was so smart or likable or handsome.

"You mean, am I going out with Gray?" When he nodded, she said, "Yes, I am."

And then she shut the door in his face.

Jack jumped out and caught up with her in three strides. She was walking quickly, her heels clipping across the driveway.

"When?" he demanded.

"I don't know."

"Are you calling him?"

"He's going to get hold of me."

"Where will you go?"

She shot him an annoyed look. "What's with the twenty questions?"

"Do you really like him?"

Callie stopped and put her hands on her hips. "No. I thought he was perfectly gruesome, which is why I agreed to see him again. Anything else you want to know?"

Are you attracted to him, he thought. Are you going to let him kiss you? Are you going to make love with him?

His stomach churned. The thought of her with his friend, with *any* other man, made Jack feel like someone had hit him with a tire iron.

And what if she really fell for Gray? Then what? The guy had quite a way with the ladies. His string of successes was almost as legendary as Jack's own. And so were the man's infidelities.

Christ, maybe he should have set her up with someone else. Like Charlie Feldman, his tax attorney, who was practically a eunuch.

"Just be careful," Jack said, thinking he'd kill Gray if he hurt her.

Callie cocked her head to one side and narrowed her eyes. "You're insane—you know that? You set me up with one of your friends and then tell me to watch myself? If he's that notorious, why did you introduce him to me?"

"I just don't want you to get hurt. Gray can be a heartbreaker."

"Something you know all about," she muttered and started walking again.

Jack cursed, wishing he had a leg to stand on, and quickly closed the distance between them. "Does that make you feel good? Getting that little dig in?"

"Not really. I hate the reminder of what you are as much as you obviously do. And at this moment, I wish you hadn't introduced me to Gray at all."

Funny, he felt exactly the same way.

Jack gritted his teeth. "What's so offensive about me trying to set you up?"

Aside from the fact that he might have to watch romance bloom between a woman he wanted badly and his best friend. Oh, joy.

"What you did is not the problem. It's how you're acting now."

"You think offering you some sound advice is wrong?"

She stopped again and confronted him. "I think you're being possessive, not helpful."

Which was, of course, precisely what he was doing.

"And it makes me wonder," she continued, "where your head is at. You have someone in your life. Why do you care what I do or do not do with Gray Bennett?"

Because he was clearly out of his goddamn mind, Jack thought.

"This isn't about me," he said.

"That's where you're wrong." She jabbed her finger at him. "This is very much about you. You've got a serious problem with that engagement of yours if you're acting jealous toward someone else."

She marched over to the house and wrenched open the back door. He was tight on her heels going into the kitchen.

"Will you slow down for a minute?" he demanded.

"I'm going to bed. Thanks for a really weird evening, Jack."

"Callie, for Christ's sake—"

She swung around, eyes flashing with anger while she interrupted him. "That's enough. I can't take anymore right now. Tomorrow, who knows? Maybe you can scare up someone else to try and pair me off with and then we can go through this stupid dance again. At least we'll both have practiced the steps once."

"Tomorrow I'm going to New York."

She fell silent.

"To see Blair?"

He nodded slowly.

She lifted her chin.

"Well, have a great time. I'm sure the two of you have a lot to catch up on, although I have to wonder whether any of it will have to do with me." She laughed harshly. "Christ, I can't believe this is happening. I'm someone's dirty little secret again."

Jack frowned. Again?

"Callie, I—"

Her hand sliced through the air as she cut him off. "Never mind. It's none of my business. Just like whatever happens between Gray and me is none of yours."

She left the kitchen, her mane of hair swinging from side to side as she rushed away.

13

FEELING POSITIVELY foul, Jack went into his study, poured himself a bourbon, and sat down.

Well, that went well. Callie was pissed off and he was drinking alone.

If he continued to run his life this smoothly, he'd have no business making doughnuts, much less being governor of a state.

He turned his chair to face the windows, kicked his legs out in front of him, and watched the moonlight filtering through the trees. The branches waving in a soft wind cast milling shadows on the lawn, but the peacefulness of the scene did nothing to lighten his mood.

She was right. He was jealous when he had no right to be.

Worse, though, was that regardless of his relationship with Blair, and in spite of his harebrained attempt to put an arbitrary barrier in his own way, he was chasing after Callie. And he didn't think he was going to stop until he had her.

"Holy hell," he muttered, resting the bourbon on his thigh and letting his head fall back. He stared at the ornate, painted ceiling above him until the cherubim and the clouds blurred.

He'd planned on going down to New York to come clean with Blair and reestablish his commitment to her. To their future.

But after tonight, he knew he couldn't. Not after the way dinner had gone with Callie and Gray. Watching her smile at his friend had been torture and Jack had had to repeatedly restrain himself from competing for her attention. With every charming thing Gray had said, with every gentlemanly gesture Gray had made, Jack had wanted to cut his friend off. At the knees.

She was dead-on with what she'd said. He was being territorial as hell.

And he needed to face facts. Callie wasn't just another chase. It went much deeper than that for him. For one thing, he thought about her a lot and not just sexually. He'd remember something she'd said that struck him as insightful or funny and mull it over, picturing just how she'd looked as she'd spoken. Or he'd read something or hear a bit of news and want to share it with her, just to find out what she thought. And he'd smile for no other reason than he was stuck in traffic, trying to get home to have dinner with her.

But the real telltale sign was somewhere south of his head and north of his hips. Recently, he'd been getting some kind of strange feeling in his chest whenever he thought of her, and that odd weight was something he'd never experienced before. He had the sneaking suspicion that it meant he was somehow becoming emotionally involved.

Entangled was probably a better word.

He was kidding himself if he thought he could just will away his feelings and carry on. He might have been able to go forward with marrying Blair if he'd just become distracted by some other woman. But Callie was no distraction.

Far from it.

Hell, for a man with a past like his, she was nothing short of a revelation. She was proof positive that even the most jaded, cynical SOB could find—

Jack shook his head, unable to believe he was actually going to use the word *love.*

He tossed back the bourbon and dialed Blair's suite

at the Cosgrove. When the voice mail kicked on, he left her a message saying he'd be in New York in the morning and had to see her immediately. And then he called Gray.

His friend answered on the second ring. "This has to be you, Jack."

"How'd you know?"

"Because I figured you'd call for details. Yes, I think she's beautiful. Yes, I asked her out. And yes, I'll take good care of her. Anything else?"

Shit.

"You sure you like her?"

"Ah, yeah. What's not to like?" There was a pause. "You got a problem with that? I thought it was your idea to introduce us."

Yes, he had a problem with it, but then, Callie had just told him she was going out with Gray. What right did Jack have to dictate whom she dated? Even if he was going to break his engagement, he was quite sure she wouldn't appreciate him warning men off of her.

"No, it's fine." Jack took a deep drink. "Listen, what are the ramifications if I run as an unmarried man?"

There was a pause, as if the question was a surprise. "I don't think it's necessarily a problem. Having a family is an asset, of course, especially considering the stunts you've pulled. Voters like candidates with wives and children; it's that whole illusion-of-stability thing. And having a family also gives you more credibility when it comes to issues like education and health care. But it's moot because you've got Blair." There was another hesitation. "Right?"

"I'll call you tomorrow."

"What's going on, Jack?"

"Tomorrow." He hung up the phone.

He thought about telling Callie he was having feelings for her when he got back from New York. Would she give him a chance if he explained himself? It sure wasn't a slam dunk; his past and his present spoke all too well for themselves. After the way he'd behaved, he wasn't sure she'd want to hear anything he had to say.

And she was also going out with Gray.

Jack picked up his glass and a feeling of unease settled into his bones. He wondered what exactly he had to offer someone like her anyway. All the other women he'd been with had been content with jewels and clothes and trips and parties, things he could supply in spades. Callie wouldn't care about all that.

Except if he stripped away the trimmings, what would she be left with? Just him. A man ruled by his ambitions. Someone who had worked himself into a stupor night after night for the past decade and showed no signs of slowing down. A guy who'd demonstrated a total lack of regard for women's feelings in his twenties and early thirties and was now breaking up with his fiancée of three weeks.

Now, there were some huge selling points.

Jack fell perfectly still.

It was, he thought, entirely possible that Callie wouldn't choose him over Gray or anybody else even if she liked the way he'd kissed her. And who would blame her. He had all the success and sophistication in the world, but that didn't mean there was enough to him for her. Because she would want more from a man than a thick wallet and an old name. Hell, she deserved more.

Rage at himself hit in a dark wave, bringing bile up into his mouth.

Jack looked down at the glass he was holding and tightened his grip. Eyeing the wall directly across from his desk, he stood up and hurled the thing as hard as he could across the room. It shattered on impact, booze and glass shards flying everywhere.

Dragging a hand through his hair, only mildly appeased by the release, he collapsed back down into the chair.

The next morning, Callie was at the window seat in her room, looking out the clear windows on either side of the stained glass, when a limousine pulled into the driveway and under the porte cochere. From across the hall,

Jack's door opened and closed and then heavy footfalls sounded out and gradually disappeared. Moments later, the limo shot down the drive as if there wasn't a moment to spare.

She closed her eyes and leaned her forehead against the leaded glass.

When she was young, she'd spent a lot of time alone because she was an only child with an odd family life. The trend toward solitude had only continued through high school, college, and graduate school. And after the turbulence of her mother's death, Callie had enjoyed the peace and ease of her own company as she readjusted to a life that wasn't all about suffering.

But solitude was not the same thing as being left behind, she thought.

She tried to imagine how Blair would react to the news that Jack had kissed another woman. Of course he'd say it meant nothing, that it was a mistake, that it would never happen again. How else could he possibly explain himself? She wondered whether the woman would cry and throw him out. Or did she have ice in her veins like his mother?

Part of her wanted to blame Jack and get angry at him for putting all three of them in such a bad situation. But she couldn't ignore her own role in the farce. The night before last he had been trying to resist kissing her in the kitchen. She'd been the one pulling him down to her mouth, so she was hardly an injured innocent. She was complicit, and the idea that she'd damaged someone else's relationship made her sick. The adage that there had to be something inherently wrong between two people for infidelity to occur just rang hollow.

There were few things in Callie's life that she truly regretted. But sitting in the clear morning light, surrounded by things that reminded her of Jack, she wished she had never met the man. She could have so easily gone about her life, perfectly happy in her cocoon of seclusion.

Instead, she was torn up.

As she continued to think about Jack, all sorts of scenes came to mind, none of them easy to bear. When she felt as though she'd been sitting forever, she checked the clock. Only half an hour had passed.

How was she going to get through the day? Or worse, the night? Even though she hated herself for it, she knew she was just killing time until Jack returned. And as with the distinction between being by herself and feeling abandoned, there was a tremendous difference between understanding that he had another woman and knowing that he was actually with her.

Callie thought of all those times she'd watched her mother wait for a visit that was canceled. All those evenings that had been spent sitting by a phone that never rang. All of the betrayals, large and small, that came with being number two. Her mother had lived less than half a life as she'd held on to a man who was never truly hers. After so many years of seeing the effects of the relationship, Callie had thought for sure she'd learned by a bad example and would never put herself in such a position.

She closed her eyes and leaned her cheek back against the stained glass, struck by a scene from childhood.

It had been her birthday. She'd just turned nine. Her mother had prepared a vanilla cake with chocolate icing and told her to set their small Formica table with three place settings. Callie had known what that meant and had barely been able to control her excitement.

He was coming. This time, her father was really coming.

In a role reversal, her mother had helped her pick out a dress to wear and they had spent time curling her hair and putting it up into bows. Her mother's mood had been light that day and Callie had taken pains to revel in it, fully aware it wouldn't last.

The good times rarely did.

They'd been sitting in the living room, her mother flipping through the same magazine over and over, Callie forced to play with her stuffed animals on the chair instead of the floor because of her dress, when the phone rang. She'd stopped moving as her mother had picked up and said a few terse words. The frozen smile sent back at Callie had meant that plans had changed and her mother was trying to be good and not yell in front of her.

Her mother had retreated into her bedroom, dragging the phone behind her, and quickly shut the door. As muffled, angry words seeped out, Callie had gone into the kitchen and over to the extra place setting at the table. She'd picked up the napkin she'd so carefully folded, the stainless steel knife, and the mismatching fork and spoon, and put them all away. She hadn't been able to reach high enough to get his plate back in the cupboard, so she'd hidden it under the sink.

Her mother had emerged sometime later, red-eyed and blotchy in the face. The cake had been brought out, the candles lit and extinguished, the presents unwrapped, but it had been no party.

Callie had gone to bed early only to be woken up much later when the door to her room had opened. The light from the hall had sliced across her blankets and her mother had stood in the beam, her slim figure a dark silhouette. The first thing Callie had noticed was that her mother's hair, which had been put up neatly in an elaborate bun earlier in the evening, had fallen into disarray. A halo of errant strands fanned out around her head, making her look like she was wearing a messy crown.

"Get up, Callie." Her mother's voice had trembled with urgency.

"What's wrong?"

"We've got to go out." Her mother had gone over to the dresser and started to pull out sweaters and pants, tossing them in disarray onto the floor. "Come on. Hurry. Put something on."

Callie had known better than to ask any more questions. When her mother was like that, the easiest thing was to do as she was told. And that night, the anger vibrating in the air had been as bad as she'd ever seen it.

Out on the street, in the cold January wind, her mother

had hailed a cab. As they squeezed inside, she'd barked out an address that Callie didn't recognize. During the ten-minute trip, the cab surged and halted through traffic lights and she'd wished she was back home. She kept thinking about her warm bed to distract herself from the way the taxi smelled and how her mother was muttering under her breath.

The cab had pulled over in front of a big private home in a neighborhood that was much better than the one they lived in. In this part of town, there was no trash in the gutters and all of the grand houses were decorated for the holidays. Each one had a pretty wreath with a velvet bow on its front door and Christmas trees twinkled through wide, clean windows.

Her mother had grabbed her hand and marched up the stairs of the mansion. When they'd gotten to the glossy front door, her mother had reached for the knocker and Callie had hoped she didn't break it. It was a golden lion's head with a ring in the nose, more majestic than scary.

Her mother had raised the ring and Callie had braced herself for when it was slammed down. But her mother had stopped. She'd just stood there, frozen in time, one hand on the brass knocker raised high, the other gripping Callie's arm.

As the pressure of her mother's grip cut off circulation, Callie had let out a whimper. "Mommy, you're hurting me."

Her mother had looked down and blinked, as if wondering what Callie was doing there with her. And then the door opened, ripping the knocker from her mother's hand. The ring fell with a sharp sound.

On the other side was a couple like the ones Callie had seen in the newspaper or on the TV. The lady had been wearing a long, dark fur coat and the man had been dressed in a tuxedo with a white scarf around his neck.

They seemed as surprised as her mother did.

"Good evening," the man had said, bending slightly at the waist. He held the door open even wider and warmth rushed out of the house along with a pool of light. As his wife had stepped onto the stoop, he'd patiently stood to one side. "Madam?"

"We're not . . ." Her mother had paused. "We're not going in."

The man had frowned and then the woman had prompted him with a tug on his arm. Before the door had closed, Callie had gotten a brief glimpse of some of the people inside. They all looked so beautiful. Like dolls on a wedding cake, she'd thought.

While her mother stared off into the distance, Callie had watched the couple walk two doors down and disappear into another fancy house with a pretty wreath. She would have liked to explore the neighborhood, but the icy wind was cutting through her coat and she'd started to shiver. She'd wondered why her mother wasn't cold. She hadn't even put a coat on over her dress.

"Mommy? Can we go home now?"

"Yes."

Her mother had started back down to the street, all the while staring through the big windows of the mansion. Before she had followed, Callie had stood on her tiptoes, trying to figure out what her mother was so fascinated by.

And then she'd seen her father.

"That's Daddy!" She'd jumped with excitement. "Let's go see Daddy."

Her mother had quickly hushed her. "Come on."

"I want to go to Daddy!"

Her mother had run up the stairs and urged her along. Callie's voice had risen to a whine. "But why can't we see Daddy—"

Suddenly, her mother was down on her level.

"I said no!" she'd hissed, grabbing onto Callie's shoulders and shaking her. "We are not going in there. Do you understand? He had his chance to see you tonight but he blew it!"

Callie had burst into tears.

"Then why did we come?" she'd sobbed.

Her mother had instantly stopped. With a sad moan, she'd crushed Callie to her chest.

"I'm sorry, baby. I'm so very sorry."

With a start, Callie came back to the present. Her father never had come to see her on her birthday. He'd had twenty-seven tries at it, but hadn't shown up once.

She let out her breath and pushed the hair from her face.

God, she hated remembering the past. It did awful things to her chest, making her feel like she was breathing through a rag stuffed down her throat.

Hopping off the window seat, she threw on some clothes and headed to the studio. When she got up to the garage, she decided to put on some music and work on the documents. She flipped through the CD collection by the stereo and decided that Norah Jones was not going to be a good call, not unless she wanted to cry all day long. When some big band swing was coming from the rafters, she went to the bin she'd pulled over to the couch and sat down.

She'd started to arrange the papers chronologically and it was a fascinating menagerie. Handwritten receipts for goods from the 1800s. A purchase contract for the tract of land on which Buona Fortuna now stood from 1871. A diploma from Harvard with the name Phillip Constantine Walker and the date 1811 on it. A scrap of paper with a scrawled Walker signature.

Reaching blindly into the box, she pulled out a pile of paper and put it on her lap. The top sheet was the beginning of a household inventory and she smiled as she read down the list of beds, linens, and dressers. The valuations were incredible, twenty dollars for a mahogany bureau and ten cents for a blanket. Going by the handwriting and the kind of paper, which was similar to others she'd seen, she figured it was probably from the late 1800s and was a record of Buona Fortuna. She hoped she found the rest of the document.

Five more pages of the inventory followed, one about kitchenware.

The next sheet of paper was a surprise. It was older and the script was difficult to read, the slanted words and faded ink almost impossible to decipher. She squinted and stared at the page.

Whilst I waited, seeing not your face coming to my window but only shadows, I pondered love and laid bare thoughts of great loss. To forge independence, I give myself to the war before us, but I cannot yield to the sacrifice without you. I waited in vain and now must go north, to Concord, with my men. Worry not. Our secret is safe. Your general will never know. Not from me.

N.W.

Callie read it again and looked over at the painting with surprise.

Could it be the first Nathaniel? Writing on the way to the Battle of Concord?

Or was she seeing hoofprints and thinking zebras again?

She put the letter aside and rushed through the rest of the papers on her legs, scanning the sheets without bothering to sort them. She put her hand into the bin again and again, but two hours later, she hit the bottom without finding the letter's first page.

"Damn it."

Her mind churned over the fragment's content again. Her knowledge of American history was average. Of course she knew who Nathaniel Walker was and she remembered a little about the Battle of Concord. But who was the general he'd gone into battle with?

Grace, she thought. Grace would know.

Callie got to her feet and headed for the house, intent on getting her address book from her room.

As she came into the kitchen, Elsie was looking clearly distraught while talking to Thomas.

"What's wrong?" Callie asked.

Elsie's eyes went to Thomas, who was standing at the sink and rinsing spinach.

The man gave a resigned shrug. "Mr. Walker died five years ago today. The missus has a hard time with it every year."

Callie was surprised. It was a little hard to imagine Jack's mother mourning anything.

Thomas turned back to Elsie. "Try Côte Basque. Tell Billy I sent you. He owes me and he'll fit her in. Then call Curt Thorndyke's mother, Fiona. The two of them will reminisce and she'll like that."

Elsie took a deep breath. "Okay."

"And don't take what she said personally. You know how she is."

"Yes. I do. But frankly, when she gets like this, I don't really care."

After the other woman left, Thomas said, "I was about to take a message up to you. Gray Bennett called. His number's on that pad over there."

"Oh, thanks. I did hear the phone ring up in the garage, but I don't feel right about answering it." She tore off the sheet, thinking tonight would be a perfect night to go out with him. Anything to take her mind off Jack.

She was on her way out when she remembered what Gray had said about Nathaniel Six. "I know this isn't any of my business, but what was he like? Mr. Walker, I mean?"

Thomas turned off the water and braced himself against the counter with his hip.

"He did a lot of good for a lot of people. And he loved Mrs. Walker. Used to say she was his finest creation." There was a pause and Callie couldn't tell whether he was trying to recall the past or choose his words carefully. "He was a handsome guy. Great athlete. Died real quick. Woke up one morning, feeling fine. Twenty minutes later, they found him dead in the shower. Brain aneurysm. He was just gone."

Although the tone was casual, the man was shaking his head as if he regretted the loss.

"He treated me real good. I met him when he was staying in Osterville for the summer. I'd just gotten out of the Navy and had a job as a caddy at the Wianno Club. One afternoon in July, I carried his bag for him. It sure was hot that day. A hundred degrees out and not a breath of wind, but he was bound and determined to finish eighteen holes. The rest of his foursome and their caddies wilted, but he and I made it all tne way around. After that, he wouldn't let anyone else carry his bag. It was he and I, all summer long. Got to the end of August and he asked me what I wanted to do. I told him I liked to cook and he got me into the Culinary Institute of America on scholarship, one that I suspect he set up just for me. When I got out, I worked in some restaurants in New York City and I was damn good. Until I lost my arm."

Thomas looked down at himself. "One unlucky move on a motorcycle and I went from being on top of the world to someone who couldn't unscrew a bottle on his own."

His smile was measured and she couldn't guess at what he'd had to go through to overcome the injury.

"Anyway, after I recovered, I got a letter from him. We'd always kept in touch. I was honest about what had happened. Two days later he called and offered me a job as his personal chef. That was near about thirty years ago. Pay's good. Got my own kitchen. I'm a happy man."

The man offered a lopsided grin, as if embarrassed he'd said so much.

She smiled back at him. "You sound like you miss him."

"Yeah, I guess I do. He was good to me even if he could be ... difficult with others." Thomas clamped his mouth shut. "Listen, if you want a phone with a private line, go to the library."

Callie thanked him, and when she came back downstairs with her address book, she found the room, sat in a leather club chair, and picked up the phone. When Gray answered, he asked her out for dinner at seven and she agreed.

Next, she called the Hall Foundation and Grace's assistant put her right through.

"Callie! How are you? I just got back from a trip and I was about to call you at Jack's this very minute. I'm so excited that you took the job."

"And I owe you some thanks for the good word you put in for me."

"It was the least I could do. How are you and Nathaniel getting along?"

"We're doing quite well. He's quiet, but his eyes follow me everywhere."

Grace laughed. "How's the rest of the family treating you?"

Callie dropped her voice. "Mrs. Walker is a bit of a challenge."

"I can only imagine. And Jack?"

"He's good. Okay. Yup, definitely fine. But how are you?"

There was a pause.

"Not all that well, to tell you the truth. I feel like everyone I know is trying to sell off a piece of me. My ex-husband is threatening to write a tell-all book about our marriage, in spite of the confidentiality provisions of our separation agreement. My former chief development officer was shopping around an exposé about the Hall Foundation and I had to level an injunction against him. And a doorman has picked up a ghostwriter and is going to write his memoirs about working in my building. Which will of course include details about me and my marriage."

Callie shook her head. "Grace, that's awful, especially considering what you've just been through. You must be exhausted."

"I am. With all these book proposals swirling around, the press is worked up. 'No comment' is becoming my middle name." There was a pause. "You know, Callie, you're the one who could do the most damage to me, to the Hall Foundation, to my mother. You could so easily cash in on your story and blow our father's reputation sky-high, but you haven't. I can't tell you what that means to me."

Callie smiled with gratitude.

"I would never betray you, Grace. I'm not going to say anything to anybody. Ever. You can trust me."

"You know, I've had a lot of people tell me that over the years. But coming from you, I actually believe it." Grace fell silent for a moment. "Trust is not something I've had a lot of experience with. Except for Ross, and now you."

"Ross?"

"You remember—my bodyguard?"

"Oh, I thought his name was something else."

"It was. But this is what he goes by now."

Callie was tempted to ask questions, but figured she shouldn't pry.

They talked a little more and then she said, "Listen, I wanted to ask you something. I've been going through some old Walker family papers and I found part of a letter from the original Nathaniel Walker to a woman. At least I think it is the first Nathaniel, but I'm not sure. It mentions the Battle of Concord and a general. Do you remember who Walker fought with at Concord? Before he was captured by the British?"

"Sure. It was General Rowe. He was a wealthy gentleman from Boston. One of the founding fathers." Grace's voice rose with excitement. "But tell me more about the letter."

Callie shared the details and the two talked over various points.

"The thing is—" Callie hesitated. "There was a very intimate feeling to it. But he didn't marry until after the War of Independence, correct?"

"That's right. He married Jane Hatte when he was in his late forties, which was ancient in those days. They had four children."

"So perhaps Nathaniel didn't write the letter. Or maybe he was writing to Jane," she suggested.

Grace laughed lightly. "I doubt it was to his wife. The Battle of Concord was in 1775. When the two of them married in 1793, she was twenty. He would have been writing to a two-year-old."

"Well, I hope I find the rest of the letter."

"So do I. This could be big news. Correspondence between Walker and any of his contemporaries would garner tremendous attention, especially if it shed light on a previously unknown relationship." Grace paused. "Tell me, what do you think of the portrait, now that you've had a chance to work on it?"

"Copley is a genius. With the old varnish coming off, his use of color, particularly in the darkest parts of the painting, is really coming out. It's extraordinary. He can make a black sleeve cast a shadow. And his brushwork is fantastic."

"Any problems?"

"No. Not really. The canvas support is sound. Paint's in really good shape for the most part. There's only one small area that I'm suspicious about but I don't think it's a big deal. There may have been some repainting."

"Really?"

"But I'm not sure. I'm cleaning around the edges first, so it's going to be a while before I get a clear view of the area. Right now, it's just my instinct talking."

"Well, don't underestimate yourself," Grace said. "Fresh eyes can find surprising things."

"Perhaps."

"Guess what. I'm going to be coming to Boston after Thanksgiving. For the Walker party. Jack's invited me and Ross to stay with you all."

"Oh. I mean, that's great!" It was the first Callie had heard about any such thing and it dawned on her that she should be making plans to go back to New York City over the holiday. If Jack was inviting people to stay over, he might want to use the room she was using.

Callie frowned with concern. "Wait. Your bodyguard is coming with you? Do you still need protection?"

"Actually, he's much more than that." Happiness suffused the words, giving them a lilt that spoke volumes.

Callie smiled. "You sound like you're in love."

"We are. It took us a while to figure things out and we're still working on it. But my life wouldn't be complete without him."

"I'm so happy for you. Truly."

After they hung up, Callie looked outside. It was late in the afternoon and the sky was a chalky white. She was surprised that Thanksgiving was so close and pictured herself back in Chelsea popping a Lean Cuisine in the oven and brooding about Jack.

Not exactly a Norman Rockwell moment, she thought.

14

By the time Jack got home that evening, he was tired. Nothing had gone as he'd expected. Or particularly well.

Blair hadn't even been in New York.

He'd called her in the morning while on the way to the airport, both at her hotel room and on her cell phone, to make sure she knew he was coming. When he'd gotten voice mail in both places, it hadn't seemed that unusual and the same was true when he'd received no calls from her in response. They'd been playing phone tag a lot lately and sometimes had gone a day or two without even leaving messages.

Nonetheless, it had been a surprise when he'd been informed at the front desk of the Cosgrove that Ms. Stanford and Mr. Graves had flown off to London the night before. The manager had explained they'd gone to see Graves's new mansion in Belgravia and would be back soon. Just how soon, the man hadn't been able to say, and going by his anxious eyes, he clearly wished he had a better answer.

Based on Blair's indeterminate travel plans, Jack had figured he'd just go back to Boston. There was no sense waiting around New York when he had business deals to watch over and planning to do with Gray. He was on the way back to the airport when his cell phone had rung. Clearly, Graves's man had called ahead. Blair was apologetic and anxious as hell about his unexpected visit. She knew unscheduled drop-ins were not a habit of his.

While she'd pressured him for details, he'd just tried to pin down when she was returning. Though she'd be home the following day, she'd refused to get off the phone and kept demanding to know what was wrong. When it was clear she wouldn't wait until they could see each other in person, he had spelled out the truth as gently as he could. Shocked silence had been her first response and then she'd been characteristically stoic. The only question she'd asked was whether he'd met someone else, and he'd been honest in his response.

The awful truth was, she hadn't seemed all that surprised about any of it.

When the call had ended, he'd gotten into his plane and told the pilot to take him to Chicago. There was a company there he'd been meaning to visit and he figured the trip would relieve his mind. It didn't work. He remained sorry that he'd hurt Blair, though he felt more sadness about losing the friendship than the intimate side of the relationship.

Shutting Buona Fortuna's front door, Jack put down his briefcase and started to loosen his tie. He wanted a drink. He wanted something to eat.

And he wanted to see Callie.

He walked back to the kitchen and ran into Thomas, who was pulling on his leather biker's jacket. Thomas informed him his mother was out to dinner and the concern in the man's voice told Jack all was not well in Mercedes's world. Jack didn't ask for details. He had enough problems in his own life to worry about.

Thomas paused by the door. "Oh, and Callie, she's out with Gray."

Jack felt a tidal shift in his body. "Oh, really? Where did they go?"

"Said something about Biba's." Thomas hesitated. "You going to be okay here on your own?"

"Yeah." Hell, in his current mood, solitude was safer for everyone.

As the door was shut, Jack headed not for the refrigerator but for his private bar. Hungry as he was, he wanted oblivion more than food.

When he got to his study, he stripped off his suit jacket, hung it over the back of a chair, and went for the bourbon. On his way across the room, he eyed the broken glass that was still on the floor. He hated having his study disturbed, so it was cleaned only once a week, and he made a mental note to take care of the mess himself.

He wasn't going to do it now, though. Picking up a full decanter and a Tom Collins glass, he decided to get good and drunk.

It was the perfect way to end an otherwise horrible day.

He was halfway through his third glass, and just beginning to feel the effects of the alcohol, when it dawned on him it was the anniversary of his father's death.

Which explained why Thomas was worried about his mother.

Jack put the glass down and felt his pinkie ring make contact with the desk, a knocking sound rising up into the still air as the gold hit wood. He twisted his hand around and looked at the crest that had been pressed deeply into the metal. The ring was supposed to be worn by a Nathaniel, had always been worn by Nathaniels, his father included.

But when Nathaniel Six had died, the seventh Nate had declared that, as Jack was head of the family for all intents and purposes, it should be worn by him. Jack had never been into jewelry before, except for his collection of cuff links, but the ring had felt right.

As he looked at the scratches and the dents in the gold, thinking of how many men in his family had worn it, he remembered the last time he'd seen his father alive. It had been the night before his death. Not surprisingly, they'd argued because his father had been into the Scotch and Jack had been determined to hold a hard line when it came to money.

After years of supporting his philanthropy habit by exchanging deeds and certificates of record for money with his son, Nate Six had nothing left to barter with. When the last interest in the house in Palm Beach had been signed over, Jack had told his father that he'd be willing to support the man's reasonable expenses, but not any more of his gift commitments. And for a while, there had been no new ones made.

On that night, however, the elder Nathaniel had announced that he'd promised half a million dollars to the MFA. He'd emphasized that he'd broken down the payment schedule into monthly sums, clearly thinking it would seem more like an expense that way. When Jack had refused to make good on the pledge, his father had been livid.

The situation would have been tough to handle at any time, but it had been ten o'clock at night, five hours after his father had started in with the drinking. The man had been past the point of rational conversation. When Jack had started to walk out of the room, Nathaniel had accused his son of being a bloodthirsty capitalist who was turning his back on the needs of the unfortunate.

Jack had reminded his father that those bloody battles in the financial world were what made Nathaniel's continued presence at Buona Fortuna possible. He'd also pointed out that there weren't many "unfortunates" hanging out at the MFA, and, if his father was truly concerned with social welfare, he should be volunteering at a soup kitchen or some worthy shelter.

When the drunken insults had continued, Jack grew frustrated at having to have the same conversation over and over again and had really let one rip. The comment had been something about his father failing at everything he'd ever done except getting his ass kissed by people after Walker money.

That had pretty much put a lid on the argument. His father had been stunned into silence, for a moment, but then struck back. Jack would never forget his words or tone of voice.

My sons are a source of inestimable sadness to me, my biggest failure. At least your brother has the decency to stay away.

And the next morning, he'd died.

Hell of a way to leave things, Jack thought, bringing the glass back to his lips and draining the bourbon dry. It was difficult to understand how his father had been able to embrace so many strangers while holding his own sons in such disdain. But then, the things people did sometimes made no sense. Which was something he was beginning to understand from his own choices.

Pouring himself another glass, Jack put his legs up and crossed his feet at the ankles on his desk. He was contemplating the color of the liquor when, from down at the other end of the house, he heard the front door open and voices in the hall.

Getting to his feet, he came around the corner and saw Gray and Callie standing in the doorway. Jack was about to say something when his friend put a hand on her shoulder and dipped his head down low.

Jack shut his eyes, feeling a burn in his gut that had nothing to do with the bourbon. He went back to his study and waited, straining to hear the door shut.

When it finally did, he hurried back out to the hall, bracing himself to see the two of them going upstairs together. Instead, Callie was taking off her coat.

"Did you enjoy yourself?" he said, stepping forward, into the light.

Her head flipped around. As if she were collecting herself, she brushed a length of hair behind her ear. "You're back."

Her eyes brushed over him, lingering on the open collar of his shirt.

"Miss me?" he asked. "Or were you otherwise occupied?"

She frowned, eyeing the glass in his hand. "How long have you been drinking?"

He looked at the bourbon. "Awhile."

She put her coat on the balustrade and stepped forward, holding out her hand. "I think maybe you've had enough."

"I'm not so sure about that."

"What do you think you're going to accomplish by drinking yourself into a stupor?"

His eyes traveled from the crown of her head all the way down her body. He went back to her lips and then her breasts. "Maybe I'll forget about you for a little while."

Then he tilted back his head and took a healthy swig.

Her voice was soft. "Give me the glass, Jack."

When she continued to stare at him with level eyes, he did what she asked. She was right. Getting liquored up wasn't going to solve anything. Hell, it only reminded him of his father and increased the chances he would do something stupid.

Like fall to his knees and beg her to pick him over his friend.

She walked past him into the kitchen. As he followed, he tracked every move she made, her hips shifting gracefully, her legs so long in the black skirt she was wearing. As his blood began to heat up, he had a very clear thought that he should get away from her. Just go up to his bedroom and pass out.

Because in the quiet darkness, all he could think about was making love to her. And if he wanted to make her see he was in some small way worthy of her, he needed to behave like a gentleman, not a caveman.

She was rinsing his glass out in the sink when she said in a low voice, "Are you okay?"

He barely heard the words over the running water.

"I could be considerably more inebriated," he said matter-of-factly. "I'm shooting for rip-roaring, welcome-to-oblivion, blackout-city drunk. At this point, I'm not even seeing double yet. And I'm still upright."

Callie pulled a dish towel out of a drawer and looked at him from under her lashes as she dried off the glass. "I know this must be a hard night for you."

He frowned, replaying the image of his friend kissing

her. Jealousy spiked and made him answer more harshly than he would have otherwise.

"How magnanimous of you. Most women wouldn't take pity on a man who traveled four hundred miles to do a hatchet job on her competition."

Callie frowned, as if she hadn't heard him right, and then her eyes became direct, her voice even more so. "I'm going to let that go because you've had too much to drink. And I'm talking about the anniversary of your father's death, not whatever happened between you and Blair today."

Jack leaned against the doorjamb, feeling like a jerk.

The regret brought some sobriety back to him and he recognized how close he was to the edge of his self-control. She was sexy and beautiful and no more than a few feet away from him. All of which left him fighting a terrible urge to pull her into his arms and put his mouth against hers until she didn't remember what Gray's kiss had felt like.

Hell, just the thought of touching her was enough to make him hard.

"You know, I think you'd better leave," he said.

"Why?"

"You've just got to trust me on this one."

Callie shrugged and put the glass on the counter.

"You know, I lost my father recently," she said. "And my relationship wasn't all hearts and flowers by a long shot. But even if it was a while ago, and even if they played a complicated role in your life, it is still hard to get over the loss of a parent."

Jack almost laughed. True, he was living with the aftermath of some seriously bad blood between him and his old man. But a far more immediate problem was standing in front of him, looking at him with concern and compassion.

She cleared her throat. "There are a lot of things I wished I'd said to my father and a lot of answers I'll never have. That creates some serious anger and frustration. I know you feel something of the same because you're obviously upset and I've never seen you drink like this. It might help to talk about it."

Jack moved before he was fully aware of what he was doing, crossing the kitchen in two strides. He took her by the back of the neck and the small of her back and brought her hard against his body. Making sure she felt every inch of his arousal, he looked her straight in the eye and did nothing to keep the lust out of his face or his voice.

"I'm not in the mood to talk and this has nothing to do with my dead father." He deliberately looked down at her breasts. He pictured his mouth finding one of the tips that had started to strain against the thin fabric of her sweater. And then he imagined what it would be like to lick her skin until she moaned his name over and over again.

Callie swallowed and her mouth parted. He could practically taste her.

Jack pulled back, cursing. What he needed to do was talk to her, not come on to her. How was she going to see him as anything other than a playboy if he couldn't keep his hands off of her?

"God *damn* it. I'm trying to do the right thing here. I really am."

Her face fell. "Because of Blair."

"No. I ended the engagement today. I'm trying to do the right thing by you."

Her eyes shot to his. "What did you say?"

"I said I ended my engagement." He put some distance between them and pushed a hand through his hair. When three feet didn't feel far enough, he went back over to the doorway.

There was a long, tight silence. "Is it really over? Between the two of you?"

"Yeah. It's done."

"Why." The word wasn't posed as a question. It was a quiet demand.

Jack sensed his answer would in some way determine their future, so he spoke with care, wishing he could trust himself more. He was liable to be persuasive when she deserved unadulterated honesty.

"I never loved her. I knew that going into it. I thought respect and friendship would be enough, but meeting you made me realize what I was missing."

Her voice dropped to a whisper. "And what was that?"

He laughed harshly, thinking he should shut his fucking mouth. He'd had too much to drink to have such a tricky conversation. God only knew what might come out of him. There was no way she'd take him seriously, for instance, if he told her he loved her.

And those three words were right on the tip of his tongue.

No, he needed to start slowly. Give her a chance to consider him as something other than a pendulum between extremes.

"Don't ask me to explain anything right now. Especially how I feel," he said. "I'm not all that articulate tonight."

"Maybe you should give it a try anyway." She leaned back against the countertop, as if she needed the support.

When he stayed quiet, she said, "I can't believe I'm going to ask you this. But, Jack, where are we headed?"

He thought of his friend bending down and kissing her.

"You mind if I ask about Gray?" he said darkly.

She flushed. "He's not for me."

"But I thought he was smart and handsome and likable." God, he hated those words.

"So are a lot of men. That doesn't mean I want to date them."

Jack laughed shortly.

"Well, then, I've recently become available and have nothing to do with at least two of those traits. I've shown some moments of true stupidity in the last couple of weeks and you've certainly spent some time disliking me—for very good reasons, I might add. As for the handsome part, I can't comment." Feeling like an ass, he shook his head. "Oh, hell. Just so you know, I'm not making any sense right now."

Callie smiled softly. "That's okay. I kind of like you when you're a little off-kilter."

Jack stared into her eyes.

He couldn't believe it, but she was looking at him warmly. The tension in her shoulders told him she was still wary, but the openness in her face suggested he might unexpectedly have a chance to be with her.

"God, Callie. I just want to be with you," he said, trying to find the right words. "Badly. And now. You're the only woman who's ever made me feel like this and I just want a shot with you. I know I've screwed a lot of things up, but I want to try and make you happy. Hell, I want to make you promises, even though I can't expect you to believe in them considering—everything about me."

He shut up. She didn't need to hear any more gory details about his failures in monogamy.

"That's okay," she said, startling him. "I don't need promises. I'm not looking for a fantasy."

Jack felt a surge of hope and clung to it. "Look, I know I'm not the best bet if you're looking for a relationship."

"You don't say. And here I was, already planning the wedding."

He studied her for a long moment. The small smile she was wearing was enough to melt him.

He wanted to reach out to her, but restrained himself. "You, ah, you make me believe in things I used to make fun of."

"As in Santa Claus?" she said, eyes glowing.

Jack smiled back. "I'm talking about love. Forever after."

Her face changed, some of the pleasure draining away. "Don't say that. Not right now."

He opened his mouth, but shut it when she moved away from the counter. She took one step, and then another, and then she was walking over to him.

"I don't want to talk," she murmured, huskily.

And Jack's body just about detonated.

Through eyes wide with disbelief and gratitude, he watched her come toward him, seeing all that red hair, those hips, her tiny waist. She moved like she knew what she was doing, and it had very little to do with just crossing the room. She also seemed a little shy, chewing on her lip as her eyes bounced from his face to his chest and back again.

Innocence and raw sex appeal were one hell of a combination, he thought, feeling his mouth go dry.

"You didn't answer my question," she said softly.

A band of sweat came out on his forehead. "Which one?"

"What exactly were you missing?"

And then she touched him, on the chest, above his heart, which had started to beat like a jackhammer.

Christ, he'd had women come on to him before, but it had been nothing like this. Standing in front of him, with her palm bridging the space between their bodies, she had total power over him. She could have crushed him.

Just by walking away.

"You," he said with a groan. "I was missing . . . you."

He bent his head down for a kiss, but she pushed against him.

"You remember when you asked me what type of man I was looking for?" He nodded. "Well, I want someone who will treat me with nothing but care and love. Who will respect me and walk through fire for me. I also want to be able to trust him completely."

Jack shifted his weight back but she put her hand on his neck and stroked him.

"Except you know what?" she said. "I've never found him. Haven't even come close. And I'm not going to pretend he's you, either. There aren't a lot of romantic heroes in the real world." Her hand moved over to his face and he turned his lips to her palm. "And I want you."

He closed his eyes, thinking those four words spoken in her husky voice were more seductive than any nude body he'd ever seen.

"Jack, I don't want you to promise me anything, but I'm going to ask you for one favor."

He opened his eyes, hoping whatever she wanted was within his control. "Name it."

"Just let me know when you lose interest *before* the next woman comes into your life." She tilted her head up, her lips so close to his he could feel her sweet breath on his mouth. "I'm only going to look at this as a short-term fling, so I have no expectations. I just want to keep my dignity, okay?"

He was about to argue that he was going nowhere fast when he saw a quick flash of mistrust in her eyes. Of course she wouldn't put faith in his words yet, he thought.

"God, yes. I promise you that."

With a groan, he put his lips down to hers, thrusting his tongue into her mouth. As his hands spanned her hips, he felt her grab onto his shoulders and lean into him. Lifting his head, he growled deep in his throat, ready to fall on his knees and beg if he had to.

"Upstairs?" he ground out.

When she nodded, he took her hand urgently and led her through the house, up to the Red Room. He hadn't even closed the door behind them when he took her in his arms again and kissed her long and hard, wrapping himself around her and holding her against his body.

He shut the door with his foot and barely heard the clap as it slammed shut because he was slipping his hands under her sweater, onto warm, smooth skin. He groaned as he pulled up her top and kicked off his shoes. Lifting her sweater over her head and tossing it to the ground, he had to close his eyes to take back some control.

If he kept going like this, they'd only be half naked when he came inside of her.

Her hands went around his neck and pulled him to her lips just as he started guiding her backward to the bed. They got tangled in a chair and he had to catch a lamp to save it from falling when they knocked into a table. Keeping contact with her lips, he ripped his shirt off with a tear only to get trapped by his cuff links and the sleeves.

He cursed in frustration and she laughed softly as he tugged and jerked.

"Stop fighting and let me do it," she told him.

He stared down at himself, willing her fingers to be fast. As she quickly freed him, he murmured, "I may never wear those goddamn things again. And to hell with the shirt for that matter."

Her smile was tremulous as she put the pair of gold studs on the bedside table. The shirt dropped to the floor in a cloud of white, and as her wide eyes went to his body, he suddenly wanted to slow down so he could remember every moment with her. She was looking at him as if she'd never seen a man's chest before, and the wonder in her blue eyes made him feel as if he was making love for the first time. As he stood in front of her, patience came to him in a cooling wave.

There would be no hurried sex tonight, he thought. He wanted them to be together the right way. Slowly. Reverently.

But as she continued to stare at him, he felt some of the urgency come back.

"You're beautiful," she said on a choked sigh. She put her hand up to her mouth, as if trying to hide her reaction.

And Jack was undone.

"Come here," he said.

Taking her hand in his, he sat down on the bed and cradled her between his legs. Her breasts were covered with thin, white lace and she was resplendent in the soft light, the contours of her body casting enticing shadows.

He put his hands on her hips and moved them slowly down to the bottom of her skirt. Sliding underneath, he stroked the backs of her knees and then moved up her thighs, feeling the warmth of her. Putting his lips against the skin of her stomach, he went searching for the zipper and the button in back.

And then the skirt was on the floor. Followed by her panty hose.

Taking her in his arms, he pulled her on top of him and they fell back on the bed. As he kissed her deeply, he rolled her over and gently touched her breasts. As she grabbed onto his arms, her body contracting with pleasure, he impatiently pushed aside the bra and took her into his mouth, looking at her face as he did. Her eyes were wide with astonishment as she arched up, spreading her legs. It was as if she had no idea her body could feel the way it did, and Jack almost lost all control.

With shaking hands, he quickly did away with the bra altogether and settled over her, feeling her fingers in his hair as she absorbed his weight in the cradle of her hips. The moment he felt her naked breasts against his chest and her heat through his pants, he had some vague thought that he might not be the same man afterward.

And that it wasn't a bad thing at all.

15

CALLIE FELT Jack come down over her and she ran her hands across the smooth skin of his back. As he kissed her neck, she knew she was making the right decision. She wanted Jack—he wanted her. Teenage fantasies of a perfect love had no place in the real world. All anyone ever had was the here and now.

And what she had was Jack nearly naked and touching her with hands that trembled.

He kissed a path down to her breasts and his hands went to her panties. Impatiently, she lifted her hips, thinking how good it would feel to have nothing between them. He slid the fabric down her legs, and as soon as she was free of the wisp of silk, he started to stroke the inside of her thigh.

"I need you," he said hoarsely. "Oh, God . . ."

She felt his mouth, warm and wet, over her belly button and the shock of his kiss was covered by a rush of heat as she felt his fingers brushing up against her core. A low sound of satisfaction came out of him and she reached for his face, needing his kiss.

When he pulled back, she let out a protest but he was only taking off his pants. They hit the floor, were followed by his boxers, and then his naked body was over her. The hard, blunt feel of him against her center made her arch beneath him and she was instantly frustrated when he stopped kissing her and pulled back.

"I can't hold on. I can't . . . Tell me to go to hell right now or I'm going to . . ." The veins in his neck were straining and his wide shoulders were rigid with tension. He was keeping himself in check. Barely.

For a split second, Callie felt some fear. This was it.

She looked into his eyes. She could say the word and they would go no further. She could wake up tomorrow morning without having known a slice of heaven. She could wake up alone. Still a virgin.

But life was too damn short to live in the shadows. So she reached up and touched his face, urging him down to her mouth.

"Make love to me," she whispered.

She felt him sag with relief and then he was kissing her again as he positioned himself over her. With one great surge, he drove into her body.

A sharp pain made her grimace, but the sting was followed by a feeling unlike anything she'd ever experienced. She let out a murmur of pleasure and then realized Jack had frozen in place.

She didn't like the look on his face. His eyes were wide with shock as he focused somewhere on the wall behind her head.

"Jack?" she said softly.

He looked down with a disarming blankness. She almost didn't recognize him, and staring at a stranger was disturbing, considering he was still inside of her.

"Are you okay?" he asked in a hollow voice.

After she nodded, he withdrew from her body slowly and carefully wrapped the duvet cover around her. Then he sat on the edge of the bed.

"Tell me that you aren't . . . that you weren't . . ."

"A virgin?" She focused on the hands that were braced on his knees. "Well, yes."

He shot her a sideways look. "And you didn't think to mention it?"

"I wasn't thinking much at the time."

His head started moving from side to side. "Jesus . . ."

"Why is it different because it happens to be the first

time? You would have been . . . fine with it if I'd had another man before you, right?"

He laughed harshly. "Christ, I can't believe I'm actually going to say this, but I'm glad you haven't been with anyone else." He stopped shaking his head. "I just wish I'd known. I would have done things very differently."

"I, ah, I thought you were doing just fine."

There was a long period of silence. She started to grow cold as she pictured him pulling on his clothes and bolting from the room like that guy in college had.

But Jack wouldn't do that, she told herself. Surely, he wouldn't.

He looked at her again. "You should have something that's worth remembering."

"I don't know, Jack. You were pretty unforgettable." She deliberately kept her tone light, not wanting to hint at the desperation she'd feel if he up and left her. Unsatisfied. Alone.

His eyes measured her gravely. She could tell he was wondering if he really had hurt her.

He cleared his throat. "I'd like to—try this all over again."

She smiled and reached for him.

Moving cautiously, as if she might be broken, he shifted closer to her. He reached out and brushed his knuckle down the skin of her cheek and then tucked a strand of hair behind her ear. His hand traveled down her jaw to her chin and he brushed the pad of his thumb over her lower lip while tilting up her face. There was a gentleness about him, a concern, that tempered the need that had returned to his face.

When he kissed her, his mouth was light on her lips, soft to the point of frustration. He refused to deepen the contact. Even though she wanted more, and twisted to get closer to him, he stayed just out of reach. His hands began to stroke her neck and her collarbone and then under her breasts and a sensual languor came over her as his lips followed.

No matter how hard she tried, he remained elusive,

pleasuring her with his hands and his mouth without letting her return the favor. Even when she let out a ragged complaint, he refused to bring his body against hers. She kept grabbing at his arms to pull him down, but he hovered above her skin, kissing her breasts and then her stomach as he stroked her thighs. The torture was deliciously frustrating and the pressure in her body kept growing and growing until she scored his skin with her nails as she held on to him.

And then he kissed where she had never been kissed before.

A blast of white heat shot through her and it was only after the waves had stopped racking her body that he lay on top of her. This time as he slid inside, she felt only a sweet rush of pleasure.

"Callie," he said roughly, "are you okay?"

It sounded as if he were talking through gritted teeth and his body was shuddering. She could feel it shake over her. Inside of her.

"You feel so good," she said against his neck.

Jack didn't move. Running her hands over the tense muscles of his back and shoulders, she was struck by a sudden thought that he was going to leave again.

"Are you . . . Is it okay for you?" she asked.

His head dropped onto her shoulder. "Good God. Yes."

She shifted under him and heard him groan at the friction of their bodies.

And then he gripped her hard and began to move inside of her. As his thrusts gained power, they carried her with him into a frenzy of heat. She let out a hoarse cry as light exploded inside of her again and she heard a guttural sound escaping from him as his body quaked.

In the stillness that followed, she felt him relax against her, though he was breathing heavily.

"Are you all right?" he asked.

Callie nodded, not trusting her voice.

She was glad she had waited for him.

As a tear left one of her eyes, she was grateful for the darkness. She didn't want to have to explain herself. It would have been too hard to make him understand how good it had felt. How good he had been to her.

Jack shifted his weight so he was lying next to her and she looked away, catching the glow coming through the stained-glass window. She felt him stroke her cheek and then stop when he ran over the path of her tears.

"Callie, what's wrong?" he asked urgently.

The choked noise she made was supposed to have been a confident *nothing*.

He tilted her head to him. "Tell me what's going on."

She sniffled and brushed her tears away. "I'm just a little emotional, that's all."

"Did I hurt you?" His voice was deep and male, velvety in the darkness. Full of concern.

Not yet, she thought to herself. And God, she hoped he didn't.

"Callie?"

As he brushed away another tear, she said, "I don't want to fall in love with you."

"Good Lord, I should be so fortunate. . . ." His voice drifted off. "You know I never want to hurt you, right?"

She nodded.

"And I'm going to do my best."

She started to worry about what would happen between them, but then she stopped herself. The present. She had the present. He was with her now, holding her tightly. Thoughts of what lay ahead would only ruin what they had at the moment. Closing her eyes resolutely, she moved in close so that her head rested in the crook of his arm.

He soothed her with a gentle caress and she eventually gave herself up to sleep.

It was early the next morning when she felt him rise from the bed. In the gray light of dawn, she watched him slip on his trousers, his head tilting down as he zipped up the fly and buttoned them. When he turned and caught her eyeing him, he smiled.

"I have to go, but may I kiss you good morning?" That silky tone was back in his voice.

"Please."

Jack sat on the bed next to her and leaned forward. She raised her mouth for his kiss, but he reached forward for her hand. Uncurling her fist, he pressed his lips to the tender skin of her palm.

"Good morning, Callie," he said. He wrapped her fingers into a ball again and squeezed. And then he kissed her softly on the mouth and walked out of her room.

When Callie woke up again and stretched, she felt a tightness in her body that was unfamiliar and not at all unpleasant. She lay on her back, looking up into the canopy over the bed and thinking about Jack. Images of what they'd done in the night were impossible to resist.

She was right. He had been an incredible lover, though not necessarily for the reasons she'd first assumed. The way he'd held her afterward was the best part of the experience.

When she finally got out of bed, she saw his button-down shirt on the floor and picked it up. Lifting the fine cotton to her nose, she breathed in, smelling cedar soap and something more elusive, more distinctly Jack.

She looked around, noting the buttons that had popped off and were dotting the Oriental rug. Getting caught with his ruined shirt in her room by the upstairs maid would send messages neither of them were prepared to deal with. She quickly cleaned up the floor, showered, and got dressed.

With his shirt tucked under her arm, she walked across the hall. There was no answer when she knocked, so she stuck her head into his bedroom and quietly called out his name.

The mahogany antiques and oil paintings she'd expected; what was a surprise was the anonymity of it all. There were no snapshots of him on vacation, no clothes draped on the back of a chair, no books or magazines fanned out on the bedside table. It might as well have been a luxurious hotel room, and she was disappointed that the place didn't reveal more about him.

Which was a lot to ask for from a color scheme, she thought wryly, eyeing the deep green walls. Even one as expertly developed as this.

The only thing that was out of order was the bed. The covers had been pulled back and the pillows propped up against the velvet headboard, as if he'd spent time deep in thought.

"May I help you?" Mrs. Walker said loudly.

Callie wheeled around, bracing herself as the woman came down the hall as if the natural order of things had been disturbed.

Mrs. Walker saw the shirt and her eyes narrowed. "Do you require something from my son?"

In a rush of levity, Callie thought, no, she'd had plenty of him last night.

Setting her shoulders, she remembered rule number four for bullies: Ignorance is bliss. There can't be a problem if you refuse to acknowledge that one exists.

Calmly, she went over to the bed and laid the shirt on top of the rumpled covers.

"Have a good day, Mrs. Walker," she murmured as she walked out.

For once, the woman seemed speechless.

As she headed for the kitchen, Callie wished like hell Mrs. Walker's timing hadn't been so good. Or maybe she shouldn't have been so conscientious. If she'd only left the shirt in her room, buried it in a drawer until she could give it back to Jack—

Hell. It was like getting into a car accident because you'd been putting on your seat belt.

Jack was reading the paper and drinking coffee when she walked into the kitchen, and the moment she saw him, she smiled. Dressed in a suit, his blue silk tie hanging from a precise knot, he looked as if he was too civilized to have done half the things he had to her in the night.

But then he looked up at her and his eyes flashed with heat.

"Good morning." His smile was slow and sexy as he put down the *Boston Globe*. "How did you sleep?"

Callie felt a flush run like a forest fire up into her face. "Well. Very well."

"Come here," he said, softly.

She looked behind her to make sure no one was around and then went to him. As soon as she was in range, his hands came out and pulled her close. Instinctively, she started to reach for his hair, but she stopped, not wanting to ruffle him.

"No, touch me," he said. "Anywhere."

As she drew her fingers through the thickness, he stared up at her. "I'm sorry we didn't spend more time together this morning, but I thought you might appreciate the discretion."

"Thank you." She dropped her lips to his and kissed him lightly, but he wouldn't let her go. As he deepened the contact with his tongue, she reluctantly pulled back.

His frustration was evident as he let her go. "You make me want to go back upstairs and start the day right. Or better yet, not get out of bed at all."

She was smiling when Thomas came down the back stairs. While he and Jack talked, she fixed herself a little breakfast and thought about the day ahead of her. When she remembered the letter she'd found, she wanted to show it to Jack.

"Do you have a minute before you go?" she asked when he stood up to leave. "I have something I'd like to show you up in the garage."

He grabbed his briefcase and quickly headed for the door. "What a fantastic idea."

She laughed as he hustled her outside and Arthur loped ahead. The morning was cold and her breath came out in a series of puffs as they walked across the driveway.

"By the way, Jack, I think we may have a problem."

"With the painting?"

"No, your mother found me in your room this morning." She glanced over, watching his eyebrows rise. "I was returning your shirt."

"Ah."

"I thought you'd want to know. She didn't look happy."

"No, I imagine she didn't."

"You don't seem too concerned," she said, opening the door to the garage.

He smiled grimly. "Just remember, my mother is not your problem. And don't worry about it. She's got a bad bark, but she's essentially harmless."

Callie thought back to the calculation behind the woman's eyes and wasn't so sure.

As they went up the cramped stairs, she was acutely aware of him behind her and found she had little interest in talking about what she'd pulled out of the box of documents.

See, this is why they tell you not to mix business with pleasure, she thought. She was so preoccupied with making love to the man, she'd be lucky to string two coherent sentences together.

And she was disappointed as hell when he walked directly to the painting.

As Jack looked down at the canvas, she turned on the halogen steam light so he could see better. The work she'd been doing in the lower left corner had spread, moving up the side of the canvas.

"You've done quite a bit."

"It's going well. I think I've hit the solvent right on the head. The only thing coming off is the old varnish and I'm happy to say the underlying paint is solid. I'm really looking forward to doing the face."

He straightened. "Now, what did you want to show me?"

His eyes were trained on her clothes, and going by the expectation in his face, he was picturing her without them. She smiled and went over to the side table by the couch.

Picking up the letter fragment she said, "I don't want to jump to conclusions but it's tempting to believe Nathaniel wrote these words."

Jack read it, holding the paper carefully by the edges. "I was hoping you'd find something like this."

She frowned, wondering what he meant.

"Come with me."

16

CALLIE FOLLOWED him back to the house and into his study. She was about to sit down across from the desk when she saw glass shards on the floor.

"What happened here?" She bent down and started picking up some of the bigger pieces. He joined her, getting down on his haunches.

"Evidently, I don't handle introspection well." He gave her a wry smile when she hesitated and met his eyes. "But don't worry. If I go into therapy full-time, I'm locking up the china."

"What were you thinking about?"

He fingered some of the broken crystal in his palm. "How different you are."

"Oh." She was hardly encouraged, considering he'd ended up throwing something.

"Did you know that I once had a woman ask me to buy her a car?"

Callie shook her head and went back to picking up the glass. She really didn't want to hear about one of his former lovers. "Doesn't surprise me."

"She wanted it to go shopping in. We were in Italy and she couldn't stomach a rental. It was too close to public transportation for her."

Callie smiled a little though she had a pit in her stomach thinking about him on some romantic getaway.

"And let me guess. We're not talking about a Ford Escort, are we?"

He shook his head. "A Ferrari. She wanted a yellow one."

She cocked an eyebrow. "To match her hair, of course. What did you do?"

"I bought it."

"That must have pleased her." When she heard the disapproval in her own voice, she said, "What I mean is—"

"It did make her happy, but not because she really wanted the car. It was a test, an absurd request to figure out how far I was willing to go." Jack shrugged. "And I showed her exactly where my limits were with pleasure. I knew she'd never forget the car that made no difference to me, especially if I allowed her to use it for a day. I bought the Ferrari, put a big red bow around it, and told her to have a ball. That night, after she got home, I informed her I didn't need to see her again and drove off in it. She called me for months afterward."

Callie got to her feet and emptied her hand in the wastepaper basket. That kind of hardball, on both sides, was way out of her league. "Are you sure it was a test? Maybe she was sincere."

"She used it to go see her other lover. No doubt to try and have him match the competition."

"Oh."

"My point is, that's something you would never do."

She laughed. "You got that right."

Jack put the shards he was holding into the trash. "This morning I sat in bed and realized I want things from you. Things I've never asked any other woman for."

"Like what?" She held her breath.

"I've had a lot of relationships that looked good from the outside," he paused, smiling coldly, "probably because we were wearing evening clothes most of the time. What went on behind closed doors, though, was just some athletic sex and not much else. Even with Blair, who I respected, there was something missing. With you"—his eyes locked on hers—"I know there is more and I want it all. I know you're looking at this as a fling, but I don't want you only in my bed. I want you in my life, too. I want to wake up in the morning and see your face. I want to come home at noontime just because I'm impatient to see you and I know you're here. I want you to trust me. And I want to earn that trust."

He threw his hands up and rolled his eyes before she could speak. "I know, I know. This coming from a man who last night reminded you he wasn't a good bet for a relationship. But I've really thought about this. Hell, I've been thinking about you nonstop for weeks now."

Believing in him and seeing a future with him was enticing. But Callie tried to remind herself that considering him as a casual lover was still the smart thing to do. They had talked a little about feelings and had a wonderful night together, but it was way too early to predict how a relationship between them would turn out.

"It's going to take time, Jack."

"I know. And I'm willing to put in the investment, if you are."

She studied him closely. "I am."

"Good." He kissed her hard on the mouth and then went over to the desk and pulled open a drawer.

"Jack?"

He looked up.

"Just so you know, I'm perfectly fine with public transportation. But that doesn't mean I want you to buy me a bus to prove your affection, okay?"

He was laughing as he took out a long envelope. "It's a deal."

The single sheet of paper he slid free was the same pale brown color as the one she'd discovered but much smaller. "This is a letter fragment I found five years ago when we were cleaning out my father's things."

She came over as Jack read from it aloud. "'My dearest heart, surely I wanted to come unto you. It was fear, not a failing of love, that kept me away. To risk all for one look upon your face seems a paltry exchange, but he would find our love as a forsaken betrayal. Your friendship, long as son to father and father to son, would be devastated. And how, thereafter, could you fight under his command? But after Concord we shall meet again at—'" He looked up. "That's all there is."

She stared at him, amazed. "May I see it?"

He handed the document to her. The handwriting was different, more curvaceous. A woman's, she thought.

"I saved it," Jack said, "because it was old and curious, but I never thought it had anything to do with Nathaniel. Many members of the family served in the military and fought in conflicts in the late-eighteenth and early-nineteenth centuries. But considering the sheet you found, it makes me think."

"It certainly does." She compared the two and was struck by how the ink had faded in a similar way.

Jack shrugged. "I've read all of Nathaniel's journals. He never mentions a woman until he gets married to Jane Hatte. He does talk about General Rowe, though, the man he fought with against the British at the Battle of Concord. The two were very close and Rowe did have a wife, Sarah."

She looked at him. "So maybe Nathaniel and Sarah had an affair."

"It might explain why Nathaniel didn't marry until much later." He took back the letter and her new find and put them both in the envelope. "Good thing Grace is coming up for the party next week. Maybe she can fill in some of the details."

Callie cleared her throat. "Listen, about Thanksgiving. I'm sure you'll have guests, so I'm going back to the city—"

"But I don't want you to go. Unless you have family to see, stay here."

The words had come out of him fast and hard, and she couldn't help but smile.

"Won't you need my room?"

"No. And even if we couldn't put everyone up, I'd send people to a hotel before I'd displace you."

Her grin widened. "What about the holiday dinner?"

"We don't really do the whole turkey thing. Not since my father died. The big event is our annual holiday party the day after. Which you are, of course, invited to."

Callie nodded, pleased. "Okay, I'll stay for both."

He smiled with satisfaction. "And have dinner with me tonight?"

"I'd love to."

"Good. I've got a tough day of off-site meetings ahead of me, but I promise to be back around six. And I'll be very hungry by then."

As he looked at her from under heavy lids, her body warmed up. Moving with obvious intent, he came around the desk, took her into his arms, and kissed her until they were both breathing heavily.

"I'll be thinking of you," Jack said. "All day long."

The feeling was mutual.

Callie spent most of the hours working on the painting, with pictures of Jack floating in and out of her mind. At four o'clock, she took a break and went out to play with Arthur in the yard. She was at the side of the house, throwing his favorite tree branch as far as she could, when a black Town Car pulled into the drive. As Arthur shot after the stick, she watched the limousine stop under the porte cochere. A uniformed driver got out and opened the rear door.

A tall, slender blond woman emerged from the car. Even from across the lawn, it was obvious she was someone important. She was dressed in a black suit and, with her short, stylized hair, she was very chic.

Callie had a fleeting thought that she'd seen the woman somewhere before. Maybe in Stanley's gallery?

The door to the house opened and Mrs. Walker emerged with arms outstretched. As the two embraced, Arthur came back with the stick and dropped it on her foot.

She threw it quickly and turned back, but there wasn't much else to see. The two women had disappeared into the house and the limousine driver was leaning back against the car as if he was used to waiting.

She returned to work, anxious for the two hours to

pass so she and Jack could get away from the house. It was curious how ten thousand square feet could still be suffocating, and she couldn't wait to be alone with him. She'd decided some necking in that Aston Martin would be a fine way to start and end an evening. Although on that logic, it was too bad the man didn't drive a Volvo station wagon.

Or a minivan.

An hour later she heard the garage door go up and the low growl of Jack's car. She whipped off her breathing mask and ran her fingers through her hair, spreading it out over her shoulders.

When he got to the second floor, she ate up the wide smile on his face.

"I missed you," he said. "How was your day?"

"I've done some great work this afternoon. Take a look at the top of his head. The waves in his hair are remarkable." Callie leaned in close to the canvas, pointing out the area with her wooden stick.

Jack came up behind her and she felt his hands settle on her shoulders. When he spoke, his voice was right next to her ear.

"I have something for you."

She looked up, feeling anticipation thicken her blood. But instead of kissing her, he put a glossy bag with satin handles down on her desk.

She tensed when she saw the Cartier name. "What's this?"

"Just a small present. Go on. See what's inside."

She took out a sizable red leather box, and when she got it open, she shook her head. Inside was a gold watch.

"Jack, I can't accept this."

"Why not?" He reached over and took the beautiful timepiece out of its satin bed. "You need a watch."

"Yeah, well, not one like this." It had probably cost ten or twenty thousand dollars.

"Try it on."

He slipped it over her hand and onto her wrist. It was heavy and felt altogether foreign.

"Fits perfectly," he said with satisfaction.

"Jack, it's too much."

Impatience flickered across his face. "The thing tells time. That's all you need to worry about."

"But so does a Timex."

Jack frowned. "Why can't I buy you a gift? People give them and receive them all the time. It's the basis of our retail economy, as a matter of fact."

She got up from the chair. "You can. But . . . your version of a *gift* and the rest of the world's are very different."

"I don't care about the rest of the world."

"Fine. *My* version of a gift, then." She faced him. "Jack, I've got to be honest with you. I don't have a dime to my name, other than what you're going to pay me at the end of this job. That place in Chelsea? That's where I live. The Chanel suit? It's a friend of mine's. I'm not from your world. Not even close."

"I know."

She narrowed her eyes.

Of course he would, she thought. He wasn't stupid.

Jack crossed his arms over his chest. "And I know where you're headed with all this, so let me just say, I don't care where you're from. Not in the slightest."

Callie studied his face closely and then looked down at the watch. "I'm not going to change, you realize. No matter what you buy me, I'm never going to be a socialite who's into dresses and shoes and parties. First of all, I hate shopping."

"So don't shop."

"And I have ridiculously wide feet so those *Sex and the City*–type shoes would never fit me anyway."

"Which means you're stable on an incline. A tremendous virtue," he said with a straight face.

She rolled her eyes. "And I hate big crowds. To be honest, I'm on the benevolent side of antisocial. I don't mind people, but I'd prefer not to have a lot of them around."

"So there'll be no going to Times Square to see the ball drop? Oh, the disappointment."

The expression of horror on his face had her laughing. "I can't believe you don't care."

"Well, I'm a little shook up there's no *New Year's Rockin' Eve* with Dick Clark in our future, but there's always TV."

Jack was smiling as he reached out and pulled her against him. He dropped a kiss on her mouth.

"I like you just as you come." He nodded down at her wrist. "If you really hate the watch, I'll take it back, provided you promise to eat lunch every day. But it is a gift from me to you and I hope you'll at least try it out."

She put her arms around his shoulders. "Fine, I'll give it a go. And thank you."

Jack nuzzled the sensitive skin of her neck. "God, you smell good. What is that perfume?"

"Eau de isopropanol."

He pulled back. "What the hell is that?"

"The solvent I'm using to remove the oxidized soft resin varnish from your painting."

"Oh, right. I thought I recognized it." He took her earlobe gently between his teeth. "Now, how about we say hello again?"

In a flash, they were on the couch. With impatient hands, clothes were thrown on the floor, shoes kicked off. As he settled between her legs, he hesitated, his eyes heated but worried.

"Are you sure you . . . Is this going to be okay?" he asked.

His awkward concern made her smile.

"There's only one way to find out," she murmured, moving her hips against his.

He slid inside of her, slowly, carefully—in spite of the passion she could feel in his body. She shuddered with pleasure. He was heavy on top of her and she liked the feel of his weight. When he began to move, she held on and carried the rhythm in her own hips until she heard him call her name in a hoarse cry. As his arms contracted around her, she let herself go over the edge with him.

Later, when her breath was no longer coming out in pants and her heart wasn't racing so much, she opened her eyes. Jack had shifted and his body was stretched out next to hers, taking up the lion's share of the couch. His face was relaxed with contentment, his eyes gleaming with satisfaction.

"How do you feel? Okay?" he asked, his voice full of gravel.

"A lot more than okay."

"I didn't want to hurt you."

"I'm tougher than I look."

He dropped a kiss on the tip of her nose. "And you don't look like a wimp either."

Her stomach let out a growl.

"You ready to eat?" When she nodded, he sat up and handed her the sweater she'd been wearing. "I thought we'd go to this diner in town that's all the rage right now."

Hell, she didn't care if they went to McDonald's and ate with plastic sporks.

Cradling her sweater against her chest, she was content to lie back and watch him move. As he picked up his shirt and pulled it on, the wide expanse of his back flexed and she noted the marks she'd left on his skin the night before.

"What are you looking at?" he asked in a low drawl.

"I seem to have done some aesthetic damage to your back."

Jack reached over and pulled her to her feet, drawing her against him. "And you can work on the front of me later on tonight."

His lips came down for a quick kiss that soon hardened with passion.

"Maybe we should put off dinner for a little while," he growled. His hands slid over her hips and she felt him, hard and ready, as his body curved around her. "God, I'm insatiable when it comes to you."

And what a wonderful word that was, Callie thought, dropping her sweater as she wrapped her arms around his neck. He pushed her over against the closet doors and lifted her up, suspending her from the floor with his arms. When she wrapped her legs around his hips, he thrust inside of her again and their bodies took over. The surging movement was frantic and she cried out as waves of energy coursed through her.

When the quaking was over, she uncurled her legs and felt her feet touch ground.

"My God," Jack muttered, putting his palms against the doors and leaning into them. His breath was coming out roughly.

Moving a hand to her hair, he smoothed the thick weight back from her face and kissed her on the forehead. His arms, which had held her up with such strength, were gentle as they cradled her.

"Callie." His breath was soft against her skin.

Before she closed her eyes to savor the moment, she saw his beautiful suit jacket crumpled on the floor, his pants hanging off the open Rubbermaid container, his tie wadded up and sticking out of the couch.

Those fine trappings of wealth meant nothing to her. It was Jack she wanted. Jack naked and trembling from passion. Jack's voice stripped of all culture and refinement, her name leaving his lips in nothing more than a guttural burst.

She leaned into him, holding on tight. She wanted Jack Walker, the man. Not the business legend. Not the newest star of his prestigious family.

When he pulled back, he said, "You amaze me."

His fingers brushed against her cheek and then lifted her chin so he could kiss her. His lips were as soft as his eyes.

"We should probably go," she said. "Why don't I meet you back at the house? I have to shut down Nathaniel's beauty spa and I'd like to change."

He placed a lingering kiss against her lips and then put on his pants. After tucking his shirttails in with sharp movements, he pulled his jacket on and casually slung his blue tie around his neck.

But he didn't leave right away. He just stared at her, a slight smile playing over his lips.

"Come here," she said, motioning to him. "Your hair looks like it's been blown dry by a box fan."

He came up to her and put his head down, standing patiently while she fixed him up.

"And we should put the tie on properly. You'll look less ravished that way." With a seductive smile, she turned up his collar, slid the silk into place, and quickly executed a pretty good Windsor knot. She nodded at the result. "You're almost perfect. But there's nothing we're going to be able to do about the wrinkles in your suit and shirt."

Jack reached for her, his arms going all the way around her body. "I can't seem to let you go."

"Which is perfectly fine with me."

When he finally left, it took her ten minutes to close up shop and head for the house. As she stepped out into the brisk night air, she felt so alive she wanted to laugh out loud. The world seemed to have expanded and she was able to find possibilities and excitement in everything, even the darkened sky. There were things to look forward to, plans she could make, places she suddenly wanted to go.

All with Jack, of course.

She pictured the two of them heading upstate and staying at some B and B in the wintertime. There would be a fireplace in their room and a big bed with lots of blankets and pillows. They would make love for days straight as the snow fell outside.

When she opened the back door, she was smiling.

She jerked to a halt.

Jack and the blond woman were staring at each other over the island in the kitchen. On the slab of granite between them was a large diamond ring.

Their heads snapped around to her.

"So you're Callie," the woman said softly. "You're the one."

17

LOOKING BACK and forth between them, Callie put it all together. It was the blonde from the Plaza Hotel hallway. The scarf and earrings that had been in Jack's suite were hers.

Callie fought a sudden urge to be sick.

"I'm Blair Stanford," the woman said, sticking out her hand and narrowing her eyes.

Probably because she was remembering their brief passing, too.

Callie awkwardly returned the gesture, shooting a glance at Jack. He met her eyes and shook his head as if he regretted the situation she'd been put in.

"I wish I could say I was pleased to meet you," Blair said, with more honesty than hostility. "This has been a disappointment, as you can imagine."

Callie didn't know how to respond, and as she looked away, her eyes flickered down to the diamond. It had a diameter the size of a nickel.

"I think I'll just go upstairs," she murmured.

"That's not necessary," Blair said. "Jack and I were just making our good-bye official."

She picked up a Vuitton handbag and nodded stiffly at Callie. Then she looked at Jack and said, "Take care of yourself. I know you always do."

"I'll walk you to the door."

"That's not necessary. Actually, I'd prefer you didn't."

She paused on her way out of the room, glancing at Callie. "Be careful, darling. He's a wonderful man on many fronts, so there's a big hole to fill when he leaves."

Callie looked away, thinking the woman was undoubtedly right.

The sound of the front door being opened and closed was followed by a long silence.

She shifted her eyes to Jack. His head was down and he was gripping the edge of the countertop.

"Are you okay?" she asked.

His chest rose and fell. "Yeah."

She waited for him to say something more. When he didn't, she murmured, "You want to hold off on dinner?"

He looked up. "Maybe. I don't know that I'd be good company right now."

Her heart skipped a beat as she wondered whether he was having second thoughts. But maybe it was just the awkwardness of Blair showing up. "I understand."

He came over and kissed her briefly. "Thank you."

After he left, she glanced over at the ring and tried to imagine wearing the thing. She couldn't picture it on her finger.

Which wasn't necessarily a bad thing. He certainly hadn't mentioned marriage to her.

She groaned. Marriage? They'd made love three times and already she was thinking about altars? She had to be out of her mind. Weekend escapes were one thing. And even then, she might have been pushing it a little.

She forced herself to consider how long they'd known each other and didn't like the answer. It was a matter of weeks, not months. They had a long, long way to go before she should be thinking more than a couple days ahead.

Jack went into his study and tried to pretend that settling in with the bourbon was not becoming a routine. After a couple of swallows, he pushed the glass and the decanter away, feeling too much like his father. What he wanted was a little peace, not a coping mechanism with nasty consequences.

But when his mother appeared in the doorway, he reached for the glass again. She was wearing a formal dress and a lot of pearls and he took the outfit as a good sign she was leaving.

Which couldn't happen fast enough for him considering the displeasure on her face.

"Where did Blair run off to? And why was this"—she held up the diamond—"in the kitchen?"

Damn it, he should have pocketed the ring when he'd had the chance.

"The engagement is off."

"Whatever for?" she demanded.

"That's none of your business."

Mercedes began shaking her head. "Jack, no. Don't do this. Don't fall for some marginal girl, especially when you could be with someone like Blair. The sacrifices just aren't necessary."

He refilled his glass. "I can assure you, being with Callie is no sacrifice for me. At all."

His mother's face tightened. "Maybe in the privacy of your own home. But what about in the outside world? You need someone who understands the kind of life you lead. Blair can support you—"

"And you think Callie can't? My lifestyle isn't rocket science. I see the same five hundred people, at the same parties, year after year. I could do it with my eyes closed and so could anyone with half a brain."

"That's a considerable simplification and you know it. Listen to me, Jack, I know how hard it was for your father and me—"

Jack didn't bother to keep the boredom out of his voice. "My father worshipped you and you've had a great time playing grande dame for the past forty years. So don't try and pretend it was all a chore, okay?"

She took a deep breath. "There's no reason to talk to me like that."

"Was there anything else you had to say, Mother?" As soon as the words came out, he regretted the invitation. Of course there was going to be more.

"Jack, you simply cannot do this. Especially if you are going to run for governor." As his eyebrows lifted, she explained, "Gray Bennett's mother called and told me that he's been here in Boston, meeting with you. It's obvious what you're planning."

"Ah, the Smith College alumni network at its best."

Mercedes came up to the desk with her particular brand of urgency, clearly prepared to force her will on him. Even though she'd never swayed him, she was always willing to try.

Man, his father hadn't stood a chance once she'd picked him out of the crowd, Jack thought.

"You know I've always hoped you'd run," she said, "and not just at the state level. Can't you see what elected office would do for you? The power it would give you? The respect? Don't you want all that?"

"I already have power, so a lot of people respect me," he said drily. "And I have a feeling that you're quite interested in being the mother of the governor, aren't you? But you're not impressing me with your logic. I fail to see how marrying Blair when I don't love her would land me in the governor's seat any more than being with Callie would prevent it."

The tone of his mother's voice hardened. "Don't think your love life isn't going to play a role in the election. God knows, your past is going to be hard enough to live down. You shouldn't compound the problem by losing someone like Blair just because you want to sleep with a member of the lower classes."

"That's enough," he said sharply, bringing the glass down hard on the desk.

His mother was not deterred.

"Jackson, I cannot let you make a mistake like this. There are ways of fixing these things."

He narrowed his eyes on her. "It's rather noble of you to try and save me from myself, but bear this in mind. If you want to keep living here, you will back the hell off and stay out of my life. Do we have an understanding?"

Her thin brows shot up into her forehead.

"But you must see that it can never work between you and that ... Callie," she said, gesturing aimlessly with a jeweled hand.

"I'm sorry. Didn't we just agree you wouldn't interfere? Or are you moving?"

Mercedes stared at him, looking almost helpless. He could imagine her frustration, to be so close to her dreams, and yet unable to control his actions.

"Jack, I'm your mother—"

"That doesn't mean you're running the show around here. Shut the door on your way out, will you?" As she continued to stare at him, he cocked an eyebrow. "Now."

When he was alone, he finished his drink and then went to look for Callie.

Even if he was out of sorts, there was nowhere else he wanted to be but with her.

A week later, Callie returned to the house following a productive afternoon with the portrait. After having worked her way around the outside of the painting, she was now far enough in so that she was cleaning Nathaniel's face. Even with the dirt and grime, he had been handsome, if rather dour, but revealed in all his glory, he was resplendent. His eyes were a dark mahogany, his cheeks a gentle pink, his hair thick with a multitude of browns. Copley had brought out the best in his subject, but she suspected that there had been a lot to work with. And with the old varnish gone, his brooding expression was less intense.

As she opened the back door, the resounding silence in the kitchen reminded her it was Thomas's day off. This meant Mrs. Walker would be out to dinner, and Callie grinned. Although she and Jack had plans to go to the movies and have dinner somewhere, maybe they should just stay home. It seemed a damn shame to waste the privacy.

She glanced at her new watch. She was getting used to it and it did serve the purpose of telling her when it was lunchtime. More than anything, though, she liked it because it made her think of Jack.

Sitting down at the table, she started to leaf through the paper, stroking Arthur's ear with her free hand.

An hour later, she looked at the watch again and started pacing around the kitchen. Jack was never late, and he'd told her he'd be home an hour and a half ago. She was wondering whether she should try him at the office when the phone rang.

Even though she wasn't in the habit of answering calls at the house, she picked up the receiver, hoping it was him.

"Hello?"

"Callie, it's Jack. I need your help."

In the background, she heard muffled voices and the sound of something shrill. Were those alarms?

"What happened?" she asked, her hand coming up to her forehead.

"I totaled my car."

Her lungs immediately stopped functioning.

Calm, stay calm, she told herself. At least he can still pick up the phone.

"Oh, God. Are you—"

"I'm fine except I broke my damn arm. Can you come pick me up? I'm at Beth Israel."

"Where? And what's around here to drive?"

"Take the other Jag."

He told her where the keys were and gave her directions to the medical center. As she flew out the door, she was imagining all kinds of what-ifs with horrid consequences. The way he drove, he could have done a lot more damage to himself than just ending up with a cast on his arm.

"The other Jag" was a convertible, and, as luck would have it, a stick shift. As she hiccuped down the driveway, she was hoping that enough of the transmission system would be left by the time she got to Boston to get them home again. The trip was interminable. She was a reluctant driver under the best of circumstances, and stress didn't improve her skills. Behind the wheel of a powerhouse engine, working the clutch and accelerator with all the finesse of a student driver, she was no Jeff Gordon.

A lifetime later, she pulled up to the emergency wing of the hospital's massive complex. She figured she'd have to ditch the car to find Jack, but then he came limping out of the double doors, his arm in a sling. She jammed on the brakes and leapt from the car.

"You hurt more than your arm," she said, eyeing the bandage at his temple.

"You should see the DB9." He shook his head and winced. "It looks like it's been through a trash compactor. This morning it was a sports car. Now it's an accordion."

Callie opened the door for him and he grimaced as he carefully slid inside. She ran around and got in, but hesitated before pulling away from the curb because she wanted to take a good look at him. His jacket was around his shoulders, his tie was hanging out of his pocket, and his untucked shirt had some dried blood on the collar. She wondered what kinds of bruises were hidden under his clothes.

"Can we go now?" He put his head back against the rest and closed his eyes. He looked tired and uncomfortable, but not as if he were on death's door by any stretch.

As soon as she was convinced he was all right, she got pissed.

"What the hell did you hit?"

He winced as her voice bounced around the inside of the car.

"How do you know it was my fault?" he asked quietly.

"Because I've been in a car with you. Damn it, you could have been killed."

"First of all, I wasn't. And I know this because I hurt all over. Secondly, the driver that swerved into my lane had a thing or two to do with the accident. Now can we please go?"

Biting back a curse, she gripped the steering wheel and eased them onto Brookline Avenue.

"How did it happen?" Callie grumbled.

"I was on Storrow Drive. Some guy in an SUV shot into my lane, and when I tried to get around him, I hit the guardrail, did a three-sixty, I think, and ended up on the esplanade." He turned his head and looked at her. "That's the strip of green between Storrow and the Charles River. Usually it's reserved for pedestrians, so you can imagine I wasn't the only one surprised to find myself in a car on the jogging path. Thank God no one else was hurt."

She shook her head. "You drive too fast."

"I know."

"You're too aggressive."

"I know."

"You could have killed yourself," she repeated, irritated by his laconic responses. "And don't say 'I know.' "

"Okay."

She shot a glare across the seat. In the glow from the dash, she saw that his eyes were closed. He looked beat and the urge to yell at him faded. Focusing on the road, she figured she would get him home and put him right to bed.

Assuming he didn't fall asleep in the car.

When she pulled into Buona Fortuna's drive, she thought she was going to have to wake him up, but he lifted his head and let out a long sigh. Carefully parking the Jag in the garage, she wondered if she was going to have to help him get out, but he stood up on his own and slowly limped out into the night air. Closing the garage door, she noted that Mrs. Walker's car was back and wondered what the woman's response was going to be. Here was her perfect son, all banged up. She was probably going to throw a fit.

As Callie came to his side, Jack was staring up at the stars with a thoughtful expression, his good arm cradling his broken one in spite of the sling around his neck.

She reached out and put her hand gently on his shoulder. She needed to touch him and not through his clothes. She had to know the warmth of his skin, to have his body against hers, to *feel* that he was all right, not just assume it from afar.

"Thank you," he murmured softly. "For picking me up."

"Good Lord, of course."

He started for the house and she followed, measuring the way he favored his right foot and the rigid way he held himself. As she opened the door for him, she thought he looked visibly relieved to be home.

"Do you want anything to eat?" she asked.

"Can you bring me something upstairs? I want to change and lie down."

When she came up to his bedroom, the confident, elegant man she knew was standing by his bed, completely tangled up in his clothes. The sling was hanging cockeyed from his shoulder, his shirt stuck around his neck, and his belt was half undone.

"You need some help?" She put down the plate and glass, swallowing a smile.

One eye glared out of the mess. "Yes. Please."

She quickly freed the buttons, stripped off the shirt, and removed the sling.

She held her breath as she eyed a bruise on his collarbone.

"That must have hurt." She put her hand out and touched him, running her fingers gently around the red mark.

When he didn't say anything, she looked up. His eyes were closed and his face was showing intense concentration as if he were drinking in her touch.

Jack's voice was rough. "When the car stopped spinning around, I was so damn dizzy and bashed up, I couldn't tell what kind of shape I was in."

She winced, trying not to imagine his broken body being pulled out of the car by paramedics.

His eyes opened slowly. "The first thing I thought of was you. The idea of not seeing you again was . . . unbearable."

Callie reached up to his face, feeling the rasp of his beard growth, the hollow above his jawline, the pulse that beat at his throat.

When she dropped her hand, he took it and put it back.

"Touch me," he said. "You make the numbness go away."

She let her hand move down over his shoulder and onto his biceps. Lightly tracing his pecs, she paused on his beating heart and went down onto the ridges of his stomach. She could felt his body tighten under her fingertips and heard his breath as it rushed out of him. When she brushed the backs of her knuckles across his belly button, he hissed, taking his lower lip between his sharp teeth.

She paused, worried that she was hurting him.

"Don't stop," he said thickly. His eyes were wild, on the edge of violence. "Christ, please don't stop."

She reached for his belt buckle, feeling supple leather as she finished undoing it. His pants hit the floor in a rush and she looked up. A fine sheen of sweat had broken out across his chest.

Jack grabbed her with his good arm, crushing her to him, burying his head in her hair. Feeling the solid wall of his chest, hearing the beat of his heart, she shuddered and opened her mouth.

Knowing that she was taking the biggest risk of her life, that it was too early, that it was not the right time, that maybe she was just speaking out of passion and relief, she whispered, "I love you."

Jack fell still and she immediately wished she could take the words back.

What was she thinking? Sure, he cared for her. Yes, he had passion for her. But love?

Callie stepped back, trying to cover up what she'd said, but his eyes pegged her with an intensity she'd never seen in them before.

He brought her back against him. "I can't believe it. I didn't think it would ever happen. But . . . I love you, too."

He pulled her close and she felt like crying. It was more than the blessing that he was home safely. That he felt the same way she did. That his words were not a promise, but a statement of fact. No, the feeling came from a sense that maybe the world wasn't quite the hard, cold place she'd always known it to be.

After so many years of being alone, she had someone of her own.

18

THE FOLLOWING evening, Jack let Gray Bennett into the front hall. His friend was obviously not happy.

"Where the hell have you been? You don't return my calls— Christ, what happened to you?"

"Car accident." He ushered Gray down to the study, closing the door behind them.

As Jack slowly lowered himself into his chair, he was more than ready to be able to move freely again. The bruises would fade soon enough, but the godforsaken arm was going to be a pain in the ass for the next month and a half.

"Jesus." Gray stared at him for a minute and then shrugged out of his coat. He tossed it over to the couch. "You okay?"

"Yeah, just banged up."

"Well, I'm glad you didn't get hurt worse. But you still should have called me back. What we're doing has taken on a life of its own and it's in your best interest to be up-to-date."

"I know." But falling in love had a way of making a man think of things other than politics. "Now, sit down and tell me what I need to know."

Gray settled into a club chair and crossed his legs. His foot started tapping.

"There something I need to worry about?" Jack asked evenly.

"I just got a call from New York and I had to track you down in person. There's a rumor going around that you and Blair have called off the engagement. You want to tell me what's going on?"

The phone at Jack's elbow started to ring and he silenced it with the flick of a switch. "We have ended it. I did, actually. I made a terrible mistake, and like most lapses in judgment, I didn't figure it out until someone got hurt. I regret what happened, but getting out is absolutely the right decision."

Gray's foot stilled. "I'm your friend first, so I've got to ask, how're you doing?"

"I'm fine. Except for feeling like shit for what I put Blair through."

"Well, I'm sorry it didn't work out. She's a fine woman." There was a pause. "Now, I'm also your political consultant, so I need to talk some shop."

"Shoot."

Jack tugged at the sling and repositioned the broken arm across his chest, trying to ease the strain in his shoulder. A meeting with Gray was overdue and he was prepared to spend an hour or two with his friend if that was what it took.

"We'll talk about the ramifications of the broken engagement in a minute. First, the election. It's getting to be fish-or-cut-bait time. Speculation is beginning to mount even though we've still got a year before the polls open. I want to know, just between me and you, where your head is. Are you going to run?"

"Unless something drastic changes, yes."

"Good. Starting this week, I'm going to quietly look for a local campaign manager. I know a couple of good ones, and hopefully they haven't been snatched up yet. This is another reason why deciding now is so important." Gray bridged his hands together and regarded Jack over the tips of his fingers. "Now, about Blair. I'm glad you didn't announce the engagement, and I'm also glad that if you had to end one this close to an election, that it was with her. She's a lady and she's got integrity, so I don't think we can expect her to jump up out of the bushes and spring a broken-heart tell-all."

Jack inclined his head. "Blair would never do something like that. We don't have anything to worry about."

"From her, maybe." Gray got up from the chair and started pacing. "I think we need to do some damage control anyway. Other people know you'd asked her to marry you. If it were to come out that you'd broken off this engagement for another woman—"

"Who said anything about another woman?"

His friend shot him a dry look. "Don't even try that with me."

"I'm not denying it. I want to know who your source was."

"Karl Graves."

Jack tightened his lips. "So it's all over Manhattan?"

"I don't think so. I've known him for a while and he called because he was concerned about Blair and wanted to know what the hell had happened between you two." Gray planted his hands on the top of the desk and leaned forward. "My point is, this is just the kind of playboy move you don't need in the papers. I think for the time being I should function as your press man. Better for me to field the inquiries first, assuming there are any. It'll give you some insulation."

"Fine." Jack looked out the window.

"Listen, I don't want you to worry. I can handle whatever comes at us. My job is to ensure that people take you seriously, and I'm going to be ready."

Jack shook his head, thinking back to all the headlines he'd made over the years. A broken engagement fit the pattern perfectly. "Christ, Gray, do you think I'm crazy to run?"

"No, but you've got some liabilities to overcome." His friend straightened. "You've never held a political office before, which is one strike against you. You're successful at business, and God knows you've got the family name working for you, but you're going to be picked apart for those bad-boy years. The good thing is that while you've been with Blair, you've been out of the papers except for good coverage. I'm only concerned right now because I don't want this thing with Blair to start the avalanche before you get out there with your platform. The more voters know about you before they're reminded of your past, the better. Which is one more reason to declare loudly and early."

"You mentioned damage control. Do you want me to talk to Blair?"

"No, I'm really not concerned about her." There was a pause. "I want you to talk to Callie."

Jack frowned. "About what?"

"She's the one who changed your mind about marrying Blair, right?" When he nodded, Gray said, "Do you plan on keeping her around for a while? Or is she just a temporary diversion?"

"What the hell kind of question is that?"

"A pretty damned important one. And later we can cover why you wanted to set me up with the woman if you were so into her."

Jack stood up and went to the bar. "You want some bourbon?"

"Bradford's?"

"Is there any other kind?"

When Jack handed Gray his drink, they both sat down.

"Callie is much more than a one-night stand. I'm in love with her."

Gray's glass stopped on the way to his mouth. "My God. You're serious."

"Very. She's everything I wasn't looking for and exactly who I want."

Gray shook his head ruefully. "I'm happy for you. Really happy. If I seem surprised . . ."

Jack laughed. "It's completely understandable. And just remember, if it can happen to me, it can happen—"

"Don't even say it." Gray took a long swallow of his drink and gritted his teeth. "Back to business. I'm going to assume Callie's a factor in the election next year.

She needs to know what she's getting into if she sticks around. She's going to get dragged into the fray, and it's only fair to prepare her."

Jack nodded while despising the truth. The last thing he wanted was to have her subjected to the media rush, but he couldn't ignore the inevitable.

"I'll speak with her."

"And it would be helpful to know a little bit about her background."

"That's easy enough." He shrugged and recited her résumé.

"What about her family?"

"She doesn't talk about them much."

"Find out why."

"Gray, I'm not going to play private detective on my . . ." He wasn't sure how to finish the sentence. Lover? Girlfriend? Those sounded weak compared to how he felt whenever he was with her.

As he struggled, his friend said softly, "We need to know."

When he swore under his breath, Gray shook his head. "This is only the beginning. Have you really thought about what the election is going to do to your life? Are you sure you're up for the scrutiny?"

"I know I want the job." Jack took a drink. "So I'll do what I have to do to get it. But I don't want Callie getting pulled into all the mudslinging. I'm willing to take the hits, but I won't stand for anyone taking shots at her."

Gray hesitated. "Listen, maybe you need to consider what you're signing up for a little more. You know I wouldn't think less of you if you decided to pull out. You can quit anytime before you officially announce."

A knock sounded at the door.

"Come in," Jack said.

Callie put her head inside. "Gray! I didn't know you were coming over. Are you going to have dinner with us?"

Gray smiled in an easy way, tossed back the tail end of his drink, and put the glass on the desk.

"No, I was just leaving." He picked up his coat. "I'll talk to you later, Jack?"

Jack nodded while staring into Callie's face.

When they were alone, she frowned. "Why are you looking at me like that?"

Because I'm prepared to kill anyone who tries to get at you, he thought.

"Jack?"

He held his good arm out. "Sorry. Come over here, so I can kiss you."

She shut the door and walked across the room. As he watched her, he felt his blood thickening in his veins and his eyes lingered on her mouth. For all the times they'd been together, he couldn't believe his attraction to her was still so fresh. That he could want someone so much, even after he'd had her, was a revelation.

But that was love, Jack thought.

Positioning her in his lap, he ran his hand down her thigh. "You know something?"

"What?"

"You're beautiful." He pressed his lips onto hers.

As she settled against his body, he thought about what Gray had said. Had he truly considered the ramifications of running? Butch Callahan wasn't going to give up without a serious brawl, and all of the other candidates were going to want to win just as badly as Jack did.

Which meant the gloves were going to come off. And everything was fair game.

The question was, how badly did he want to win? And how much was he willing to sacrifice to make sure he did?

"Jack?"

"Hmmm?"

"Do you ever get away? You know, take a vacation?"

He swept her hair aside and kissed his favorite spot on her neck, the one right behind her earlobe. "What did you have in mind?"

"Maybe after the holidays, we could go up north. Just for a weekend. We wouldn't be gone that—"

He cut her off with a kiss that went on and on. "Let's take a week."

The smile she treated him with made Jack think being gone even longer might not be a bad idea.

Later that week, they were lying in her bed and Callie was on the verge of falling asleep when Jack said, "I want to ask you something."

"What?"

"Why did you wait so long to have se—to make love with someone?"

For a moment, she wasn't sure how to answer him. She'd tell the truth, of course, but the wording was difficult.

"Well, aside from being an introvert to begin with, I had to work my way through college and grad school, so it seemed like every minute of the day I had something I needed to do. When I got out of NYU, my mother was sick and getting worse fast. She had multiple sclerosis, and with her increasing debilitation, someone always had to be with her. We didn't have money for round-the-clock nursing." She shrugged. "You need time and discretionary energy for relationships, and I had neither."

She knew he was frowning by the displeasure in his voice. "You shouldn't have had to deal with your mother's illness alone. What about your father? Where was he?"

"He was— Ah, it was a difficult situation."

Jack propped his head on his hand and let his cast fall between them. In the dim light, she could tell he was looking at her with his characteristic intensity.

"So you handled everything by yourself?"

"I had no other choice," she said. "I just coped, and sometimes not well. There were a lot of nights when I couldn't stand the pressure and would have done anything to get away from my mother. I cringe at some of the things I felt. She didn't choose to get sick, to suffer, to wilt in her own skin until she died. But I felt so . . . trapped. I didn't want to leave her because I was afraid something would happen, but I just wanted to get out of the house sometimes. I could have been better, I think. I could have—"

"You stayed," he countered. "That's what counts."

Callie released her breath in a sigh. "I wish I could do so much of it over again."

"I think you're too hard on yourself." Jack brushed his lips softly over hers. "And I don't know how your father could have stood by and done nothing."

"Frankly, it was easier than having him involved. Things could get really messy when he was around."

"What was he like?"

She looked up at the ceiling, figuring it was probably okay to let some anonymous details out. "He was . . . larger than life. Whenever I was around him, I always felt as if I were in the presence of greatness. He was a tall man, almost as tall as you, and I felt tiny around him. Insignificant."

"Were you close?"

"Not at all. He was confident, very sure of himself, until he tried to talk with me and then he became so awkward. I think he avoided me because he didn't like the way he felt when he was with me. Powerful people tend to be comfortable only when they are in control of themselves."

"That's a hell of a way for a father to act," Jack muttered. "What did he do for a living?"

Her eyes flashed to his and she began to think of ways to change the subject. "He was a businessman. But I don't know much about that side of his life."

"Was he gone a lot? Working?"

"I guess you could say that."

"What kind of business was he in?" When she didn't answer, Jack frowned. "You're leaving out a lot, aren't you?"

As she stayed silent, he stared at her for a long moment.

"Let's talk about something else," she suggested softly.

"Okay." She was relieved until he said, "So why don't you want to tell me about your father?"

Callie felt herself bristle. "I just don't want to talk about him, okay?"

"Don't you trust me?"

"What do you mean?"

"If you have to ask that, I think I know your answer." He rolled over onto his back.

"I'm just not interested in talking about the man."

He turned his head on the pillow. "But maybe I want to know."

Callie sat up and wrapped her arms around her knees. "What does it matter, anyway? The past is the past. He's dead and I've moved on from whatever problems I had with him. It's all a nonissue."

There was another long pause.

"Callie, I think we need to talk."

The tone in his voice was grim and she felt her skin shrink. "About what?"

"Us. The future."

She looked at him over her shoulder. He'd cradled his head in the palm of his good hand and his bare chest was only partially covered by the blankets.

"What do you have in mind?" she asked, hoping like hell she could bear his answer. He'd told her the night of the accident that he thought he loved her, but they hadn't talked about what was going to happen after she was done with the portrait.

"Have you ever thought of settling in Boston?" he asked. "You could work from here just as well as you could in New York."

Her slow smile returned. "True."

"And we could see each other. A hell of a lot."

She felt herself loosening up. "I'd like that, Jack. I really would."

He reached for her, pulling her down.

"Me, too," he said, against her mouth.

He kissed her once, but then stopped.

"About the election." He smoothed her hair back. "If

I decide to run, it's going to get rough. If you're going to be at my side, you need to be ready."

"To duck and cover if they pelt you with tomatoes?"

"Well, yes." He laughed softly. "But I was thinking more about the press. You should be prepared to get hit with some inquiries into your life."

Cold dread coursed through Callie, wiping out the rush of relief she'd felt a moment before.

"What do you mean?"

"The media, my opponents, they're going to crawl all over me. My past, our relationship, your background—everything's going to be examined closely."

She jerked upright, trying to imagine what would happen if anyone looked into her life. Her father's secret, the thing she had protected for so long, would be prime fodder for reporters if it was discovered. She could just imagine the coverage.

And there was Grace to consider. Callie had promised never to betray her, and even though she wouldn't be selling out her half sister on purpose, the end result would be the same. The whole world would know the details of their father's infidelity, and Grace would be the target of more tell-alls.

Jack sat up, having obviously caught the wave of her concern. "I'll take the brunt of it, of course, and Gray and I will take care of you."

She searched his face. "You said *if* you decide to run. Is there a chance you might not?"

He seemed taken aback. "Why don't you tell me what you're worried about?"

She thought about explaining everything to him and felt her throat close up. It was probably just as well that she keep quiet. The story wasn't hers alone to tell. Jack and Grace might have been friends, but exactly how close were they? After having made a promise never to speak of the past to anyone, she wasn't about to break her word.

"I just don't want the press in my life," she said. "That's all."

Jack frowned, his eyes growing shrewd. "What exactly do you have to hide?"

She looked away.

"Tell me, Callie."

"I can't."

There was a long, tense silence.

"Why not?"

When she remained quiet, he got out of bed and roughly pulled on his pants.

"Where are you going?" she asked.

"I don't know what happened in your past, but it's hard to imagine what you can't share with me."

"Jack, don't be like this." She reached out to him, but he brushed her hand away and yanked his shirt on. "Look, I don't know why this has to be a big deal. You haven't decided to run yet, right?"

He shot her a harsh look. "What I'm worried about right now is how little you trust me."

"But I do trust you."

"Then tell me."

When she remained quiet, he looked away.

"Christ," he muttered, stuffing his feet into his loafers. "I thought honesty was something I'd never have to worry about with you. I can't believe you're being like this."

How she was being? As if she'd asked to be born to a father who was horrified by her very existence?

A surge of defensive anger got her out of bed and she wrapped a blanket around her body.

"What's really going on here, Jack? Are you just concerned about us? Or are you worried about how my past might influence your success at the polls?"

He stopped moving. "I'm going to try and forget you said that."

She closed her eyes, immediately wishing she could take it back.

"I'm sorry."

"Yeah, so am I," he said, heading for the door.

"Jack, wait—"

"I don't really want to talk right now, if you don't mind."

After he'd left, Callie sat down on the bed and closed her eyes, feeling her heart pound.

Keeping her father a secret had been drilled into her for so long, she couldn't imagine talking to anyone about him. Even Jack.

God, how well she'd been trained. And how early.

She could remember being eleven years old and standing in Grand Central Station with her mother. As they'd waited for their train, Callie had looked over at a businessman who was getting his shoes shined. The man had had a paper up in front of his face, but she could tell he was someone like her father because he dressed in the same kind of clothes.

She'd been watching him, wondering what it felt like to have shoes cleaned while they were on your feet, when he'd flipped the paper around and she'd seen a picture of her father. Excited by the image, she'd hurried over and proudly started to explain to the man just whose daughter she was.

Her mother had pulled her back sharply, making excuses and smiling. "She thinks everyone in a tie is her father."

"No, I don't."

"Excuse us."

The man had nodded and gone back to reading but, as Callie was dragged off, he'd dropped the corner of his paper and had given them a measured stare. Her mother had caught the look and done her best to block his view, drawing Callie into a corner.

Her mother was obviously shaken. "You shouldn't do things like that. Remember how I told you that your father is a secret? A secret between the three of us?"

Of course Callie had remembered, but she was getting tired of keeping her mouth shut. No one else's father had to be kept hidden.

"I was just telling some stranger."

"But if you tell a secret, what happens?" her mother had prompted.

"You don't have to keep it anymore," she'd retorted, putting her fists on her hips.

"No. No— Callie, look at me. If you share a secret, what happens? You lose something special."

Callie had started shaking her head. She was tired of the lecture, tired of keeping the stupid secret. Besides, it wasn't like she was gaining much by being a good girl. Whether she followed her mother's rules or not, her father still didn't look her in the eye when he came to visit.

"Callie, I'm serious."

At that moment, she hadn't cared how stern her mother was getting. "So what! If I tell people about Daddy, I'm going to lose him? Who cares!"

Her mother had gripped her shoulders and put her face down so close that their noses had almost touched. "If you tell, we're both going to lose him."

Looking into her mother's pale face, Callie had felt the fight drain right out of her.

As she came back to the present, she heard the sound of Artie chasing groundhogs in his sleep. She glanced over the side of the bed, watching his paws twitch and hearing him yodel deep in his throat.

God, she wished she had a different story to tell. But she didn't.

And breaking through years of careful schooling was not something she could do easily. After a lifetime of guarding the secret, letting it out felt all wrong even though she reminded herself that it was Jack who wanted to know.

If she could tell anyone, surely it would be him.

And what about the election? The press? It wasn't a fait accompli that a reporter would find out what she was hiding. But considering what there was to lose, namely Grace's peace of mind and security, was she really willing to chance exposure?

Artie jerked and let out something that was close to a bark.

"Wake up," she murmured, reaching down and patting the dog. "Come on, now."

His eyes opened halfway and he seemed grateful as he looked up at her. Maybe the groundhogs had been coming after him this time.

Abruptly, she felt like she knew what being chased was like. She'd been trying to outrun her father's dubious legacy for some time now, but damn it, history was proving fast and tireless.

She stroked Artie's head until he fell asleep, and then she put a pillow against the headboard and leaned back. As she stared at the Caravaggio over the fireplace, she let the debate between her past and her present fill the dark, quiet hours.

19

THE NEXT morning, Callie put Artie on a leash and headed off at the crack of dawn for a walk. By the time they came back down Buona Fortuna's driveway, the dog was exhausted. Unlike her, he didn't have to work off anxiety and dismay, two great energizers along the lines of caffeine and rocket fuel.

They'd walked along the side of the road for miles, all the way into Weston, the next town over. She'd finally forced herself to turn back, because however keyed up she was, walking to the New Hampshire border wouldn't accomplish anything other than wearing out her running shoes. Besides, Artie was starting to droop.

When she approached the house, the garage doors were open and Mrs. Walker's Jaguar was gone, which meant Jack had left for the day. He'd taken to driving his mother's car because it was an automatic and he couldn't shift with his arm in a cast. Looking at the empty bay, she was disappointed that she'd missed an opportunity to try to apologize to him again.

After she let the dog into the kitchen, she said good morning to Thomas and went up to the garage. She'd just turned on the big light and settled in when she heard footsteps come up the stairs. She turned and was surprised to see Jack.

His eyes met hers, but he didn't smile.

"I'd thought you'd gone," she said, putting down the wooden stick she was about to wind with cotton.

"I'm working from home today." He walked across the room to a window, hands in the pockets of his jeans, a thick Irish sweater bringing out the darkness of his hair. Weak sunlight fell across his face as he scanned the sky.

"About last night," she began. "I really want to apologize. I was frustrated and angry—"

"And honest, maybe?" He looked at her over his shoulder.

"Jack—"

"I need to make something clear."

"Okay," she said, putting her hands on her knees and leaning forward to ease the tension in her shoulders.

"I told you I wanted more out of this relationship than sex and a little affection. I'm greedy by nature, so I won't settle for second best. I never do. I want all of you, Callie. Not just the pretty bits and pieces." He faced her. "I want to know about your past because it's part of you. Not because I'm worried about how it will affect me."

"I believe you."

"So talk to me."

She started to shake her head. "It's not that simple."

"You say you love me, but how can you if you don't trust me enough to share all the parts of your life with me? Are you worried something will change my opinion of you? Because nothing will. There isn't anything you could tell me that would make me pull back."

She glanced down at her hands and wondered whether she was really worried about that. Did she honestly think he would bolt just because she was a bastard? Of course not.

Jack's voice darkened. "I'll tell you what, though. This silence could drive me away."

Callie looked up, searching his face for the courage she knew she needed to find in herself. She took a deep breath.

This was Jack, she told herself. This was Jack. This was Jack. This was—

Feeling like she was leaping into a black hole, she blurted out, "My father and mother were never married."

His face changed instantly. It was as if he'd relaxed and become saddened for her at the same time.

"My father was married to another woman. He had a family, a whole life, outside of my mother and me, and we were the lesser of the two. He never acknowledged me in any formal way; his name's not even on my birth certificate."

Jack came over and she felt his strong hand on her shoulder. "I'm so sorry."

"I—I grew up knowing that we were always second best. That he loved my mother just enough to never let her go free." She leaned into him, resting her head on his hip. As she did, he made some sort of quiet noise, an encouragement to keep talking mixed with the regret he was obviously feeling. "I watched his burial from a stand of birches, fifty yards away from the gravesite. I only knew about the ceremony at all because I followed my half sister without her knowing it."

He brushed her hair back.

"I . . . This is hard to talk about for me because I've never told anyone before. I was taught to keep quiet. It was the only way he would stay in our lives." She tried to smile but couldn't pull it off. "Old habits and all that."

"I'm glad you told me."

Wrapping her arms around his waist, she murmured, "So am I."

Jack's hand rubbed her back in circles.

She tilted her head so she could look up into his eyes. "I don't know what I thought would happen if I actually told someone. If I told you. It's not like my head exploded or anything. I suppose I thought it might." She tried to laugh a little, but the sadness she felt came out raggedly instead. "It was hard growing up. Other girls talked about their fathers with such . . . ownership. *My* father did this. *My* father did that. I had *a* father. After a long time of hoping he'd come around and be who I wanted him to be, I realized I was never going to make the possessive pronoun fit. Talking about him as *my* father was like claiming something that wasn't there."

Jack took her hand and urged her out of the chair. "Come over here. I want to hold you for a while."

Which was what she wanted, too.

They settled on the couch, and he pulled her onto his lap. "You know your father's bad judgment was not your fault, right?"

"I know."

"You deserved a hell of a lot better."

She hadn't really thought about that much. Growing up, she'd been too busy trying to please. As an adult, she'd been preoccupied with trying to forget.

"So am I forgiven?" she said against his shoulder.

"Absolutely."

"Because I don't want to lose you."

"I'm not going anywhere." His hand stroked the back of her neck.

"I really wanted to tell you, but—"

He silenced her with a soft kiss. "Don't worry. I understand completely. And when it comes to the election, I don't want you to be concerned. This is not going to be a problem."

She pulled away. "Excuse me?"

"The press would only care if your father was someone already in the public eye. We can easily protect you and argue there's nothing newsworthy in your past."

"I can't possibly be hearing you right," she muttered in disbelief.

"Callie, I'm not downplaying the effect this had on you," he said. "Not at all."

She started shaking her head. They were back to square one. "You don't get it. I still don't want to answer anyone's questions, especially not a journalist's."

"But you don't have to worry. It's going to be okay. Nothing is going to get out in the media."

Callie gripped his shoulders. "Yes, it will."

Jack's eyes narrowed. "Who exactly was your father?"

She dropped her hands. She couldn't go that far. Even with Jack. "Isn't it enough to know what happened?"

"Clearly not. Who was he, Callie?"

She broke free and walked across the room.

"You're shutting me out again," he said darkly.

"Stop pushing me, okay?"

"Callie," his voice was sharp, "if I'm pressuring you, it's because I only have half the story. You're leaving out the most important part."

She wheeled around. "I would have hoped the most important part was me."

"I didn't mean it like that."

"But you do, Jack. You truly do. You're trying to force me to fit into your plans."

"Because I want you in my life," he said, throwing up his hands.

"On your terms."

"Don't hit me with that, Callie. I'm trying to make this work and you're putting up an obstacle. Something that seems fairly arbitrary to me, I might add, unless you're willing to tell me the whole story."

"Can't you just trust me?" she whispered.

He put his hand on his chest. "How about you trusting me?"

She looked away.

He let out a curse. "So what are you telling me? If I run for governor, you're out of here?"

She closed her eyes, thinking, Oh, God, was that where they were headed?

"I don't know, Jack. I just don't know."

When she didn't see him for the rest of the day, and he didn't come by her room that night, she figured he was cooling off and giving her an opportunity to do the same. But after a couple of days passed with no more than cursory meetings in the kitchen, or hallway, she knew Jack was avoiding her.

She put down the wooden stick and cotton bud she was working with and checked her watch again. It was late, very late, and Jack still wasn't back from the office. He'd taken to coming home well into the night and he disappeared into his study as soon as he walked in the back door, even if it was nine or ten o'clock. She kept hoping he'd come to her room, but every morning she woke up having spent the night alone.

The night before, she'd cracked. She'd sat in the kitchen, halfheartedly doing a crossword puzzle and prepared to wait until dawn. When he'd finally come through the door, she'd followed him down the hall, trying to get him to talk about something, anything. He'd been silent, but at least he'd made eye contact with her as he'd poured himself a bourbon.

She'd been on the verge of steering the subject to them when he'd sat down and started flipping through the piles of documents that had sprung up all over his desk. When she'd asked what he was doing, he'd given her a curt answer, something about that blood company deal he'd been working on.

She'd lingered in the doorway, willing him to look up at her again, but he'd been lost in his papers. Going by the furrow in his forehead and his single-minded focus, he'd clearly not been prepared to be interrupted by anything. Or anyone.

When she'd finally turned away, after he'd seemed to have forgotten she was there, she'd been on the verge of tearing up.

Callie closed up her jar of solvent and shut off the light, knowing that she was looking at another dinner alone. Another night spent tossing and turning in an empty bed. Another dawn that held the promise of a day she could only hope to limp through.

She couldn't go on like this. Tonight, she wasn't going to play it soft. She was going to demand they talk. She might have had trouble opening up to him, but he was shutting her out completely.

She went back to the house and was fixing herself something to eat in the kitchen when the back door was thrown open and a tall man walked inside.

It was Jack. She squinted. Well, not really. The long hair and the roughed-up leather jacket were nothing like the man she loved, but pretty much everything else was.

"Hello there," he said, in a low, appreciative tone. "Who are you?"

She looked out the windows behind him, at an old Saab that was parked cockeyed between the coach lights in the driveway.

"I'm Callie. You must be—"

"Nate." He stuck his hand out. "Jack's brother. Is he around?"

As they shook hands, she thought there was something instantaneously likable about him. Maybe it was the rakish grin. Or the fact that she was looking into a pair of familiar hazel eyes without seeing cold reserve in them.

"He should be home any minute."

"Working his tailbone off as usual. I've got to get that boy loosened up." Nate cocked his head and regarded her seriously. "Are you his . . ."

The question dangled between them and she forced a smile, trying to keep her emotions in check. "Well, that all depends on the noun you were going to finish up with. Employee fits. I'm working on a portrait."

"That's right, the Copley."

She nodded and he smiled.

"And how long have you been with my brother?" Nate cut off her stammering with a shake of his head. "Don't bother with the denials. You're wearing one of his shirts under that sweater. I can tell by the monogram on the cuff."

She looked down and knew she'd been caught. She'd put the shirt on that morning, figuring no one would notice if she covered it up. Jack had left it in her room the other night, before things had gone badly, and she'd put it on because it was the closest she could seem to get to him.

"No offense," Nate said, "but you don't seem like Jack's type. Which is a really good thing."

She was shaking her head and smiling when Mrs. Walker's Jaguar pulled into the garage. She tensed up, and tried to feign nonchalance as Jack came striding toward the house. As he walked inside, she thought he looked exhausted, but he grinned as soon as he saw his brother.

The men embraced, clapping each other on the back. Jack spared her a nod and then focused on his brother.

"It's good to have you home, Nate."

"Happy to be here. You've clearly gotten into some trouble." He nodded at the cast.

"Ah, hell, it doesn't hurt much anymore. And it makes an excellent weapon. I threatened a securities and exchange lawyer with it today. You eat yet?"

"Two hot dogs and a bag of licorice since Rhode Island."

Jack rolled his eyes. "And I thought you were a gourmand."

"Got to keep my nitrate level up and Twizzlers are an acceptable substitute for sorbet if you have to clean your palate on the road. Is Thomas here?"

When Jack nodded toward the ceiling, Nate shouted upstairs, "Hey, where's the cook in this place?"

As Thomas bolted down the back way, Callie met Jack's eyes.

She was determined to make him talk tonight. She'd had it with the silence.

With Nate and Thomas catching up in the kitchen while Callie ate, Jack changed into a pair of running shorts and a ratty T-shirt and headed down to the basement. He'd installed a gym there ten years ago, when his schedule had started getting really hectic. He worked out on a regular basis at dawn and sometimes again at night, especially when he had a lot on his mind.

And he sure as hell did now. Things were going south in his personal and his professional lives, and the raging storm of disasters was making him feel like he'd lost control of things.

Which was not something he tolerated well under the best of circumstances.

Of the host of problems he had, his estrangement from Callie bothered him most. He hadn't expected her to have something to hide or for there to be problems between them if he ran for governor. He'd figured the hardest part was over. He loved her, she loved him, and even if he was still gun-shy on marriage, he was making future plans with her in mind.

Instead, everything was a fucking mess. He wanted to talk to her, but his emotions were about as level as his temper. One minute he was mad enough to walk out on the relationship; the next he was having trouble not begging at her door just to hold her. He knew the former wasn't something he really wanted to do. It was out of frustration and . . .

God, *hurt* was the word. The fact that she didn't trust him enough to take care of her, to guard her secret, stung like hell.

Looking into the future, he had to assume things were over between them if he ran for office. Other than keeping *her* a secret, which was not only disrespectful but also impractical, there seemed to be no other alternative. God knew he'd been searching for days for some sort of solution.

Going over to the treadmill, he fired the thing up to a rubber-burning pace and pounded himself into the ground. Forty-five minutes and six miles later, he was covered with sweat, his thighs were on fire, and his shoulder was screaming from having to support the weight of the cast. He juiced up the machine a little more and did his last mile at breakneck speed.

When he stepped off, he sucked back half a liter of water and sat down on a bench. Leaning his head against the wall, he felt the sweat dripping off him and hoped his physical exhaustion would give him some clarity.

Clear thinking had been elusive for him lately. Courtesy of all his emotions about Callie and their situation, he was looking at a lot of things in really weird ways. It was as if he couldn't turn his feelings off anymore about anything, so the unfettered objectivity he was known for was difficult to get ahold of.

At an earlier stage in his life, he would have been convinced he was losing his edge.

Hell, for the first time in his professional life, he was torn as to the appropriate course of action in a deal when all the financial indicators were clear. It was that damn blood processing company. The technology the McKay brothers had patented could truly improve the delivery of blood products around the globe, helping thousands and thousands, maybe millions of people. But the two inventors had seriously diluted the company by having given shares of it away to what sounded like every conceivable member of their family.

The McKays needed a big influx of cash if they were going to succeed, but if Jack put his money into the company with all of those people holding an interest, he might as well bury the stuff in the yard for all the return he was going to get on the investment. There were just too many fingers in the same pie.

He knew no other venture capitalist was going to touch them for the same reason, but nonprofit grant support and government funding could take them only so far. To succeed, the brothers needed the kind of money only a Walker Fund could provide.

As recently as six months ago, the solution would have been totally obvious to him. A no-brainer. Hands down he'd have passed on the deal and found something that would make him the kind of returns he demanded.

Now? He was torn.

Hell, maybe it wasn't just Callie who was getting him to think differently. His general counsel's daughter had taken a turn for the worse. The little girl was receiving hospice care at home now and Jack had taken to occasionally stopping by the house on his way back to Buona Fortuna at night.

Between watching that family mourn, dealing with the dilemma with the blood brothers, and trying to decide if he would run for governor even if it was going to kill his relationship with Callie, Jack felt like he was about to explode.

Damn it, he was back to grinding his teeth at night. One of his molars had started to ache and he recognized the sign. Two years ago, when he'd gone to war over a bioengineering firm and almost lost his shirt, he'd chewed up his teeth so badly he'd had to get two caps put in back on the left side.

Jack opened his mouth and prodded the tooth, feeling it answer the inquiry with a shot of pain into his jaw.

Christ. The last thing he needed was a trip to the dentist.

"Hey, brother," Nate said, ducking to get under the low clearance of the door. "How're you doing?"

Jack wiped his face off with the bottom of his shirt, shrugged, and lied.

"Well enough. And yourself?" he asked. "To what do we owe this visit? Did Thomas call you in as reinforcement for the party?"

"Thomas called me, all right." Nate sat down next to him on the bench. "But it was about you."

Jack frowned. "Oh, really."

"He's a little worried."

"About?" Jack took a long slug of water, feeling a strong urge to walk out of the room.

"He says you've been working yourself to the bone."

Jack lowered the bottle. "Like that's a big news flash?"

Nate shrugged casually, but was obviously choosing his words. "He said you ended your engagement. Got into a car accident. Haven't slept in your room in nights because you're at your desk until dawn. What's going on?"

Jack stared over at the treadmill, wondering if he could squeeze another couple of miles out of his legs.

"Talk to me, Jack. Or I'm going to have to go big brother all over your ass and get it out of you myself."

Jack finally looked across the bench. "I'm in love."

Nate smiled slowly. "Really. With the redhead?"

He nodded.

"Very nice, brother."

Jack stretched and tossed the empty water bottle across the room. It bounced on the rim of the trash bin and for a moment he thought it was going to go in. When it rolled off and hit the floor, he watched the drops shimmer inside the plastic.

"I don't know if things are going to work out. We've hit an impasse." He cleared his throat. "I want her. But I might have to change the entire course of my life to keep her."

"That's a bitch."

"It sure is."

Jack got off the bench and went over to the bottle. He flipped it into the trash and faced his brother.

"I want to run for governor."

"So I've heard. I think you'd be damned good at it, by the way."

"Me, too." He dragged a hand through his hair, feeling the sweat. "When I first thought about it, years ago, it was mostly to get in a good dig at Dad. I figured that would really piss him off. My ambitions running out of control and all that. When I told him, though, he was actually delighted."

"And you didn't lose interest?"

"Not at all. That's how I knew I really wanted it. I've planned to run for years. Built up a base of support. Pressed a lot of palms. I want this."

"But she doesn't want to be the wife of a public servant?"

"We haven't gotten that far. She doesn't want to go through the election. Which is going to get rough." Jack went over to the bench and picked up the sling, which he had to take off before he could run. He put the thing back around his neck. As he slid the cast inside, he said, "You ever been with someone that makes you feel—hell, makes you believe there might be a God up there after all?"

"No."

"Yeah, well, neither had I. Before her. Letting her go feels all wrong."

"So it sounds like you've made up your mind."

Good God, had he?

He thought about it for a minute and realized, yes, he had.

For Callie, he would give up everything. Even the goddamn governor's mansion. To have true love with her, he would give up his dream.

So he could live another.

Jack's breath left him in a rush as the solution became clear, at least on his side.

He would absolutely give up his political aspirations for her. No question. But that was only half of it. If he was going to make that kind of compromise, she was going to have to be completely truthful with him. He would need to know everything.

He focused on his brother. "Thanks, Nate. This has been really helpful."

Nate looked a little confused, but then slapped his hands on his knees and got up. "Always glad to help. Even when it's just listening."

They started for the door.

"So how long are you here for?" Jack asked.

"Thought I'd hang around for the party and then go up to Montreal to see Spike and Louie."

Jack killed the lights and they headed upstairs. "How are those two nut jobs?"

"Still out of control. So naturally I'm thinking of going into business with them. We might buy a restaurant together."

"The rolling stone is thinking of settling down?"

"Not at all. I'm just buying a joint, brother." Nate shrugged. "Anyway, I've saved some money."

"You have?"

"Don't sound so surprised. It's not your kind of money, but it's enough to get us started."

Jack stopped as they emerged into the hall. "Look,

if you find something, just let me know. I'll be happy to give you—"

"Don't even go there. You have enough dependents and I don't want to be a charity case."

Jack paused, thinking back to Callie saying those very same words to him at the Plaza. It felt like a lifetime ago.

"Well, keep me in mind if you want a loan."

"Will do, brother." Nate grinned. "But don't hold your breath."

Callie opened the door to her bedroom and looked out into the hall. The only sound she could hear was Artie smacking his chops after a yawn and rearranging himself on her bedroom floor.

She quickly crossed the hallway and knocked on Jack's door. There was no answer.

"Looking for him?"

She wheeled around. Nate was coming down the hall, a book in his hand, a grin on his face.

"Ah—yes."

"He's down in his study." The man paused and whispered, "Don't worry. I'm discreet as hell. Oh, and avoid the third stair from the bottom. It creaks like a bitch if you hit it wrong."

He shot her a wink and sauntered down to his bedroom.

Moving quickly, Callie made her way downstairs, judiciously avoiding the stair Nate had warned her about.

When she got to Jack's study, the door was open. He was sitting in a pool of light, facing the window behind his desk. His hand was on the phone as if he'd just hung it up.

His head moved, as if he'd seen her reflection in the panes. When silence stretched out between them, she said, "We need to talk."

"Now?" His voice was so low, it almost didn't carry.

She cleared her throat. "Yes."

There was a long pause and then he said, "Okay."

Callie frowned as she realized something was very wrong with him.

"Jack? What's going on?"

He slowly turned the chair around and faced her. His face was frozen, his mouth set in a grim line.

"She died this afternoon."

Who? Callie wondered.

Oh, no, the little girl.

"Oh, Jack . . ."

His voice was utterly devoid of emotion, as if he was holding himself together with that iron will he was known for. "The funeral is going to be tomorrow afternoon, in the Jewish tradition. I'm going to go, of course. I've decided to close the office. Everyone is going to go. And then her family will be sitting shiva for the next week."

Wordlessly, she went around the desk, hoping he would let her take him into her arms. When he leaned into her, she could feel him shudder.

He took a deep breath. "I've been sitting with her and her family at night. That's why I've been getting home so late. They had this fantastic nurse from hospice. The care was amazing." She could feel his chest rise again. "I'm going to set up an endowment at the hospice center in her name. It will be—" He cleared his throat. "It's going to be the first charitable donation I've ever made."

Callie held him tightly, wishing there was more she could do. When he finally lifted his head, he looked up at her.

"I know there are things left unsaid, things we need to talk about. But stay with me tonight?" he asked.

When she nodded, he took her hand and rose from the chair.

20

EARLY THE next morning, Callie sat on her stool, grabbed one of the solvent jars, and cracked it open. After adjusting her breathing mask, she dipped a cotton bud into the isopropanol and carefully brushed the solution over the surface of the painting. She was all the way into the center of the portrait now, right at the edge of the mirror, having logged countless hours while she and Jack were at odds. There was not much left of the cleaning to do.

She glanced up. Outside, the sun was bright in a clear New England sky.

She couldn't stop thinking about the night before. They'd made love and Jack had held her long afterward. They hadn't talked very much, but it had been enough just to be with him, to close the distance between them even if it was only physically. And she'd been relieved that he'd allowed her to be with him at a vulnerable time and that she'd had the opportunity to console him.

In the morning, as he'd left her room, he'd promised her they would talk tonight.

She was hoping that he was going to tell her he wasn't going to run in the election and that they could go back to the way things had been. In her heart, she knew that both were unlikely and she tried, once more, to reconsider the ramifications if he did get into the race.

The outcome wasn't any better than it had been all

the other times she'd thought about the situation. He was right; if her father had been a private citizen, the papers would have no real cause to follow the story. Unfortunately, Cornelius Woodward Hall's infidelity was going to be huge news.

If Jack ran, she had to back out of his life. That was the only way to keep the past from coming to light. But the idea that she wouldn't end up in Boston, by his side, was intolerable. Whenever she pictured herself going back to New York and never being with him again, her heart just about shattered.

Callie took a deep breath, looked back down at the painting, and shot up in a panic, knocking her chair over. She barely heard the slamming noise of the thing hitting the floor or Artie's terrified yelp and scatter.

"Oh, no, no, no . . ."

She threw the swab down and grabbed a rag, though it wasn't like she could do anything with the damn thing.

Suspended with horror over the painting, she stared in disbelief at what she'd done. She'd burned a hole right through the varnish and into the paint layer. She bent down farther, hoping that closer proximity would reveal it was just superficial damage. It wasn't. Across the face of the mirror, in a swath about an inch square, Copley's original paint had been eaten up.

Callie cursed as she quickly looked at the jar she'd opened. By mistake, she'd picked out the strongest solvent she'd brought with her and had compounded the error by leaving the damn stuff on as she'd stared out the window. The chemical had had plenty of time to seep in, infecting a larger area than just the part she'd applied it to as it spread outward.

A hot flash ran through her body, bringing sweat to her palms and her underarms and her forehead.

She'd marred a great work of art. She'd never work again. Jack was going to kill her.

And all because she'd let herself get distracted.

Of all the stupid, neophyte—

But now was not the time to beat herself up. God

knew, there would be plenty of opportunities for that as she waited in line to collect unemployment.

She needed to focus. Focus and assess the situation and the remedies. Then she would call Gerard Beauvais.

She hovered above the painting, her eyes moving desperately around from the damaged area to all the work she'd done so well.

Screw it. She needed to call Beauvais now.

Callie reached into her tool kit for his card and dialed the number on the back, praying her voice would work if he answered. And God help her if she burst into tears. Looking weak as well as incompetent would just about put the finishing touch on a total nightmare.

She got his voice mail and left him a message to call her as soon as he could.

After a couple of deep breaths, and with a resolve not to keep picturing herself careerless and tossing pizzas for a living, she bent over the painting again. The solvent's appetite hadn't waned. The damaged part was getting bigger.

It was like watching an evil tide.

Yeah, and that path of destruction was wiping out her professional future as well as all that paint, she thought.

She propped her head on her hands and told herself that Beauvais's shop could do a repaint on the mirror, just as he'd done for the Fra Filippo Lippi. They'd match the paint tones and brushstrokes with as much precision as possible so that it would be virtually impossible to tell that anything had gone wrong.

Which was a cold comfort, she thought. Even if the damage was hidden masterfully, she had still irrevocably diminished the value of the painting.

Abruptly, Callie frowned. Blinking her eyes a few times, she told herself she was seeing things.

It couldn't be.

She bent down so low she felt the heat of the chemical reaction and her eyes burned.

From out of the mess, a shape was emerging. Underneath the blistered and melting layers of paint, she could see the outline of . . . a face.

She rubbed her eyes.

No, there was definitely a pattern coming through. Behind the pale creams of the mirror's surface, it looked like . . . the shape of a face.

Her heart started to pound for an altogether different reason than career suicide.

When the phone rang next to her, she grabbed it, hoping to pick up before anyone else did at the house.

Gerard Beauvais's cultured tones were the sweetest sounds she could imagine hearing.

"Oh, God, I screwed up," she began, her words running together, just like the melted paint. "I was working over the mirror and I used the wrong strength solvent and I melted part of the paint layer—"

"Okay, okay, *cherie*. Slow down."

Somehow Beauvais's calm voice reached her inner ear and she forced herself to stop jabbering.

"Now," he said, when she had herself under better control, "tell me exactly what happened from start to finish. And what the chemical composition of your solvent is."

After she was finished, her throat was tight as she waited for his response.

"I must know," he said quietly. "What was underneath? In the mirror."

"A dark figure, actually." Her voice dropped to a whisper. "In the shape of a head, I think."

Beauvais laughed tensely. "Well, perhaps your mistake is fortuitous. Did the paint layer there react differently to the solvent than the other parts of the portrait?"

"Well, I didn't burn any of the rest of it off, thank God, so it's hard to say. But no, I don't think it did. It came up easily but that could be explained by the increased strength of the solution."

Beauvais was silent for a moment. "I must see it for

myself. But do not move the painting. I will come to you tomorrow. I have family here now and cannot leave. In the meantime, say nothing to Jack or his mother. I don't think you should go to them until we know what our plan to remedy the situation is. There is no reason to upset them, if it can be avoided."

Callie's breath came out in a shudder. "God, I feel awful. Jack's going to fire me. I'm never—"

Beauvais laughed easily. "Jack is not going to fire you. And you are going to work again, trust me. The conservation science is administered by human hands and we make mistakes. There is nothing we cannot fix together, but let us not be foolish. I will call on you tomorrow and we will decide what to do."

"How am I ever going to thank you?"

"That, my dear, is simple."

She laughed with a choked sound, finding it hard to imagine she could offer him much of anything.

"You, Callie Burke, are going to do the same thing for someone else when you are well along in your career and a younger colleague has a problem. Twenty-five years ago, I was working on a Titian when I managed to spill raw turpentine in one corner." When he heard her gasp, he laughed merrily. "It was awful. After I retired to *la salle de bains* wherein I revisited my lunch in a most unpleasant way, I came back, told my mentor what I had done, and the two of us took care of it. The painting is hanging in the Uffizi to this day, and every time I go for a visit, I make sure I take a hard look at that canvas. I can still see the strip we had to repaint. Few others can, of course, but it always reminds me of my folly. I will say this. Egos are far more damaging in our line of work than mistakes. So when someone calls on you years from now, remember this experience and do the right thing. Help. Do not judge."

"I feel so ashamed," she whispered. "That I have to come to you like this."

"And that is good. What your regrets will do to you will be far worse than the harsh words of someone else.

We all go through this, *cherie*. Just make sure it is only once."

When Callie hung up the phone, she wiped her eyes with her palms and looked down at Artie, who'd come over to offer his condolences. He gave her a little wag as he put his head on her thigh.

Her sense of failure warred with her relief that Beauvais was willing to help, and it was a while before she could go back to the house and face anyone. Not saying anything to Jack made her feel uneasy, but she trusted Beauvais implicitly and she knew the man was right. It would be far easier to present the problem to an owner if the solution were offered as well.

As soon as she opened the back door, she was enveloped in a wall of cooking smells. It was like being hugged.

"You call that dough?" Thomas was saying to Nate while gesturing with a wooden spoon. "It looks like something you'd put wallpaper up with."

Nate cracked a smile as he kept kneading on the counter. "Why don't you give those onions a stir, old man. Before they have to be taken out of the pan with a jackhammer."

"Hey, Callie!" Thomas grinned. "Welcome to my nightmare. Two cooks, one kitchen."

As gratitude for some uncomplicated friendship washed her eyes with tears, she knew she was in a vulnerable place. If she was smart, she'd go up to her room and stay there. Now was not a real good time for her to be around other people. Particularly nice ones.

When the front door knocker sounded, she volunteered to answer it and nearly let out a cry of joy when Grace and her bodyguard were on the other side.

She embraced her half sister. "I am so glad to see you."

The hug she got back was just as strong as the one she gave.

When they pulled apart, Grace motioned to the imposing man behind her. "You remember Ross?"

Callie smiled as she felt her hand taken in a firm grip.

"It's good to see you again," she said, looking up into his stark face. The smile he gave her made him look almost approachable, in spite of his black leather jacket and his hooded eyes.

She motioned the pair inside. "Come on in. It's cold out there."

Ross bent down and picked up a couple of leather bags like they were weightless.

"Where's Jack?" Grace asked, taking off her coat.

"He's still out, I think. But Nate's here."

"You're kidding me."

As Callie shook her head, the man in question came around the corner while wiping his hands on a dish towel. "Gracie!"

Grace let out a laugh and went to him. As they embraced, she said, "It's good to see you, stranger."

"You, too. Who's this?" Nate looked over at the other man.

"This is my fiancé, Ross Smith."

Callie gasped. "Congratulations!"

"Thank you. It just happened last night. We couldn't be more thrilled."

When Grace and Ross were seated in the kitchen, having a drink while Thomas and Nate cooked, Callie found the shouts of laughter and private jokes a little hard to bear.

Making a quick excuse, she slipped upstairs to her room, promising to return when the meal was on the table.

Jack parked his mother's Jaguar in its bay, turned off the ignition, and stared at the back wall of the garage. He was suddenly exhausted, but didn't want to close his eyes because he'd only replay scenes from the synagogue and the graveyard. He couldn't get the image of that small coffin out of his mind, no matter what practicalities he tried to distract himself with.

When he finally walked over to the house, he saw

Grace and his brother through the windows, laughing while one poured dressing on a salad and the other tossed. Standing in the pitch dark, looking at two of the people he loved most in the world, he was grateful to be home. Grateful that his loved ones had not suffered as the family of that little girl had. As she herself had.

He opened the door and frowned when he didn't see Callie.

"There he is!" Grace exclaimed, rushing to him. She pulled up short when she got a load of the cast. "I heard all about your accident. I'm glad you're okay."

"And all the better for seeing you."

He gave her a quick hug and a kiss, but when he pulled back, she held on to his good arm.

"Hey, how are you really doing?" she whispered as she gave him a shrewd stare. "I also heard about you and Blair. I'm sorry."

"Thanks." Jack smiled and nodded across to the big, silent man in the corner. "John Smith, right?"

"My fiancé's name is Ross," Grace interjected.

Jack cocked an eyebrow at the name change and the announcement.

"Well, congratulations," he said, meaning it. As he shook hands with his friend's fiancé, he approved of the way Smith put his arm around Grace and brought her close to him.

"Hey, brother, go get Callie, will you?" Nate said from the stove. "We're ten minutes out. She went upstairs."

Jack put down his briefcase and went up to her bedroom. When he knocked on the door, she answered softly.

When he walked in, he saw her sitting on the big bed, a pillow in her lap. She smiled. "I was hoping it was you."

He closed the door just as a wave of laughter drifted upstairs. "I don't blame you for wanting some quiet. It's pretty rowdy down there."

He sat beside her and the feel of her hand covering his was like a balm.

"How did today go?" she asked.

"The service was beautiful and incredibly sad. Afterward I went to the hospice center and gave them a check."

"They must have been very grateful."

"Yes, they were." He put her hand on his thigh and began to smooth the skin of her palm.

She opened her mouth to speak, but he cut her off.

"I've been talking to Gray." He could feel the tension come into her fingers. "It's time for me to declare what my plans are for the election."

"What are you going to do?" she asked.

He looked into her eyes, as if that would help her understand what he had to say.

"You know, walking through the hospice facility today, I remembered exactly why I want to run." He shook his head. "I'm not saying I had some mystical experience. Actually, it was all very practical. I ended up in the executive director's office poring over P and L spreadsheets. In the process of going through their numbers, I could see where they could improve their operations so they would have more cash. I *knew* what needed to be changed. I understood how I could help."

She listened to him with quiet intensity, but there was heartbreak in her eyes.

"My vision for this state is starting to take shape, Callie. My head's been spinning with ways to balance spending and drive revenue. I know where things need to be done differently. I won't be able to accomplish everything I want to. I won't be able to fund every program or save every center or shelter. But I can sure as hell try to help some of them. And I *want* to try. This is important to me." Her eyes went down to their hands and he intertwined his fingers with hers. "I want to put my hat in the ring because that's the only way to get where I want to go. So I can make a difference."

"I'm happy for you," she said, though she looked dejected. "I truly am."

"And I talked to Gray about your situation."

"You told him everything?" she asked, clearly horrified.

"I had to get his perspective."

"But what I said to you was private. Between you and me." She brushed her hair back from her face impatiently. Nervously, he thought.

"He won't say anything."

"That's not the point. I never expected you to tell him. Or anybody else."

Jack frowned, feeling frustrated.

"Who are you protecting?" When she didn't answer him, he squeezed her hand. "Who? Tell me."

"The only family I have left," she said urgently. "And I'm not at all comfortable with having private conversations broadcast to everyone else on the planet."

"Gray is hardly a stranger."

"Maybe to you, he's not."

Jack steadied himself, trying to get past her defensiveness. He chose his words carefully. "I also told Gray that I might not run."

Shock widened her eyes. "You did?"

He nodded slowly. "Even though I want to be governor, I would walk away from the election in an instant. For you."

Callie hesitated, as if she couldn't believe it was true, and then threw her arms around him. "Oh, Jack—"

He held her back.

"I would give up anything for you, even a shot at leading this state. But I'm not going to do it unless I know the whole truth. I'm not going to turn away from this thing I've spent years preparing for unless you can be real with me. A relationship with only part of you is not worth the sacrifice to me."

She closed her eyes and dropped her hands. "I understand. I totally understand. I just need some time, a little time. I need to ... talk with someone."

"My exploratory committee is meeting in secret at my offices this weekend. I want to be able to commit to them one way or the other on Saturday afternoon." Jack stood up, not encouraged by the fact she wasn't meeting his eyes. "Talk to whoever you want to and let me know what you decide. But I have to say this. If you can't trust me, I can't be with you. No matter how much I love you."

She nodded without lifting her head.

He paused. "Nate wanted you to know that dinner's ready. Do you want to come down?"

"Tell them I was asleep."

When he closed the door behind him, he felt hollow and spent.

Not wanting to deal with anyone, he changed into running shorts, made his excuses to the people in the kitchen, and hit the gym.

21

THE NEXT day, the prospect of Gerard Beauvais's arrival was all that got Callie motivated to go up to the garage. As she looked at Jack's ancestor, assessing and reassessing the mess she'd made, she was convinced nothing in her life was ever going to be right again.

And she was not looking forward to talking with Grace.

But it seemed like the only choice she had. Grace had a right to know what was happening with Jack and what he wanted to know.

Callie would have preferred getting the conversation over with as soon as possible. But when she'd gone down to the kitchen that morning, intent on getting her half sister alone, she'd learned that Grace and Ross were gone for the day on a tour of private Early American art collections. With the party tonight, Callie was going to have to catch Grace the moment she returned.

To pass the time before Beauvais arrived, Callie decided to sort through the final box of documents, but she found herself walking from window to window, as if one of them might, against all odds, show her a view that gave her some peace of mind.

At nine o'clock sharp, Beauvais walked up the stairs.

"Thank God," she breathed.

They barely exchanged pleasantries before leaning over the painting and discussing various options. Finally,

Gerard took off his reading glasses, sucked on one of the earpieces, and regarded her with his bright little eyes.

"It has to come off. The top layer of paint at the mirror must be totally removed."

Callie sat in her chair. She wasn't surprised by the conclusion but it hit her like a ton of bricks anyway. "Okay."

"At least we will find out what is under there." Beauvais smiled. "Which is something I have wanted to know for quite a while."

"You saw the imperfection in the mirror's surface when you examined it for the Blankenbakers, didn't you?"

He nodded. "I advised them that the portrait should be cleaned and they promised to follow through. Alas, they did not."

Callie looked down at the Copley. "I have to tell Jack."

"Tell me about what?"

She looked across the studio in surprise. Jack's expression was cool as he approached them. He was dressed in a suit, the sleeve of the jacket hanging loosely on the side of his cast.

"So that's your car, Gerard," he said. "I was wondering why there was a silver Audi in my driveway. How are you?"

The men shook hands.

"What brings you to Wellesley?" The question was more pointed than polite.

Callie looked at Beauvais, who inclined his head toward her ever so slightly.

"I've made a mistake," she blurted.

Jack's eyes narrowed on her and then moved to the painting. "What kind of mistake?"

She told him quickly and pointed out the area on the portrait. Jack's expression gave nothing away as he studied the damage.

"And what are you proposing to do now?"

"We've decided that removing the top layer of paint

is the best course of action. We will make a further assessment once that is done, but a repaint is probably in order."

"How does this affect the value of the portrait?" Jack directed the question to Beauvais and the man tilted his head at an angle, now working the earpiece of his glasses with his teeth.

"It depends on what is revealed." When Jack frowned, the conservationist went on to explain, "There is an image under the paint that is rather curious."

Jack bent down closer to the canvas. "That dark shape might be something?"

"Indeed."

"And if it isn't?" he demanded.

Beauvais cleared his throat. "After restoration, I don't believe there will be any serious decrease in worth. It is such an important painting, the loss will be relatively small compared to its overall value."

"How small?"

"I would say one hundred to two hundred thousand dollars."

Callie felt the floor underneath her feet heave. If Jack came after her for restitution, that would wipe out the nest egg she'd planned on socking away after the project was done. Most conservationists were insured, but she hadn't bothered with the precaution. Couldn't have afforded it until Jack paid her, anyway.

"How much time will it take until you know what's under there?" Jack asked her.

"A couple of hours."

"I'll be back then. And thank you for coming by," Jack said, extending his hand to Beauvais. "Callie, we'll talk."

It was only in the wake of his departure that she realized he'd hardly looked at her at all. Caught up in her thoughts, she was surprised when Beauvais took off his tweed jacket.

"Shall we begin?" he said cheerfully, eyeing her tools and supplies.

*   *   *

Beauvais left four hours later. He'd volunteered to stick around until Jack came back to look at the painting, but she'd declined his offer. It was her project and she needed to be the one who talked with the owner about the future of the portrait.

Callie stared down at the work she'd done with Beauvais. What had been revealed was extraordinary.

In the flat plane of the mirror, there was a miniature portrait of a dark-haired woman. Both she and Beauvais had agreed that the depiction was undoubtedly Copley's work. First of all, the brushwork was obviously in the master's style. And secondly, following the stripping process, it became clear that the lower paint layer was made of precisely the same kind of elements as the rest of the portrait's oils.

What was likewise interesting was that the paint that had bubbled up and been removed appeared under the microscope to also be of the same composition and age as everything else. The appropriate inference to be made, therefore, was that Copley had painted the image and someone, probably him, had covered it up relatively contemporaneously.

Beauvais had been delighted by the discovery. Tickled pink, as he'd put it.

Callie was enthralled because she knew about the letters and was tempted to find a connection between the mystery woman and the love affair that had been hinted at in the old pieces of correspondence. The date on the portrait was 1775, so it could have been painted while Nathaniel was consorting with the beautiful Mrs. Rowe, because the Battle of Concord was waged that year. All it would take to establish whether the woman was in fact the general's wife would be a comparison between the depiction in the mirror and an existing portrait of her.

As for the rest of the conservation project, Jack needed to see the woman's face and consider whether he wanted the mirror's image covered up once again. He might well decide to preserve his ancestor's untarnished reputation, and Callie would support him in whatever he chose to do. The urge to hide a family's immoral past was something she was very familiar with. Given her own commitment and sacrifices to protect her father, she couldn't very well fault Jack if he chose a similar path.

While waiting, she looked outside. Trucks and vans had been pulling up to the back door all day long as food for the party was delivered. She'd assumed there were going to be a lot of people coming, but there seemed to be enough supplies to feed an army going into Thomas's kitchen.

After checking her watch, she walked over to the second bin of documents and decided to get to work. She was about halfway done with what was left in the Rubbermaid container. If she wanted to finish the sorting before she left, she had to get going on it because she was almost done with the portrait.

It was hard to believe, but a small part of Nathaniel's hand was all she had left to clean. Depending on what Jack decided to do about the woman's face, she might be finished as quickly as tomorrow or the day after. If there was no repainting to be done, the final step of the conservation would just be the application of a fresh coat of varnish, and that would not take long.

Sitting down on the couch, she began to methodically sort, page by page, the remaining documents. She was scanning a letter of credit from 1929 when Jack and Grace both came up the stairs. She put down what she was reading and rose to her feet.

"So what have we got?" Jack asked briskly.

He was still in his suit, but had taken off the jacket and the tie. The pale pink button-down he was wearing made his hair and his eyes look especially dramatic.

"See for yourself," she said softly, nodding to the painting.

As they looked over the portrait, Grace gasped. "Oh, my God. It's a woman's face."

Callie measured Jack's reaction. His brows dropped

low over his eyes as he studied the canvas, but she couldn't tell whether he was upset or intrigued.

"Well, that's a bit of a surprise, isn't it," he said casually. And then he looked at her. "And it sheds some light on those letters."

"Letters?" Grace questioned. "There's more than the one you told me about?"

Callie nodded while Jack spoke.

"I'd found one with a similar tone years ago, and if they are indeed a pair, it appears that Nathaniel might have had an affair with, or at the very least a romantic interest in, the wife of General Rowe." He looked back down at the painting.

"What are you going to do?" Callie asked him. "Do you want to have the face covered up again?"

There was a long pause.

"Even if it is General Rowe's wife, I think not." As she glanced at him in surprise, he shrugged. "Whatever the implications, I believe the portrait wouldn't be authentic without it."

Grace frowned. "These letters, you're sure they're between him and the general's wife?"

"You should look at them yourself," he said, "but the circumstantial evidence suggests it was her."

"And you think this woman"—Grace pointed at the painting—"is the one he was in love with? Sarah Rowe?"

Callie interjected. "The general's wife was a known associate of Copley's, right? I mean, there are notes in Copley's journals that stated she often visited his studio before he left for London because she dabbled in painting as well. Nathaniel commissioned this portrait. It's not inconceivable that he'd put his lady love's face in it but, because of the clandestine love between them, have it covered up. A secret pledge of his feelings, perhaps. Quite romantic, actually. And the timing's right—1775."

Grace laughed softly. "That's a fine theory and I don't doubt some of its merits. There's only one problem. The general's wife was a blonde."

Both Jack and Callie turned their heads.

"How do you know?" he demanded.

"I have some expertise in American history," Grace replied with a dry grin. "There are very few portraits of the general's wife. Maybe two at the most, one of which happens to be a miniature owned by the Hall Collection. She most certainly was a blonde."

"So who the hell is that?" Jack asked, frowning.

"Are you sure the letters make reference to the general?" When Jack nodded, Grace said, "Then it could be his daughter, Anne. She was a brunette, took after her father in that regard."

"Really?"

Grace nodded and looked up at the ceiling, tapping one high-heeled shoe.

"Let me see if I can do the math properly. This portrait was done in 1775. Anne would have been sixteen, I think, and Nathaniel Walker would have been about twenty. That sounds on the young side now for a love affair, but back then, girls were married off in their teens regularly." She looked at Jack. "General Rowe's writings suggest he was very protective of his daughter. At one point, I recall reading that he wanted Anne to pursue a spiritual life, and I take that to mean he might even have pushed her to join a religious order. I can certainly see why, if she were falling in love with Nathaniel, she'd want to keep it from her father. At least until there was an engagement and it would be too late." Grace's eyes went to Nathaniel's face. "But Anne died in 1775, if I remember correctly. Of typhus. Quite a tragedy. Her father never recovered."

They all stared at the painting.

"Perhaps," Callie said softly, "her image was too hard for Nathaniel to bear so he had it covered up."

"It would explain a lot," Grace hazarded. "Especially why it took Nathaniel so long to marry. It was twenty years later when he finally walked down the aisle with Jane Hatte."

"Christ," Jack muttered under his breath. "What a story."

Grace put her hand on his arm. "But you really should show those letters to a few more people first. All we have is a theory at this time."

"I have a feeling that we're right," he murmured.

Grace checked her watch and smiled. "Well, unless you have any other mysteries to solve, I better get changed. The party starts in an hour, right?"

Jack nodded and gave her a kiss on the cheek. "Thanks, Grace."

"No problem. Just remember to pick up the phone the next time I call you for investment advice."

"Deal."

After Grace left, Jack went back to staring at the portrait. "You've done wonderful work."

Callie's laugh was awkward. "That's kind of you to say considering the mistake I made."

"But you've transformed the painting. He has such life in him now. Before, he seemed so gloomy, but now I see him differently. He seems younger, more vibrant. You've done very well."

"I've just revealed what Copley did." She walked over to Jack, catching the scent of his aftershave. It hurt just to breathe in the smell. "Look, if there is any diminution in value, I will make you whole."

"Make me whole." His laugh was short. "What an interesting choice of words, considering I've recently concluded that filling up a bank account doesn't work for me like it used to."

When he looked at her, his eyes were so dark, it was as if there were no color in them at all.

"Forget about the problem with the painting and keep your money." He nodded down at the portrait. "All you really have left to do is put on a new coat of varnish, right?"

She nodded.

"And then you're finished."

"I am." A yearning tightened her chest. "Jack, I really want to end up in Boston after the job is finished."

She waited for him to respond, but he just turned away.

"See you back at the house," he said.

22

STARTING AT six o'clock, a steady stream of cars began to arrive at Buona Fortuna. From the window seat in her bedroom, Callie watched them come up the lighted drive, disappear under the porte cochere, and then get parked by uniformed attendants on the lawn. They were a fleet of luxury, every make and model that cost an arm and a leg. She even thought she'd made out a Bentley or two.

All those flashy cars were not inspiring her to join the party. She imagined the people getting out of them were every bit as glamorous as their choice of transportation. As someone who avoided crowds to begin with, getting thrown in with a bunch of corporate raiders and beauty queens was like the second ring of Hell to her, and she was debating the merits of hiding in her room. It smacked of cowardice, sure, but she was almost guaranteed to have a better time.

Besides, she wasn't feeling festive. When she'd come back from the garage, she'd gone upstairs looking for Grace. The door to her half sister's room had been shut, however, and the sensual, masculine laughter coming through the panels didn't prompt a good knocking. Callie had gone to her room to change, resolving to talk to Grace the minute the party was over.

She looked down at her black skirt, the one she'd worn out to dinner with Gray. Twice.

The one that Jack had taken off her body that first night they'd made love.

She thought of burning it just to get away from the memories.

There was a knocking sound and then Grace put her head in the door. "Are you all set? Ross and I are ready."

Callie stood, smoothed down the skirt, and squeezed her feet into her heels.

"You look lovely," she said to Grace with a smile.

Her half sister was wearing a dark red sheath dress that fell, strapless, from her pale shoulders. With her blond hair cascading down her back, she was almost too beautiful to be real.

"Well, thank you. So do you. Those simple lines really suit you." Grace went over to the window and leaned in, looking at the cars. "I used to come to Jack's holiday party religiously, but in the last couple of years I've had to bow out. There are so many friends to catch up with! And I'd like to introduce you to a couple of eligible men, if you wouldn't mind."

Oh, no. Not that.

Grace turned around, a smile on her face, but the expression faded. "Callie? Are you all right? You don't look well."

That was funny. She didn't feel well, either.

"I'm fine. But I need to talk with you."

Concern lifted Grace's perfectly arched brows. "Is everything all right?"

"No, it isn't. After we get through this evening, can we find a quiet place?"

"Of course." Grace eyed Ross, who was waiting in the hall. "Do you want to talk now?"

"I think later would be better." She didn't want the pressure of keeping Grace from the party and had no idea how long the conversation was going to take. "Just promise me. By the end of tonight."

Walking downstairs behind Grace and Ross, Callie felt as if she were wearing concrete shoes. Or maybe lead-lined underwear. Her body was impossibly heavy and she gripped the railing as she approached the crush of people in the front hall. There was a jam as guests came in the door and handed their coats to more uniformed staff. The foyer was filled with the sounds of the party, and the volley of talk and laughter made Callie wince as her senses became overloaded. There was too much noise, too much light, too many perfumes competing for the same air space.

As Grace got swept up in some woman's arms, Callie blindly went into the living room and immediately knew she'd taken a wrong turn. She was lost in a sea of people. There must have been a hundred already there and more kept squeezing in from the hall. Moving through the throng, she went over to one of the bars that had been set up and ordered a glass of wine, not because she was thirsty but because she felt like she needed something to do.

She'd just accepted a Chardonnay when a woman wearing a dramatic gold dress stepped in front of her and said crisply, "Oh, good. And my husband wants a martini."

The woman snatched the glass out of Callie's hand and turned back to the man she'd been talking with.

I'm out of here, Callie thought.

But before she left, she tapped the brunette on the shoulder.

The woman pirouetted around and then smiled at the man next to her. "Oh, darling, your drink's here already."

"No," Callie said politely, taking her glass back. "That one's mine. If you want to be waited on, you could ask one of the men in tuxedos who are passing trays. Otherwise, you can stand in line at the bar."

As the woman began to sputter, Callie walked away, leaving the glass on a side table as she tried to get back to the stairs. The congestion in the hall had gotten worse, though, so she decided to head for the rear of the house. She was moving through the dining room, which was filled with some truly gorgeous food, when she saw Jack in one corner. He was talking to someone intently, his back to her.

Callie stopped, forgetting the feel of people brushing up against her.

Jack had changed into a tuxedo and he looked good in formal clothes. The jacket stretched over his broad shoulders and the stark white of the shirt's jaunty collar played well against his dark hair.

He turned to shake a man's hand and she saw he'd been talking with a woman. Like so many of the other ladies, the long-haired blonde was wearing a dress that was right off the runway, and she'd accessorized it with plenty of important jewelry. Jack turned back to her when he was done talking to the man and she said something in his ear, a smile playing over her lips as she ran her hand over his cast. Jack laughed and pointedly stepped back.

It could have been innocent, probably was, at least on Jack's part, but at that moment Callie wasn't inclined to hang around. Her head was spinning from the noise and the people and so much more. If she didn't get away from the party, she was going to disintegrate and do something ridiculous, like elbow that woman right out of the room. As quickly as she could, she fled to the kitchen and left through the back door.

The night was cold and she was grateful because the chill helped quiet the buzz in her ears. Wrapping her arms around herself, she walked across the driveway and went up into the studio. She just couldn't bear to be in that house, not until after the party died down. She wasn't part of Jack's world and she couldn't pretend to be. Not tonight.

She went over to the couch and sat down by the last of the documents. One by one, she picked pieces of paper from the bin, in search of Nathaniel's truth.

Jack saw Gray through the crowd in the dining room and excused himself from a conversation about highway funds. There were a lot of people who wanted to discuss issues involving the state and it was clear that rumors about his candidacy were getting around.

Waving his arm, he caught Gray's attention and motioned the man over.

"Glad you came," Jack said as they met in front of a platter of poached salmon.

"I just talked with Senator McBride. I think you're going to be pleased." Gray lifted his glass in salute at a congressman who had just walked into the room. "The preliminary reports from the exploratory committee are highly favorable. You'll hear all about it tomorrow, but so far you've got some big backers on the fund-raising side and your name recognition is through the roof. There's heat, Jack. We've got some heat."

"That's great," he said for his friend's benefit.

"It's a hell of a lot more than great. And I've heard some interesting news. Were you aware that Butch Callahan physically threatened his deputy director when the woman didn't get behind him on those construction awards last year? You know, the ones that went to half his family?"

"Jesus. No, I wasn't."

"Yeah, well, no one else has heard about it either."

"Gray, how do you find this stuff out?"

"You don't want to know. Anyway, what this means is we've got something to barter with—"

"Later." Jack nodded toward his mother, who'd just come into the room and was eyeing them both with purpose.

Mercedes's arms stretched out widely as she approached. "Gray, dear, how are you?"

"Mrs. Walker, you look lovely."

As she accepted Gray's kiss on the cheek, Jack eyed his mother objectively. She did look good in the dark blue gown she was wearing and he noted that the collar of diamonds and sapphires at her neck had been a wedding gift to her from his grandparents. Which meant it was one of the few pieces in her safe that he didn't technically own.

"Now, Gray, I understand you and Jack have been

hard at work, plotting. I want you to know I thoroughly approve." Gray made a noncommittal noise as she tucked her arm into his. "I can't tell you the number of people here who are prepared to vote for my son. There's going to be a stampede to the polls."

As Gray did the social dance with his mother, Jack searched the room. He'd been looking for Callie all night long, but she was nowhere to be found. Hell, maybe she was avoiding him on purpose. After all, the deadline he'd given her was up tomorrow. Maybe she was just running the clock down.

"Jack?" his mother prompted him.

"What?"

Mercedes let out her social laugh, the one that carried like wind chimes through the small group that had gathered around her. "Isn't that just like my son? Always deep in thought. Jack just has so much going on. Now, if you all will excuse us, my son and I need a moment alone."

"We do?" he drawled.

She was smiling and nodding as she grabbed onto his good arm and led him into the butler's pantry. She slid the pocket door in place and glared at him.

"What happened to that painting!"

Even though he knew exactly what she was talking about, he muttered, "You want to be a little more specific?"

"She's *ruined* it."

"And who did you hear this from?"

"Gerard told me everything."

"Then I'm quite sure he didn't phrase it like that."

Mercedes threw her shoulders back and hit him with the full regal routine. "Jackson, I do *not* understand what that woman has done to you. She comes into this house, destroys your relationship with Blair, and then does untold damage to that priceless piece of art, and you defend her?"

"Mother, relax. Grace and I reviewed the painting with Callie this afternoon. It's perfectly fine."

This stopped Mercedes in her tracks. "Grace has seen the devastation?"

He tightened his lips. "Let's get this straight. The painting is not ruined."

"What about that face! Who is it?"

"We have a theory, and if it proves to be correct, the value of the painting has probably been enhanced."

His mother's eyes narrowed. "Well."

He lifted a brow and waited to see if she came up with some other way to try to blow the situation out of proportion.

Instead, she hit him from a fresh angle.

"And what of the party at the MFA?" she prompted him. "I thought we were going to have a reception when the painting is mounted next to the Paul Revere. I've already started to invite people, but Gerard says you're being evasive."

"If there's a reception, we'll have it here. No matter how great my ancestor would look next to the Revere, that painting's going back over my fireplace where it belongs."

"But that's where your father is!"

Like the man, and not a portrait of him, was mounted on the wall.

"Actually, I'm going to move that picture."

While his mother stared at him as if he'd committed blasphemy, Jack checked his watch. It was seven o'clock on the West Coast. Perfect, he thought.

"If you'll excuse me, I have some business to attend to."

He knew that was the only way his mother would let go of him. She'd forgive him anything that had to do with the Walker Fund. Mercedes, he thought, had always kept her eye on the prize. And the prize was almost always green.

But she took his arm in a sturdy grip. "I'm very concerned about you."

"I don't know why. The cast comes off in a week or two."

"Be serious!" Her eyes flashed. "I just don't know

what you're thinking anymore, Jackson. But I refuse to let you lose sight of the big picture."

"Lucky me," he said as he opened the door.

Moving quickly through the party, Jack shut himself in his study, picked a note card off his desk, and dialed the phone.

The voice was harried on the other end of the line.

"Hello?" There was a muffled noise and then, "No, no, honey, Daddy's got the phone."

A wail sounded out.

"Bryan McKay?" Jack said.

"Yes." There was a loud sigh. "Listen, I don't accept phone calls from telemarketers—"

"This is Jack Walker."

Pure silence. And then, "Oh, my God. Ah—hello, how did you get my home number? Never mind. You must have people who— Oh, my God. What can I do for you?"

"Take a deep breath first."

Jack laughed as the good doctor actually did it.

"Dr. McKay, I'm going to invest in your company. I'm going to fund your entire operation for the next three years, down to the cost of lightbulbs and floor mops."

There was another resounding silence and then, "OhmyGod—ohmyGod—"

Jack smiled, feeling good about his decision.

"Now, listen, we're going to have to work out some details," he said crisply. "I'm not just investing. I'm going to help you guys make it. Your family and I are going to be in business together."

Callie reached into the bin, took hold of a piece of paper, and then felt it slip from her grasp on the way to her lap. The page scooted under the couch and she muttered a few choice words as she got on her hands and knees, hiked up the slipcover's kick pleat, and stuck her hand into the darkness.

When she felt paper under her fingertips, she sat back up and brushed off the darkened, half-torn sheet.

Her breath caught the moment she noted its deep brown color. It was old. Very old. Carefully holding the two sides together, she could barely make out the words because the ink was so faded.

She leaned over to the light and tried to read the sprawling script.

Dear Nathaniel~

    It is with great sorrow that I must detail the passing of my beloved daughter Anne. She went unto the Lord's gentle hands. My sorrow is boundless, coming to me in the night and under the sun likewise. In the disposition of her things, I found your letters to her and I return them herein to your care as a matter of discretion. Had I but known of her feelings for you and yours to her, I would have been o'erjoyed at the prospect of a marriage. I cherished her like nothing on earth, but would have granted her passage into your house because I know of the man you are. 'Tis a double loss to my heart that I came so close to calling you son.

    Our angel is with the rest.

Yours faithfully,
J. J. Rowe

Callie looked up. Over the tattered edge of the paper, she saw the portrait.

She reread the letter and went to the painting.

Reaching out, she brushed her fingertips lightly over Nathaniel's cheek and then stared at the reflection of the girl he had loved and lost.

The Battle of Concord had been staged around the time of her death. Which meant that Nathaniel and Anne's failed midnight meeting had been a matter of weeks before she'd died. Afraid of her father's reaction, Anne had missed her last chance to see the man she loved, but it had been for no reason. If the general's letter truly reflected his feelings, he would have approved of the union after all.

Callie looked into Nathaniel's eyes, shaking her head sadly at what he had lost. And what might have been.

Good Lord, to have missed so much out of a fear that was ultimately unfounded.

Anne would still have died, in all probability, but who knew what would have come of that meeting? A marriage proposal? Perhaps Nathaniel would have taken her with him somehow and she wouldn't have contracted typhus in the city.

Callie wondered what kinds of regrets Anne had had. By the time the girl fell ill, it would have been too late to get word to Nathaniel, so her destiny to forgo a last good-bye was sealed. Her father and her love were fighting and away from Boston. Even if she had sent for Nathaniel, it was doubtful she could have reached him in time, given the constraints of communication and the confusion of battle. It was hard not to imagine the sickened girl yearning to see the man she cared for so deeply.

Callie put the letter down and wandered over to the windows that overlooked Buona Fortuna. The mansion was stunning in its illuminated glory. For a house that appeared so dour in the daylight, at night, with lights shining in all the rooms, it was dazzling.

And the party was in full swing. Through the first-floor windows, she could see shapes passing by as people in beautiful clothes mingled with one another.

Somewhere, Jack was among them, she thought. And she was, once again, on the outside looking in.

Recalling the evening she'd stood in front of that mansion with her mother, watching her father be with people who were friends to him and strangers to her, she was struck by how her life had come full circle.

The difference was, now she was choosing not to go inside. There was nothing holding her back, nothing keeping her out of Jack's life, but herself.

She pictured Anne again, lying on her deathbed.

And with a sudden, sickening clarity, Callie relived the last moment between her parents. She saw her mother, weak, unable to speak, her eyes the only things that moved. She saw her father, bent down low, face contorted in an anguish that was clearly from the heart. The words he had spoken washed over Callie and the pain they caused came swiftly, harshly. Immutably.

As she heard what he'd said once again, she realized it wasn't just Grace she was protecting by keeping the past out of her life. She, herself, was hiding from the worst truth of them all. It was as if, by not speaking her father's name to anyone, what had happened, especially at the end, had not been real.

But it had happened. It was real.

And Callie knew with complete conviction that if she couldn't acknowledge the past openly, she was going to lose the one shot she had at everything she had ever wanted. A man who loved her. A family. A place where she belonged.

Someone who was *hers.*

She knew what she had to do.

On her way out, she picked up the letter, and holding it with care, she headed back to the house.

23

When Jack left his study a half hour later, he was surprised by how good he felt, considering he was pouring $100 million or so into something that would at best be a break-even proposition. But part of it was Bryan McKay's reaction. The doctor was over the moon and so enthusiastic that he was still stuttering a little when they'd hung up.

Hell, Jack figured, if he couldn't make things work out for himself, at least he could play fairy godmother to a few others. All he needed was a wand and a tutu.

Now, there was a campaign ad.

"Jack! How are you?" The CEO of one of the state's largest insurance companies was coming down the hall. "Listen, I wanted to talk to you about worker's comp."

"I'm all ears."

He and the man spoke for quite a while until Jack's mother appeared in the hall. Nate was with her, dressed in chef's whites and looking like he was anxious to get back to the kitchen.

"It's time," she said.

Taking both her sons by the hand, Mercedes led them to the living room and put a halt to the procession when they were in front of the fireplace, right under Nathaniel Six's portrait. A hush fell over the party and people began to press in close to make sure they could hear her speak.

Looking across the room, Jack saw Gray leaning against a column in the back, his arms crossed in front of his chest, his eyes narrowed on Mercedes.

"If I might have your attention for a moment," she began.

Jack hoped the speech was going to be quick this year. At every one of the holiday parties, Mercedes paid homage to his father in a litany of praises that stopped just short of being a eulogy. She seemed determined to keep the legend of Nathaniel Six alive. When Jack was feeling charitable toward her, he tried to see love in the gesture, but he was never totally convinced that her motivations were pure. He suspected she wanted to remind everyone exactly whom she'd been married to.

But what was the harm, he thought, eyeing his brother over her snow-white chignon. Nate was looking as awkward as he felt.

"My husband . . ."

Jack tuned out the words and looked around idly, coming to attention only as he saw Callie and Grace edging their way through the front hall. They went halfway up the stairs, until they cleared the heads in the room, and stopped to listen to the speech.

As he stared across the crowd, he had eyes only for Callie.

Standing amid the fleet of high-stepping women and men in sleek tuxedos, she was dressed simply in a black-and-white outfit he'd seen before. Her hair was falling over her shoulders in a glorious red wave, and unlike so many of the other ladies, her makeup was soft, natural.

To him, she was the most beautiful woman at the party. Hands down.

At the foot of the stairs, he caught a couple of men eyeing her and talking. One shrugged, as if to indicate he didn't know who she was, and then they both stared over their shoulders at her.

The appreciation and hot speculation in their expressions had Jack curling his hands into fists. He wanted to tear through the crowd and kick them out of his house, even though one of them was his squash partner and the other he'd known since kindergarten.

Callie didn't seem to notice the attention, though. She was looking at something in her hand, and when she finally lifted her head, their eyes met. A yearning went through his body and he had to stop himself from taking a step toward her.

With a soft smile, she lifted a tattered piece of paper up and waved it slowly in the air.

Had she found the answer?

Mercedes's voice cut into his thoughts. "And then there is my son Jackson. As you all know, he's made his father and me so proud with all he's accomplished, and he's about to take on another challenge. I'm simply thrilled to say that he will be running for governor of this fine commonwealth next November!"

Jack snapped his head around. As a wave of cheers rose up into the air, he stared at his mother in disbelief.

"How the hell could you do that," he said through his teeth.

But she was too busy soaking up the adulation to hear what he said.

Frantically, he looked out to the stairs, but he couldn't see through all the hands that were in the air. *Fuck*. He could only imagine what was going on in Callie's head.

"Speech! Speech! Speech!"

Knowing he wasn't going to be able to get away until he said something, he held his hands out and quieted down the guests.

"I don't have anything to formally announce one way or the other at this point." Supportive shouts drowned him out. "But thank you for your vote of confidence."

As the clapping started again, he met Gray's eyes. His friend was shaking his head, knowing exactly what would happen next. His mother had effectively announced his candidacy to three hundred of the most influential people in Massachusetts. And almost every one of them had a cell phone in their pocket. The news was going to be all over the *Globe* and the *Herald* tomorrow morning.

When the fervor began to die down, Mercedes turned to him, all smiles, and exclaimed, "Isn't it fabulous! They love you!"

Jack leaned in closely, so no one else would hear. "Mother, you're going to regret this."

She gasped and pulled back, but he was already walking away. He *had* to get to Callie.

She'd disappeared, probably heading for her room. Jack was on his way to the stairs, deflecting congratulatory handshakes, when Gray stepped in his path.

"We need to deal with this. Now." Before he could speak, Gray said, "Did you know she was going to do that?"

"Hell, no."

Gray's cell phone went off and he took it out and frowned at the number. "We've got to caucus and prepare a statement to the press. Then we're going to have to reach all of the members of the exploratory committee, including those who aren't here tonight. Pissing off the people who've been helping you is the last thing you need to do right now. None of them expected this announcement."

Welcome to the goddamn club.

Jack was infuriated. He had all this shit to deal with because of his mother's need to be a power broker, and all he wanted to do was to find Callie.

When Jack's mother made her declaration and the crowd went wild, Callie closed her eyes.

"I can't believe this!" Grace exclaimed. "How exciting!"

Callie forced a smile. "Yes. He really wants to run."

So much so, he hadn't even bothered to wait for her answer.

In the corner, she saw Gray cocking a cell phone and putting it up to his ear.

She had to give Jack and his friend some credit. Having Mrs. Walker announce the candidacy, while under the portrait of Jack's father, was a brilliant piece of maneuvering. It was a perfect act of calculated spontaneity, a staging that emphasized his family's lineage and service to the state and country. And doing it at a holiday party, without the press, was ideal. Word was going to get around just fine; hell, the cell phones were already being flipped open. The reporters were going to be forced to come to Jack for details, giving him an opportunity to grant interviews as a form of patronage. As a press strategy, it was magnificent.

He'd arranged the situation to his advantage beautifully.

As Jack held his hands over his head and smiled, assuming the quintessential politician pose, she looked away. She had no interest in what he had to say.

She couldn't believe he hadn't bothered to wait. He'd promised to hold off until tomorrow, but now it was all over. He was running. And she was out of his life.

With half an ear, she heard the guests quieting down obediently, Jack's deep voice speaking, and then there was an eruption of clapping and shouting again.

"Callie?" Grace shouted over the uproar.

She snapped to. "Yes?"

"You wanted to go upstairs to talk?"

Not anymore, she thought. Or not for what she thought she was going to say.

"I just want to show you what I found," she replied.

"You found another letter?"

"*The* letter, as it were."

Callie followed Grace to her room.

Once inside Grace and Ross's bedroom, she took a seat on a chintz-covered chaise lounge in the corner. Kicking her shoes off, she tucked her legs under her as Grace took the letter over to a lamp and read.

She'd been so ready to take the leap, Callie thought. To tell Jack everything and beg him to find a way for them to be together. And she'd decided that even if Grace was uncomfortable with Jack knowing about their past, it didn't matter. She was going to speak the truth anyway and choose Jack over everything she'd spent her life protecting. As well as what little family she had.

Only she'd been too late. Or maybe he hadn't been serious about not running, after all.

"This is extraordinary." Grace looked up. "We were right."

Callie glanced at the paper. "*You* were right."

"Have you shown this to Jack?"

She shook her head. "I'll wait until tomorrow. He's got a lot on his hands right now."

"He certainly does." Grace put the sheet down on a bedside table. "How much do you have left to do on the portrait?"

"I finished the cleaning this afternoon. All I have to do is apply the fresh varnish coat and the project is done."

Grace sat down at the foot of the chaise. Her fingers went to work on the heavy diamond studs she was wearing in her earlobes. "And then what?"

Callie laughed quietly. "And then I'm heading back to New York."

At that moment, the door opened and Ross walked in. He was wrenching his bow tie off like he hated having the thing around his neck, and he stopped when he saw Callie.

"Am I interrupting something?"

Callie got up and retrieved the letter. "Not at all. I should go. It's late. What time are you leaving tomorrow morning?"

Grace followed her to the door. "Right after breakfast."

"I'll see you first thing in the morning, then. Good night, Grace. Night, Ross."

As she went down the hall, she thought that tomorrow she would show Jack the letter, put the varnish on the painting, and then it would all be over.

She was surprised that she was actually looking forward to going back to her studio. However modest it was, everything in it was hers. She wasn't sure what she was going to do for a job, but she figured she'd solve that problem eventually.

After she shut her door, she hesitated. And then she slowly turned the lock.

She had a feeling Jack would come to her tonight, and she didn't have the energy left to deal with him. She just wanted peace.

And she would never find it with Jack Walker in her life.

24

It was two o'clock in the morning by the time Jack could get himself out of his study. Members of the exploratory committee and Gray had turned it into command central and they'd all spent hours working every phone line he had. Calls were coming in from reporters, legislators, and business contacts. He did eight interviews with the press before midnight.

Although it wasn't as if he had much to say.

Against the overwhelming consensus of opinion in the room, Jack had stood firmly behind a noncommittal holding statement. Even Gray had hotly disagreed with him, convinced that capitalizing on the rush was a good idea.

But Jack refused to make it official before he got to Callie. Even if it would be messy, it still wasn't too late for him to back out, and he had hope that she would still come around. Slim though the optimism was.

After thanking Gray and the two advisers who were still in the room, he went upstairs to find her.

Striding down the runner in the hall, he thought he should have known his mother would pull a stunt like that. A woman who could change her entire identity, and walk away from her mother, father, sisters, and brothers without ever looking back, was capable of anything when she put her mind to it.

And she'd made it very clear how badly she wanted him in office.

Well, first thing tomorrow morning, he was going to take care of his mother.

Jack stopped in front of Callie's door and tried to prepare himself for whatever was going to happen. He knocked, and when there was no answer, he went to open it. The knob didn't turn.

Unable to comprehend the problem at first, he jiggled the brass with a curse.

And then he slowly released his hand.

He couldn't believe it. She'd locked him out.

He was about to start pounding the door down, had raised his fist and leaned forward, when he stopped himself.

Jack dropped his hand to his side. Sat back on his heels. Stared at the door.

Not only didn't she trust him; she clearly had no faith in him, either. She hadn't even bothered to let him explain that his mother's announcement had been rash, unexpected, and *wrong*.

Abruptly he felt as though he couldn't breathe. With an uncoordinated hand, he undid his bow tie, loosened his collar. Opening his mouth, he dragged some air into his lungs.

So this is how it ends, he thought.

How appropriate that it was with him being locked out of her room.

Jack laid his palm against the door.

He wasn't sure how long he stayed like that, but eventually he resurfaced and knew he needed to face up to reality.

No matter what she said, Callie didn't love him enough. She'd made her choice. She didn't want him in her life.

So be it.

Jack let his hand fall from the door and walked away.

He wasn't sure where he was going or why. The only thing he was certain of was that standing in front of her locked bedroom wasn't where he wanted to be when the sun came up.

When he found himself downstairs, there were waiters still milling around. The men and women were carrying trays of dirty glasses into the kitchen and stripping the dining room of the remnants of the food. It dawned on him that he'd missed saying good night to the guests.

Probably just as well, he thought, heading for his study. He wouldn't have been able to stomach all of the good wishes for his candidacy.

Gray was in the room by himself, packing up papers.

"Hell of a night, huh," his friend murmured.

You have no idea, he thought.

He stared at Gray for a minute and then spoke sharply. "Tomorrow morning, I want the committee members downtown in my office early."

"Fine, but it shouldn't take more than a couple of hours to hear the reports—"

"Tell them it's going to go all day long. We've got a campaign to launch."

Gray looked up from the folder he was holding. "What the hell are you talking about? I thought you were still on the fence. We *told* everyone you were on the fence."

"Not anymore."

"Jesus Christ, Jack." Gray slammed down the folder. "We missed a prime opportunity tonight!"

Jack marched over to the desk. "I don't need this from you right now, okay? Do your job, call those goddamn people, and let's get this candidacy started."

He sat down and watched Gray compose himself.

"You mind telling me why the change?" His friend's voice was even now.

But Jack had no intention of exposing his pain to anyone.

Because how he felt was no one else's fucking business, he thought.

"I don't have anything to lose. Not anymore."

Jack was still sitting at his desk when the sun came up. As the first rays of dawn fell across the lawn, he shifted in the chair and moved his cast to another position. He felt a sturdy ache in his shoulder, but it was the pain in his chest that held his attention. He figured it was either angina or a broken heart, and it was hard to decide which would be worse.

Although that was probably because he was all alone, watching a beautiful sunrise, and feeling pathetically melodramatic.

"Hey, Governor."

Jack looked over and saw Nate standing in the doorway. He smiled even though he felt half-dead. "Don't jump the gun with that title. It's a long way to the finish line."

"Yeah, and when have you ever failed at something?"

Jack couldn't bear to entertain the joke. "I'm surprised you're up this early considering what you and Thomas pulled off last night. The food was fantastic." Eyeing the duffel bag hanging off Nate's shoulder, he asked, "You headed out?"

"Yeah, I want to be up in Canada before nightfall. Spike, Louie, and I have an appointment to see a restaurant that's for sale."

"You know, I was serious when I offered you the money. Even if you insist on just borrowing it."

"Thanks."

Jack stood up, loosening the stiffness in his back. "When are we going to see you next?"

"Christmas."

"Good." They walked out, heading for the kitchen, and Jack made a quick detour to pick the *Globe* off the front step. As he uncurled it, he saw a picture of himself below the fold on the front page. The article quoted him as still being undecided, but the reporter speculated it was only a matter of time before an official announcement of his candidacy was made.

That guy's editor was going to be pleased, Jack thought. Because the Walker campaign was probably going to release something by the end of the week.

"So you really are going to do it," Nate said over his shoulder.

"Yes, I am."

As they went into the kitchen, he scanned the article. Butch Callahan's response was as he expected. Barely polite.

Jack threw the paper down on the table.

And so the fight begins, he thought.

"Breakfast?" he asked Nate.

"Naw. I'll grab something on the road."

Jack walked his brother out to the old Saab Nate had driven since graduating from Harvard.

"I hope that thing keeps going."

"Me, too." Nate tossed his bag in the trunk and got in. With a sputter and a roar, the car's engine came alive and he leaned out the window. "Take care and remember, my cell phone's got voice mail, so you can always find me. Let me know if you need to talk."

"Will do, brother."

Jack waved as Nate shot down the driveway.

Before he went back in the house, he looked at the garage and wondered if he'd ever be able to see the damn thing and not think of Callie.

Briefly, he entertained a scenario of what-ifs, like what if his mother hadn't sprung the announcement. Or what if Callie had given him a chance to explain. Or what if she'd trusted him enough in the first place.

But then he reeled in his thoughts, and as he went back to his study, he knew he had some work to do.

Sitting down behind the desk, he called a real estate agent he knew. The message he left authorized a full-price, cash offer to purchase a condo at the Four Seasons Hotel. He knew one was available because he'd seen one advertised in the paper the week before. His next call was to a moving company. Assuming his lawyers worked quickly, he figured the closing could be in as little as two weeks, and he wanted to make sure he got the movers lined up.

He was hanging up the phone when his mother materialized in the doorway. Dressed in a pale silk robe that fell to the floor, and with her hair loosely coiled on her head, she looked fresh even at her age.

"Speak of the devil," he said.

His mother's smile was conciliatory but her eyes held a certain satisfaction. She knew, he thought, exactly what she'd done. But then, why should he be surprised? His mother was a very smart woman.

"Jack, darling, I missed the opportunity to say good night to you after the party." She came into the room. "I wanted to thank you for everything you did to make last night a success."

"Tell me, Mother," he said, idly fingering some papers on his desk, "when are you thinking of going to Palm Beach for the season?"

"The day after tomorrow."

"You might want to delay for a week."

"Not so eager to get rid of me? That's a pleasant change," she chided, her smile becoming more genuine.

"I just think you'll want the extra time to adjust."

She shot him an inquisitive glance. "To what?"

"You're moving out of this house."

Mercedes seemed to stop breathing. "Whatever are you talking about?"

"I am purchasing a condominium for you at the Four Seasons. So I imagine you'll want to be there to direct the movers when they put your things in your new home. Unless you want a decorator to do it."

His mother turned ashen. "My God, Jack, what have you done?"

"I'm cutting the proverbial cord."

He watched as Mercedes backed over to the couch and sat down. She seemed to collapse, looking very small surrounded by all that luxurious silk.

"You can't do this. You can't send me away. I live here. I couldn't possibly leave Buona Fortuna to live in a *hotel*."

"I'm not sending you to a Motel 6, for Christ's sake. It's the Four Seasons."

"But this is our home."

He stood up. "Let's be very clear. This is *my* home. And you are leaving. End of story."

His mother's lower lip trembled. "Jack, don't do this."

"Frankly, I'm sorry that I waited this long. Now," he said briskly, "I'm heading into the office and I doubt I'll be home for dinner."

As he went by her, she gripped his hand. He noted dispassionately the tears in her eyes.

"But why?" she asked.

He stared at her long and hard. "You know *precisely* why. Do you have any idea what you did to me last night?"

"I only wanted to help," she whispered fiercely. "And, Jack, you need me."

"Maybe if you behaved less like an enemy of mine. But as you are now, no, I don't."

Callie walked into the kitchen and immediately wished she'd stayed upstairs a little longer.

Jack's mother was in tears and Thomas was looking at the woman as if he was going to have to catch her if she fainted.

"He can't do this!" Mrs. Walker wailed. "I need you to talk to him. Make him understand that I can't possibly go. He'll listen to you."

"I don't know if—" Thomas stopped talking when he realized they were not alone.

Mrs. Walker wheeled around. The moment she saw Callie, she tried to pull herself together by lifting her chin up and bringing a tissue to her nose. Moving with noble forbearance, she wiped her eyes briefly, and when she spoke, her voice trembled only a little.

"I should like my breakfast in bed this morning, Thomas. Please tell Elsie to bring it up when she arrives."

And then Mrs. Walker glided by as if she hadn't just been hysterical.

Callie glanced over at Thomas. He was leaning back against the stove and shaking his head.

"I should have seen this coming," he muttered.

"What happened?"

The man looked up. "Jack kicked his mother out of this house."

"Excuse me?"

"Kicked his own mother out. Though I could see how he feels like she deserved it."

"But why—" Callie felt the blood drain out of her face.

Last night's announcement.

"Thomas, I need to know. Why?" She asked the question, even though she suspected she knew the answer and was horrified by its implications.

"That little speech she gave last night. Evidently, Jack wasn't prepared to announce anything."

"Oh, no," she whispered.

"Mrs. Walker said she'd tried to apologize, but he wouldn't hear of it. Frankly, I don't know what the big deal is. So she jumped the gun a little? Unless he wasn't going to run, after all."

A nauseating wave came over Callie as she realized the mistake she'd made. The terrible mistake. God, she had to find him and explain—but maybe it was already too late? His candidacy had been formally announced. He couldn't possibly go back, right? Or maybe he could—

"Will you excuse me?" Callie didn't wait for a reply before she tore out of the room.

She raced to Jack's study, and when it was empty, she went upstairs and pounded on his door. She threw it open, but he wasn't there, either.

She told herself that the exploratory committee wasn't meeting until the afternoon. There had to be time to catch him before he left for the office. But where was he?

She was briefly stalled in the hallway when Grace and Ross came out of their room with their bags packed.

"Grace! I need to talk with you."

Her half sister's eyes widened. "Certainly, where would you—"

Callie pulled the woman into her room and shut the door.

"I don't have much time but I need to— I'm in love with Jack and I've made a terrible mistake. An awful, hideous . . ."

"You're in love with Jack!"

"Oh, God, assuming I haven't completely blown it with him, I need you to understand something. I've told him a little of my past, but he doesn't know the whole story because I couldn't be completely honest without exposing you. He feels as though I must not love him because I can't trust him."

Grace's eyes widened even farther.

Callie took a breath before she lost her voice. "You've got to understand. I have to explain everything to him, even if you don't want me to. If I don't, he and I have absolutely no future together. And I can't let that happen."

She waited for a response, but there wasn't one. Grace seemed totally frozen.

"I'm sorry," Callie said, reaching out. "I know I made a promise to you. But I can't hide anymore. Not when I have so much to lose by staying silent."

She heard a clicking noise and looked down. Grace started to fiddle with her watch, clipping and unclipping the latch. When she broke away and walked across the room, Callie held her breath. She wasn't prepared to keep quiet, but that didn't mean she wanted to cause Grace any pain.

"I— I'm sorry, Grace. Truly. I never expected—"

Grace whirled around and pegged her with hard eyes. "Don't you be sorry. Don't you ever be sorry. This is our father's fault. *All* of it. Not yours."

There was a long silence as Callie watched Grace's face grow increasingly dark. The depth of anger was a surprise.

And then Grace marched over, grabbed Callie's hands, and said, "Tell Jack. Tell him *everything.*"

Callie blinked. "Everything? And you'll still be—"

"I'll be just fine."

Callie felt an immense gratitude, but it passed as she remembered she still didn't know where Jack was.

Or whether he would let her talk. Her only hope was if she apologized well enough, he might forgive her. Maybe.

But where was he?

She thought about the commotion of the night before. She was willing to bet he was meeting with the exploratory committee early. Considering everything that had happened, he had probably moved up the time of the meeting. Because God knew he and his advisers would have plenty to talk about.

"He's probably left already!" She looked at Grace. "Are you going back to the city now?"

Grace nodded.

"Will you give me a ride to Jack's office downtown?"

"Sure. I know where it is."

Callie whipped the door open. She and Grace grabbed hold of Ross and raced him down the stairs. Moments after they had confirmed with Thomas that Jack had headed for his office, they were in a black Ford Explorer with Ross hitting the gas.

They shot onto the Mass Pike and were heading for Boston when Grace frowned and looked into the backseat.

"And after you tell him, then what?"

"I have no idea. Hopefully, he'll forgive me." Callie smiled weakly. "It may be too late anyway. But I have to try."

"But what if it isn't too late? Then what happens?"

Love, family, the whole bit, she thought, not even daring to put such optimism into words. But happily-ever-after probably wasn't what Grace was concerned about, anyway.

"You mean about his candidacy?" Callie said. "You don't have to worry. He said if I told him the whole truth, he would stay out of the election."

Grace considered her thoughtfully. "Do you really

want him to give up all that? You said yourself how much he wants to run."

It felt premature to be discussing their future, given how upset Jack probably was with her. But Callie answered the question anyway.

"Of course, I don't want him to stop. I hate the thought of what he would be leaving behind and I worry that he'd resent me later. But there's no other choice."

"Yes, there is."

Callie frowned, unable to comprehend what Grace was suggesting. Perhaps she just didn't understand.

"But Grace," Callie explained patiently, "if I'm with him and he runs, my past—our past—is all going to come out. Somehow, some reporter is going to put the pieces together and then it will be everywhere. You think the tell-alls are bad now? Wait until you see our headlines."

Grace regarded her gravely. And then said the most unexpected thing.

"Maybe so. But I don't really feel like keeping our father's secret anymore. Do you?"

Callie was stunned. She was willing to go through anything to be with Jack, even expose herself to the press. But Grace? Why would she put herself through that? She had nothing to gain, everything to lose.

Callie shook her head. "But the consequences, to you, to your mother, would be ... tremendous. I can't imagine you'd want to deal with it all."

Grace looked over at Ross, meeting the man's eyes.

And then she turned back. "At a different point in my life I might not have been able to handle it. But I've changed and so have a lot of my circumstances. With the success of this year's gala, my position is secure at the Hall Foundation. I have a man who loves me and isn't afraid of anything."

Ross reached over and took her hand in a solid grip.

"And I have you, Callie." Grace paused. "Our father cheated us both and I can't call him on his conduct because he lied until the day he died. I'm not inclined to protect him, certainly not considering how it will affect your life and Jack's. Let it come out. Let the whole godforsaken thing come out. We'll get through the storm together, and once we're on the other side, we're free."

"You'd do that?" Callie whispered.

Grace's green eyes were fierce. "For you, I would. I have nothing to hide. I'm proud that you're my sister."

Callie clasped her hands over her mouth and squeezed her eyes shut. The possibility of such acknowledgment, such support, had never occurred to her.

She felt Grace reach out and stroke her hair, but she couldn't meet anyone's eyes at that moment.

"We're family, Callie. Which means we're going to stick together."

Family.

When Callie finally spoke, it was hoarsely. "He was so ashamed of me. He could barely look at me most of the time. While he was alive, I lived in fear of the truth getting out because I was terrified it would drive him further away. And after I met you, I was afraid I would lose you."

Grace's voice was strong. "That's not going to happen. I'm not going anywhere."

Callie slowly opened her eyes and saw her sister's tears through her own.

"Listen to me, Callie. We're not going to let our father rule us from the grave anymore. The time for hidden truths is over."

25

JACK PARKED his car under One Financial Center and took the elevator up to the Walker Fund's offices. As an electronic chime marked the passing floors, he had about as much interest in his candidacy as he did in any other part of his life. There were phone calls to return, documents to be reviewed, the deal with the McKays to finalize—he couldn't have cared less about any of it.

He was worn-out and not because he'd stayed up all night.

When he'd walked away from Callie's locked door, he'd figured he was taking his first steps to accepting a life without her and he'd convinced himself that eventually he'd be back to normal. But driving into town, he realized he hadn't banked on the length of the road ahead of him. He wasn't going to get over her in a night, or a day. Or a month. He had an awful suspicion it was going to take a long time.

Like maybe forever.

Which was ridiculous, he told himself. There was no forever with this kind of thing. There were four—no, five steps to grief, right? And he seemed to have zoomed right past denial, given how terrible he felt.

Four more to go and then maybe he'd feel halfway decent again.

The elevator doors opened and he walked up to the receptionist who covered weekends. "There are some ladies and gentlemen coming to see me. An invitation list should have been left for you. Will you please show them down to the big conference room?"

"Of course, Mr. Walker. And I've had breakfast set up for you all."

"Good thinking, Latasha. Thanks. And we'll be in there through lunch, too."

He headed down the hall and waved to a couple of his people who were behind their desks, working in sweaters and khakis. When he got to the conference room, he pushed the double doors open. For confidentiality purposes, the only windows in the room faced out of the building and he went over and looked at the view.

He tried to imagine how he would feel in a year. Would he still be thinking of her?

Gray arrived next and then the members of the committee began to file in.

When everyone was seated around the glossy table, Gray leaned over to him and whispered, "Are you going to make your announcement first?"

Jack looked at the assembled group. The men and women in the room were culled from all sectors of Massachusetts political life and there were two with national ties to help strategize about the long term. It was a powerful crew and fully capable of helping him get where he wanted to go.

Funny, how he'd been prepared to give it all up and never look back.

"Jack?" Gray prompted. "Are you ready?"

He nodded, forcing himself to get on with the rest of his life.

He was standing up when there was a commotion out in the hall and the door was cracked open.

"Excuse me! I don't believe you are a part of this meeting!" Latasha hissed.

Jack was about to demand what the hell was going on when Callie burst into the room. She stopped short as all the attention around the table focused on her.

Oddly enough, his first thought was that her hair was

down, just the way he liked it. And then he did himself a favor by remembering that what she looked like was no longer his concern.

Although where she was mattered if she was on his property.

"This is a private meeting," he said, trying not to look into her eyes. He had no interest in seeing that particular shade of blue again.

"I'll call security," Latasha muttered while reaching for a phone.

"That's all right. I'm sure Ms. Burke is just passing through."

"Actually, I'm not."

He cocked an eyebrow, not really in a big hurry to indulge her. But as she put her hands on her hips, he had a feeling she was not going to leave unless she was dragged out or she had a chance to say her piece.

Jack shrugged. He wasn't about to sic a security guard on her. And there was no reason for the two of them to have it out in front of three judges, a senator, the Speaker of the House, a DA, four CEOs, and a clergyman.

Although maybe Father Linehan would make a good referee.

"Ladies and gentlemen, would you give us a moment?"

Gray shot him an amused look as he left the room with everyone else.

When they were alone, she clasped her hands together and took a deep breath.

"So," he drawled, "what's on your mind?"

"I'm sorry to interrupt, but this is really important. I have to talk to you."

"You want to sit?"

She shook her head.

"Jack, I made an awful mistake last night. I'm so sorry. I should have known you'd keep your word. You always have. I jumped to the wrong conclusion about that announcement."

He sat in his chair and stared down the long table at

her. If she thought that was what bothered him most, he wasn't going to correct her. He'd had it with trying to reach out. Now he was more concerned with getting over her.

"Thanks for saying something." He looked at his watch.

"I just wasn't thinking straight. I've been so torn."

He nodded, but stayed quiet, not having much to say. There was a period of silence.

"If there isn't anything else," he got to his feet, aware of a feeling of disappointment.

Christ, he still had hope? What an idiot he was.

"Jack, I didn't come here to say I love you and expect you to forgive me."

"Good."

"Because saying I love you wouldn't be enough."

He narrowed his eyes on her face. He could see she was having trouble choosing her words.

She cleared her throat. "Right before my mother died, my father came to the apartment. He brought a dozen roses with him. The moment I looked into his face, I knew he had come to say good-bye. She was getting worse. . . . He knew it was time."

Jack slowly sat down in the chair. He had a feeling she was going to tell him everything.

"I was at her bedside, and I knew they wanted to be alone. I went into the living room but the apartment was very small, so voices carried. Even the very quiet ones." She looked at him. "I heard my father say that he would have married her. He would have left his wife and m-married her. If it hadn't been for me."

She took a deep, shuddering breath.

"He, ah, he told her that it was impossible with me around. He couldn't very well marry a woman who already had a twenty-some-year-old daughter who looked like him. His indiscretion would have been so obvious. I—" She tapped her chest. "It was me who he blamed for keeping them apart. *Me.*"

Jack got to his feet and came around the table, unable

to stand the way her voice sounded. He wanted to take her into his arms, but she started to pace.

"After he left, I went to my mother's bedside. She looked up and I *knew* he wasn't the only one who regretted having me. I mean, God, it was her whole dream. To be his wife. I tell you, I hated them both that day. I hated them and what they had done to each other. And what they did to me."

She stopped and faced him. "There were a lot of reasons that I didn't want to tell you what had happened. One of them was noble because I wanted to protect my half sister. But the real reason was—" She straightened her shoulders, breaking his heart with how strong she was trying to be. "But the real reason was me."

She pushed a piece of hair out of her eye. Or maybe it was a tear. "I didn't want to relive any of it and I had convinced myself that with both of them dead I would never have to. Telling you the story was hard enough. Telling you who he was, though, would bring it all back. I could barely get through the events when they actually happened. I couldn't see how I could—"

Her voice cracked.

"Callie." He walked over and he was relieved when she let him wrap his arms around her. He wanted to do something more to ease her pain, and he felt helpless.

Whatever he had expected, the truth was harder than he had imagined.

He heard a sniffle and then she stepped back sharply, lifted her head, and looked him straight in the eye. Her voice was completely unwavering.

"So I didn't come here to tell you that I loved you. I came here to tell you that my father's name is"—she took a deep breath—"Cornelius Woodward Hall."

Jack felt his chest contract, convinced for a moment that he couldn't possibly have heard her right.

She cleared her throat again and repeated, "My father was Cornelius Woodward Hall."

As if she was getting used to saying the words out loud.

"Oh, my God." Jack scanned her face and her red hair. He hadn't noticed the resemblance before, but having known the man rather well, he could see it now.

"Grace is my half sister. As far as I'm aware, she and I are the only ones who know the truth. Well, and her fiancé knows, too." She let out a long breath. "She's all the family I have left, really. I was afraid . . . I don't know. I assumed she'd be upset if I told you, even though you were a friend of hers. It has always been a secret, Jack. My father never wanted anything to be said about me. I only approached Grace after he was gone out of desperation. Loneliness."

Jack's mind started spinning. He'd known Hall, had respected the man, but all that went out the window as he imagined everything Callie had been through.

"How the *hell* could he do such a thing?"

"I've decided to stop asking that question."

He reached for her again, drawing her against his body, thinking that he was never, ever going to let her go.

He pictured Hall, swanning around the Congress Club in New York, all smiles with his wife and his daughter. The man had always spoken of his family in such glowing terms, with such conviction. And it had been lies. All of it.

That *bastard*.

Jack felt like kicking over the man's gravestone.

Callie spoke against his chest. "Last night, I finally realized that Grace wasn't the only one I was protecting. I decided I was going to tell you everything. But then the announcement came out and I lost sight of . . . everything. Who you really are, what you promised me. I wish I could go back and unlock that door, Jack. I really do."

"It's okay."

The forgiveness, he thought, was so easy. So simple. So complete.

"This morning, when I learned you'd kicked out your mother, I suddenly realized I'd read the situation completely wrong. And I spoke with Grace." She pulled back. "But I want to be clear. I did not ask her permission to tell you. I told her I was going to explain everything to you, because I had to or I was going to lose the man I love. And nothing would be worth that."

He gently took her face into his hands. As their lips met, he would have done anything to avenge her if he could have, but that time had long passed. Now he could only protect her. And that meant his candidacy was off.

She was absolutely right. A reporter would find out about Hall somehow and blow the story up into an exposé that would rob Callie of the privacy she held so dear.

She took a deep breath. "And I can't get Anne out of my mind."

Jack frowned. "Anne?"

"Last night I found a letter from General Rowe to Nathaniel. We were right. It was Anne in the mirror. And her father would have supported a marriage between the two of them after all." She shook her head. "Anne lost her last chance to see the man she loved. Last night, I was determined not to have that happen to us, but then I thought everything had changed. I thought we were over."

As he bent his head down to her shoulder, he thought they were lucky. Lucky to have found each other. Lucky to get past the obstacles even if it hurt.

We cut it so close, he thought, and then laughed.

"Your timing is good," he said. "I was about to formally announce my candidacy, but obviously I'm not—"

"No. Don't call it off!"

He pulled back and shook his head. "Good God, how can I run now?"

"I'm not going to hide anymore. I'm not going to protect him and neither will Grace. If you don't think I'll hurt your chances too much, I want to stand beside you when you run. I don't want you or me or Grace sacrificing anything for that man. He didn't deserve it when he was alive. And now—I just refuse to believe it matters anymore."

"Callie, are you sure you want to do this? It's not going to be easy."

"There isn't anything I wouldn't do for you. I just wish I wasn't such a liability."

Jack stared into her eyes with disbelief. "You are *not* a liability to me. And besides, the voters have to choose me because they believe in my vision for the state. God knows, I have enough scandals of my own. If my platform, my convictions, aren't enough to override my own past, it's not going to matter what your father did or who he was."

There was a pause and she smiled softly at him. "So you're going to run? Because I think you would make a fantastic governor."

Jack couldn't believe the way she was looking at him. She was so steady, so certain, even though he had the sense she knew what she was in for.

"Okay. I'll run."

Out in the hall, Gray Bennett looked over as the DA for Suffolk County tapped him on the shoulder.

"Listen, Bennett, I'm due at my kid's soccer game this afternoon and we're wasting time out in this hall. How much longer do you think he's going to be in there?"

Gray opened the door to the conference room a crack. He took one look at Jack and Callie kissing and shut it with a smile.

"I think it might be a while. Why don't I give you a call?"

The man smiled slowly and then nodded with a knowing grin. "Sounds good. Hell, if that redhead wanted to see me, I'd give her the time, too."

Epilogue

"Callie, look at the time." Gerard Beauvais's voice broke through the silence of the conservation lab. "You will be late!"

Callie glanced at her watch and leapt from her chair. "Oh, not again. I totally lost track of—"

She began frantically screwing on lids and putting brushes away.

"No, I will do that," Gerard said, shooing her away. "You must go."

She grabbed her coat and her backpack. On the way to the door, she was talking to Gerard over her shoulder. "About the Tintoretto. We need to—"

"We will talk of it tomorrow! Go!"

She ran for the stairs and burst out through the back entrance of the MFA. Breaking into a jog, she fumbled for her keys as she went over to a silver Volvo station wagon.

When she was speeding down Huntington Avenue, she flipped on the radio.

"With the polls just closing now, we'll have the results of this year's elections in a matter of minutes. The hotly contested governor's race, between Jack Walker and incumbent Butch Callahan—"

She turned the thing off, unable to bear the tension. Heading into town, and running a couple of yellow lights along the way, she tried to pay proper attention to the road. She didn't want to smash up the first and only car she'd ever bought for herself on a night like this.

Eight minutes later, she pulled up in front of an office building just on the edge of Chinatown. She went once around the block looking for a space and then parked the Volvo up on the curb next to a Dumpster in the back, hoping she didn't get towed.

Rushing into the building, she heard the noise of an excited crowd out in the lobby and went right for a sign that read JACK WALKER FOR GOVERNOR. She wrenched open the door under it and hit a wall of people.

The room was good-sized and filled to capacity. Down at the far end, she could just make out the stage that had been erected. On it were a huge TV set tuned to the local news and a lectern with a microphone. To one side of the platform, there was a bank of desks with people moving around furiously. She saw Gray with his jacket off and his sleeves rolled up, one ear plugged with a finger while he tried to talk on a cell phone. To his left was Cookie Sanchez, the campaign manager.

At the edge of the action, she saw Nate, Thomas, and Mrs. Walker. They were standing apart from the crowd, Thomas looking a little overwhelmed and Mrs. Walker working her gloves with nervous hands. Nate was smiling, as if he had no doubt as to what the results were going to be.

And then she saw Jack. Her breath caught, as it still did whenever she walked into a room and put her eyes on him. Pride in everything he had done over the past year, in the way he'd presented himself, in what he believed in, in how he had stood by her side when the story about her father had come out, had her chest swelling. It had been a grueling year for him, full of traveling across Massachusetts, meeting thousands of people, refining and redefining his vision for the state. And through it all, she had his full love and support. Even five minutes before the final debate last week, he'd been holding her hand and looking into her eyes as if there was nothing else going on in his life at all.

He was looking around the room when Gray grabbed him, stared him intensely in the eye, and whispered something in his ear. Jack seemed momentarily stunned.

And then the newscaster said, "And it's just now official. Jack Walker has won the governor's seat by a small margin over—"

Callie shouted in happiness as the room exploded. People let out cries and yells of victory as everyone started hugging one another. She lost sight of Jack in the melee but could only imagine what he felt like.

He'd won. He'd really done it.

Blue-and-white balloons began to fall from the ceiling as she collapsed back against a blackboard, grinning so widely her lips hurt. Some kind of music came over the loudspeakers and then Gray and Cookie were pushing Jack up onto the stage. He seemed to be fighting them and craning his neck around as flashbulbs went off everywhere.

The moment he was in plain view, the room fell completely quiet. Everyone wanted to hear what the first words from the governor-elect were going to be.

As he stepped up to the microphone, someone yelled, "What do you say, Governor Walker!"

Jack smiled. "Has anyone seen my wife?"

There was a roar of laughter and people began looking all around.

"She's right here!" a man said next to her, pointing over Callie's head.

The crowd began to part, and just as she started for the stage, Jack leapt off the dais and strode toward her, kicking up a wake of balloons.

They met in the middle of the room and he threw his arms around her, to the crowd's booming approval.

"I couldn't have done this without you," he said fiercely, in her ear.

"I'm so proud of you. I knew you could do it. And I'm sorry I'm late. I—"

"Forgot to check your watch?" he finished indulgently.

She nodded, trying not to cry, she was so happy for him.

The people were still cheering when he pulled back and kissed her soundly on the lips.

The rest of the night went by in a frenetic blur. There was a huge party immediately following the election results, but Jack and Gray had to spend most of that time talking to the press. It was well past two in the morning by the time Callie and Jack returned to Buona Fortuna.

As they walked into the Red Room to settle in for the night, Jack shook his head.

"I guess everyone's going to have to start calling me Governor now," he said as if he was still amazed.

Callie walked up to him and his smile was the slightly lopsided one that he reserved for her.

"Well, Governor Walker, I've got another title for you." She put his hand on her belly. "How's Daddy sound?"

Jack froze and then wobbled in his wing tips. "Callie?"

"Yes." She laughed softly as he seemed to melt in front of her. Wonderment, love, joy filtered through his hard features.

When he took her face gently into his hands and dipped down for a kiss, she said, "If she's a girl, can we name her Anne?"

Read on for a sneak peek of

AN UNFORGETTABLE LADY

by J. R. Ward writing as Jessica Bird

Available from Signet.

JOHN SMITH checked his watch and looked around the Plaza Hotel's ballroom.

Things were going well. According to the report that had just come over his earpiece, the ambassador's plane had landed safely at La Guardia and the man would be arriving at the party on time.

Smith's eyes passed over the glittering crowd. It was the same kind of flashy scene that always revolved around $5,000-a-plate dinners. Women in jewels and long gowns, men in tuxedos, the collective net worth of the room up into the stratosphere. In the midst of the shifting throng, deals were being made, affairs were getting started, and social slights were exchanged with smiles. The place was choked with air kisses and hand pumping.

Underneath the chandeliers in the elegant ballroom, the whole lot of them looked as if they had the world by the throat. Smith knew better. He'd been hired by quite a few, had learned their dirty secrets and their hidden vices. He'd even watched as some got their wake-up call to real life.

Being the target of an armed stalker—that was something to worry about. Your kid gets pinched by some madman looking to hose you down for a couple million? That was a problem. Whether or not your mistress's boob job was symmetrical paled in comparison.

Danger, like illness, was the great equalizer, and the rich learned fast what really mattered when tragedy came knocking at their door. Courtesy of the visit, they also picked up a few lessons about their inner depths. Smith had seen hardened businessmen break down, sobbing from fear. He'd also witnessed great reserves of strength appear in a woman who'd only worried about her clothes before.

Being a personal security specialist was a dangerous line of work but it was the only thing he could imagine doing. With his military and intelligence background, and the fact that he didn't take orders well, it was a good fit. An observer, a protector, a killer if he had to be, Smith was at the top of his field and his small firm, Black Watch, Ltd., handled everyone from statesmen to financiers to international figures.

For some, it would have been a hard life. His chosen profession had him flying around the world, sleeping in hotel rooms, staying in other people's homes, moving on to the next job without a break. To him, the lack of continuity was appealing. Necessary.

An army duffel full of clothes and two metal briefcases of equipment were his only possessions. The money he'd earned, a tidy sum, was spread around in various offshore accounts under several different names. Without a valid social security number, and with neither the Internal Revenue Service nor any other government agency having an unclassified record of him, he was, for all intents and purposes, a ghost.

But this didn't mean he went unnoticed.

A woman in a tight black gown sauntered by him, eyeing him with an invitation he imagined a lot of men would find irresistible. He looked past her, through her. He wasn't interested in a quick fling with a social diva. Experience had taught him to stick with his own kind.

The women he'd been with tended to be members of the intelligence community or in the military. They understood his life and expected nothing more than a shared night or two, a body to warm their bed. Civilian women tended to look into the future after they had sex and dealing with their misplaced expectations took time and patience he didn't have to spare.

His earpiece went off. The "package" was in his limo, heading to the Plaza.

"Thanks, Tiny," he said into a small transmitter on his wrist.

The ambassador had been receiving death threats, which was how Smith had ended up in a tuxedo at the party.

As he scanned the crowd, he didn't expect trouble. The place was crawling with his men. He knew and trusted them all, having handpicked them out of elite military corps. Black Watch was the only place he knew of where former Rangers, Marines, and Navy SEALs could work together without throwing punches. If something went down tonight, they'd work together and do their damnedest to protect the ambassador.

Except Smith wasn't worried because he knew something no one else did. The man after the ambassador had been killed about five hours ago, in a deserted outpost in his native country. Smith had been tipped off by an old friend of his, and considering the source, he was confident the intel was solid. It didn't mean the ambassador was out of the woods, as assassins could be easily replaced, but it decreased the odds of trouble on this particular evening.

Despite the reduced level of threat, Smith wasn't any less alert. He knew where all the bodies in the ballroom were, in what patterns they were moving, how they were entering and exiting the space. Even the best intelligence in the world wasn't going to change the accuracy of his peripheral vision or his rapid assimilation of information.

The watchfulness was second nature to him. As immutable as his eye color.

Smith sensed someone approach from behind. He turned and looked down into the worried face of Alfred Alston, the gala's host. The man was a typical Social Register type, with a full head of prematurely white hair and the requisite horn-rimmed glasses. Smith liked him. The guy had been easy to deal with.

"I'm terribly sorry to intrude, but have you seen my wife?"

There was a slight English cadence to his vowels, no doubt left over from when his family had crossed the Atlantic. Back in 1630.

Smith shook his head.

"She should have been here quite some time ago. She would hate to miss the ambassador's entrance." Alston's thin fingers came up and fiddled with his bow tie. "Although I'm sure she will turn up."

The strain around the man's eyes was more truthful than his words.

"You want me to send one of my men over to your place?" Because Alston had been such a good sport, Smith wouldn't have minded the extra effort. Besides, it wouldn't take long. His boys had a way of getting through traffic that made NYC taxi drivers look like they were from the Amish country.

Alston offered a worried smile. "Thank you, that's very kind, but I wouldn't want to trouble you."

"Let me know if you change your mind. The ambassador's on time, by the way."

"I'm glad you're here. Curt Thorndyke was right. You put a man's mind at ease."

Smith resumed looking around the room. In another twenty minutes, the ambassador would show up. There'd be the requisite photographs and genuflecting and then dinner would be—

Smith's eyes caught on something.

Or someone, rather.

He stared through the crowd at a blond woman who had just arrived. Dressed in a shimmering silver gown, she was standing in the elaborate entrance to the ballroom looking too damn radiant to be real.

He recognized her immediately. But who wouldn't?

The Countess von Sharone.

Conversation in the ballroom dropped to a hush as people registered her presence. The social status of the gala, already high, shot through the roof with her arrival, and the crowd's approval was palpable.

If these fancy types hadn't all been carrying drinks, they'd have burst out in applause, he thought drily. As if she were the honoree, not the ambassador.

Still, he had to admit she was a looker. With her blond hair twisted up high on her head, she was a classic beauty with delicate features and dazzling green eyes. And that dress. Molded to her body, it moved like water as she stepped into the room.

Christ, she was *beautiful*, he thought. Assuming you liked that patrician, butter-wouldn't-melt-in-my-mouth type.

Which he didn't.

Alston went up to her. She extended a hand and accepted air kisses on both cheeks from him, her expression warming. Someone else approached her and then another, until she was carried into the room on a wave of ingratiation. Smith tracked her every movement.

She'd been in the papers recently, he recalled, although it wasn't like she was ever really out of them. Her clothes, her parties, that extravagant wedding she'd had—they were fodder for the tabloids and the real papers alike. What had he read about her lately, though? Her father had just died. That was it. And there'd been some spread about her and five other women in the Style section of the *New York Times*. He'd seen it lying faceup on the front desk of the Plaza.

Talk about being born with a silver spoon in your mouth, he thought, eyeing the heavy pearls and diamonds that were around her throat and dangling from her ears. Her family's fortune was in the billions and that count she'd just married wasn't exactly pulling down minimum wage either.

As she came deeper into the room, she turned in his direction and met his gaze. Her brows lifted regally when he didn't look away.

Maybe she resented being stared at. Maybe she sensed he didn't belong even though he dressed the part.

Maybe some of the lust he was feeling had crept into his face.

He hid his reaction as she scanned him. He was surprised by the shrewd light in her eyes and the fact that she lingered on his left ear, the one with the piece in it. He wouldn't have expected her to be so observant. A first-rate clotheshorse for haute couture, sure. The favorite arm candy of some wealthy man, yeah. But hiding half a brain under all that fancy window dressing? No way.

The countess continued into the room as Tiny's deep voice came through the earpiece. The ambassador was fifteen minutes away. Smith glanced down at his watch. When he looked up, she was standing in front of him, having broken away from her admirers.

"Do I know you?" Her voice was soft, a little low for a woman. Incredibly sexy.

The smile she offered him was gentle and welcoming, nothing like the aristocratic, chilly grimace he would have predicted.

His eyes flickered over her. Her breasts were concealed by the silver gown but they were perfectly formed and the waist below them was small. He imagined that her legs, which were also covered by the dress, looked every bit as good. He also noticed her perfume, something light and tangy that got into his nose and then his nervous system.

"Haven't we met?" she repeated, putting out her hand and waiting for an answer.

Smith looked down. She'd given him her left hand

and he caught a look at the jewels on her ring finger. She was wearing a monstrous sapphire and a thick band of diamonds.

The rings reminded him he'd just mentally undressed a married woman.

He glanced up into her eyes, wishing she'd go the hell away. They were beginning to attract attention as she stood there with her hand out.

"No, you don't know me," he said roughly, gripping her palm.

The instant he touched her, a flare of heat shot up his arm, and he saw an echo of it flash in her eyes. She pulled back sharply.

"Are you sure we haven't met?" Her head tilted to one side while she rubbed the hand, as if trying to get rid of an unpleasant sensation.

His earpiece fired up with another update on the ambassador. "Yeah, I'm sure."

Smith turned and walked away from her.

"Wait," he heard her call out.

He didn't stop, just kept heading for the back of the ballroom. Pushing open an unmarked door, he stepped into a corridor that was filled with extra chairs and tables. Bald lightbulbs were suspended from the squat ceiling and they cast harsh shadows on the concrete floor. The hall would take him to the service entrance the ambassador was going to use.

When he heard a clicking noise behind him, he turned around. The countess had followed him.

Even under the glare, she was breathtaking.

"What are you doing?" he demanded.

"Who are you?"

"What's it to you?"

She hesitated. "It's just that you were looking at me as if we'd met."

"Trust me. We haven't."

Smith started walking away again. The last thing the countess needed was another man panting after her. No doubt adoring simps were a dime a dozen in her life.

And speaking of simps, why wasn't her husband drooling all over her tonight? She seemed to have come to the party alone.

Smith glanced over his shoulder.

The countess had turned back to the door. Her head was down, as if she were bracing herself before going back into the gala.

His feet slowed. Then stopped.

"What's wrong with you?" he called out, his voice bouncing off the bare walls. The instant he asked the question, he wanted to take it back, and muttered, "Someone show up wearing the same dress tonight?"

The countess's head snapped toward him. She straightened and regarded him coolly.

"There is absolutely nothing wrong with me." Her voice was steady, the words coming out clean and sharp. Maybe he'd imagined the vulnerability. "You, however, are sadly lacking in manners."

Smith frowned, thinking that she was damn efficient with the put-downs. With one sentence spoken in level, calm tones, she'd made him feel like a total heel. Then again, she'd no doubt had plenty of practice cutting people down, had probably perfected the skill on a whole retinue of servants and waiters over the years.

Well, he wasn't one of her lackeys. And she had no business getting in his way. Even if the ambassador's assassin was dead, the last thing Smith needed was to have someone like her hurt in the middle of one of his details. She needed to go back to the party now, so he could do his job.

Time to be a hard-ass, he thought.

Smith sauntered over to the countess and had to ignore the tantalizing scent of her while glaring into her eyes.

"Is there something you have to say?" she asked primly. "Or do you just want to loom over me?"

As she regarded him with that even stare, Smith was surprised. People backed off quickly when he glowered. The blonde was holding her own.

He pushed his face closer to hers, feeling irritated.

"I'm sorry if I merely offended you," he said. "I meant to piss you off."

"Now why would you want to do that?"

"Because you're in my way."

"How so?"

Time was passing, the ambassador was getting closer, and the countess's tenacity was beginning to get under his skin.

Just like her proximity was. Staring down at her, he felt an urgency that had nothing to do with timing.

And everything to do with hunger.

Wrong woman, wrong place, he thought. Get rid of her.

"Tell me, Countess, do you always beg for attention like this?" His voice was cold, disdainful.

"I'm not begging you for anything," she said smoothly.

"You pick the only man who has no interest in you and follow him out of the party. You think that's standoffish?"

He was itching to be free of her but there was more. His reaction to her, the strength and inappropriateness of it, made him wary. She was like standing in front of a fire.

And he was a man who had no intention of being burned.

FROM
#1 *NEW YORK TIMES*
BESTSELLING AUTHOR

J. R. WARD

THE BLACK DAGGER BROTHERHOOD NOVELS

Dark Lover
Lover Eternal
Lover Awakened
Lover Revealed
Lover Unbound
Lover Enshrined
Lover Avenged
Lover Mine
Lover Unleashed

jrward.com
facebook.com/jrwardbooks

Available wherever books are sold or at
penguin.com

S0073